Jennifer Johnston is one of the foremost writers of her, or any, generation. Her many awards include the Costa (formerly the Whitbread) Prize (*The Old Jest*) and the *Evening Standard* Best First Novel Award (*The Captains and the Kings*). She was also shortlisted for the Booker Prize with *Shadows on our Skin*.

Praise for Jennifer Johnston:

'She has created a world of her own . . . of such material is the finest literature made' *Irish Times*

'The best writer in Ireland' Roddy Doyle

'A brilliant storyteller' *Literary Review*

'The quiet, elegiac prose is well sustained' *Guardian*

'One of Ireland's finest writers' *Sunday Tribune*

'[A] radiant descriptive gift' *Spectator*

'Written in Johnston's usual haunting prose, where no word is unnecessary' Maeve Binchy

'Stunning' *Daily Express*

'Superb' *Irish Sunday Independent*

'A very nearly perfect novel of broad, regretful vision and magical intimacy' *Sunday Telegraph*

'Her writing is a joy: dialogue snaps with life while Johnston's distinctive prose is at once supremely comfortable and delightfully brisk' *Daily Mail*

'The Costa prizewinner and Booker-shortlisted Johnston knows how to tell a story succinctly . . . [she writes with] the deceptive ease of a skilled craftswoman . . . further proof of her skill as a writer' *Irish Independent*

# Jennifer Johnston

## Naming the Stars

A duo companion with *Two Moons*

TINDER
PRESS

TWO MOONS first published in Great Britain in 1998 by HEADLINE REVIEW
An imprint of HEADLINE PUBLISHING GROUP

NAMING THE STARS first published in Great Britain in 2015 by Tinder Press
An imprint of HEADLINE PUBLISHING GROUP

First published in this omnibus paperback edition in 2016 by Tinder Press
An imprint of HEADLINE PUBLISHING GROUP

2

Cataloguing in Publication Data is available from the British Library

ISBN 978 1 4722 3471 1

Typeset in Cochin by Avon DataSet Ltd, Bidford-on-Avon, Warwickshire

Printed and bound in Great Britain by Clays Ltd, St Ives plc

Headline's policy is to use papers that are natural, renewable and recyclable products and made
from wood grown in sustainable forests. The logging and manufacturing processes are
expected to conform to the environmental regulations of the country of origin.

HEADLINE PUBLISHING GROUP
An Hachette UK Company
Carmelite House
50 Victoria Embankment
London EC4Y 0DZ

www.tinderpress.co.uk
www.headline.co.uk
www.hachette.co.uk

*For my two wonderful grandsons with hope and love,*
*Sam and Atticos*

# Jennifer
# Johnston

*Naming the Stars*

TINDER
PRESS

Six o'clock in the evening.

My name is Flora.

Some people think this is not a great name to have been landed with. They find it a simpering sort of a name, the sort of name that makes them smile an embarrassed smile; personally, I quite like it. My mother and father must have chosen it with care, well, my father anyway. I think though that my mother would have preferred another boy. She always preferred men to women, but still she would have chosen my name with care, because she knew he would have liked her to do that. Had he picked me up in his long hands and looked into my face with great love and said, 'She is like a flower.' I seem to hear his voice and her reply. 'A rose, perhaps.' Roses have thorns, she might have thought, and smiled her secretive smile. I remember all his gestures so well; he would have pushed his hair back from his forehead, blond, floppy hair. 'It's easy to see I must be descended from a Norseman,' I heard him say once. 'None of this Anglo-Irish nonsense for me. I am a Dane. Hamlet the Dane. Look at my Danish hair.' I must have been very young, as the joke meant nothing to me. Mother laughed. She used always to laugh at his jokes. Bad or good, they were always followed by the gentle tinkling of her laughter. I don't think my name was a joke, though. Funnily enough, he hardly ever called me Flora; chicken, chicky or even chuck-chuck were what he preferred to shout with glee or whisper secretly in my ear when he was carrying me on my way upstairs to bed. He loved his daughter; I had no doubt about that. He never told lies; of that I'm sure. And she, well, she was different to anyone else I have ever known in my pretty long life. She seemed to love lying. 'Daddy will be home soon,' she used to say. 'Won't that be great. You must be good. That will make him happy. We all want Daddy to be happy, don't we?' I remember Eddie muttering, 'Bullshit' once when she said that and I tried hard not to giggle. She pretended not to hear.

Six p.m., and across the autumn fields strolls the sound of the angelus.

The sky was lacquered indigo.

'Bong,' said Flora aloud and put her book down on the table.

A brilliant star, the only one in the sky at that early moment, winked at her from a million miles away. Flora winked back at it.

The other old woman looked at Flora and smiled; she stuck the needle through a fold in the sheet that she had been mending and blessed herself.

'I thought you might have fallen asleep,' said Flora, 'and missed the holy moment.'

'How could I have fallen asleep and all this mending to do?'

Nellie picked the needle up and continued with her work: her hands were never idle, she never sat without a basket of mending, darning, stitching, sewing buttons, making lace for the Communion dresses of the girls in the village, or lace collars.

She always wore a white lace collar herself, clipped neatly on to the top of her dark blue dress and held in place with a pearl brooch that had been left to her by the mistress.

'Five minutes, then I must be off about the dinner, just time to finish this sheet.' She pulled the needle out and smoothed the linen over her fingers. 'Mr Taggart sent the boy up with some kidneys and a nice leg of lamb. And a couple of garlic bulbs. I told you, didn't I, that he grew real French garlic in his garden?'

'Every time he sends us up some you tell me.'

'So I do. I find it of interest. I expect we're the only people around who he shares it with.'

'Times have changed, Nellie dear, we're all used to garlic here nowadays. It keeps the arthritis at bay and of course the werewolves and vampires.' She laughed at her own joke.

Nellie bit the end off the thread.

'Well it's there now, in the oven, sizzling away under the lamb – we'll feast on it – and I've made a blackberry and apple crumble. There's no doubt but we'll eat well this evening.'

'We eat well every evening.'

'I thought I might run down to the cellar and bring up a bottle or two of the Gruaud-Larose.'

'There can't be much of that left.'

'It'll see us through.'

She folded the sheet neatly and laid it on top of the basket that held her sewing accoutrements. She pushed herself up from her chair with care.

'French garlic or no French garlic, the arthritis is creeping up on me. The joints creak.'

'Perhaps we should go and live in the South of France. Wine, garlic and a soothing climate, very good for old age pensioners.'

'Such rubbish you talk.' She put the basket over her arm and headed for the door. 'I always feel like a thief in the night, creeping down to steal the master's wine. What would he say to me at all, if he knew?'

'He'd laugh. He'd be so pleased to think that we were making good use of it . . . and Nellie, bring up a bottle of port while you're at it, may as well be hanged for a sheep as a lamb. I'll just sit here a while longer and watch the sun go down.'

'And catch your death of cold.'

'It's only September. The summer warmth is still hanging round. You're such a fusspot, Nellie. Fuss, fuss, fuss, always have been.'

Nellie stopped at the door.

'Haven't I kept you well with my fussing, and me besides. If it had been up to you, we'd have both been dead years ago.'

She stooped and put her basket on the sitting-room floor. She raised her voice to make sure that Flora heard. 'Isn't Dr Carey always telling me how pleased he is with the pair of us, never a spot of bother. That's what he always says to me: You're a wonder, Nellie, never a spot of bother.'

Flora laughed.

'Well we don't cause him any bother anyway, he gets enough of that from the rest of his patients, and God knows he got enough of it from Mother.'

'I'll shut the door over so the damp won't come into the house.'

Flora waved a hand at her. The door squeaked as Nellie pulled it towards her and a wisp of cloud floated across the sinking sun. This corner of the house, the western edge, looked at that moment as if it had been built of gold, and the windows flashed private signals to the distant hills.

She cuddled herself back into the comfort of her chair.

Mustn't tease Nellie, she thought to herself, no indeed. She knew too well where she would be without Nellie, out there in the cold, unkind world. Mmm hmm. Out beyond grandfather's trees: chestnut, ash, beech, hornbeam, and that mighty avenue of oaks. 'There's a fortune in them trees,' someone, she couldn't remember who, had said to her once, and she had laughed and said, 'Maybe that will come in handy some day.' But no matter what misfortune fell, you couldn't cut grandfather's oaks. She could see them now, tall, marching it seemed down the hill towards the village, sturdy, their green leaves just beginning to turn. No Gruaud-Larose, no indeed. I mustn't tease Nellie. I must keep my giggles to myself. I would hate to be a woman alone. That was what Mother used to say to us, to make us behave ourselves.

'Your father is battling in the desert and I am a woman alone. You must help me by being very, very good.'

She used to say it to other people too.

'Paul is battling in the desert. Poor dear Paul.'

Paul, Father, Daddy. And of course they called him Major when he was away in Africa battling in the desert.

It was his second war. Flora used to feel quite sorry for him when she thought of that. He got the tail end of the first one, eighteen, straight from school. There are pictures of him all round the house looking so handsome in his uniform. So very handsome. Men always look handsome in uniform, I have never been able to work out why that is. He was my dear friend, she thought, but he never explained to me why he felt he had to go and leave us all, leave grandfather's trees, leave Mother to be a woman alone. I missed him so much when he went away.

I missed him so much when he never came back. He had this wonderful hearty laugh. He used to throw his head right back and roar with laughter. Eddie used to do that too. He had that same laugh. Father used to lift me in his arms and put his lips to the side of my neck and blow warm air on to my skin. I remember that, I remember shivering with joy when he did that.

'You'll ruin that child, Paul,' Mother would say.

I dreamed I would marry him when I grew up; all in white as she had been. 'Chicken, I will love you for ever,' he said in my dreams and blew warm air on my neck. 'Bye, chicken,' was what he said when he left. 'We'll meet again some sunny day.' He never even mentioned the possibility of death. I was not in any way prepared for that.

Death.

Either time.

No. Not death.

El Alamein.

We had this map of North Africa on a table in the drawing room, with all those names on it. Tobruk, Mersa Matruh,

Himeimat, Benghazi, El Alamein. They make a pattern in my head, even now, the sound of those words.

After we got the news, she drew a little black cross by El Alamein in indelible pencil, and a few days later she rolled up the map and put it away as if the war didn't exist any longer.

'We don't need that any more,' were her words.

At school, Miss Ross taught us history: the slave trade, the Boer War, Khartoum. She had a fine black moustache above her upper lip, but she was decent enough. I put my hand up.

'Yes, Flora?'

'Is Khartoum near El Alamein?'

'No. Africa is a very large country, you know, Flora.' A giggle swept around the classroom. She blushed. 'That is enough.' Her voice was embarrassed. 'I'm sorry, Flora. So sorry,' she said. 'We're all sorry.' I would have liked to tell them about him, about the black cross in indelible pencil, but the words stuck in my mouth. Dry words like biscuit crumbs stuck to the roof of my mouth. Maybe it was just as well. You learn as you get older that there are things you should keep to yourself. Not go blurting everything out of your head. I am afraid that I find this hard to do, I am afraid that I am a blurter.

Then there was the song; on quiet evenings like this I can hear the woman singing it in her gravelly voice. I don't remember her name, just the low timbre of her voice.

> *Vor der Kaserne bei dem großen Tor*
> *Stand eine Laterne und steht sie noch davor*
> *So wollen wir uns da wieder seh'n*

7

*Bei der Laterne wollen wir steh'n*
*Wie einst, Lili Marleen*
*Wie einst, Lili Marleen.*

That's it. I can still remember all the words. It's as if she was standing down by the gate, singing that mournful tune.

Mother used to play it on the wind-up gramophone.

'What's that song you play every night?'

'I didn't realise that you could hear it all the way up the stairs. "Lili Marleen". Daddy listens to it in the desert.'

'But it's German.'

'They all listen to it. He says so in his letters to me; all our enemies and all our friends, tired men lying out under the desert stars. Trying to fall asleep, trying not to think about the next day. I call it "The Desert Lullaby". Isn't that a good name?'

I remember being angry when we had that conversation. I remember the little bubbles of rage that burst in my chest. I so desperately wanted him to write to me. I didn't just want messages at the bottom of her letters. Love to chick-chick. Kisses to my favourite chicken. That sort of thing. I really wanted him home.

This was of course before Alamein, and when I heard the singer's voice drifting up the stairs I used to think of him lying under the stars, thinking of us, of home, of me. His chicken. It was comfortable to think of us both listening to the same woman singing us to sleep.

After we got the news, she never played the record again. She probably broke it in pieces. That was the sort of thing she used to do; banging the shellac against the edge of a marble mantelpiece or cracking it under her heel.

She never wore black. That was considered strange round here.

Eddie and I had black bands sewn on to the sleeves of our good coats.

Respect and sorrow.

That was what the black band meant. Nellie told me that when I asked her; she bit through the black thread and then she said that, respect and sorrow.

'He never liked me in black.' I heard Mother say that to someone. I used to listen carefully; that way, you hear a lot of useful things. I could hold my breath and become invisible. You learn a lot of things that no one would tell you, if you can do that. I always wanted to learn a lot of things that I could tell Eddie when he came home from school for the holidays. I was always so afraid that he would get bored with only having me to play with. He heard me singing that song to myself one night when he was passing my door.

*Steht 'ne Laterne, und steht sie noch davor . . .*

'What the hell are you singing that for, Flora? That's not a song you should be singing. That's the song of the enemy. The *sales Boches*. Where did you learn it? The men who killed Daddy, they sing it. It's their song.'

'They all sing it, everyone. Out in the desert. Every night. Mother had a record of it. She told me. Daddy used to listen to it. It made him happy. That's what she said.'

'Well they're not in the desert any longer and I bet they don't listen to it any longer either and you shouldn't be singing it and I'll tell Mother if I catch you at it again.'

'Blah, blah, blah,' I said to him, but I stopped singing the song.

I never sang the words or tune aloud again, but I sang them inside my head. I told nobody. I hadn't the foggiest idea what the words meant, but they kept Daddy sleeping in my mind, not dead.

'After all, what is death?'

Flora asked herself the question aloud. She looked up at the sky, now almost navy in places away from the fiery west. 'Only a long sleep, and when you're tired, what is better than a long sleep?' She laughed aloud. Poor Nellie, she thought, she doesn't think I know what day it is today, but I do. I know all right. I knew when she bustled in and pulled my curtains this morning and slammed down the window muttering about autumn and draughts and pneumonia and all that sort of stuff. Hear me, Nellie. I knew.

She settled back into silence once more. Daddy had told her once that if you kept very, very quiet you could hear the grass growing. She had believed him, but in all her years she had never been able to find that perfect stillness.

Mother had sent her away to school. Flora had begged and begged to be left at home, but her mother had been adamant.

She never learnt German at school.

'You must broaden your horizons,' Mother had said.

She was too busy being a woman alone and running the place

to be able to occupy herself with broadening Flora's horizons.

No German. A modicum of Latin: *a, ab, absque, coram, de,* that sort of thing.

'You'll meet girls of your own age,' Mummy had said. 'You'll make friends.'

Algebra, arithmetic, geometry; the square on the hypotenuse is equal to the sum of the squares on the other two sides. All that wearisome stuff.

'It's what Daddy would have wanted.' Mother's voice sounded as if she was bored by the whole conversation.

The Statutes of Kilkenny, the Diet of Worms, the repeal of the Act of Union, the abolition of the slave trade.

In one ear and out the other. In, out. In, out.

A little shiver of autumn wind touched her ankles. I must go in before I get cold. I must go and partake of the feast that Nellie has prepared.

I wonder if she will have lighted candles?

She stood up and walked slowly across the dampening grass. At the door she stood for a moment and looked at the sky. The sun was gone and a pink glow was all that remained, and the bright star was now directly above the house; it appeared to wink at her again. With a little wave in its direction, she went into the drawing room and closed the door behind her.

Nellie had indeed put candles on the table, and two small posies of flowers, one in front of each place.

The old ladies ate always in a corner of the kitchen at a round mahogany table that had once sat in one of the windows in the dining room.

'Aha,' said Flora as she came into the room. 'Should we change for dinner?'

Nellie laughed; she pushed a pot from one side of the Aga to the other.

'Have you clean hands?'

Flora held her hands up in front of her.

'Clean as clean can be.'

'Then sit you down and have a glass of wine. That's a nice dry September sort of wine there, suitable for us to drink now.' She nodded to a bottle on the table. Open, ready for pouring. 'Did you close the door behind you? With the lights on in the house these evenings the bats come in. We don't want bats in the house, do we?'

Flora sat down in the wicker chair, which crackled as it took her weight. She shook her napkin open and placed it neatly on her knee. Nellie poured two glasses with great care.

'You know, Nellie, bats have a most sophisticated radar system. I saw a programme about them on television not long ago. I really don't think that they will come in and bother us.'

'They get in your hair, that's what I've always been told, and they cling. Imagine a bat clinging in your hair.'

'Well they seemed quite charming little things to me. No danger to life or limb. But to put your mind at rest, I did shut the door.'

'Here's your wine.' Her hand trembled slightly as she handed the glass to Flora.

Flora stared for a moment at the reflection of the candle

flame deep in the glass, like a small animal struggling to get out. She smiled.

'Who shall we drink to? Give me a name, Nellie.'

Nellie laughed nervously.

'I have only the one name.'

'That won't do at all. Here's to Paul, the Major, Father, Daddy. Peace be with you.' She hoisted her glass in the air. 'And Paul, Major, Daddy, darling Father, thanks for the wine.'

'The Major.'

They both swallowed lavishly. Flora giggled and thumped back down into her chair.

'I always thought I would marry him when I grew up. Imagine, such silliness.'

'I never seen him even. He was gone just before I came here. Far away out in that desert. A gallant gentleman, everyone said he was. She never wore black.'

'It didn't suit her.'

They both drank their wine in silence for a few moments, their minds back in the past, and a little wind blew up from the south and rattled the windows.

The silence was broken by Nellie.

'D'you remember I used to go to the pictures on Thursdays?'

'A vague recollection.'

'On our bikes. I used to go with Bernie from the post office. We would pedal in to Bray . . . mostly Bray, though we had to push the bikes up a lot of that hill. We'd do the shops, have our tea and pop into the picture house. Hail, rain or shine we did it. It was touching the world, not just stuck at the bottom of a muddy hill in County Wicklow; we touched the world on Thursdays. And then on the way home we would sing the songs from the film we had seen. We never could remember all the words, but we stitched it together as we pedalled, and then we would name the stars . . .'

'Name the stars?'

'Yes. All those thousands of stars, hanging there above us, and we'd throw the bikes in the ditch and we'd give them names: Mickey Rooney, Clark Gable, Judy Garland, Claudette Colbert, Fred Astaire. We could have gone on for ever giving names to those beautiful winking stars, and we'd dance little dances, singing the tunes that Judy Garland had taught us.' She laughed. 'It was fun. I asked the mistress once if I could bring you one Thursday; you could have sat on the carrier and you'd have loved it, but . . .'

'She said no.'

'She said no. She said . . .'

'It doesn't matter what else she said, no was what mattered. No was what she always said.'

'She had a hard life.'

'What rubbish you do talk.'

Nellie filled up her own glass and then Flora's, then she headed across the kitchen, leaving Flora to think about her mother's hard life.

The holidays were almost over.

Two thirds of Ireland remained indomitably non-combatant; there was very little petrol and no bananas.

Flora had become a weekly boarder at a small school in Dublin, and Eddie braved the war and submarines to remain at the school in England that he had been at when Daddy was killed. Mummy wouldn't hear of him retreating to the safety of Ireland.

'It was your father's school,' she had said, and that was that, no arguments. 'Do not argue with me,' she would say. 'I cannot cope with arguments.' She would leave the room.

Now the long summer holidays were almost over. In less than a week their cases would be packed, name tapes would have been sewn on every article of clothing, the bottle of whiskey and the smoked salmon for Eddie's headmaster and the dozen eggs for the housemaster's wife would have been carefully stowed and the house would have become quiet again. Mummy would be able to take up her argument-free life again.

The playroom faced downhill, towards the village; it was possible on very still nights to hear the last bus, or on Saturday nights the music from the Capitol Ballroom, and even the laughter from the young people as they spilled out into the dark at eleven o'clock sharp and collected their bikes and began the journey home, or wherever it was they were going.

*If you were the only girl in the world and I was the only . . .*

The record was scratched with overuse and sighed as it rotated.

Eddie let go of Flora's hand and did a splendid reverse turn, ending with a flourish and a bow in her direction.

'It's quite simple really.'

'It's all very well for you, you've had lessons. We don't get dancing lessons at school, unless you stay there at weekends, and anyway you have to be fifteen. It's so unfair. I bet if I had lessons I could be as good as you.'

'You need the aptitude.'

'I have the aptitude. Just as much as you anyway.'

'And a sense of rhythm.'

He rattled his feet on the floor.

*There would be such wonderful things to do. If you . . .*

'You're such a show-off. A bloody show-off.'

'Naughty, naughty, what would Mummy say?'

'What she always says. N. O. D'you know that Nellie asked her last week if she could take me to the pictures and she said no. How nice of you, Nellie, she said, very nice, very kind, but it's too soon.'

Eddie saw tears rising in his sister's eyes and threw his arms around her. 'Dance,' he ordered, loud and clear. 'Slow, slow, quick, quick, slow. That's a great girl, you'll be a splendid dancer one day.' They whirled across the parquet floor and he hummed the tune in her ear. *If you were the only girl in the world and I was the only boy.* The music stopped and they stood looking at each other and the gramophone needle went round and round and round: whick, whick, whick. Eddie walked over and turned it off.

'She doesn't mean to be unkind, you know. She feels she has a duty to keep us safe.'

'Safe from what?'

Tears had left their tracks on her face.

'The comments of the hoi polloi. Cruel comments. Perhaps you're too young to have heard the way people make comments, quite decent and kindly people. The world's quite wicked you know. Dangerous.'

'I don't see anything dangerous in going to the pictures with Nellie. It's not Tobruk, it's bloody well not Tobruk, and anyway she lets you go to school over there, where there's a war on. A blitzkrieg. That's what one of our teachers calls it. A horrid word, don't you think? I just don't understand.'

'You will. When you're older. I'm sure she has her good reasons.'

'I'm only two years younger than you and they always say that girls grow up quicker than boys. Their understanding of things is in advance of boys. They do say that. I have heard people say that.'

'Oh do stop snivelling, Flora.'

'I'm not snivelling.'

'Yes, you are.'

'You're being mean.'

'Oh God, it's so boring here. I can't wait till I'm back on that boat again, steaming down the Liffey, seeing the last for a while of smoky Dublin and you and Mummy waving your handkerchiefs. It's so boring, boring, boring.'

He stamped his foot on the floor. He did a little tap dance. Heel, toe, heel, toe. His mood lightened as his feet tapped the floor. Heel, toe. Tippy tappy. He smiled at her. He held out a hand towards her. Come and tap-tap, the hand said. She shook her head. She smiled as his feet tippy-tapped.

'You're good,' she said. 'Nellie would say you're good. Nellie knows all about dancing. She goes to all those pictures.

She tells me about them. Fred Astaire, Judy Garland. I do wish Mummy would let me go. Even just once.'

He put his arm around her shoulder.

'She will. She'll have sense one of these days. One of these days she will see what she is doing to us. She'll see that we're prisoners and she will let us go free. I have plans in my head.'

He bit his finger and stood looking at her.

'Plans?'

'Oh nothing really. I didn't mean to say that.'

'Plans, Eddie, what plans do you have?'

'Isn't it odd the way you can say something that you don't mean to say. The words just sort of fall out of your mouth.'

'What plans? You'll have to tell me or I'll tell Mummy that you're up to something.'

He walked over to the window and stared out into the darkness.

'You know I think that girl is a bit of a snooper.'

'What girl?'

'That Nellie girl. Every time I turn a corner, there she is, always watching.'

'Watching who? Watching what? She works jolly hard. She's at Mummy's beck and call all the time. Fetch this, mend that, where is the child – that's me, I'd have you know. She doesn't call you child. When will she stop calling me child?'

'She's Mummy's snooper. I bet she knows everything we do, everything we say, everything we think.'

The trees bent and swayed; soon, he thought the leaves would start to fall and the ground would be orange and red and he and Wilkinson would have put their plan into action and no one would be able to stop them. His heart beat fast. He looked at the reflection of Flora in the window. She was only a child yet and Daddy was gone. He would have let her go to the pictures with the snooper; he had been a man who created fun and lightness wherever he went. I will be like him, Eddie thought, I will make people happy. He turned from the window and went over to his sister.

'Come and sit by me, dear Flora. We have a while yet before she comes calling you. Missee Flora.' He thought he was imitating Nellie's voice, but it was nothing like. Flora grinned at him and settled herself on the sofa beside him.

'Missee Flora, your bath is run.'

'It's not a bit like her.'

'I'd like to tell you my plan. I've been wanting to all hols, but I promised not to mention it to a soul.'

'Promised who? You never have secrets from me, Eddie. Who?'

'Don't get worked up or I'll not tell you a thing. I promised Wilkinson not to breathe a word. We swore just to keep it tight inside ourselves, but I trust you. Honestly, I really do. Love you, baby pigeon.'

She folded her hand into a fist and pummelled his arm.

'Who is Wilkinson?'

'He is my friend.'

'You've never mentioned him to me.'

'Why should I? What can I say to you about Wilkinson, Baggot, Evans, Baillie? What would they mean to you? You don't know what they look like. You don't know the sound of their voices. I might just as well tell you fairy tales. They don't belong in this life. Nor do I any more. This is a prison we live in here. You know that as well as I.'

'Wilkinson, Baggot, Evans, Baillie.'

'My friends. We mess around together. Talk. We go on long route marches over the hills. Wilkinson and I . . . well. His father's gone too. Missing believed . . . We have that in common.' His voice trembled for a moment. He bit his finger.

'Wilkinson, Baggot, Evans, Baillie. What's his name?'

'His name?'

'Yes, dopey. He must have a Christian name. Everyone has a name.'

Eddie stared at her.

'Yes, of course. His mother calls him Patch . . .'

'You've met his mother?'

'But I think his name is Patrick. To us, the rest of us, he's Wilkinson P. H. He has a younger brother, Wilkinson R. J. He's only thirteen. Quite a decent kid.'

'How silly it all is, not to know people's names.'

'It's all right, you know. We're friends.'

'Well?'

'Well what?'

'What about telling me this great secret, this Wilkinson secret, or have you changed your mind?'

He stood up and bit once more at his finger.

'Eddie . . .'

'I promised. I want to tell you, I really do, but . . .'

He ran quickly to the door and opened it. There was no one in the passage. There was no one outside in the garden hiding in the swaying trees. There was no sound in the house at all. Just emptiness.

'I do think you're mean. Indescribably mean. When have I ever told on you? I promise I won't breathe your secret to a soul. You know you can trust me with your life.'

He took a deep breath and then the words streamed out of his mouth.

'We're going to join up, Wilkinson and I. It's all arranged. Friday. The day after tomorrow. I'm getting off the train at Crewe. He's going to meet me there.'

She didn't understand what he was saying. She clutched at his arm.

'Eddie . . .'

'He's found out all the know-how. He's great like that. He's an organiser. I got a . . .'

'No, Eddie. What are you saying? You're going to join . . . No.'

'. . . letter from him saying it's on. Imagine . . .'

'No . . . no.' She began to slap at him ineffectually with her hands.

'Imagine, Flora, in three days I will be in the war.'

'No. You . . .'

'Yes. I will be preparing to be a soldier.'

'You're too young. They won't let you. They can't . . .'

'They can, you know. I'm nearly eighteen. We could have joined up at the end of last term, but we wanted to see our people before we set out. We're going to the depot at Crewe and . . .'

Flora jumped from the sofa and ran towards the door. He was after her in a flash and caught her by the arm.

'Where do you think you're going?'

'To tell Mother. You're such a fool, Eddie. She won't let you go. You're still at school. You're hurting my arm. Let go of me. You can't do this. You mustn't leave us. You . . .'

He shook her so hard that one of her shoes fell off, clattering across the floor.

'Stop making that racket. You'll have the snooper in on us. Flora. Flora, for God's sake, shut up. Come on, sit down. Stop that noise. Sit. Here. We must talk. You promised. You know you promised.'

He picked her up and threw her on to the sofa and then quickly sat on her legs. He pulled a handkerchief from his pocket and shoved it into her hand.

'Now shut up, wipe your face. You're behaving like a little kid. Blow your disgusting nose. Why oh why did I tell you? Why could I not keep my mouth shut? Do stop crying. I'll be OK. Mop up, darling Flora. Everything will be fine.'

'You'll be killed.'

He laughed.

'Of course I won't be killed.'

'Daddy was killed.'

'That's no reason why I should be. And I know, I positively know that he would have wanted me to go.'

'He would not, he would have wanted you to stay at school. He would have . . .'

'You're too young to know anything about it. I only told you because I thought you would think it was a lark. I didn't want you to think that I was deceiving you, and now you're behaving like a baby.'

'I am not.'

'You're spoiling it all. You're making me feel rotten.'

'Oh Eddie.'

She threw her arms around his neck. He could feel the heat of her face through his clothes.

'Come on, baby. Don't cry. Please. Smile, just a little smile. I'll miss you. I'll write to you, I promise, and the war will be over and I will be home. I will be a hero, just fancy that. I know it's what Father would have wanted me to do. Step into his shoes.'

'And I can only say no and go on and on saying no.'

'It doesn't matter what you say. It's all arranged. I can't back out now, even if I wanted to. I have promised and you must promise too. Please, Flora. A secret. Just between you and me. Please. We mustn't be enemies. Look, tomorrow night we'll dance. Here. Just you and me. My last night at home. I'll pick out all the best records. We'll put on our best clothes and we'll dance our feet off. It will give me something to remember. Hey? What do you say?'

She mopped at her face with his handkerchief. He shifted himself from her legs and stood up. He held out a hand towards her.

'I don't know,' she said. 'It's a bit like a seal of approval, isn't it?'

'Silly. You mustn't think of it like that. It will be a ball. Our ball. Like the night before Waterloo. We'll have candles . . . yes, and champagne. Why not? There's all that champagne in the cellar that Father bought. We mustn't let it go to waste. And we'll dance until our feet give up and then I'll be off in the train and no one will be the wiser. Please say yes, Flora.'

She put her hand in his and he pulled her up from the sofa.

'You always win, don't you?'

'That's the girl.'

He pulled her towards him in a great bear hug, and then putting his lips to her neck he blew warm air on to her skin. She jumped away, pushing him as hard as she could.

'Never,' she shouted the word, 'never do that again.'

Then suddenly through the door came the sound of Nellie's voice.

'Missy, Missy Flora.'

Calling.

'Missy Flora, your bath is run.'

'Missee Flora, your bath is run,' echoed Eddie.

The two of them looked at each other and then burst into laughter, great swoops of laughter.

'Missy Flora.'

Nearer.

'Coming.'

Flora's voice was quivering with laughter. She picked her shoe up from the floor and ran to the door.

She turned at the door and curtsied to her brother.

'Missee Flora gratefully accepts your kind invitation.'

She was gone.

That was a close shave, he thought. He wandered over to the window. He opened one side of the glass door and stepped out into the garden. He could hear the sound of music from the dance hall, and above his head a million stars stared down at the earth. He felt enormously happy; his life was about to begin. His real life, his life with a capital L.

Flora sipped her wine and thought her thoughts — well, they were recollections rather than thoughts; that, she decided, was the boring thing about being what seemed to her incredibly old. When you sat down peacefully to think about life, death and things of that nature, memories kept getting in the way, or sleep. She wondered why you needed so much sleep when you never did anything to tire you out. Nellie does all those things. She bicycles down to the village to give the orders in the shops and visit the post office, she goes to Mass on Sundays and confession, though God alone knows what she has to confess. Knocking back the vino, perhaps, and of course the gambles that the pair of them took on the horses once a week, and a bit more often if the great classic races were being run. Never did any harm to anyone. Never, never. She looked across the kitchen to where Nellie was beating something in a bowl with a fork. She had offered to buy one of those neat machines for beating things but Nellie had shaken her head most vehemently and said that she'd beaten eggs with a fork all her life and she would continue to do so till the day she died and if Flora didn't like the way she did things she could find herself another housekeeper. She was singing now.

'"... in the ranks of de-ath you'll find him ..."'

Was that Tom Moore? She couldn't remember. She did know that Nellie had a great partiality for Tom Moore, and of course for Julie Andrews, Judy Garland, Pavarotti and others whose names she couldn't recall at this very moment.

'"His father's sword he has girded on and his wild harp sluuuung ..."'

'Nellie.'

'I thought you'd dozed off.' She raised her eyes from whatever was in the bowl. 'Did I wake you with my singing?'

'I wasn't asleep. I was just wondering, what do you think they call us in the village? That pair of old winos? Isn't that the word they use nowadays?'

Nellie laughed, and put the fork down on the table beside the basin. She picked up the bottle and came over to Flora. She filled up her glass.

'That's not a very nice thing to have in your mind. If they knew about the master's wine, they'd never use a word like that.' As she filled her own glass, she was thinking. 'Conisurio. That's it. That's what we are, conisurios. It's the class of wine we drink makes the difference.'

Flora raised her glass.

'Here's to us. Two conisurios.'

'Long may we last.'

'Long may Daddy's wine last.'

'Amen.'

The candles flickered, the glass and silver shone. Flora squeezed Nellie's arm.

'How beautiful it looks, and grand. Sometimes it's good to be grand. So tell me, Nellie, what is tonight's anniversary? I really feel we should have changed our clothes, put on something more formal.' She looked expectantly at Nellie.

'You know well. Will you carve or I?'

'You always carve, and I don't know, my mind is in a muddle this evening. Not a serious muddle; a sort of misty one. Nothing to get worried about. There will be no need for Dr Carey and his soothing potions. Before we eat, I think we should drink to Eddie.'

Nellie put her glass down on the table and clasped her hands in front of her as if she was about to burst into a prayer.

'He's very close to us tonight. I can almost see him over by the window. Look, look, Nellie. Is he a ghost or a figment?'

'I don't believe there's such a thing as ghosts and I don't know what a figment is. I think you're teasing me, pulling my leg.' Her voice trembled.

'Yes. I suppose I was. I suppose . . . I'm sorry.' She put out a hand and squeezed Nellie's shoulder. 'What do you remember, Nellie? Out of all those long years, what remains in your head? When you've nothing else churning in your mind, can you browse on the past? Can a sound or the sight of some silly thing transport you back?'

Nellie looked puzzled. 'Back where? Back. Sure I can click my fingers and I can remember anything I want. Is that what you mean? Haven't I a memory like an elephant. The dinner will be ruined if I don't attend to it.'

She plonked her glass down on the table and walked back

over to the huge black range, her shoes creaking as she walked. She clattered and banged, she picked up the long whetstone and began to sharpen the fearsome-looking carving knife, whick, whick. Flora sat back into her chair again and wondered to herself about Wilkinson. All his fault, she said in her head. Wretched, wretched Wilkinson, but then how could it be his fault? You had to look at it sensibly; it was as much her fault as Wilkinson's. If she had told Mummy, that would have put a stop to the whole thing, the whole D-plus-one fiasco on some damned Normandy beach. One day in the year I can moan and groan. I can throw blame around, I can mourn in my own way, not just for his fiasco, but for mine too. Nellie's mourning takes the form of eating and drinking; mine is bewailing my own devastation. That was something Nellie did not know about.

Whick, whick.

'Nellie.'

Whick, whick.

'Nellie.'

'Just coming in a minute.'

She pulled the dish with the lamb on it over to a suitable place and drew the sharpened knife gently across the meat.

'Yes.' She muttered the word to herself. 'Yes, yes.'

The smell of garlic drifted across the room. Flora smiled.

'He never lets you down. You know, when I came here first, all those many, many years ago, I saw myself becoming a person of consequence. Miss Maher, everyone would call me. Full of respect.'

'They are full of respect, Nellie. It's just that times have changed. Respect and love for you. Everyone has that. What could be better?'

'Not a soul calls me Miss Maher. Even the little kids call out "Hello, Nellie" to me from their pushchairs.'

'And you smile at them and give them sweets. Why do you want it to be any other way? Nobody calls me Flora, except maybe behind my back. I think that their heads are filled with misconceptions about me and I don't think I care what they call me. No, I don't.' She took a swig of wine. 'That's good wine, Nellie. Well chosen.'

'We conisurios only drink the best.'

They laughed. They were friends.

Yes. Yes, that was it. She put her knife and fork down on her plate and patted at her mouth with her napkin.

'I remember what it was that I wanted to ask you. Wilkinson. Did he ever talk to you about Wilkinson?'

Nellie frowned.

'Who?'

'Wilkinson.'

'Never heard of him. Who would be talking to me about someone I've never heard of?'

'Eddie, of course. This is Eddie's day. What other person would I be talking about?'

'He hardly spoke to me. I don't know why you'd be thinking otherwise. Good morning, Nellie. Nice to see the sun shining. Take care of yourself on that bike of yours. Good night, Nellie. I remember every word from him. Always the same. Never anything about someone called Wilkinson, never what you might call conversation. He never conversed with me.' She stopped talking and gazed back into the past. When she did speak again, her voice was so low that Flora could barely hear her. 'I longed for conversation with him. Tell me about Wilkinson.'

'I don't know anything except that they were friends. Bagot, Evans, Baillie and Wilkinson. He mentioned them for the first time the night before he left. He just said their names really, except for Wilkinson. He told me about their plan. They were going . . . just the two of them . . . they were going . . .'

'They went.'

'Yes.'

'Why didn't you stop them?'

'I promised.'

'Promises!'

'We have to keep promises. I know I should have told Mummy. I should have run away from him as fast as I could. I should have shouted for her. For help. I should have . . . but he turned my thoughts away from sneaking. That's what he would have called it. Sneaking. I couldn't bear to sneak on him, be thought of as a sneak. So I let him go and be killed.'

'And Wilkinson?'

'I don't know what happened to him. Did he live or die? Was he there to hold Eddie's hand when the end came? Did they die side by side like the heroes of old? I used to have terrible dreams . . . terrible dreams. I . . . Oh dear . . . You know he didn't even know what he was fighting for. He told me that Daddy would have wanted him to go, but that can't be true,

Daddy would have rather he'd stayed at school than be killed. I used to have terrible dreams.'

She picked up her knife and fork and began to stuff her mouth with food, as if she could block up the rush of words. Nellie stared across the table at her.

'I never knew any of this.'

'I . . . we . . . thought you knew everything.'

'No.'

'Eddie said you knew everything. You were always there, he used to say. Listening, staring, waiting in passages or out in the garden, stitching, mending, but always listening. You were like a spy, he said.'

There was a long silence between them. Nellie's face was burning hot; finally she spoke in what was barely louder than a whisper.

'He shouldn't have said that. He got it all wrong. All. I . . .' Her voice died away. She poked at the corner of her right eye with a finger. 'A spy! How could he say such a thing? I always hoped that he would smile at me or say something, not just good morning, Nellie. Not just . . . not just . . . Mind the child, the mistress said, look after the child. That's your job. See she comes to no harm. So I watched you like a hawk, so I did, and the stitching kept my fingers occupied. I enjoyed sewing and making little collars of lace and turn-ups for the ends of the children's sleeves. A little lace turn-up and a collar spreading out around the neck makes a tired dress into something new and smart. I often wondered if I might get a job in one of those posh Dublin dress designers, but then things didn't turn out the way I wanted.' She jumped up from her seat. 'Can I get you more?'

'He was only joking when he said that. I promise. He didn't mean it. He used to make silly jokes. I'm sure that going to the war started out as a joke and then became a reality they couldn't do anything to stop. No, no more, thanks.' She waved her hands at Nellie to sit down. Nellie remained on her feet.

'You never made me any lace collars or cuffs, at least I've no recollection of any.'

'The mistress didn't hold with such things. You ran around the place in shirts and shorts, like a boy might. She thought you would have more freedom like that.'

'Maybe she was right.'

'You were a lonely little girl. I always used to think that.'

'I had my books and all Daddy's books. It always seemed like millions of books. You know I don't suppose I've read them all yet. I wondered sometimes if he managed. Some of them are pretty dry and boring. He would have been too gay and cheerful to plough his way through such dry stuff. Those terrible Brontës. I've always loathed them, all mists and moaning. I bet he never read them. John Buchan would have been more his style. You know, Nellie, you've got the wrong day. Tomorrow. The twelfth of September, that's the day we should be doing our feasting. That was his last day with us. You went to the pictures, and he and I . . .' She threw her head back and roared with laughter. 'We had such fun. Definitely the twelfth, Nellie dear.'

'In the name of God . . .' Nellie ran over to the kitchen table and picked up the newspaper. She peered at the top corner, she screwed up her eyes. She gave a little scream. 'Bloody feckin' glasses, I thought I'd manage to the end without them. Today's the eleventh. You're right. You're right. Tomorrow's the day. Tomorrow's the twelfth. Amn't I the old eejit? What'll we do?'

Flora continued to laugh and after a moment or two Nellie joined in.

'We'll do it again tomorrow.' The words puffed out of her mouth between the hiccoughs of laughter. 'We'll have another drink and our pudding and go to bed early, so we'll be ready to do it all over again tomorrow, and then the next day we will go and see about glasses for you. Here's to tomorrow.' She picked up her glass and waved it round. The laughter had turned into silence. 'Maybe tomorrow I will tell you something you don't already know. There are things I have never told you.'

'I know everything.'

Flora shook her head slowly from side to side. She sat down in her chair again and picked up her spoon and fork, then like a child might she began to bang them on the table.

'Pudding, pudding,' she shouted as she banged.

The next day was the twelfth of September.

As it was the last day before he went back to school, Eddie had been allowed to choose what they would have for lunch. He was traditional in his tastes and always chose the same meal: roast leg of lamb followed by apple and blackberry pie covered with great blobs of thick, yellow Jersey cream. The countryside was glowing under the golden autumn sun and the swallows were gathering together, preparing for their flight; in rows they sat and twittered on the telegraph wires, like notes on the staves in the music books on top of the piano. Flora watched them from the playroom window and wondered how they communicated with each other, who was the boss, who said now, we will go now. Ready steady go. They must be waiting for some sort of signal; this was the third day they had gathered. Sometimes impatience seemed to get the better of a few and they would curl up into the air and fly around for a short while before settling back into their places again. Then one day soon they would all be gone. Not a swallow to be seen. She wondered if she were to spend all day, until darkness had driven them back to their nests, and then all the next day from what Eddie called sparrow's fart, but only when there were no grown-ups around, if she would find out what the message was, who was the messenger. Would she be the only human being in the world to have this information? What good would that do anyone? We seem to store up information in the huge store cases of our minds and it just sits in there in the dark. And then if you do need it, you can't find it.

Is information merely useless baggage?

She thought about this enormously important question and stared out of the window at the same time.

The stuff you learn at school.

I suppose it's what you do with all that information that matters; that's what they teach you at school. How to make sense of all that stuff that gets shoved into your head. Of course you don't have to listen.

She laughed out loud at herself, at her nonsensical thoughts.

The rows of birds quivered in the wires and she turned away. This was her moment to steal from Mummy's dressing room the perfect dress to wear tonight. She must dazzle Eddie. She ran down the passage and up the back stairs, which came out just beyond the dressing-room door, and she slipped in unseen. Her mother's dressing room was like a dim treasure house, the lights reflected and re-reflected in the mirrors and looking glasses and in the polished surfaces of the furniture. Everything had its place, its exactitude and position. Since Daddy's death her mother had hardly used anything in here; her daily clothes she kept in the more mundane presses in her bedroom. When Flora was certain that her mother was not around, she used to slip into this room, open all the cupboard doors and sit breathing in the luxurious smell of silk and velvet and listen to the whispering as the dresses moved slightly on their hangers, murmurs and creaks, secrets being told and retold, memories. It was to Flora a room full of ghosts.

This visitation, however, she knew what she wanted and she moved across the floor to the centre of a long cupboard and pulled open the doors. The dresses on their hangers swayed softly together, like dancers she thought. A pale grey crêpe de Chine dress was what she had in her mind. She remembered her mother wearing it to a party one night and it had swirled gently round her body, now stroking, now floating, making her look like a misty princess from a book of French fairy tales. She found it and pulled it out. I will be the belle of this ball, she thought. It seemed to weigh nothing over her arm. She held it up against herself and did a few dancing steps. Oh yes, it must be the most beautiful dress in the whole world. She hunted round for a pair of silver sandals, suitable for dancing in, then cautiously opened the door out to the landing. Not a soul to be seen. She scooted down the passage to her room. 'I will be the belle of the ball,' she sang as she closed her bedroom door behind her.

The dining room was cold; it wasn't until October that the fire was lit, and before that it was like eating in a huge green cave with dead men and women staring from the walls, criticising, Flora always thought, the way we carry on today. That evening Mummy arrived for dinner in her dressing gown and her hair tied up in a colourful scarf.

'Darling Ma.' Eddie was surprised.

She waved her arms in the air.

'I've worked so hard in the garden all day, I thought a really hot bath would be a good thing and then bed, full of hot-water bottles.' She ignored Flora. She picked Eddie's hand up and kissed it. 'Last night. Sorry, sorry, dear boy. We will miss you.' She sighed. 'This terrible war will be over soon. I do hope so. My modest prayer drifts up to God each night.' She smiled at him, then sat down and spread her napkin on her knee. 'So what have you dear things been doing all day? Eddie's last day?'

Flora felt her face going red.

'Nothing in particular. N . . . nothing. Nellie went to the pictures.'

'I'm not really interested in what Nellie did.' She turned towards Eddie and smiled.

'I went riding. For miles and miles. Up over Calary bog. It was fantastic.'

'Memorable?'

'Most memorable.'

'That is good. You should always do something memorable on your last day.'

He laughed.

'You make it sound like my last day on earth. I'm merely going back to school.'

Flora crossed her fingers.

'What would you do,' asked their mother, 'if it really were your last day? What would you want to die remembering?'

Eddie laughed again.

'How absurd you are, Mummy darling. I'm never going to die, or not until I'm ninety anyway.'

'I hate this conversation,' said Flora.

'Your father always said that no one ever dies, we all just move on somewhere else.'

'Nomadic life and death for eternity; maybe we will all drift from planet to planet. Meeting, touching, passing, loving and hating. Hey ho, what do you think of that, Flora?'

'I hate this conversation.'

'Don't start fighting. I am in no mood for fighting, children. Eat up your dinner quickly so I can get back to my hot-water bottles and quietude. I do so love quietude.'

Later that evening, the house was silent, good nights had been said, Mummy was tucked up well, surrounded by warmth and books.

Flora pushed open the playroom door. The room was dim with flickering candlelight; they stood on the mantelpiece, the tables, the escritoire, and the high windows reflected the dancing flames. The tall man in uniform turned as he heard the door opening. He held out a hand towards her. He moved with confidence towards her and then for a moment the confidence left him and he stopped. 'I . . . oh . . . Mother . . .'

Flora threw her head back and laughed, a boisterous, childish laugh, as her father might have laughed.

'I fooled you. Didn't I? What do you think? Don't I look a dream?' She began to dance around the room, the grey dress floating round her as her body twisted and turned and the laughter bubbled out of her.

'I fooled you.'

'Just for a moment . . . I thought you were . . . That's all. Just one moment.'

'Yes. I fooled you. Nellie was out at the pictures so I slipped into Mummy's dressing room and there . . . Well, everything was so beautiful. Butterfly clothes, silk, velvet, satin, dresses and cloaks and marvellous shawls of all colours. How beautiful she must have looked then, before the war. So beautiful . . .'

'Yes. Just like you.'

She stopped twirling and looked her brother up and down. She moved slowly towards him, until she was close enough to put out her hand and touch his uniform. 'Is that Daddy's? His . . . ?'

Eddie nodded.

'I thought I might surprise you. Instead, you have surprised me.'

'Perhaps you shouldn't have.'

'Why on earth not? Who's to know? Nobody ever opens

those boxes of his. Tell you something, though, it stinks of mothballs. Rather disgusting.'

They stared in silence at each other, almost as if they didn't believe in what they were seeing. Eddie was the first to break the silence. He gave a little giggle.

'Anyway,' he said, 'I went down to the cellar and got some . . .' He waved his arm towards the table. 'Some . . .'

'Champagne?'

'Two bottles. The real thing. We can get sozzled. Won't that be fun?'

'You pinched it and their beautiful Venetian glasses. You know we're not allowed to use them. What a wonderful evening of sin. I bet you can't open it without it fizzing all over you.'

'I can so. Wilkinson showed me how.'

'Oh bloody old Wilkinson again.'

'Tut, little girl. Now watch carefully. This may come in handy. It's always useful to be able to open a bottle of champagne.' He picked up one of the bottles. 'Veuve Clicquot. *Salut.*' He kissed the side of the bottle and pulled off the gold cap that was covering the cork. His fingers twisted the wire. 'See. You take off the wire and then you put your hand, like this . . . Watch, Flora, no giggling, just watch. Quite firm, and then . . . Quick, a glass, quick, it's coming.'

A few bubbles splashed on to the sleeve of his jacket and sank into its darkness; she caught the rest in the beautiful gilded glass. Eddie poured wine for each of them and they stood staring at it, almost not daring to drink it, so beautiful and dangerous it seemed to them.

'Now we must drink a toast.' He held his glass up between them. 'Our wonderful future.'

She touched his glass with hers.

'Our wonderful future.'

The bubbles rushed up her nose and she sneezed.

'Oooh. Ooooh. This is wonderful. When I'm grown up, I shall drink nothing but champagne. Ooooh.' She sneezed again and he refilled their glasses.

'You know, Flora, you look incredibly beautiful drinking champagne.'

She laughed, she felt happy as she hadn't done since Daddy had been killed.

'It's the stolen dress, anyone would look beautiful in it.' She whirled away from him, spraying champagne from her glass on his uniform.

'Hey. Take care. It's for drinking, not throwing around the place.'

'I feel so incredibly happy. Come on, Eddie, music. Only dancing could make me feel happier. Music, maestro, please.'

The candlelight danced in her eyes. He put out a hand and touched her face gently.

'I chose all the records that I like best. Here, fill our glasses and I'll put on number one. I think it's one of the best of their records. We must remember, darling Flora, that this is their evening.'

Plinky, plinky.

Light music.

Plinky, plinky.

He held his arms out towards her, and she walked into them.

*They asked me how I knew*
*My true love was true*
*I of course replied*

He held her close to him.

*Something here inside*

She smelled sweet.

*Cannot be denied*
*They said some day you'll find*

She was light on her feet.

*All who love are blind*
*When your heart's on fire*
*You must realise*
*Smoke gets in your eyes*

He nuzzled his head into her long, soft hair.
　　She sighed.
　　'We have so little time left,' she said.
　　She sighed again.
　　'Melancholic,' he whispered in her ear. 'This is not a night for melancholic thoughts.'

*So I chaffed them and I gaily laughed*
*To think they could doubt my love*
*Yet today, my love has flown away*
*I am without my love*

Plinky plinky plink.

*Now laughing friends deride*
*Tears I cannot hide*
*So I smile and say*

With a slight whisk of his arm, he twirled her round.

*When a lovely flame dies*

And she came back close against him once more.

*Smoke gets in your eyes*

'More champagne?'
'Of course, but you mustn't stop dancing. My feet want to go on dancing for ever.'
He danced her over to the table and filled their glasses.

*Smoke gets in your eyes.*

The voice stopped.
'Oh Eddie.'

'Two moments.'

He wound the handle. She danced, humming to herself and sipping from the glass, her eyes tight shut.

'Will you miss me?'

He took the old record off the turntable and slipped on the next.

'Of course, you silly girl. How could I not miss you?'

'What fun they must have had . . . all that dancing in the days of their youth.'

'It's all ahead of us.' He held his arms out for her. 'Just think what fun we'll have. How beautiful you will be, Flora, very, very beautiful. I will be quite jealous of all your lovers.'

She laughed, threw back her head and laughed, again just like her father used to do.

'Darling Eddie, it's so difficult to think of lovers when your head is being stuffed full of French irregular verbs and Archimedes' principle . . . "I wandered lonely as a cloud that floats on high o'er" . . . Stuff like that.'

'You'll forget all that. You'll forget this evening.'

'Oh no. How could I ever forget this evening? My first perfect evening.'

'Will you miss me?'

'Silly boy. School will start, no time for missing brothers, and you will have . . . No . . . you won't be at school. You won't have Baggot, Evans or Baillie; it will just be you and Wilkinson out on the battlefield. Will you have your guardian angel hovering overhead? Oh Eddie, I do hope so.'

'Such a baby you are.' He pulled her really close to him and kissed the side of her face. Suddenly she became aware of the music.

'Where did you get this? "The Desert Lullaby". I imagined she had broken it into bits. It's wonderful to hear it again.'

'Wilkinson gave it to me.'

'Bloody Wilkinson.'

'One day, when the war is over, you'll meet him and you'll really like him. Why do you call it "The Desert Lullaby"? I think its real name is "Lili Marleen".'

'That was what Mummy called it. I thought it was a good name. Daddy said they all used to lie under the stars in the desert listening to it. Them and us. Imagine, just imagine. Mummy told me all about it after he had gone. Lullaby seemed right to me. Did Wilkinson have a name for it? Why did he give it to you anyway?'

'He said he wanted it out of the house.'

'*Vor der Kaserne bei dem großen Tor, Stand eine Laterne und steht sie noch davor* . . . There you are, I can remember the words. How's my German? *Gut? Ja?*'

'You'll make a first-class spy.'

The singer began to sing, and they danced, and at the end of the record they poured themselves more champagne and put the record on again and danced some more.

'I feel wonderfully woozy,' she said after the fifth record. She staggered towards the sofa.

'Have some more champagne.'

'I'd better not. I had better not. I might get lost on my way home.' She threw back her head and laughed again and fell on to the sofa. 'You shouldn't drink champagne too fast. All those bubbles make you drunk, so they do.'

'Well I don't care about getting drunk. I'm going to have some more. I think you should join me. I can see you safely home. I promise to see you safely home. Now, before I sit down beside you, just a drop. Be a pal. You wouldn't want me to drink alone, would you?'

'A drop, then.'

'A drop is all there is. One for you and one for me.'

He emptied the bottle into their glasses.

A few drops and a little fizz.

Her feet were sore, her belly was sore, her head throbbed, she felt as though her eyes were stitched shut. She pulled one of them open; light streaked in through a crack in the curtains. She heard the pony shifting restlessly in the shafts, its harness jangled. She pushed the heavy bedclothes off her naked body and pulled open the other eye. A murmur of voices. She wondered vaguely what day it was, what time it was, who was below her window with the trap. She felt ill, her heart was bumping. Why was she naked? She stretched out a hand and felt the piece of paper; she forced herself to sit up and focused her eyes on it. Black ink. *I kept my promise to bring you safely home. Goodbye, dear one.* Her head turned for a moment, toppled and fell back on to her pillows. Eddie. The pony stamped once more.

She slithered carefully out of the bed; her feet hurt as they took her weight. She walked slowly to the window and peered out through the crack in the curtains. The boy was just climbing into the trap, the reins gathered in his hand. Eddie and his mother stood at the bottom of the steps; he was holding her hand, wondering, Flora thought, whether to kiss her or not. He ducked his head quickly and touched the side of her face with his lips, then put his foot on the step of the trap and swung himself in. He glanced up at Flora's window but she stepped quickly back. She waved, she blew him a kiss, both were lost in the folds of the curtain. She stood listening to the sound of the pony clopping down the avenue; after a few moments there was no longer any sound at all and she peered out of the window again to see Nellie, forlorn, standing on the grass, her face streaked with the misery of tears.

'Why did you cry?'

'Crumble,' said Nellie, putting a plate down in front of Flora. 'And a few late loganberries, just for fun. Would you like to go on with the red, or would you prefer some white?'

'Why didn't you answer my question?'

Nellie walked back across the kitchen to collect her own plate of crumble and a little bowl of berries. She placed them on the table and seated herself.

'What sort of a question is that? You have never seen me cry. I am not a crying type. Even in my own privacy.'

Flora sighed.

'The day Eddie went away. September 1943. You stood on the grass and you cried.'

'So long ago, so very distant. I don't remember crying. As I

46

said, I'm not a crying type; even as a child I was dry-eyed. Red or white?'

'I saw you. Red, please.' Nellie pushed the bottle across the table towards her. 'The trap drove away and Mummy went into the house and you just stood there on the grass, crying, as if he were your ...'

'He didn't even shake my hand. He didn't wave. He didn't seem to know that I was there.'

'His head was probably too full of other things. He was, after all, just about to go and be a hero.' Flora thought for a few moments that Nellie was going to cry then and there, sitting across the table with her hand clamped round the stem of one of Mother's beautiful red Venetian glasses. She was tapping her fingers on the table as if she were calling up yesterday's shades, thoughts that she had packed tightly away for ever, happenings that she had never wanted to think of again.

'Then,' she said at last, 'I went into the playroom. 'Twas very early, the sun barely rising, but I thought to myself I might as well start my work as go back to bed, and there didn't I find a mess to beat the band. What, I wondered to myself, were that pair of scallywags up to at all? Empty bottles and the broken red scattering of one of those precious glasses. I whisked them away out of sight first, in case the mistress came down and caught me at it. Then when I had the room to rights I found her dress, her grey silk dress, rolled up and thrown in the wastepaper basket. I took it out and shook it ever so carefully and it floated, so fine and soft was the silk, and I held it close to my face to feel the softness on my skin. It was torn beyond my mending, so I sent up a little prayer to the mother of God that the mistress wouldn't go looking for her grey silk dress ever again.' She gave a little laugh. 'I don't think she ever did.'

'Oh Nellie, how shocking of us not to have cleared up the mess we made. I don't remember a thing except for dancing and how sore my feet were the next day. And of course the champagne. We drank too much champagne. That was the real problem. Yes. How odd, I never thought to blame the champagne before.'

'Blame?'

Flora's face went vague for a moment, blank, as if disconnected from her mind.

'Just things, things.' She came back to normality again. 'Anyway, that's the past. Pretty horrid it was too. It's odd looking back into the past, so much of it is pretty horrid, and then there are moments of such happiness that you forget the horrors completely. I've always wondered why the Americans consider happiness to be a right; of course it isn't. It's a prize that comes, sometimes for no reason at all. What do you think?'

'Blether. Sometimes you do blether so. I listen. That's my role in life, I listen. All those years you were away, I listened to the mistress. I sewed and listened. I knitted and listened. I crocheted and listened. Over and over again she told me the same things. She didn't want me to say anything, only to . . . She had lost everyone.'

'She hadn't lost me.'

'You might as well have been dead. You never even wrote her one letter. She didn't have that to look forward to. She, poor lady, didn't have anything to look forward to.'

'It's strange to think how two people can have such different views of one other person.'

'You were only a child. A giddy child. You were too young to have views about why grown-ups behaved the way they did. They knew what they were doing.'

'She didn't.'

'How can you say such a thing?'

'All too easily. She either didn't know what she was doing or she was a woman filled with evil, and I don't want to believe that about her.' She took a drink of wine and let the liquid lie warm in her mouth. She shut her eyes and Nellie could see the pearls that were clinging to her lashes.

Nellie wondered to herself why it was that during a silence time seemed to move so slowly. She had cried. She remembered she had looked at her face in the glass over the fireplace in the playroom as she folded up the grey dress and she had seen the streaks on her skin and she had rubbed them away with the soft grey silk.

'I did cry,' she said, quite loud. 'But only for a moment or two. I was sad to see him go. I thought how lonely we would all be without him. The house would be quiet. Yes, I do have to say I cried a little. You've no idea what the house was like with you two gone away to school.'

'You've no idea what school was like.'

'You were learning stuff, weren't you, and you had all those other little girls to play with, to talk to. I remember you told me once that on Saturday afternoons you were allowed to go out of the school grounds with a friend or two and walk in the streets and look in the shop windows and maybe even have a cup of coffee.'

'We did that, yes. Once we were fourteen we were allowed to do that. Personally I'd rather have been at home, just messing about. Here. You know, I've never wanted to be anywhere else. He was wearing his grey flannel suit, his school suit, and I wanted to throw the window open and shout down at them, "He's going to the war with Wilkinson!" That would have put the cat among the pigeons, but I remembered my promise. Damned promises. Damned, damned . . . Perhaps, Nellie, we are all ruined by the promises we make.'

'Ssh,' said Nellie. 'You're getting heated. Remember what Dr Carey says about getting heated.'

Flora shook her head; she flicked a finger against her glass. 'Heated, my eye,' she said. 'Dr Carey, my eye. I'm just getting drunk. It's a day for getting drunk — well it's not really, but I'm going to pretend it is, and tomorrow I will have a tumultuous hangover and I'll stay in bed all day and you will fuss and cluck like an old hen and then the next day we will be back to normal. Two sweet old ladies. Go and get us a bottle of champagne.'

'There's only two left.'

'So?'

'Shouldn't we keep them for special occasions? When we win the Derby. That'd be a time for celebration. For being flahoola.'

'If we ever win the Derby, I promise you, Nellie, we will buy some more. We'll replenish the master's cellar. Now, are you going or am I going to make the adventurous descent?'

'You'd only fall and break your neck. And then we'd have you in the hospital and you wouldn't enjoy that, not one little bit . . .'

'Oh for heaven's sake. Will you go or I go?'

Nellie got slowly up from her chair.

'I hate them old cellars at night. You can hear the mice scuttling round in the dark, and there might be worse things than mice.'

Flora laughed as she watched Nellie moving across the room. She saw for a moment her nimble, slender brother, or maybe it was Daddy. The major himself, making the adventurous descent down to his carefully tended bottles. The words of the German song came back into her head.

> Vor der Kaserne bei dem großen Tor
> Stand eine Laterne und steht sie noch davor
> So wollen wir uns da wieder seh'n
> Bei der Laterne wollen wir steh'n
> Wie einst, Lili Marleen
> Wie einst, Lili Marleen

Maybe it was Daddy, just over there by the door, in his uniform. I have never seen him in his uniform, she thought. Just photographs, not the real man.

And that woman's voice.

*Aus dem stillen Raume, aus der Erden Grund*
*Hebt mich wie im Traume, dein verliebter Mund*

The real man was so sweet. Would Eddie ever have become such a sweet man? I don't suppose so. I don't think he would have lived here. He didn't have the appetite for country living.

That woman's voice.

*Wenn sich die späten Nebel drehen*

Grey, like Mother's dress. Yes, grey. But not soft like the dress, not melting; it had been a tragic voice, broken by war, and all those men in the desert – schoolboys, fathers, lords and commoners – they had listened to that rough, sad voice. Friends and enemies. Strangers. Yes.

*Wie einst, Lili Marleen*
*Wie einst, Lili Marleen*

They had all dreamed.

Eddie had not been there, only Daddy.

Eddie had only lasted one day. D plus one. Then, in loving memory, the end of the line. A long, long line.

'In loving memory.' She heard her voice say the words.

'I was right. Now there's only one bottle left.'

Nellie put the bottle gently on the table and began to clear away the plates.

'We'll have no nonsense with it. That'll be for a big race.

The National, the Derby, the Prix de l'Arc, now wouldn't that be a great one to win. That might be a two-bottle win. It's not as cold as it should be, but it'll do us. Sometimes champagne is too cold. Were you crying?'

'No. Just musing. No tears. Push over the bottle and I'll open it.'

'All in good time. All in good time. I've the tidying-up to do, and then we must do our choosing tonight as you'll be in no fit state to choose anything tomorrow.'

As she spoke, she moved with amazing speed, shifting the plates and dishes, leaning over to give the table a wipe, piling pots and pans into the sink, filling the dishwasher.

'I'll be asleep and you'll have to bring the bottle back to the cellar if you take much longer.'

Nellie laughed. 'Get away out of that.' She pulled open a drawer in the sideboard and took out some pieces of paper, a little red notebook, two ballpoint pens and the sports section of the *Irish Times*. She plonked them in front of Flora. 'Get your head arranged. I'll be with you in a moment,' and she was away off out of the room, rather like, Flora thought, one of the mice that she complained about in the cellar.

She picked up the paper and spread it on the table in front of her. She ran her finger down the names of the runners. What idiotic names people put on racehorses. Such great times she and Nellie had had when they used to go to point-to-points in the spring. Mr Doris had taken them in his taxi cab and had enjoyed the fun as much as they had. Sometimes they arrived home with money jingling in their pockets, sometimes not a farthing. They once contemplated going to Cheltenham, that would have been such an adventure, but Nellie changed her mind about it almost at the last moment. Flora had always thought that Dr Carey had had some hand or part in that decision. He never appeared to interfere in her life, but she sensed his guiding hand steered her comings and goings in a benign fashion, which when she was younger and had more energy she resented, but gradually she drifted into acceptance of the way he and Nellie thought she should live. She, in spite of what everybody thought, had never been mad, never would be mad. Mummy had done her homework very well and in the eyes of the world she was a little soft in the head. Poor Flora. She smiled to herself as the words passed through her mind. Poor, poor Flora.

Nellie arrived back in with a red Venetian glass in each hand.

'Tra-la.' She waved the glasses in the air before she put them on the table. 'Now you may open the bottle.'

She settled herself at the table and pulled the papers towards her, she spread the *Irish Times* wide in front of her and took the top off her pen. She looked expectantly towards Flora, who was sitting with her fingers laced, unmoving.

'Which would you prefer, Nellie, champagne or port? I never thought to ask you. I just sent you scurrying off down to the rats and mice in the cellar without finding out which you might like.'

Nellie carefully wrote *Leopardstown 2.15* on the paper in front of her. The ink was very bright blue.

'Champagne. I would always vote for champagne. Port lies heavy on my stomach. But we must get our choosing over with before we have a drink and I will pedal down to Moran's first thing in the morning. I might even be able to persuade Mrs Moran to give my hair a going-over.'

'Your hair is perfectly all right.' Flora's fingers twisted the wire on the bottle.

'She'll put a bit of shape on it. She's a great hand with the scissors.'

'Quick, quick, Nellie, a glass.'

Nellie pushed one of the glasses across the table just in the nick of time. The cork flew out between Flora's fingers and the bubbles were neatly caught in the glass.

'Hooray.'

Flora filled each glass and they both admired the bubbles and the way the reflections of the candlelight bobbed and flickered in the wine.

'Almost too pretty to drink.' Flora raised the glass to her lips.

'Mary, Mother of God be with the pair of them.'

'Amen. I hope they have access to champagne.'

Both women giggled and drank.

'Conisurios.'

They raised the burdened, twinkling glasses towards each other and drank again. Nellie put her glass on the table with a thump and picked up the paper. She bent towards it and closed one eye.

'You know, I think I need glasses. I'm finding it very hard these days to see the small print. I wonder should I have a word with Dr Carey when he comes next. The letters scurry away like tiny insects running thither and yon. Maybe it's the wine. What do you think? Does too much wine affect the eyes? It's probably old age. That's what he'll say. We're not getting any younger, Nellie. Silly thing to say, anyway. Don't we all spend our lives not getting any younger?'

'Nellie . . .'

'Mr Marmalade, Line Dancer, Carrowleena . . . Mmmm . . .'

'There's something I've wanted to ask you for a long time.'

'Ask away. Champagne Charlie . . . now there's a name. Don't you think that's a good name for us? Champagne Charlie. Mind you, it's twenty to one. We'll put a few bob on it, just for fun.' She put a tick by the horse's name with the ballpoint pen. She waved the pen towards Flora. 'Ask away.'

'It's something I've always wondered about. Fifty years of wondering. That shows what a lazy person I am. Lethargic is perhaps a better word. You could have had a life. Do you never regret that?'

There was a long silence between them. Nellie wrote the word *life* in large letters on the piece of paper in front of her and then crossed it out with long, deep strokes, each stroke almost tearing the paper with its ferocity.

'What have I had?' she said finally. 'What is this I'm living? Isn't my belly full of good food and drink? I'm at peace. What more can anyone want? I never had high expectations for myself, you know. When I came to work here, sixteen I was, sweet sixteen, I thought I might rise to be housekeeper. My mother always told me that a housekeeper was a person of importance.

A person with dignity of their own. That's what I had in mind. Miss Maher. Miss Maher, when I walked down to the village and went into the shops. Perhaps I might have had a little car, so that I could drive up to Dublin, or to the pictures on my Thursday evenings. One of those nice little Morrises. I'm sure I could have managed one of them.'

Flora looked startled.

'Oh, dear Nellie. If you'd only said, I'm sure we could have got you a car. We still could. I'll talk to Mr . . .'

'Don't worry your head. You have to have a certificate these days to drive a car. I'd never manage that. Anyway, I've grown accustomed to the bike. I like the old bike, except when it's raining cats and dogs.'

'Maybe I might get a bike too. Keep you company. They say that cycling is very good for the health.'

Nellie hooted with laughter.

'It's no laughing matter. I'm sure I remember how to ride a bicycle. They say once you know, you never forget. I seem to remember that I used to be very daring. No hands, that sort of thing. I'm sure it would come back to me in a flash.'

She swooped her hands across the table, like a small child might, delighted with the vision of herself on a bicycle.

'Would you stop your foolishness,' said Nellie. 'Just think of the trouble I'd be in with Dr Carey if he saw you scooting down the hill to the village with no hands.'

'A pretty amazing sight, but . . .'

'But me no buts . . .'

'Shakespeare.'

'Rubbish. My mother said it all the time.'

'That doesn't mean it isn't Shakespeare.'

Nellie took a drink from her glass.

'I suppose I should answer your question.'

'Yes.'

'Well, I promised her. You know, in spite of all the carry-on of her down the years, I really think I loved her. I suppose I had no one else to love. And she had no one either, with you over there gone mad . . .'

'I had not gone mad, Nellie. You know that well.'

'She made me put my hand on the Bible and swear that I would mind you here for ever. You would come home here and I was to mind you and I promised. It's the only place for her, she said, and then perhaps God will forgive me for what I've done. That's what she said all right. Whatever she was talking about I don't know, but I made the promise. She said they'd keep you there in that place if I didn't do what she wanted. The moment she was dead, Dr Carey and I were to go and fetch you and bring you home. That was the one and only time I've been to England. We travelled in an aeroplane, the doctor and I. He was only a young lad then, new to the job. I never asked him if she made him swear too.'

'I don't suppose she did.' Flora almost whispered the words.

She remembered the journey back; she had been frightened by all the people, menaced by their closeness and by the noise they made as they moved around the airport. She had clung to Nellie's arm; she had been afraid to touch the doctor. She had thought the journey would never end. Her grandfather's trees had grown enormous; they had seemed like giants to her as they drove under them that sunny afternoon. She had been dizzy as she stepped from the car outside the front door. Home, a voice had shouted in her head. This is my home. I will never leave it. Never, never. Oops, Nellie had caught her arm as she stumbled. No, let me go. This is my home. Without any helping hand from anyone she had run up the steps and taken the shining brass knob in her hand and gently turned it, and the heavy door had slowly opened. Dr Carey had stood at the bottom of the steps and clapped and then without a word he had jumped back into the car and driven off.

'She held my hand, gripped it hard as if she thought I might throw the Protestant book on the floor, but never such a thought came into my mind. Never. I made the promise before God. Her God or my God, it didn't matter.'

'No one,' Flora's voice was angry, 'should be bound like that.'

'Well, yes or no, I made it. There was no escaping her.'

'Eddie managed it.'

'That's not a very nice thing to say.'

'No. I suppose it's not. Mind you, looking at it from here and now, I don't think he'd have come back, even if he hadn't been killed.'

'Why would you think a thing like that?'

'He really missed Daddy. He was lonely for him and lonely without his school pals and lonely because she never let us do anything, go anywhere. He couldn't wait to get away. To escape. That's what he used to say. Escape. D-Day plus one was his escape. Isn't that a thought? I often wonder when we look at those old newsreels about the war on the TV will I see him. I scout those faces to try and catch a glimpse of him. That makes me laugh. Would I recognise him, Nellie, after all those years? What do you think?'

'I'd recognise him.'

Flora didn't hear her.

'Did he drown, weighted down with all that stuff they had to carry? Was he shot by a sniper? Blown to smithereens by a German shell? Did he lie wounded for hours on a stony beach? No one ever told me, I don't think. Was he a hero or a coward? To me he was a stupid schoolboy who didn't know what he was fighting for. He was just escaping. And what about Wilkinson? Did Wilkinson survive? What do you think? Was he escaping also?'

'I never heard tell of Wilkinson. I told you that and you shouldn't be thinking such morbid thoughts.' Nellie rattled the newspaper. She dipped her head towards it, straining to see the print. 'We must get on with the choosing. Tallulah, Sea Master, French Toast . . .'

'One thing, just one thing I've always wanted to know: would you have kissed him if . . . if he'd asked you?'

'If, if ifs and ands were pots and pans . . . and I suppose you'll tell me now that's Shakespeare too.'

'Don't be cross with me, Nellie.'

Nellie put the paper back down on the table and threw the pen on top of it.

'And why shouldn't I be cross? Stirring up all this old rubbish. Rubbish. That's all it is. Isn't that why you were shut up all those years over there? Your head was teeming with rubbish. They had to clean out the inside of your head before you could come home. They had to stabilise you. That's what she said to me. One day she'll be stabilised and then she can come home again. You were such a good little girl. I wanted you to come home and be stabilised. It was really lonely here with no young people round. I was never able to work out why I stayed on. I could have got a job in Dublin easy enough. I was good at my job and I was good at the sewing too. I suppose I got used to the life. Anyway, she used to say that you'd have to stay over there in that place if I left. I used to ask her all the time, when will Flora be coming back, and she would eat the face off me. Mind your own business, Nellie, she would shout. Flora will come back when she's ready and not one day before. I sometimes wondered if she was keeping you over there for her own ends; life was easier for her here without you around. Then I would say to myself, don't be thinking such bad thoughts about the poor mistress. Hasn't she had enough of suffering? I used to pray for her. You can smile, but it was all I could do. All I knew about.'

Flora sniffed.

'You asked me and I told you. I made a solemn promise, just like I said, just like you did. We both kept our promises and this is where we ended up, and if you want an answer to your other question: yes, I'd have kissed him. Oh yes, I'd have kissed him.'

She pulled the bowl towards her and began shovelling food into her mouth.

Deep red juice trickled down her chin; she picked up her

napkin and blotted at her face. There was juice on her white lace collar, looking like spots of blood, Flora thought. She had seldom seen Nellie dishevelled; it shocked her.

'You were such a good little girl.'

Nellie pushed her chair back from the table and got up stiffly and walked over to the window, the napkin clutched in her hand. A white flag, Flora thought. To whom, she wondered, did she think of surrendering? She smiled, silly joke, as always. Nellie stood by the window staring at the blackness, quite quite motionless. Flora wondered if she were crying, and if she were, how on earth could she have tears left for something that had happened so long ago?

Did we drain her youth and energy away? Mummy did, of course, but did we, Eddie and I?

Hiding from Nellie's watchful eye was a game we used to play.

Watch the child was what Mummy used to say to her, and we did our best to hide from her. Silly young scamps that we were.

Missy Flora.

We used to giggle. We never hid for long, just long enough to catch the sound of irritation in her voice.

Missy Flora.

And Eddie's mocking voice, close to my ear.

Missy Flora, your bath is run.

My bath is still run, even at this late hour of my life.

Where would I have been without you, Nellie?

You'd have got on all right. You'd have got your little car and everyone would have respected you, just as they do. You'd have had your friends, not just me and my silly ways. We guard my secret, you and I; that perhaps is the meaning of our lives. But then, of course, life may not have any meaning, and of course you do not know my secret.

She smiled to herself; she always enjoyed her own silly jokes. She must remember to keep them to herself.

Nellie rubbed once more at her face with the napkin and then shuffled back across the floor to the table.

'I was upset,' she said. 'When they closed down the picture house in the village. I really felt I had lost a lot of friends. Judy Garland, Myrna Loy and all those others. All those others. I used to love Myrna Loy. Yes. Best of all, I think.' She pulled out the chair and sat down. 'I tried biking into Wicklow town, but it was too far. I hated that long ride back in the dark, and all those hills.' She threw the napkin down on the floor and reached for the papers. 'Anyway, they showed a different sort of picture then, pictures about wars and disasters, cruel sorts of pictures. I like dreaming pictures, pictures with hope in them. Fred Astaire and Ginger Rogers. They were a lovely pair. You say he called me a spy?'

'He didn't mean it in a bad way. It was just joking.'

'I just wanted to be near him, to learn everything I could about him. I wanted to know things about him that I could keep in my heart for ever. "Bye, Nellie," he might have said to me when he jumped into the trap that last morning, "we'll meet again some sunny day."'

Flora laughed. A small burst of laughter which she smothered with a hand.

'You can laugh. I believed him. I was able to see that sunny day, like it used to be in the pictures. I didn't know he was going to the war. I didn't know he had such a thought in his head. To me he was just Mr Eddie, off to school again, and he'd be back some lovely sunny day. I didn't know he thought I was a spy.'

'A joke.' Flora spoke the word with certainty. 'Honestly, Nellie, we were always joking. We used to joke about Mummy, too. He said it was the only way he could cope with the way she carried on. Come on, Nellie, let's do our choosing.'

'Yes. I suppose we should do that.'

She picked up the crumpled newspaper and smoothed at it with her fingers. She peered down at the print.

'One o'clock, Kempton. No great shakes there. Can Can Charlie. Nah. Not worth thinking about. You know, I think I need glasses. I'm finding it very hard to see the small print these days. I wonder should I have a word with Dr Carey. The letters slither away from me sometimes. Maybe it's the wine. What do you think? Does too much wine affect the eyes? On the other hand, it's more likely to be age. That's what he'll say anyway. We're none of us getting any younger, Nellie.' She gave a little laugh. 'A silly thing to say when you come to think of it. Don't we all spend our lives not getting any younger? Perhaps I should say that to him sometime. Perhaps though he might think me cheeky, above myself. He might frown and curl his lip.'

'I don't think so, Nellie. I think he'd be amused. He's a decent man.'

'Macushla, Highwayman, Mr Marmalade, now that's a

name appeals to me, not much form though, fifteen to one. We might chance a quid on Mr Marmalade. It's such a droll name.'

'Each way.'

Nellie picked up the pen and wrote something on the paper in front of her.

'Paperchase, Captain X, Champagne Charlie. What do you think about that? That sounds like the horse for us all right.'

'Nellie . . .'

'Not much form either. We might be throwing our money away. Think how cross we'd be sitting in front of the telly tomorrow afternoon watching Champagne Charlie limping in last.'

'Nellie . . .'

'You're not concentrating. What have you got on your mind?'

'There's something I want to tell you.'

'It can wait, can't it, till tomorrow. We'll put five pounds to win on Champagne Charlie.' She scribbled with the pen. 'Twenty to one. Imagine that. We might win a hundred pounds. Larry O'Hara is riding. Now why would you put Larry on a horse with no hope? Hunh? I ask you that. And I can see by the look on your face that you're not listening to me.'

'I really should say there's something I have to tell you and I think that it would be best if I were to tell you now, while we have the heat of all that drink in us. The courage. We both need courage, me to tell and you to listen.'

'Is it about Master Eddie?'

'I suppose it is. Yes. I suppose it is.'

* * *

I watched her walk, head down, looking inconsolable. Towards the door into the schoolroom she went, her feet leaving streaks in the dewy grass. The boy rattled the reins on the pony's back and the pony's feet crunched away down the avenue and I wondered why Mummy hadn't sent him to the station in the car and I wondered why Nellie looked inconsolable and in the end I fell into bed and fell asleep until Nellie came knocking on the door announcing breakfast.

'Missee Flora, Missee Flora, your porridge will be cold. Up, up. It's past nine o'clock.'

Oh my God. I leapt out of bed and threw on my clothes and then remembered that he was gone, and remembered where he had gone, and everything slowed down and I didn't care any longer about cold porridge and I wondered if in the end he had told Mummy or if he had changed his mind and was now just another schoolboy on his way back to another year at school.

Mummy didn't come down for breakfast.

'Wasn't she up at dawnlight to see Master Eddie off, wouldn't she need a little time for herself after such an early start to the day. I brought her some coffee and toast on a tray.' I loved dawnlight; I rolled the word round inside my head. I didn't speak it. I wondered why I had never heard it spoken before, nor read it in one of Daddy's books. They were my source of knowledge, far more so than school.

I have found *a, ab, absque, coram, de* to be pretty useless in the life I have led, just a patter of words that marches from time to time across my mind, unbidden. *Sine, tenus, pro and pre* . . . I could go on for several more lines, but what would be the point?

I wondered if she had forgotten about me; not, I thought, beyond the bounds of possibility. In a few weeks she might meet me in a passage and say, Oh, hello, Flora, how nice to see you after all this time, and I would giggle and we would be back to normal once more. But she hadn't and she came looking for me later on that morning. I wasn't in the playroom as she would have expected, but in Daddy's library, looking for a book by Siegfried Sassoon that would tell me what war was like, tell me truthfully, not with *Boy's Own* heroics. I was up a ladder when she opened the door and looked into the room. For a moment she didn't speak, she just stared up at me.

'What are you doing?'

'Looking for a book.'

She came into the room and closed the door behind her.

'These are your father's books.'

'Yes.'

'You're too young to be reading such books.'

'I'm fifteen.' I put the book that was in my hand back on the shelf. My fingers were grey with the dust that had lain on the books since Daddy had gone. People seldom came into this room now and no one ever lit the fire, so even now at the end of the summer holidays there was a damp smell and the air was chilly. I climbed slowly down. I wiped my fingers on the seat of my trousers.

'Too young.' She repeated the words. 'I suppose they're really Eddie's now.'

'Eddie doesn't read.' I could feel fury rising up inside me.

'Don't be silly, darling, of course he reads.'

'Not like I read. He doesn't gobble up books. He doesn't drink them, pour them into himself like he does cham—' Oh God, I nearly let the word fall out of my mouth.

'Sham what?'

'Just the sort of books he reads. Adventures, war stories, thrillers, ghosts. That sort of stuff. He wouldn't read the sort of books that Daddy did. I know that.'

'Daddy, Daddy, Daddy,' she said and turned to leave. At the door she stopped. 'We've no petrol, so you'll have to go to the station tomorrow in the trap. I've told Nellie to have your case ready in time.'

She came with me to the station. Of course she did. To her I was still a child. She saw me into an empty carriage and I watched her through the window as she gave a half-crown to the guard, who tipped his hat to her. She waved to me and we both set off in our different directions.

I didn't complain about school, you must remember, not like I complained about so many other things. I quite liked it, in fact. I liked being with other girls of my own age. I liked playing games. On Saturdays we could go to concerts, or to the theatre. I remember seeing *The Playboy of the Western World*, which we had read in class, and *Romeo and Juliet*. I didn't believe there was such a thing as sorrow until I saw that play. I missed Daddy. I kept having dreams that I would find him. When I left school I would go to El Alamein and I would stand up high on a sand dune and sing as loud as I could . . .

*Vor der Kaserne bei dem großen Tor*
*Stand eine Laterne und steht sie noch davor*

Loud. As loud as my vocal cords could manage, and he would come, walking slowly across the sand towards me. A tired man who had fought and now was coming home.

*So wollen wir uns da wieder seh'n*
*Bei der Laterne wollen wir steh'n*
*Wie einst, Lili Marleen*

And just as he reached me I would wake up and that would be that.

Maybe I have always been a little mad. Maybe they have all been right.

Even now, all these years later, I from time to time have shadowy dreams. It's odd there is never any sign of Eddie. He never follows in Daddy's footsteps, dragging his army boots across the sand. No sign of him at all. Just his name in the church. Father and son and of course Mummy. I don't want to have my name there, not with hers. Don't say a word. I will tell my story and then you can speak all you want. Yes. You may lecture me, tick me off. What you will, really, what you will.

Christmas was coming and we were allowed to go into town to buy presents, look at the lights, though because of the war and shortages and all that, the lights were no great shakes to look at, but we had that lovely freedom to wander where we wished. I hadn't been feeling well for a couple of weeks and had told the school nurse and an appointment had been made for me to see the doctor in his rooms in Fitzwilliam Square. Four o'clock and don't be late. It was getting dark and a savage east wind was blowing. Smoke from the turf fires stung my eyes and I wished that I was back in Bewley's Café with my friends. Nowhere was warm in Dublin, not even in the carpeted grandeur of the doctor's rooms; the east wind seemed to be blowing through them too. I kept my eyes shut as he examined me. He didn't speak. His hands were cold, like the wind, as they touched my body I cringed. As I dressed behind the screen I could hear him washing his hands. I imagined the warm water running over his long fingers. He cleared his throat and then called out to me.

'Have you really no idea what the matter might be?'

I came out from behind the screen. Cold.

'No.'

He stood by the basin, the towel in his hand, and looked at me for a long time without saying a word.

'I hope it is nothing serious.'

'Nothing life-threatening,' he said. 'You can go now. I'll speak to the head.'

It wasn't until the next morning that the axe fell. During the Latin class. Miss Murphy, who I had never liked; Virgil's *Aeneid*, which I had never liked either. *Facilis descensus Averno; noctes atque dies patet atri ianua Ditis* . . . see how easily you can recall it, when you don't really need to . . . *sed revocare gradum superasque* . . . How truly batty the mind is. I used to stumble and tremble over those words when I needed to let them rip from my head; now they dance off my tongue, as if they had lived forever in the forefront of my mind.

The head came for me herself.

. . . *evadere ad auras, hoc opus, hic labor est.*

'Excuse me, Miss Murphy, but may I take Flora?'

I shivered; I shiver now when I hear her voice in my head.

'Of course, Miss Morrison. Put your books in your desk, Flora, and run along with the headmistress.'

I followed the head along the passage and up the stairs to her study. It was a charming room with two tall windows facing south and the watery sun. Paintings covered the walls and a fire crackled in the hearth. She pointed to a chair. I sat and waited until she had settled herself behind her desk.

'Well now, young lady, what is all this?'

I wanted to ask 'All what?', say it back to her, but I didn't think she would take it kindly. I shook my head. She waited a while before she spoke again.

'The doctor has telephoned to tell me that you are pregnant.'

The word bewildered me.

'Pregnant?'

'That was what he said. That was the word he used.'

I shook my head again.

'No.'

'Flora.' Her voice was impatient. 'You are pregnant. You are having a baby. What have you got to say for yourself?'

'How can I be having a baby? How? I don't understand. I . . . I . . .'

It began to dawn on me. I began to remember. I began to put two and two together.

'No.'

Panic.

'I have informed your mother . . .'

I began to cry.

'No.'

'I have informed your mother and she is coming up on the first train. Your case is being packed and I would like you to stay in this room until she arrives.'

'Oh no, no, no, no.'

I have to say she wasn't too bad. She shoved a couple of handkerchiefs into my hand. She sent for a cup of tea for me. From time to time she patted my shoulder. I couldn't speak, all I could do was cry. She had to go and get me another handkerchief. I knew she was afraid, not for me, but for her school, her reputation; afraid of the pointing fingers, the whispers. It took so little time to tear down a reputation. As my crying came to an end, I realised that there were things I couldn't tell anyone. It would be better not to speak at all than that I should say the wrong things, that I should speak the truth.

So I became mute.

My babbling mouth became silent.

From the moment the door opened and Mummy came in with the head, I didn't say a word. How could I have told them what had happened? Better that they should think that I had been skiting off with some boyo from the village than that they should know the truth.

It was as if I had some infectious disease. I was bundled out of the school, into a taxi and out of the country. I saw no one, not even to wave to. No one called out my name, no one smiled in my direction. There was just the weight of my mother's cold hand on my arm, the rapid beat of her feet. I had become invisible. I used to wonder what the girls at school had been told about my disappearance. I suppose some harmless lie, something or other that would not disturb them in any way. Something or other that would not reflect badly on the school. And what had Mother told Eddie in those weekly letters she used to write to him? I don't think she ever mentioned me at all. *Flora sends her love* would have been the most she might have said. *Flora sends her love.*

'Did you know?' Her voice on the telephone had been full of angry tears. It was about two weeks after term had started. Before my interview with the head.

I knew what she was talking about.

'Know what, Mummy?'

'About Eddie.'

'What about Eddie? I haven't heard a word from him since he went back to school.'

I knew, of course I knew. My heart was hammering.

'I was telephoned a couple of days ago by the school to say that he hasn't returned. They say he has . . .' There was a very long pause, then she cleared her throat. 'Joined up.'

Oh Eddie, you did it. Every night I had prayed to God that you might change your mind.

'Did you know?'

Of course I knew.

'Joined up?'

'Yes. Did you know?'

'How could I possibly know?'

'You children always have secrets. He never . . .'

'No.'

'I've tried everything. I've rung everyone I know who might be able to help, but they've been useless. Useless. He might at least have written and let me know where he is. He could be anywhere at all. He's only a child.' There was another very long silence, then she blew her nose again. 'Well,' she said at last. 'Not much use in talking to you about it. There's nothing you can do. I just thought he might have said something to you.'

I wondered if she had been told about Wilkinson.

I wondered if I should mention his name.

I decided not.

If I say too much, I will be bound to say the wrong thing.

Better stay mum. Silence is golden.

I listened to her breathing. I wondered if she had said all that she was going to say. What if I were quietly to put down the receiver and leave her to her own silence? Not a good idea.

'If you hear from him you will let me know, won't you?'

'I don't imagine he'll write to me. He never has.'

'Good night, Flora. Don't worry. I have to say that. We mustn't worry. He will be all right.'

'Yes.'

That was the end of our conversation. D-Day plus one never entered our heads.

* * *

In the home, they hung lights in the trees for Christmas. Blue, red, yellow, green. They were lit every evening at four o'clock and were switched off at eleven thirty. We were all supposed to be asleep by then. I honestly don't know where the house was situated. I did ask them, but they would just smile and say things like 'You'll find out all in good time, dear.' They were kind, though, and they had little parties for us all from time to time and interesting people came and gave talks or sang. I mean to say, it wasn't one of those ghastly places where you sit staring at the wall all day. I gardened, I enjoyed that, and I read a lot. It was not bad, but you felt you were in prison, all the time you were being watched. You could hear doors being locked, foot-steps outside your door at all hours of the night, soft slippered feet; they would pause and then pad away again. I was frightened by this at first, but once I had realised that no harm was meant to me by the sounds I heard, I paid no more heed to them.

At least I was safe there, the baby and I were safe. I spoke only to the child inside me, as I gardened, or just walked round under the trees or sat by the window in my room, looking out at the winter rain and watching the branches dance, and thought about Grandfather's trees and longed to be at home; last thing at night I spoke, very quietly so that the person with the slippered feet wouldn't hear me. I told the child about my life, the house and the avenue down to the village and how you could hear the music from the dance hall on Saturday nights. I sang 'Lili Marleen' for the child and told it about Daddy lying under the stars listening. On the desert sand, with all those other men from all corners of the earth, all listening to the gravelly voice singing in a language that many of them couldn't understand. I spoke about the millions of stars watching down on us all and how Nellie and her friend used to give them names on their way back from the cinema. I spoke my whole life to the child: Latin verbs, and bits of history, the Statutes of Kilkenny, the repeal of the Act of Union, the sad famine, *Alice in Wonderland* and *Pride and Prejudice*; everything I knew I told that child, except I never mentioned Mummy or Eddie. I couldn't say their names to the child. I spoke about everything under the sun; I love you, I love you, little baby, I would whisper. I wanted it to know everything when it came out into a possibly unfriendly world and I wanted to remain able to speak when the moment came, as I was sure it would. I didn't want to lose the facility of speech; to be without words was so mournful. I spoke about King Arthur and the Knights of the Round Table, of Cuchulain and the Knights of the Red Branch, of the discovery of America, of the Armada and the retreat from Moscow. And always, I love you, little baby. Always those most important words.

I was busy talking, but not to the world.

It was a home from home for the harmlessly insane. I'm sure it cost my mother an awful lot of money to keep me there for all those years. When I learnt after I had come home how many girls had been treated so badly, how in fact their lives had been destroyed by the treatment they had received in homes where their parents had buried them to hide the family's shame, to bury them and their babies for ever, I merely lost any belief that I might ever have had in God. Money kept me safe, and of course the fact that Mummy died and you were here still to look after me. We've managed quite well, haven't we, Nellie? Apart from the fact that we might have had other lives. I won't say better lives, just different. Yes. Very different. I would like to have travelled abroad, France, Italy, seen their landscapes, felt their sun warming me, smelled all those new smells. Think of all the wine we could have tasted, we really could have become true conisurios. We would have gone to the desert, to El Alamein, and seen where Daddy spent his last few days. Camels loping over the sand and the ghosts of all those poor men who died. And after dark the voice singing.

*Aus dem stillen Raume, aus der Erden Grund*
*Hebt mich wie im Traume, dein verliebter Mund*

I see such foolish things in my mind . . . and poor Eddie and Wilkinson, blown to flitters in Normandy. Well, maybe Wilkinson wasn't, of course. Maybe he is an honoured member of society, a retired solicitor, captain of the local golf club, filling his grandchildren's heads with stories of his own St Crispin's Day. *He that outlives this day, and comes safe home, will stand a tiptoe when this day is named, and rouse him at the name of Crispian.* Imagine after all these years, that speech comes tripping into my mouth. I could say all the rest of it, only you might think that I was crazy. So many years have passed. Fourteen I think I was when I learnt that speech.

I have to laugh at myself. Forgive me for laughing. There was so little to laugh at when I was over there, I feel I must make up for lost time.

She never came to see me. She used to speak on the telephone about once a month, a few short sentences, and that would be all till next time. I didn't utter a word and I often wondered if she had appeared, posh in her London clothes, if then I might have spoken to her. Probably not. Even when I had the child she didn't come, she didn't come to tell me about Eddie's death. Poor Eddie. D plus one. I wonder what happened? Was he fighting his way up a road inland from the beach? Had he made his way on to French soil, become a liberator of the unfree, a hero, as he had wished, and his reward was death? He's there still, some of him anyway. I always wanted to go and see his grave. Poor Eddie, only just eighteen. We could have done that, you know. I believe lots of people do, make that sad trip. Birds sing in the trees and there is amazing peace in those places. I have read about that peace. Yes, we should have made that journey. How foolish of me not to have suggested it. We're too old now. We could have remembered it in our heads, the stretches of green, the trees, the distant sound of the sea, the birds, and Eddie, 2nd Lieutenant Edward Paul Morgan, with his cross and the neatly clipped grass, always neatly clipped. The French are like that, always so conscious of the neatness of death, the importance of quiet dignity. I could have told him about the child, his son, the baby I never saw or held. I would have brought a little campstool with me and set it up beside his grave and talked to him as I had talked to his son, only this time I wouldn't have had to whisper, I could have shouted if I had wanted to, except of course my shouts would have been very inappropriate in such a silent place. I have it all in my imagination.

If I had known that I was carrying a boy, I might have been tempted to call him Eddie, but it didn't occur to me; I was sure it was a girl inside me. I would have liked it to have been a girl. We could have minded her well, you and I, Nellie. You would have loved her too and you could have stitched her beautiful dresses, and cut her hair for her, in the way that makes the curls spring out. I'm sure you could have done that, and I would have taught her to read all those books that are here still in the schoolroom: *Ameliaranne and the Green Umbrella*, I always loved it. *Peter Rabbit, Squirrel Nutkin* ... As I spoke those books inside myself to her, I could see them all, Winnie-the-Pooh and dear batty Tigger. She would have laughed and clapped her hands. Clap hands, clap hands for Mummy. But it wouldn't have made any difference, they would have taken her too. Snatched her away as they snatched him.

Please. I held out my arms for him. Please, and without a word the nurse took him away. It was the first word I had spoken since I went in there. Please, and I stretched out my loving arms for him. Please, oh please. It's for your own good, they said, all for your own good, and the nurse carried him away. My little damp creature. He had to go, they said. I was only a child. He would be better off with a father and a mother. I would be better off without seeing him, holding him. I would be better off. They promised me that, but I wouldn't listen to them. I put my hands over my ears and I screamed and they put me into darkness. That was their punishment for me. Exhausting darkness, and I would lie there too tired even to cry. A nurse was with me night and day, not the nurse who took away my baby, I never saw her again. They were afraid, they told me, that I might do myself some damage. Or the little baby. I didn't want to damage anyone, only to hold my baby, to whisper in his ear: I love you, chicken, I will love you for ever, and he would be able to hold those words in his head for ever. They would be there through thick and thin, those simple words. A minute, that's all I want, a minute. I wanted to photograph him into my mind as I spoke the words so that I, also, would have him for ever. He's gone, they said, and I screamed again and they put me once more into darkness.

She never came to see me, not even with the news about Eddie. The matron told me about that, she used her gentlest voice. She sat and looked at me with sympathy in her eyes, she poured me a cup of nice hot tea. You mustn't go bothering your poor mother about this. She has enough to bear without that. No telephone calls, no hysterical letters, just leave her be. She'll be over to see you as soon as she can make it.

He was the father of my child.

I said it one afternoon to the matron, who had popped into my room to visit me. A little after-lunch chat, she used to call it. This day the sun was shining, the window was open wide and a warm breeze rustled the curtains. She walked across the room and closed the window, then she sat down beside me on my bed and took my hand in hers.

'Who would that be, my dear?'

Her fingers were cool. She was using her gentle voice again. I couldn't quite think why I had said it. Perhaps, I thought to myself, I had made a big mistake.

'Flora?'

'Eddie.'

'Eddie?' She sounded puzzled.

'Yes. My brother Eddie. The one who was killed.'

'My dear child, you shouldn't say things like that.'

'It's the truth. You want me to tell the truth, don't you?'

She looked at me for a long time; I had disturbed her, no doubt about that. She pressed her lips together, she scratched her chin for a moment. When she spoke, her voice was no longer gentle.

'If what you say is true – if, I repeat, if – I must let your mother know this piece of news. I presume she does not already know.'

She stood up.

'Flora. Does your mother know this . . . this . . .'

I shook my head.

'Your poor mother.'

She left the room, closing the door firmly behind her.

Poor Mummy. I whispered the words. She'd get the shock of her life, but maybe she would sit down at her desk and write me a letter.

Darling Flora, now that poor Eddie is dead you are all that is left to me in this world, you must come home. You must bring your little baby with you. We will love him. We will care for him. This will always be his home. Your loving mother.

I could see her quite clearly, sitting at the little desk in her bedroom. It was by a window and you could look down across the lawn at a wide border and behind it the grey stone wall of the farmyard. But it was all in my mind. She never wrote; she sent me message after message to say that when I was stabilised, I could come home. No more lies.

Stabilised indeed.

That was the first time I heard that word. I told them and told them the truth. I begged them to believe me.

Tell us the truth.

I told them the truth. It wasn't Eddie and me that did that thing; no, it wasn't. It was Paul and Mummy. We watched them. We saw their joy and pleasure. We felt their joy and pleasure. I now know the meaning of the word ecstasy. And the next morning he left. He went to the war, as Daddy had done, only this time I knew he wouldn't come back. Over and over again I told them, and they shook their heads and put me into darkness. I became weak and weary, and one night as I lay there I realised that I had to become stabilised. This could go on until I died. If I wanted to live, I had to tell them the lies they wanted to hear. Or rather that she wanted the world to hear. So I taught myself to smile and make my silly jokes again. They let me out into the garden and my skin became bonny once more and I wrote to her and said, Please, dear Mummy, come and see me. I am well now and I miss you so much. I don't know if they posted the letter or not, but she never came. I never saw her again.

Over twenty years.

A prison sentence.

For not doing anything more criminal than tearing a grey silk dress.

You know I often thought, after I had been home and felt

the safety of home, that I should look for the boy, put the wheels in motion; after all, this is his house that we two mad old ladies occupy. He might have loved it. Grandfather's trees and the rookery at the bottom of the big field below the house, Daddy's library – he would surely have got pleasure from that? Though perhaps not as much pleasure as I had got down through the years. But common sense broke in. How could I meet him and not tell him the truth? Who could I say his father was? I couldn't lie and lie. I couldn't pretend. I could say nothing or I could leave him be.

I probably made the right decision. I will never know.

After the words had stopped flowing from Flora's lips, there was a long silence in the kitchen, then Nellie got up from her chair and moved slowly over to where Flora was sitting. She put her arms round Flora's shoulders and hugged her gently.

'Missy Flora.' She whispered the words. Flora gave a little splutter of laughter. 'All that stuff locked up inside you. My poor pet. If I'da known what the pair of you were up to, I'd have put a rapid stop to it, I can tell you that.' There was another long silence. 'I'll make us a good strong cup of tea.'

'No. Don't do that. There's still wine in the bottle. We wouldn't want to waste that, would we?'

'She never said a word to me. Never one word. Aye, you're right, why waste time making tea. You'd think she'd have mentioned about the little baby.'

She let go of Flora's shoulders and walked slowly back to her chair.

'You'd think she'd have liked to have the little lad around the place. We'd have minded him well. Wouldn't we?'

'Yes. I think we would have minded him well.'

'She made me believe that you were mad. From time to time she would talk about that; about what we'd do when you came home, about how you might be altered by madness, about how she missed you and was longing for you to be allowed to come home.'

'Lies,' muttered Flora and reached for the bottle.

'She spoke as if she was telling the truth.'

'Well she damn well wasn't.' She emptied the champagne, a few bubbles into each of their glasses. She sighed; it was a deep sigh, almost like a moan. 'I've thought about this for years and I keep coming to the same conclusion.' She swigged down her champagne and pushed the empty glass away. 'I hate my conclusion. I hate it because it makes me hate her. I never wanted to do that. I wanted to love her. I wanted her to love me, but . . . but . . .' The word hung around their heads.

'She did, she loved you. She spoke of you with such love. You were always in her mind, you were all she had left.'

Flora laughed.

'I am a woman alone, remember how she used to say that to us. To everyone, if the occasion arose, and her beautiful eyes would tremble with tears, and we would all do exactly what she wanted. Everyone rallied round. Remember?'

Nellie nodded.

'That was who she really loved, that woman alone.'

'You shouldn't say such things about her. You weren't there to see how she grieved for you.'

84

'Grieved, my eye.' Silence overtook them once more. There was a long time of silence. 'I'm sorry, Nellie. I really don't mean to be rude to you. But for so long I was lost, imprisoned. Locked away and lost. Her grieving did that to me. Everyone was kind when I came home, but they all thought I had been mad, was still a bit crazy. I was just someone who had been reborn at the age of forty-nine and had to teach myself into the way of the world.' She gave a little laugh. 'I didn't succeed very well. I can't blame her for that. My own lethargy. Something like that anyway. If things had been different, if I'd had a chance, if none of this had ever happened, if, if, if. I'd have left home when school was over and probably never have come back. I don't think that even Eddie could have lured me back if he'd been alive. Not while she was around anyway. Cutting off your nose to spite your face, some people call it. But I'd have lived a life, and so would you, Nellie. You'd have got married and had dozens of babies.'

'Away with you. Who said I'd have wanted dozens of babies. Sometimes you talk too much for me. You use too many words.' Nellie's voice was plaintive. 'You make my head reel with all the words you use.'

'Tell me, Nellie, I've often wondered. What will you do with this house when I've gone? Dead, I mean. When I'm dead. It will be yours, you know. I've left it to you. The whole shebang. Maybe then everyone will call you Miss Maher.'

Nellie took a handkerchief from her pocket and blew her nose.

'You can't do a thing like that, Flora. Honest to God, you

can't. There must be someone who it should go to. There must be someone who has a right to it. No matter how distant. Somewhere there must be a letter from some legal person, something signed meaningfully, telling you who it should go to. Someone who will hold the place together, like the Major would have done. Seen to things. Yes. When I first came here, things were seen to, like as if he were going to come home the next day.'

Flora banged on the table with a clenched fist.

'You. You deserve it. You can do what you like with it. Sell it, let it fall down, turn it into an old people's home, burn it to the ground, even give it to the Church, if you're so inclined, if you didn't think that Mother would come back from the grave and haunt you. You've minded it and us for so long, with such care. I've talked to Mr O'Brien and he thinks it's good. Yes. Good. That is good, Flora, were his very words to me. So that is that, all signed and sealed and it will be delivered in the fullness of time. Mind you, I may live to be a hundred. What are you crying for? You should be clapping your hands and shouting yippee, not snuffling. Stop snuffling, for heaven's sake. Yes, go and make us some tea, that would be such a good idea. I would love a cup of tea. I'd rather have tea than snuffling. Smile for me Nellie.'

There was a long silence.

Nellie got to her feet. She gave her nose an almighty blow and shoved the handkerchief back in her pocket. She walked slowly across the floor back to the old black range. She picked up the kettle and put it on the hot plate.

'What would I do with a place like this anyway?'

'Use your imagination.'

'I don't think I have one.'

'You have, you have indeed, dear Nellie. You'll have a bit of money to help you along. A nice little B and B. You'd like that, you like meeting people, you like minding them.'

'I'd have to put in the central heating to have a B and B. Mrs Shaughnessy had to do that. It cost her an arm and a leg, so it did. And I'd worry about the hot water: supposing five people all wanted baths at the same time?'

Flora laughed.

'Wait till it happens. There's no point in getting all worked up about that sort of thing in advance.'

'I always saw myself ending up in a nice little cottage, white-washed every spring, with a small garden out the front, that I could look after myself, and a few hens out the back and lovely fresh vegetables. That would suit me well. I'd try to have hens that laid nice dark brown eggs, and I'd have a run for them with a strong little house for them to sleep in that the fox couldn't penetrate. No fox would get my hens. Maybe too a field with an old donkey in it. A couple, perhaps, to keep each other company. I've always liked donkeys, I'd like to mind them, they work so hard and then people disregard them, leave them to die.'

She put two spoons of tea into an old tin pot and put it on top of the range to warm up.

'Well when I die . . .'

'You're not going to die. Not yet, not for an age. For God's sake, you're five years younger than I am.'

'Frail. That's the word they use. I am frail.'

'You're as tough as old boots. Dr Carey says you'll outlive us all.'

'Yes. You've told me that before.'

'He says it each time he calls. After he's prodded you and questioned you and knocked back his glass of Jameson's and you call me to bring him to the door, he asks after me. Am I well? Am I bearing up? Have I any worries about myself? We couldn't manage without you, Nellie, he says, and then, She'll outlive us all.'

'We must ask him to dinner soon.'

'Well give me good warning so I can get something pleasant from the butcher. A good sirloin roast, or perhaps a pheasant. He likes pheasant and all the accoutrements. We've got a couple of bottles of Léoville-Barton below. That would please him.'

'That, Nellie, would please us all. Remind me to give him a ring in the morning. Now, how about our choosing? We really should get on with that.'

'There's something I'd like to ask you. If you didn't mind.'

'Why should I mind?'

Silence.

The kettle spat for some angry reason of its own. Nellie picked it up and poured a stream of boiling water into the waiting teapot. Flora wondered why she always used the old tin pot instead of a nicer one; there was a cupboard full of teapots – china, silver, large, medium and small – yet Nellie always used this battered object. Odd, she was so meticulous about other things, things, it seemed to Flora, of less importance. Starched table napkins, for one, and washing gumboots, now that seemed pointless, but not to Nellie. She became aware that Nellie was speaking.

'Sorry, Nellie, I didn't hear.'

'You fell asleep.'

'Not at all. I was thinking. That's all. Just lost in thought.' She laughed briefly. 'I lost you, I didn't lose myself. So tell me, what were you saying?'

'I like my milk in first.' Nellie picked up the milk jug and poured a splash of milk into a cup. 'I never can understand why some people like it the other way round. My mother used to say that Protestants always had their milk in last, but I have never been sure about that.'

'It's habit.'

'Habit?'

'Habit. Yes. The first cup of tea I ever had, the tea was poured in first and so it has always been. Habit. Nothing to do with God or what religion you might happen to be or anything like that at all. In fact it tastes the same whichever way you do it. It's habit.'

Nellie sniffed, disbelievingly. She carried the two cups of tea over carefully to the table and put them down.

'Biscuit?'

Flora shook her head.

'A nice little piece of fruit cake?'

'No thanks. Sit down, for heaven's sake. You're making me nervous.'

Nellie sat down.

'Well?'

'Well it's just I don't know if I've got your story straight. It's just not what she told me. She told me . . .'

'Mummy?'

'The mistress. Yes. She told me different. Not like that rigmarole of yours at all.'

'I bet.'

'So who do I believe?'

Flora laughed. 'Whoever you want to believe. That may not be the truth, mind you, but it will make you happy.'

'I think I didn't really understand what it was you told me in your story. My head is confused. She told me that you were ill in your head. She told me that you might kill yourself if you didn't have the right care. You needed someone there all the time to see that you were all right. Until the illness cleared up. That's what she said, until that moment, and then you could come home and lead a quiet life here, with us. She told me you had had an illness, not a . . . not a . . .'

'Baby?'

'Not a baby. No . . . an illness. Not mad. An illness in your head. Stabili . . .' Her voice faded away. She stared at Flora across the table.

Flora stared at the ribbons of steam that drifted up from her cup of tea. She wished that she could think of what to say, she wished that she hadn't told Nellie the whole damn story, she wished that she had let sleeping dogs lie.

'I have never been mad,' was what she said eventually, her

voice quite conversational. 'And if I had been allowed to keep that little boy, I would have called him Edward Paul, after his father and his grandfather. Mummy was probably right, I would have flaunted him round the countryside and disgraced her. He might have been sitting here with us now. Imagine that, Nellie. He might have been drinking champagne. We might all be happy. People get used to curious circumstances in time. You must remember that, Nellie. I'm sure that Shakespeare would have put that better, well, anyway with more mellifluity.' She laughed with pleasure at the sound of the word. 'You know I can't imagine what he looks like. This man, he walks around the world, he is my son, and I know nothing about him, not even the colour of his eyes, though I do expect that they might be grey, that dark grey that Eddie's were, and my father's. It would be likely that they would be that colour. I wonder what he has become. Not a soldier, I do hope not a soldier. Of course he will be an Englishman, an Englishman who doesn't know that he isn't an Englishman.' She laughed again. 'I wonder if that makes him a wolf in sheep's clothing. More likely a sheep in wolf's clothing. We don't have wolves in this country. Wonder why not. What do you think, Nellie?'

'Some people talk too much.'

'Paul Edward sounds better, though. It scans; well, almost scans. Names should scan. Do you really think I talk too much?'

'At this moment you are talking too much. It's maybe the drink, and anyway, I don't like what you're saying to me. So many sins. That frightens me.'

'Sins?'

'If you're saying the truth. Either you or the mistress lied to me, down all those years.'

'I have never lied to you. I admit I didn't tell you the whole truth. I thought that might upset you and wasn't I right. I didn't realise that her lies had been so comprehensive. I thought she must have let you know the truth in dribs and drabs. Perhaps she began to believe her own lies. I am a woman alone.' The last five words sighed out of her mouth. 'I suppose I must only feel sorrow for her. For us all, perhaps. No . . . I find I can't do that. It's not in my nature to be mournful. I do my mourning last thing at night. I see grey-eyed men walking towards me down a cobbled street, one, two, three. The eldest comes first, he raises his hat and bows his head in my direction, the second blows me a cheery kiss, and the last, the youngest, who looks unbearably like the other two, digs his hands deep into the pockets of his jeans and averts his eyes.'

She stretched her arms way out in front of her and laughed. Nellie looked at her for a while.

'Will I call the doctor?'

Flora shook her head.

'Not at all. Don't be foolish.' She gulped the words out, between the little bursts of laughter. 'For so long, so bloody long, Nellie, the truth has been evaded, pushed away. Now I feel energised. I am not ill, energised, more like, by the unwrapping of truth. You know, in spite of the story I have told you, I almost feel happy. I've got it off my chest. After all these years.'

After.

All.

These.

Years.

The words echoed round inside her head.

Nellie's face looked angry, and somewhere a clock struck. Flora counted each stroke.

'Ten,' she said as the sound died away.

'Ten,' echoed Nellie.

'Bed. I think bed.'

'No,' said Nellie, her voice a little gruff with crossness. 'We have to do our choosing. You know that well. You're not trotting off to your bed leaving me here on my own.' For the umpteenth time that evening she stretched her hands out for the papers. 'I will read out the names and you can choose.' She put the notebook and pen down in front of her and rustled open the newspaper. 'Here we go. I hope you're listening.' She bent her head down close to the tiny print.

'Mr Marmalade, Champagne Charlie, Metroline, Hot Stuff, Gemstone, Mickey Dazzler, Lady be Good . . .'

Meaningless names scuttered past her ears.

I am not concentrating, Flora thought. I have made her cross. I have upset her. I have told her of my sin, rather than my sickness, and she is a good devout woman who doesn't believe that you ought to sin. The signpost to hell, especially my sin. Incest. How stupid we are in this wild world . . .

'Tananarivo, Hot Cross Bun, Billy the Kid, Merrygo-round . . .'

Whirling world. I never believed them at school when they told us about the whirling world. After all, you could see the stars and planets whirling and the moon waxing and waning and whirling as it did so, all around us, here, the firm centre of everything, and I felt so safe here, so protected from danger like everyone used to think until Galileo came along and told them they were all wrong. He cut their safety away from them. Death was too good for him, they said, and they cut him off from God. I thought he was wrong too, but I could never have punished him so mercilessly, and in the end the old man was right and they, those others, were the fools, like I have been a fool. Perhaps my boy is another Galileo, a discoverer, a finder of the truth. That makes me laugh. Is there any truth, or do we just live on, feed on, grow on lies? She was nourished by her lies, the woman alone . . .

'Green Fingers, Robin Hood, Crocodile, Ruby Red, Billy Bunter . . . such daft names, don't you think?'

'Umm? What? Oh yes. Daft. But then we're daft too, sitting here reading them out like that.'

'We make the odd few bob. Have you any thoughts? Will I read them out again?'

'No. No, no. Give me the papers, I'd better have a look at the form, otherwise we'll lose money. That would never do, have a fight and lose money, all on the same day.'

Nellie rattled the papers in her hand, but didn't hand them over.

'I can say no, no, no also,' she muttered. She bent her head once more to the words. Her mouth opened and shut but no sound came out. She wrote something in her notebook. 'I don't want to fight. I just worry about you and all that sin. I want you to go, when the time comes, a clean spirit, that's what I want, to heaven. You deserve that. But you have to be . . . well, clean. You know the word I want. I can't find it at this moment.'

'Shriven. Would that do you?'

'That's a word I never heard before.'

'It's old. It's beautiful, it means what you said, forgiven, clean, free of sin. At least that's what it means to me. I could of course be wrong. Absolution is your word.'

'Yes, that's right. I loved it when they used to say the Mass in Latin. The words were like soft rain on your head and shoulders. You couldn't understand it but you knew it was good. God's loving words. They should have left it like that. *Orapronobis*. I remember how I used to say that . . . *orapronobis* . . . gently, straight to God, thanking him for all his kindness. I can hear the sound of my voice now speaking that word in my head. *Orapronobis*,' she whispered.

Flora wanted to laugh, but she didn't. 'Pray for us, three words. That's what those words mean,' she said out loud. 'Now,' brisking her voice up, 'let's get on with those damn horses.'

'Father Sullivan is a very nice man.'

'I believe you.'

'Well, would you not . . . ?'

'No thanks. I don't have the need for that sort of conversation, Nellie. You should know that by now . . . considering all the years you've been protecting me, washing my clothes, mopping up my tears and drinking Daddy's wine. We lead pretty sinless lives, you and I.'

Nellie shook her head.

Flora snatched the paper from her hand, Nellie leaned

across the table and snatched it back. She spread it down on the table and poked at the creases with a finger.

'No one is sinless,' she muttered. 'We are born full of sin. They tell us that all the time.'

'It's rubbish they tell you. Every sweet baby that is born is pure and clean and innocent. We teach them to sin. We teach them all the horrible things that men are capable of and they become sinners. But nobody can tell me that my sweet baby was anything but innocent when he was born, in spite of the sin that they said we had committed. He didn't carry my sin anywhere. I carried my own sin. I paid for my own sin, and my sin was the sin of innocence. Or perhaps, one should say, ignorance.'

During the long silence that lay between them, a branch, blown by the wind, tapped softly on the window, and for a moment the light bulbs flickered and Flora's heart went bump. The mad thought entered her head that if she were to run to the window and pull the curtain back she would see a man standing there and she would know it was her son. She stayed anchored to her chair. She recognised madness when she saw it. She smiled in the direction of Nellie.

Tap, tap, the branch against the window made its presence felt again. Nellie searched for the pen.

'Innocence, *mar dhea.*' She spat the words like little pebbles from her mouth. She found the pen and wrote *Billy Bunter* on the paper in front of her; she looked at it for a moment or two and then crossed it out. 'Fat,' she said. 'Billy Bunter was a fat boy, wasn't he? A fat boy doesn't win.'

Flora laughed.

'So, we will remove Billy Bunter from our list of possible winners. No fatties allowed. But just think how angry we'll be if he thunders past the lot of them, tail spread out behind, neck gracefully stretched out in front. "Billy, Billy!" everyone will shout. "Billy wins by a neck. Hurrah for Billy."' She clapped her hands with vigour. Nellie continued to scribble out the words in front of her.

'The Fat Owl of the Remove has won. All those books were in my father's shelves. I read them. I don't think that Eddie did. I think that Eddie thought they were foolish. Kids' stuff. Maybe they were, but they were fun. I'm sure that Daddy thought they were fun too or he wouldn't have kept them for all those years. I wonder if my . . . if . . . if my baby boy ever came across . . . across . . . Stop it, Flora, sometimes you make such an ass of yourself.' She shut her mouth tight.

'I'm sure he's been well reared. With kindness and love. He'll be a happy man. Now here's a coincidence. Happy Fella. I don't think we can miss out on that. Five to one. What do you say? Happy Fella, yes or no?'

'I think it has to be yes.'

'That's Champagne Charlie, Happy Fella and . . .'

'Two's enough.'

'But . . .'

'Two is enough.'

She sounded splenetic. Splenetic. Splendid word. It made her smile. It shouldn't make me smile, she shouted inside her head. One of my problems is that I laugh too much, I smile too much. I don't take life seriously enough, I have always been too protected. Suppose I had been in Nellie's shoes, then I would have had cause for spleen.

'Mr Marmalade. That was the one I chose earlier. That's a winning name. If you won't have anything to do with him, I'll put a couple of euro on him out of my own money. To win, and I'll laugh to see your face when he romps home.'

'If.'

Nellie wrote something in her notebook and then slammed it shut. She laid her hands flat on the cover of the book and stared down at them.

'Twenty to one,' she whispered. 'Think of that. Just think.'

'Such an optimist you are. We'll put ten on, each way, and see what happens. Now I must go to bed. I feel so tired out tonight.' She pushed her chair back and stood up. 'I've been a bit cranky. I'm sorry about that. I've wound up the energy in order to tell you my deep secret and now I feel quite exhausted, and sad. I think of that boy every day, you know. I muse and wonder about where he is and how he is and is he better off without me in his life.'

'Such rubbish you talk. What's done is done and it was all for the best. She was right. The little lad will have had a family. Love, security . . .'

'How can you have security when you know that someone has already given you away? How? Answer me that. Without a cuddle even, or a song. How the hell can you have security with that hole in your life?'

She stamped her way across the kitchen floor to the big window that gave on to the herb garden that she had insisted on making herself so many years ago. Neat box hedges surrounded the beds, and little flagstone paths criss-crossed the area, giving it the look of a chessboard. Parsley, thyme, sage, rosemary. She had planted bulbs of garlic, but without success; unlike the butcher's efforts, they hadn't enjoyed her attentions. Chives, basil, fennel, four small well-pruned bay trees; all eventualities were catered for, and dotted among the herbs were lilac bushes and wonderful explosions of bright orange marigolds. Oregano and horseradish; now there was a vegetable that she couldn't persuade Nellie to use. She would throw them in the bin rather than make that hot, hot sauce; she would scowl, and it took quite a lot to make Nellie scowl; so the horseradish remained unused, uncared for.

She pulled back the curtains. In the garden, everything was silver.

'Why do you not like horseradish?' Her voice was soft, no sound of spleen.

'It's poison. The devil's draught. That's what I was always told. My gran told me that. The devil's poison, never touch it. That's what she used to say.'

'You never told me that. An old wives' tale I'd say that was. Millions of people eat it and they don't die, or they don't grow horns or anything like that.'

'Everyone believed my gran. My mother used to say she was a saint. Your granny is a saint, she used to say to me, real low, as my gran used to get angry if she heard people saying that. She wore a black hat from the moment she got up in the morning till the moment she went to bed at night. Always the same hat, all, all the time. I used to wonder if perhaps she had no hair. I asked my mother once and she gave me a slap for being cheeky.'

'That was unkind of your mother.'

'I suppose I annoyed her. She was generous with her slaps.'

Flora laughed.

'You never slapped me. And I'm sure I must have annoyed you quite a lot.'

'I had no right to slap you. There was many a time I was tempted, I do have to say, but by and large you were a good little girl.'

'Mummy probably wouldn't have cared if you had.'

'Tut.'

Flora sighed.

'I would like to have loved my mother.'

A small cloud blew across the moon and for a moment the garden became dark.

'She didn't seem to want me to, though. It was odd, she didn't want me to have friends and she didn't want to be my friend. It was like as if she wanted me to be invisible. Eddie was my only friend and he was mostly at school. Away. With those boys who he never spoke about: Baggot, Evans, Baillie and of course Wilkinson. Boys he never spoke about, until the end. All English, all without names. So odd I thought that to be.'

The cloud had passed away on, away in an eastward direction; the mica in the granite paving stones reflected the stars. A breeze quivered through the branches of the trees.

'I could have been your friend.' Almost a whisper, like the wind.

'I didn't know that then. I knew so little. Like I said before, total ignorance. My childhood was one long stretch of ignorance. No one taught me how to apply the knowledge that I learnt or just read about to being alive. I had to teach myself that. Later on. Yes, much later on. I often thought that I'd be a good yard girl. I used to imagine that one day I would run away and go and work in someone's yard. I was good with horses and ponies; I loved them. I was calm with them and they liked me. You must remember, I rode well and I looked after my pony. Do you remember that little Shetland that I had? Hamish, his name was. *"Is there anybody there?" said the traveller, knocking on the moonlit door.* I remember saying that one to him and he whickered and snuffled all the way through, as if he were saying it with me. He was a friend. I suppose I was about nine or ten. *And the horse in the silence champed the grasses of the forest's ferny floor.* Dear old Hamish. I haven't given him a thought for years. He wasn't much bigger than a large dog. I used to take him for walks, when I really felt I was too big to ride him any more. The dogs and I and Hamish. Quite funny really. The dogs used to tease him, nip his heels and make growling noises, and he would kick out at them. He seemed to laugh at them as he tossed his feet in the air. I don't think you were there then. Were you? Do you remember Hamish?'

Nellie shook her head.

'No. No horse called Hamish comes into my mind.'

'James, Seamus, Hamish, they're all the same. Oh dear, that was all such a long time ago. Before . . .'

After a very long silence, Nellie spoke.

'Before what?'

'Oh, you know, all that . . . misery. You know, Nellie, I sometimes don't believe myself. Maybe Mother was right, maybe I really was mad. Maybe I . . . maybe . . . maybe . . .'

She remembered the cold hands of the doctor in his Fitzwilliam Square rooms. She shut her eyes and turned away from the silver garden.

'Nothing life-threatening. You can go now.' Cold, clear voice and he rubbed at his fingers with the towel as he spoke. 'I'll speak to the head.' She wondered what he had said, how he had positioned his words to fire them into the telephone, precise and unequivocal.

'You mean you've been telling lies to yourself?' Nellie's voice cracked into her head. 'As well as me and the doctor and whoever else you've been telling this tale to.'

'I don't know. Honestly, Nellie, I don't know. You have to know if you're telling a lie or not. A lie is not a lie if you believe it to be the truth. At least, I don't think it is.'

'A lie is always a lie.'

'And I haven't told this tale, as you call it, to anyone. You know that well. Nobody, absolutely nobody, knew everything, except Mummy and me. Poor old Eddie hadn't the foggiest idea about what had happened. Mother's letters to him would have been one series of lies after another. I have often wondered, if he had known, would he have perhaps run away from the war and come home. Would he even have written me a letter or would he have magicked up another awful lie to try and save him from the pointing fingers? I would have loved a letter. I would love to have known that he knew, that he was on my side. I'm sure that he wouldn't have allowed them to lock me up for all those years. What do you think? Can you imagine him doing that?'

Nellie shook her head.

'Families,' she said. 'You'd never be sure what they'd do.'

Flora put out her hand and took a hold of the key in the back door. She turned it and gave a little pull. The door sighed and gave a little moan as it moved slowly open.

'We really must get this door seen to,' she said as she stepped out into the darkness. She laughed. 'How many times have I said that down all the years?'

No answer.

'About a thousand, I suppose. Or perhaps two. Good evening, stars. I have come to wish you good night. I've never done that before.' She waved up at the crowded sky. 'Nellie.'

Again no answer.

'Tell you what, stars, when she comes, we'll name you, give you the names of wonderful human stars. Nellie.'

No answer.

I really do need you, Nellie, she said inside her head. You're the one who knows the names. She bent and pulled some leaves from a rosemary bush. That's for remembrance, *pray you, love, remember*. Or we could call you after Shakespeare's names. Portia, Viola, Juliet. Oh dear, Nellie, why did I tell you my history? You knew enough without me doing that. You may go. You may feel encumbered with my sin, or what you consider to be my sin. You may go and find yourself that cottage that you spoke about. You could pray there for all the sinners in the world and crochet collars and cuffs for all the little girls who lived around, and what would I do, Nellie dear? What on earth would I do? Stare out of the window at Grandfather's trees? Weep for my baby boy? Dream that every time the doorbell rang it would be he. That some miracle would happen, that he would find me here at the end of this long avenue, that he would be looking for me, that at the eleventh hour he would find me. Then would be the time for celebration, for drinking Father's champagne. The very time. The time that truth made us happy. I laugh. Oh yes. It's better than crying. We are rejuvenated by our laughter. If I laughed hard enough maybe I could return to the age of fifteen. I could perhaps then change my history, and indeed Nellie's also, and poor dead Eddie and his friend, what was his name? *Pray you, love, remember* . . . Wilkinson. Yes. Such foolish thoughts and dreamings get into my head.

'Nellie. Where are you?'

'I'm here. I'm here, Missy Flora. You'll catch your death of cold so you will. Strolling round out here with nothing over your shoulders. It's not the summer any longer. We'll have Dr Carey ticking us off. You don't have a notion how to take care of yourself. Here, let's tuck this round you.'

She shook out the pale grey cashmere shawl that was folded over her arm. It floated like smoke, flickered like the blur you could see on a distant hillside when they were burning the whins, and it settled on her shoulders. Nellie smoothed the warmth down around her back and arms, tucked the ends into the neck of her dress.

'There now. That'll keep the chill out. The mistress always loved that shawl when the evenings became chilly. It had warmth, she used to say, and no weight. It's been lying up there in a drawer all these years, and this seemed the right moment to bring it back to life again.'

'It smells of mothballs.'

'I wouldn't complain if I were you. No indeed. If it didn't smell of mothballs it would have been nibbled into a thousand holes by the little buggers. Cashmere is the best for them, like champagne for us. So be thankful for small mercies.'

Flora laughed. She put out her hand and took Nellie's arm.

'Look up, Nellie. All those stars. Let's name them. Well, just a few of them. The really bright ones. You said you used to do it on your way back from the picture house. Let's do it again tonight. In honour.'

'In honour of what, may I ask?'

'Truth.'

The two old ladies stood, their necks stretched back, their faces bathed in starlight. The silence whispered around them.

'Deanna Durbin,' said Nellie after a long time of thinking.

'I quite distinctly see the Marx Brothers.' Flora pointed upwards.

'Bette Davis.'

'Gary Cooper.'

'Bing Crosby.'

'Shirley Temple.'

'Dear Myrna Loy.'

'Eddie.' Nellie whispered.

'Yes. Oh yes.'

Flora put her arm round Nellie's shoulder. 'And Daddy.'

'The Major.'

They stared up at the sky in silence. The wind stirred through the branches of grandfather's trees and a fox barked in the distance.

'I wonder would we . . .'

'Who?'

'. . . Perhaps not.'

Flora began to laugh.

'What asses we are. Wilkinson. Dead or alive. Of course.'

The two old ladies lifted their heads and shouted 'Wilkinson Wilkinson,' and the moon went behind a cloud and the fox barked again.

# Jennifer Johnston

*Two Moons*

TINDER
PRESS

Everyone called her Mimi.

Her real name was Eleanor. A name she had never been able to bear, so when Grace as an infant called her Mimi rather than Mummy, she embraced that name with energy.

In her more flirtatious and youthful days she used to smile at certain people and say, '*Je m'appelle* Mimi.'

This used to make Grace squirm. Even as a child she could never bear it when her mother behaved like that.

Now she was a shadow: only the name was left to remind people that once she had moved with gaiety and authority through the world.

People looked through her now.

Indeed she sometimes wondered if she had become invisible, gradually, in the last few years losing her substantiality.

She liked the light.

She sat always in the brightness of window embrasures, or on warm days in the sunlight in the garden . . . out of the wind of course, in case she might be blown away. She perhaps hoped that some of the brightness of the sun might attach itself to her, make her for some moments visible again.

On a sunny afternoon in June 1996 she sat, her hands folded in her lap, in an upright chair as she could no longer cope with the unfriendliness of a deck chair, outside the sitting-room window of her house, looking down the gently sloping garden towards the sea. Behind her the rose Albertine climbed with astonishing vigour towards the bedroom windows; she was enveloped by the sweetness of its scent.

The sea was bright with sun sparks and away out on the horizon the car ferry headed for England.

Somewhere in the house someone hoovered; a comfortable sound. Mimi remembered that she had never much enjoyed hoovering, or dusting, if it came to that, or washing curtains, ironing or polishing brass.

Had she ever polished brass?

She let her mind dwell on that for a moment and decided that she probably hadn't.

'I'm sure I could have if I'd wanted to,' she said aloud.

She wondered who was working the Hoover.

Not Grace.

It couldn't be Grace.

Grace was otherwise engaged.

Grace was taking part in another play.

Ever since she had left school, and that wasn't today nor yesterday, Grace had been taking part in plays.

Benjamin had tried to stop her, but there was never any stopping Grace when she got the bit between the teeth.

She just went to England and got on with her life there.

Mimi thought about Benjamin for a moment.

She couldn't conjure him up these days, as she used to be able to do for several years after his death. There were various photographs of him round the house so if she needed to she was able to refresh her mind as to his appearance. She didn't bother doing it very often. She presumed that if she saw him again . . . if . . . and that was pretty unlikely . . . but if she saw him again he would look different. Transformed by immortality, touched by his God. She didn't really wish to see him ever again. Even the thought of him caused her painful little spasms in her head.

She wondered again who was hoovering.

The noise was getting closer or maybe it was an aeroplane.

That was probably it.

Taking people away.

Bringing them back.

More and more people moving around the world.

Enlarging their horizons?

She laughed and then felt unkind for having done so.

Grace did a lot of coming and going.

Mostly going really.

She went to London a lot, but you could hardly count that as going anywhere much. Just down the road. It takes about the same time as getting to North Dublin from here in the rush hour.

Across the pond. Seagulls do it all the time . . . Grace went to New York, Los Angeles, Toronto, Sydney. A much-travelled lady.

She sighed.

I mustn't joke. It is spleen that makes me joke. It is spleen that makes me think of Benjamin.

I do not wish to be a splenetic old lady. Apart from everything else it's very bad for the liver. I would like to keep my liver intact to the end; unpolluted, except of course by the odd glass of whiskey, a drinkable Côtes du Rhône and, with luck, a few glasses of champagne at Christmas.

Unlike Benjamin, she thought, staring at the shadows of the trees as they trembled on the sloping lawn.

Daisies. He would never have countenanced daisies on his lawn. His lawn was always immaculate. His flower beds weedless. His hedges clipped.

I think I prefer it this way, she thought. I prefer an element of disorder in the world.

A man was coming up the garden. She shook her head to shake away any shadows that might be there.

But he was still there walking across the daisy-scattered grass, his shadow in front of him, short and black. As if he owned the place, she thought.

He must have jumped over the hedge. Benjamin's hedge, no longer clipped to a uniform three feet.

She wondered if he were one of Grace's actor friends.

He wasn't dressed like a bank manager anyway.

A silver-grey track suit and a small round hat on his thick black hair.

A tourist, perhaps, who had lost his way.

He was heading straight for her.

Now she could see the smile on his face.

She could see his black eyes.

American perhaps?

She'd seen men who looked just like that on the TV.

His hand was stretched out towards her.

She struggled to stand up.

'Don't bother getting up. Please don't.'

His voice was low and quite sweet. A slight foreign accent, she thought. Definitely not American.

So she held her hand out and touched his.

He bowed slightly and taking her hand in his, he kissed it.

His lips were soft and warm. She blushed at even having noticed such a thing.

He noticed the red flush on her cheeks.

'Don't be alarmed, Mrs Gibbon.' He pressed her fingers and then let her hand go. 'There is nothing to be alarmed about. You are Mrs Gibbon, aren't you?'

'Yes, I . . .'

'That's great. Sometimes, in the past, I have made little errors. I don't like to do that. No error this time.'

She wondered if he were one of those men who insinuate themselves into your house and try to buy your furniture. They give you a lot of money for something worthless and then buy the rest for a song. She'd seen a television programme about such people. He didn't look like a criminal, merely foreign.

'Should I know you?'

He shook his head, then he darted behind her and came back dragging an ornate wrought-iron chair.

'Mind if I sit down?'

He put the chair beside hers and sat looking into her face.

'No. You shouldn't know me. I hope we will become friends though. We don't have to, if it doesn't suit. We don't have to do anything if it doesn't suit you.'

'Could you explain who you are? You have the advantage of me.'

He stood up and bowed politely in her direction.

'Bonifacio di Longaro, at your service. BONIFACIO. CI is pronounced *ch* as in cheese, church, cheetah. But maybe you already know this.' He sat down again.

'Are you working for a charity of some sort? Looking for money? Saving souls? Anything of that nature? Because I don't give to charity and my soul is quite safe.'

'I assure you I have no ulterior motive.'

'The furniture belongs to my daughter now, I thought it was sensible to pass that over to her. Death duties and that sort of thing. I don't think she would be willing . . .'

He stretched his hand out to her across the table.

'Mrs Gibbon, please believe me.'

Definitely a slight foreign tinge to his voice.

Such deep black eyes.

If only, if only I were twenty . . . well, perhaps thirty years younger, I could lean across towards him and smile. I could say, '*Je m'appelle* Mimi,' and then I could laugh to show him that this was just a little joke between us. I could dive into his deep black eyes and swim around for a while. What fun that might have been.

Benjamin.

She remembered Benjamin. He had never been pleased when she had let her mind wander down such paths.

'You're smiling,' he said.

'Yes. Tell me, how did you get into the garden?'

'I came up from the sea. A hop, skip and a jump.'

He waved his hand exuberantly towards the sea.

'You must be very fit. Only the very young can hop, skip and jump up that hill without getting puffed. I haven't been able to do it for many a long year. Most people arrive by car these days.'

He smiled at her and shook his head.

'Alas, Mrs Gibbon, I do not drive the car.'

He was foreign.

'I suppose you had better tell me what you want. Here in my garden . . . or perhaps I should say, my daughter's garden. I take it your purpose is benign. You look benign.'

He laughed.

'Thank you. In a nutshell, Mrs Gibbon, I am an angel.'

She thought perhaps she hadn't heard him properly.

Both Grace and Polly kept telling her that she was losing her hearing, or else that she no longer paid attention to them when they spoke to her. So much of what they said was not really very interesting, that perhaps indeed her attention did wander from time to time, but she could hardly say that to them.

'I beg your pardon?'

She leant across the table so that she could catch his words with more ease when next he spoke.

'I am an angel.'

She looked at him with interest.

'Don't angels have wings?' She asked the question because she couldn't think of anything else to say.

'Only in paintings.'

'Really?'

'Really. You see those painters had to differentiate between the mortals and the immortals. To give the angels wings was an easy way out. Wings are beautiful in pictures, that's true, but they would be such a bore. Think of the size they would have to be to sustain one in the air. Think how difficult it would be to wear clothes . . . and it's really very inappropriate to go around the place naked. Wouldn't you think so?'

'You would probably be arrested.'

'And all those feathers. I can't bear feathers. I suffer from hay fever.'

She laughed then.

He looked pleased to have amused her.

'Bonifacio?'

He nodded.

'Very well, Bonifacio, suppose you are an angel. Suppose that sort of thing is possible. What are you doing here in Dalkey, County Dublin?'

'I've come to mind you.'

'Mind me? Why? I don't need to be minded. I am very well minded. I also take very good care of myself. I am cautious on stairs and don't smoke cigarettes in bed.'

'Nonetheless, I have come to look after you. To keep you company perhaps would be a better way of putting it.'

She considered this for a long time.

'I don't believe in God,' she said at last. 'In fact I find the notion of God quite disagreeable.'

He spread his hands out towards her . . . a very continental gesture, she thought.

'I haven't talked to too many people about this . . . well, no one really. It didn't seem to be anyone's business but mine. I have found life to be much less confusing since I stopped believing in God. I hope I'm not offending you.'

She peered anxiously across the table at him. He looked slightly absurd perched on that uncomfortable chair. If he were going to be around for a while, she thought, she'd have to find something better for him to sit on out here in the garden. Maybe, though, angels didn't feel pain.

He shook his head.

'You're not offending me, lady. You're at liberty to believe or disbelieve in what you wish. That's not why I'm here. I don't want to change the way you think. You see, sometimes we come to people and they don't see us or hear us. We just walk with them for a while, quite unnoticed. You, though, see beyond reality. Some people do, not many.'

'Is that a good thing?'

He gestured again with his hands.

'You say a while. What does that mean?'

He smiled.

'Who can tell.'

She looked out past him at the sea. The ferry was no longer visible. Grey clouds were starting to pile up on the horizon.

'You'd better call me Mimi,' she said.

In the house someone switched off the Hoover.

She pushed herself up onto her feet and stretched her back; sitting for a long time made her stiff.

'We'll walk down to the end of the garden. I like to stir my bones from time to time. You can tell me about yourself. There is always the possibility that I would prefer you to vanish.'

She picked up her stick and walked very carefully down the three steps onto the grass.

Grace turned the key in the door.

*'Oh gentle son!*

*Upon the heat and flame of thy distemper sprinkle cool patience.*

*Whereon do you look?'*

She said the words aloud.

*'Whereon do you look?'*

Hoover-sound impinged on Shakespeare.

Christ!

Upstairs.

What day is it?

Thursday? No. Friday?

It bloody well must be Thursday.

No Mrs O'Brien on Thursday.

'Who is hoovering?' She shouted the words loud, up the stairs.

If it's Friday, I have lost a day. A precious day gone. *O gentle son . . .*

The sound of the Hoover stopped.

'Hi, Mum,' shouted Polly's voice. 'It's only me. I'll be down in a tick.'

I thought you were in London.

I really don't want you here hoovering, not just at this moment in my life. I have so few precious days.

Keep that thought inside your head, Grace.

Smile and smile.

She went across the hall and into the kitchen, practising her smile as she went.

She filled the kettle.

*Alas, how is't with you that you do bend your* mind on, no! Your eye. Eye. *Eye on vacancy.*

She put the kettle on the stove and lit the gas.

*And with the in-cor-por-al air do hold discourse?* Hum. *Eye on vacancy.* Eye.

Polly's arms around her neck and a kiss on the cheek.

The smile was still there.

'Hello, darling, how nice to see you. What are you doing here?'

'I got a few days off work, so I thought I'd come home to Mum.'

'I hate being called Mum.'

'Joke.'

'It gives me the shivers, joke or no joke.'

'You are of course happy to see me?'

'Of course. Don't expect much attention though, I am steeped in omelette. Perhaps if you had let me know I might . . .'

'Oh God! I had forgotten. How's it going?'

Grace shrugged.

'It'll be all right on the night. What's all this hoovering in aid of?'

Polly walked across the room before answering.

I know I know I know, thought Grace. She has invited someone. Yep. Invited . . . a man. A suave and handsome bloke in banking whose home is dust-free and smells of furniture polish. Whose mother is *Hamlet*-free.

But I will not be diverted from my cup of tea.

'What on earth is Mimi up to?'

Polly was staring out of the window.

'Look, Mother.'

'I'm not looking at anything till I've made some tea.'

Grace picked up the teapot and poured steaming water into it.

'Do come and look.'

Grace walked over to the sink.

Through the window she could see Mimi down at the bottom of the garden talking, gesticulating, smiling benignly at the air.

Grace began to laugh.

'What's funny?' said Polly.

'*Alas, how is't with you, that you do bend your eye on vacancy?* Go and give her a shout like a good girl. Maybe she'd like a cup of tea too. Oh and before she comes, you'd better tell me who's coming to stay.'

Polly looked, just for a moment, cross, a child discovered at something forbidden.

'I didn't think you'd mind,' she said.

'I quite like to know.'

They waited in silence for a moment while Polly put the right words together.

'A terribly nice man. Honestly. I know you've always hated the men I've liked. But . . .'

She scratched at the bridge of her nose with a finger. She

looked out into the brightness of the garden. Her grandmother was laughing merrily, leaning sideways on her stick and laughing at the escallonia hedge.

'I never actually hated them,' said Grace. 'I just never thought they were quite . . . quite good enough for you.'

'Has Mimi gone completely batty?'

'Don't change the subject.'

Polly sighed.

'Paul is different.'

Abruptly she held her hand up as if to stop her mother from speaking.

'I mean to say, you were right. Yes. I do have to admit you were right. Looking back, I do have to give you that.'

'Paul?'

'Paul Hemmings. Quite, quite different. Funnily enough he's an actor too. So . . .'

She moved towards the door.

'I'll go and call Mimi.'

The kettle whistled. Grace put out a hand and turned off the gas. 'So what?'

'So you'll both have something to talk about.'

Polly stepped into the darkness of the hall and went towards the garden.

Grace popped two tea-bags into the teapot and poured boiling water in on top.

She hated herself.

She hated tea-bags.

At that moment she also hated Polly.

There didn't seem to be any point in hating Paul whatever his name is.

Yet.

'Mimi.'

Polly's voice floated through the sunshine.

Mimi didn't answer.

She never answered calls; she just either came or she didn't.

'Mother's making tea.'

Grace put some cups on the table.

Got the milk from the fridge.

Got the biscuits out of the cupboard.

Decided against the biscuits and put them back in again.

Polly came back into the room.

'I don't really want anyone to talk to,' said Grace. 'Not at this moment. I want . . . well, just to be alone with Gertrude.'

'Don't worry, darling. He'll understand. He's an actor. Mimi really is up to her eyes in conversation down there. Don't you worry sometimes about her?'

Grace sighed.

'I worry . . . But, at this moment in time, I only have worrying space in my head for Gertrude. I do think you should have . . .'

'It will be all right. He's nice. He can hear you your lines. Give you helpful hints.'

'Sometimes you are such a pain.'

They heard Mimi's stick banging on the floor in the hall.

'It'll only be for a few days. I only have a week off. I thought we might go somewhere. Connemara, somewhere like that. Could we . . . ?'

'No, you may not borrow my car. Pour out the tea, there's a good girl. In the kitchen, Mimi. When is he coming anyway?'

'Who?' asked Mimi, coming in through the door.

'Come and sit down, darling. I've just made tea.'

She pulled out a chair for her mother.

'Some friend of Polly's who is coming to stay.'

'A man?'

'Yes,' said Polly, pushing a cup of tea across the table towards her grandmother. 'You like men coming to stay, don't you, Mimi?'

'I can take them or leave them.'

The old lady lowered herself cautiously into the chair.

'You'll like this one anyway. I can guarantee that.'

Grace picked up her cup.

'I must go and take my shoes off. You still haven't told me when he's arriving.'

'Tomorrow. I said I'd pick him up at the airport. May I . . .'

'No,' said Grace, leaving the room. 'I have a very heavy day tomorrow. I need the car. I need the car, Polly. I'm getting too old for hopping on and off public transport. You'll have to collect whatsisname by taxi.'

As she went up the stairs she heard Mimi say to Polly, 'I hope he's as nice as the one in the garden.'

Bonifacio.

Bonnyfackio.

Boneyface.

Bonnyface.

Bunnyface.

CI is pronounced as in cheese, church, cheetah.

I think however I'll call him Bonnyface.

That's what he has.

A mite swarthy perhaps, but that's because he's Italian.

I like that. I like the notion that here in this last section of my life I will have the pleasure of a sexy companion, no matter how swarthy.

I don't really mean sexy; I mean someone who reminds me that I am alive, not just a shadowy weight.

Or a weighty shadow.

A shadow of eighty. Ha ha.

'Mimi.'

Mimi focused her eyes.

Polly was sitting across the table from her, a cigarette in her fingers, smoke spiralling from its tip.

'I thought you were in London.'

'I was. I am. I'm taking a few days off.'

Polly's hair was more golden, more full of soft waves than Mimi had seen it before.

'Dyed your hair?' she asked.

'It's called highlighting.'

'Nothing is ever the same. I like things to stay the same. I like to know where I am. I find it hard to remember what people look like. Like your grandfather for instance. I don't think I'd know him in the street.'

Polly took a deep drag on her cigarette.

'You probably would. What one in the garden?'

Mimi looked puzzled.

'I don't know what you're talking about.'

'You said . . . I hope he's as nice as the one in the garden.'

'Ah, yes,' said her grandmother. 'So I did. I wonder what I meant?' She smiled.

From over their heads came the sound of Grace throwing shoes around. It was quite normal: Grace was given to throwing shoes around.

Then she remembered.

'Bonnyface,' she said.

She looked past her granddaughter's head out of the window. The sun was at last showing signs of sliding and more than half the garden was now in darkness, the other half an almost blinding green. There was no sign of any person, neither angel nor human, and she wondered if she had imagined the episode.

'A dream,' she said aloud.

Polly wasn't listening.

'Or perhaps . . .'

Grace came into the room, wearing a long towelling dressing gown.

'I'm going down for a swim before the sun goes. Mimi? Polly? I'm driving down.'

'It'll be freezing.'

'You've gone all Londonish. You've forgotten. Mim? Care for a drive?'

'Yes. I'll come. I'll sit on a rock and admire you.'

\* \* \*

There were still children and dogs on the long beach even though the shadows were now moving fast towards the sea. Grace lay on her back and looked up at the sky, small waves rocked her and her hair was stretched on the surface of the sea.

She spoke aloud to the sky.

> 'One woe doth tread upon another's heel,
> So fast they follow; your sister's drowned, Laertes.'
> 'Drowned! O, where?'

The sunlight glittered on the still wings of a hovering seagull.

She kicked with her legs and a lazy trail of bubbles followed behind her.

Now I am clean.

All that dusty thinking has been washed away.

> There is a willow grows aslant a brook,
> That shows his hoar leaves in the glassy stream;
> There with fantastic garlands did she come.

I know this. I can call this out to the seagulls.

I learnt this at school.

> Of crow flowers, nettles, daisies, and long purples,
> That liberal shepherds give a grosser name.

She turned over and looked towards the shore.

Her mother was sitting obediently on a rock and the hill

was growing dark behind her.

Grace waved.

*But our cold maids do dead men's fingers call them.*

Mimi waved back.

A dog barked somewhere and a gull swooped down, landing neatly on the surface of the sea. It preened its wings for a moment and then settled like a bath toy, bobbing.

Mimi watched the bird and thought of angels and feathers and the time that she had found a dead cormorant on the edge of the sea, its feathers dark and stiff with oil. Benjamin, who had hated beaches, had shrugged and said, 'Why waste tears on a bird?' It had been the way the bird had died that had made her cry, not the fact that it was dead; the careless cruelty had made her cry.

'Oil is more important than birds,' he had said.

She hadn't believed him, but, of course she hadn't said so.

'I feel so much better.'

Grace's voice surprised her.

She was squeezing the water from her hair.

'I always used to wear a bathing cap,' said Mimi. 'They say salt water is bad for your hair.'

'They are probably right, but I hate the bloody things. I get a headache if I wear a cap and that takes away all the good of the bathe.'

She put on the towelling coat and rubbed briskly at herself. She wriggled out of her togs and then tied the belt tightly round her waist.

'You were a million miles away, weren't you? What were you thinking about?'

They began to move at Mimi's snail's pace up the beach towards the road where the car was parked.

'Your father.'

Grace looked surprised.

'Good Lord! Dad. Do you still miss him?'

She took her mother's arm and squeezed it gently.

She felt suddenly guilty that perhaps there were areas of her mother's life to which she had never paid enough attention.

Mimi laughed.

'Miss him? No, no, no. I've never missed your father. But sometimes he pops into my head unasked. That's all. Quite uninvited.'

A woman trudged past them carrying a screaming child. A bag full of sandy towels and clothes was slung across her back.

'I do not want to go home. I want to stay. Stay. Stay. Mammy.'

The child's feet flailed.

'Stay. Stay.'

'If you don't shut up I'll give you a good hard . . .'

She caught Grace's eye and said no more. Grace smiled.

'I know the feeling,' she said.

The woman grimaced. The child continued to scream all the way to the road, then stopped as if switched off.

Mimi was blethering on: 'Of course when I say a thing like that I don't intend to belittle your father in any way. I'm just pointing out that I've got used to living without him. Yes. I mean to say, ages ago. Ages and ages. You never lived with a man as long as I lived with Benjamin.'

A little bubble of laughter came up in Grace's throat.

'That is certainly true.' She took the car keys from the pocket of her dressing gown and opened the car door. She opened the back door for her mother. 'Hop into the back, darling, so that you don't have to brave the traffic.'

'Hop.' Mimi's voice was angry. 'I haven't hopped for years.'

'Manner of speaking.'

Mimi put her bottom on the seat and painfully lifted her legs into the car.

Grace turned round and smiled at her.

'Okay?'

'I am not okay. It is a long, long time since I have been okay and you know it. I don't know why you ask such silly questions.'

Grace put the car in gear and edged out into the traffic. The road was narrow and at this time of day crowded with commuters leaving the station and people going home from the beach. Grace, though, was probably the only driver who was naked under a towelling dressing gown.

'I wonder what Polly's man will be like?'

She glanced at her mother in the mirror as she spoke. She was wearing her sulking face. More and more these days she wore her sulking face.

Is this my fault, she wondered. Am I not giving her her fair share of my attention?

I used to wonder that about Polly too. I remember that. I used to wonder if she would turn out neurotic, paranoid, criminal even, any one or all of those things . . . Now when I look at her normality I still wonder on bad days how thin that shell might be. Will it crack one day? Will I, in the throes of coming to terms with Madame Arkadina, or the wretched Mrs Tyrone, have also to grapple with yet more guilt?

Why make a stick to beat your back with?

John used to say that to her quite a lot.

Thanks, John.

Always full of helpful hints you were.

Quite endearing for a while.

Became tedious; very British, very stuffed.

At least Polly has one normal parent.

Run of the mill.

God, you're horrid.

Think only on Gertrude. Do not be diverted.

She didn't do too good a job on Hamlet, did she? Taking everything into consideration?

Grace laughed out aloud, throwing her head back and almost hitting the kerb.

'I don't think you're concentrating,' said Mimi from the back seat.

'Sorry, darling. A silly thought just popped into my mind.'

'Has she got a new one?'

'Who? A new what?'

'Man. Polly. You said she had a new one. I must say I quite liked the old one. Whatsisname. He was always very nice to me.' She thought for a long time. 'Yes.' She said at last. 'I have always liked Italians.'

There wasn't a car parked across her gateway. Miracles

sometimes happen, she thought, swerving violently in through the gate.

'He wasn't Italian, darling. Polly's never had an Italian boyfriend.'

'Ah,' said Mimi. 'Someone was Italian. Someone I've met quite recently.'

Grace got out and opened the back door for her mother. She held out her hand. Mimi brushed it aside.

'I can manage perfectly well, thank you.'

All fingers and thumbs.

The weight of the *Shorter Oxford Dictionary* hurt Mimi's wrists, her elbows, even her shoulders. She let it fall with a thud onto the table and sat down slowly, gasping a little for breath.

Upstairs Grace was running a bath. Grace always seemed to be running baths, even as a child she had shown an unusual disposition towards cleanliness. I have warned her and warned her, said Mimi to herself, about the dangers of drying up the natural oils in the skin; the oils keep the skin resilient, flexible. I have told her all that. I have told her many times.

She never listens.

'As long as I can afford hot water, Mim, I will have as many baths as I like.' That was what she said the last time the subject had been spoken of.

However, Mimi had to admit, Grace did look quite good. Not dim, like some fifty-year-olds you saw about the place. Perhaps there was something to be said for all those baths after all.

Her eyes fell on the large book on the table in front of her. She pulled it towards her and began to turn the thin pages.

Angel.

She fumbled in her pocket for her glasses.

Let me see. Angel.

Hieroglyphics. Presumably Greek. Useless.

*Messenger.*

She kept her finger on the word and thought about that for a moment.

*A ministering spirit or divine messenger.*

*One of an order of spiritual beings, superior to man in power and intelligence, who are the attendants and messengers of the Deity.*

*One of the fallen spirits who rebelled against God.*

*Guardian or attendant spirit.*

Messenger.

She closed the book.

I'll leave it for someone else to put away, she thought.

I suppose I know what the message is. No big surprise, really. Come in Mimi, your time is up.

She smiled.

'What a nice smile you have.'

He was standing on the other side of the table, between her and the window. She couldn't see his face, only the darkness of him silhouetted against the fading light.

Her heart fluttered briefly as she wondered if this was her moment but, as if he knew her thoughts, he spoke.

'There's no need to worry. No need to be frightened.'

'I have been looking you up in the book.'

She nodded towards the dictionary.

'What does it say?'

'Messenger.'

'There's a bit more to it than that, really.'

'Do you consider yourself to be superior to man in power and intelligence? Or are you fallen? Have you been defying God in some way?'

He laughed.

'No, no, none of those things. I'm more of a minder really. I thought I could mind you for a while.'

'A while?'

He nodded.

'May I ask …?'

'No, no. Most certainly not.'

She was aware of a delicious smell filling the room.

It couldn't be Grace in her bath, lubricating her skin with oils and unguents.

It couldn't be the peperonata she knew that Poppy was making in the kitchen.

'Wonderful smell,' she said.

'Guerlain,' he said. 'Nothing but the best.'

'Did someone send you?'

He shook his head.

He turned and looked out into the garden and she studied his profile: a slightly beaky nose and full lips, his chin jutted forwards and jowls were beginning to gather, but he had a good head of hair. She was pleased to see that. She had always preferred men with thick, shining hair. Benjamin sprang to mind; you couldn't ever have faulted Benjamin's hair.

'Nobody send me.'

She smiled and wondered whether it would be proper to correct the grammar of angels.

'I am . . . well . . . I do it freelance.'

He turned towards her and spread his hands.

'You say freelance?'

'Oh yes.'

'That is what I do. I am freelance. I make my own decisions. Actually, this is the first time I do this sort of thing.'

He put his hands on the table and leaned towards her. He lowered his voice as if he didn't want to be heard.

'I was tired of being invisible. So.'

It was very nearly dark in the room now and she had to peer to see him.

'So?' she asked after a long silence.

'Just, so,' he answered.

She heard Grace's bare feet on the stairs.

'Here's Grace.'

As she spoke the words, the door opened and Grace came in.

'Here I am, indeed,' she said. 'Do you want to be in the dark, darling, or will I . . . ?'

Without waiting for an answer she pressed the switch by the door. The room became full of friendly light, but apart from the lingering scent, there was no sign of Bonifacio.

'I find this unsettling,' said Mimi.

'I'll turn it off if you like.'

'No. Don't bother. I was just thinking of something else.'

'Wonderful smell. God, how I love the summer. It must be Albertine. Dad was right, wasn't he? About Albertine? Messy but worth it. Wasn't that what he said? I'm going to shut the window though. It gets chilly quite suddenly these evenings and I don't want you to be catching cold.'

She crossed the room and pushed down the bottom half of the high sash window.

She was dressed in a red silk dressing gown, tied round the waist with a black sash. Her feet were bare and her hair was bundled up into a turban of towel. Steam still seemed to rise from her as she moved and her face had an oily sheen.

'I think a glass of white wine would be nice and then food. I'm absolutely starving.'

'If anyone is going to catch cold,' said Mimi in a peevish voice, 'it's going to be you. How many times have I told you not to go slopping round the house like that?'

'Millions.'

As she passed her mother on her way to the kitchen, she touched her lightly on the shoulder.

'And millions.'

'Chills. Walking round in your bare feet gives you chills. And your feet spread. Just look at your feet. You have the feet of an old country woman. Flat, spread. Size seven, for heaven's sake. My feet are still worthy of admiration.'

Polly was in the kitchen, looking as if she was about to go out.

'What is she going on about?'

They could hear Mimi's voice quite clearly.

'Feet,' said Grace, opening the fridge and taking out a bottle of wine. 'She says I have the feet of an old country woman. Do you want a glass of wine?'

'So you do.'

'Oh God, how I hate you all.' She filled two glasses and held the bottle poised over a third.

Polly shook her head.

'I must rush. I'm eating with Barbara and we're going to the pictures. May I . . . ?'

'The keys are on the hall table.'

'You're a pet. And your feet aren't too bad really. Leave some peperonata for tomorrow. Paul is partial to it. I'm exploiting his love of food. See you, darling.'

She was away, jangling the car keys triumphantly.

'Bye Mim, see you tomorrow.'

'If I live that long.'


There was a full moon.

Two, thought Grace; one suspended in the globe of blackness, the other flickering in the sea below.

How lucky I am, to be suspended here between two moons. Gertrude and I.

Away out beyond the reflected moon a light flashed in the darkness.

*Hamlet, thou hast thy father much offended.*

If I were younger, years younger, I would go down now and swim in the moon.

Would Gertrude, had she been younger, have done the same

thing? Would she also have in her head the memory of phosphorescence spilling from her hands and arms as they rose and fell through the water?

Maybe, of course, kings and queens never tasted such simple pleasures.

Where would she have swum?

The Baltic? The North Sea? The Skagerrak?

Nought for geography, Grace.

She sighed.

Poor lady.

*Come, come, you answer with an idle tongue.*

What would she have said now, had she been alive now?

How would you translate this acrimonious dialogue?

Chill Hamlet?

Chill, Hamlet.

It would make the play much shorter if we all spoke in today's vernacular.

'Would you please concentrate,' she said aloud.

*Come, come, you answer with an idle tongue.*

*Go, go, you answer with a wicked tongue.*

Chill Hamlet.

Somewhere a bell rang. She wondered if the sound was from Mimi's television set.

*Why, how now, Hamlet!*

What's the matter now?

It was a bell.

It was the doorbell to be quite specific.

I will not answer the doorbell. It is ten thirty at night and I am not dressed for answering doorbells. Like Gertrude, I am in my dressing gown and ready for bed.

Someone put their finger on the bell and held it there.

Bloody Polly had forgotten her keys.

I will give her a piece of my mind.

She stood up and threw her book onto the bed. It was still quite warm and through the open window she could hear the distant sound of someone's radio playing and smell the nocturnal smell of tobacco plant from the flower bed below her window. Good old Dad. You had some good points.

She went out onto the landing; there was no light coming from under Mimi's door. That was good. Some nights Mimi never slept and then had to spend the following day in bed, grey and a bit shrivelled and in need of quite a lot of attention.

She ran down the stairs and across the hall, hoping to get the door open before Mimi woke up.

'Honestly . . .' She spoke the word with anger as she pulled the door towards her.

A tall young man was on the step, one finger on the bell, a suitcase by his right foot.

She pulled the dressing gown round herself.

'What do you want?'

He took his finger off the bell and looked uneasily at her.

'I'm sorry . . .'

'Who are you?'

'Em, Paul.'

'Well? Do I know you? What do you want? It's late for visiting.'

'I'm Polly's friend. Oh my God, don't tell me she hasn't . . .'

'Tomorrow,' said Grace somewhat despondently. 'Yes, definitely it was tomorrow, she said.'

She punched at the door with her fist.

'She can be a little unreliable,' said the young man. 'Would you like me to go away and come back tomorrow?'

'No, no, no, no. Come in. She's gone to the pictures.' He stepped past her into the hall and she closed the door.

'I nearly didn't answer the bell.'

He put down his suitcase and they stood and stared at each other.

'Then I thought, maybe that silly girl has forgotten her key. So I . . .' She gestured with her hands.

'Come in and have a drink.'

She walked into the sitting-room and started to turn on lights.

He followed her.

'Have you eaten?'

'I . . .'

'Aeroplane food is so disgusting, isn't it?'

'Well . . .'

'Maybe you didn't come on a plane. Maybe . . .'

She turned and looked him up and down; head to toe and then again.

To her surprise he blushed.

'I'm her mother.'

She held out her hand towards him.

'Grace . . .'

He took her hand and held onto it.

'. . . is my name. Grace. Just in case you thought . . .'

'She told me. Yes. She . . .'

Grace pulled her hand from his.

'Paul.' He gave a little bow.

'Well, I'm going to have a glass of red wine. You can have stronger stuff if you want it. Whiskey? Something like that?'

'A glass of wine would be lovely. Thank you.'

'And peperonata. You could also have some peperonata.'

'Just wine.'

'She said you liked . . .'

'I do, but not just at this moment . . . thank you.'

They stood for a moment caught in some web of silence.

'Paul what?' Grace asked eventually.

'Hemmings.'

'Ah.' She noticed a slight waft of alcohol from him and remembered that she had offered him a drink.

She went across the room and got two glasses from the cupboard, and a half-empty bottle of wine. She pulled out the cork and took a quick sniff at the bottle.

It seemed okay. Good enough anyway for late-night inter-lopers. She filled the two glasses. He never moved. That was something anyway if he was an actor, if Polly had been speaking the truth about that. You had to know how to be still if you were an actor. She held out a glass to him.

He took two steps towards her and took the glass from her hand. His hand trembled for a moment and wine ran down over their fingers and dripped onto the floor.

'Oh Lord, I am sorry,' he said. 'Can I . . .'

'Don't worry. That carpet's seen worse than a few drops of wine.' She wiped her fingers on her dressing gown.

'Polly can be a real pain in the neck,' she said and walked over to the window.

The garden was silver and black, like a set for an opera, she thought. The golden nest of the room was reflected in the window. She watched him raise his glass to his lips and drink. Through him she could see the dark shadows in the garden. She liked that notion, that transparency.

'Badly brought up.'

'I wouldn't think so,' he said politely.

'You can take it from me.' She turned round towards him. 'I don't know what arrangements she has made about . . . well . . . sleeping. I only saw her for a few moments when I came in. So . . .' She waved her wineglass at him. 'I recommend that you make yourself comfortable here until she comes in. I would hate to make some unforgivable error.'

He started to laugh.

'I am going back to bed.'

He continued to laugh.

'I have a very busy day tomorrow. So, if you'll forgive me.' She waved her glass again round the room. 'Lots of books, the telly, comfortable chairs. Be my guest.'

She swept past him, glass in hand.

At the door she stopped. He had stopped laughing and was staring at her, his eyes very wide and green.

'There's more wine in the cupboard, if you finish that bottle.'

'Thank you. I'll probably just snooze on the sofa till she comes. I . . .'

She shook her head at him suddenly and left the room.

Maybe I've been behaving like Lady unmentionable Macbeth, she thought as she went up the stairs, but really Polly is the end. The ultimate bloody end.

Mimi had slept well.

She hadn't heard the to-ings and fro-ings, bells, voices and the disconcerting creaking of the stairs that only seemed to happen at night, when no one was moving at all.

She had dreamed of Benjamin; not something she did very often.

He had been swiping the heads off the daisies with his father's dress sword, which used to hang over the fireplace in the dining-room until Grace had taken it down one day and given it to the Abbey Theatre for its wardrobe department. 'Suppose a burglar were to get in and get a hold of it,' she had said, as she threw it into the back of the car. 'We might all be murdered in our beds.' That was Grace all over. Impetuous.

Mimi looked out of the window just to check that the daisies were still there. All was well.

She got dressed slowly. Sometimes when she bent down these days she got so dizzy that she had to hold onto the wall or a chair for several minutes before she could continue with life. She didn't like that. She worried about falling and not being able to get up; she worried about Grace coming home from rehearsal and finding her unconscious on the floor; she worried about blood, urine, vomit, creepy things like that. She also had to struggle with buttons from time to time, pushing them with ungainly fingers through holes that were far too small, or so they seemed, or misplaced, so they seemed. Grace would refasten them for her if she got them wrong. 'We can't have you looking like a ragbag, Mim darling,' she might say, as her slim fingers did the job in double-quick time.

She wasn't too bad, Grace; preoccupied, but not too bad.

Mimi went carefully down the stairs. Grace had left the house about half an hour before, slamming the hall door, slamming the car door and driving off without, no doubt, looking either to left or right.

Benjamin had always thought that women should not be allowed to drive cars; sometimes, in Grace's case anyway, Mimi had almost agreed with him. Not that she had ever said that. No. It wasn't always wise to discuss Benjamin's prejudices with him. Smile was what she used to do. She used to have a pretty smile. She thought she probably still had. Fundamental things like smiles didn't change with age.

There was an agreeable smell of coffee coming from the kitchen.

She went in through the door and found Bonifacio sitting at the table, a cup of coffee steaming in front of him.

He stood up when she came into the room.

'Signora Mimi.'

He took her hand and kissed it.

'I hope you have slept well?'

'Yes, thank you. And you . . . ? Where . . . ? I hope you were all right.'

'I have no problems. Sit down. Have some real coffee. What else will you take? Toast? Fruit? Eggs?'

'Goodness me.' She sat down and he poured her a cup of coffee.

'I'll just have some toast. I don't like to eat much in the morning. Where did you get this coffee? It's delicious.'

He put two pieces of bread under the grill and smiled at her. 'We are allowed to perform inconspicuous miracles. I consider a decent cup of coffee to come under that heading. I hope I'm right. Sometimes we get in trouble.'

'I'm so glad to see you again. I thought this morning when I woke up that perhaps you were a figment of my imagination.'

'I am no figment.'

'I can see that now. You look most substantial. I must say I enjoy being looked after. I don't mean that to be a criticism of Grace. She is very good. She is very busy. Benjamin always thought that a woman's place was in the home. Sometimes I found this notion irksome. Of course things were very different then. That was fifty years ago. More. Over half a century. Doesn't it sound a long time when you put it like that?'

Bonifacio put three pieces of toast on the table in front of her and sat down again.

'Yes,' she said, 'irksome.' She put a piece of toast onto her plate and began to butter it.

'I have always liked being cared for, watched over, protected . . . whatever you like to call it.' She chewed carefully. At her age it was only sensible to chew carefully. She looked past him out of the window, the endless blue of the sky was reflected in her eyes. She sighed.

'People are always going away. Sometimes I feel like a monument, just sitting here waiting; reminding everyone of all sorts of things they don't want to be reminded of.' She laughed.

He put down his coffee cup and reached towards her. He touched her hand with a finger. He kept his finger there, pressing warmly against her wrist bone.

'What age are you?'

What a rude and stupid question to ask, she thought, as the words slipped out of her mouth, but he didn't seem to mind.

'I am no age. I suppose I was at my prime . . . no . . . no . . . I was in my growing phase . . . well, not to beat about the bush, I was born in 1429.'

'You were born . . . ?'

'In 1429.'

'I didn't think angels were born. I thought they just were. Cosmic beings.'

'Maybe I am eccentric?'

He looked at her apologetically.

She drank some coffee.

'I like it,' she said eventually. 'I think I prefer you to be unorthodox. I never had the courage.' She wondered if this were the truth or not. Perhaps she had merely lacked imagination, energy. That was probably it. She had always preferred lassitude to energy.

'I miss being alive.' He pressed gently on her wrist with his finger and then took his hand away.

She was surprised; she would have thought that being alive back in 1429 would have been fraught with terrible dangers, disease, violence, the constant notion of hell gaping if you stepped out of line.

'I think we should go into town. I like to shop. We could eat a lunch somewhere, have a glass of wine . . .'

She shook her head.

'No. Stop. I couldn't possibly do that. I walk so slowly now it would take us all day to get to the bus. I am sorry. But you could go on your own.' She pointed a finger towards the window dramatically. 'Phhhht. Like Batman or whatever he's called. Sometimes I watch him on TV. Perhaps he's some kind of an angel too. What do you think?'

He laughed.

'We'll take a taxi and then we will walk very easy. We will do a little shopping. I think you need shoes. Your shoes are horrible.'

She agreed with him. Her shoes were horrible; her shoes were sensible; her shoes helped her to stay on her feet.

'I used to wear lovely shoes,' she said. 'But now . . . well, I have to be sensible.'

'Those shoes are not sensible.' He got up and came over to her. He knelt down beside her and slipped the shoe off her left foot. He turned it upside down; he tapped the sole; he tried to bend it. He looked up at her.

'This is no good. Look. It is solid like a stone. No shoe should be like that. The human foot is not solid like a stone, it must be able to move, to breathe. Your feet cannot move in such shoes. They are in prison.'

'I have been told . . .'

'You have been told everything wrong. You have good feet. For a woman of your age, you have very good feet. You must let them be happy. I know, dear signora, what I am talking about.' With care he put the shoe back on her foot and stood up.

'You will not know yourself when you have good, happy shoes. Italian shoes. We will go into town and find them. Soft little suede boots that will be like gloves. Hand made, with tiny heels to stop you getting cramps in the backs of your legs.'

'I think such little boots would cost a lot of money.'

'So?'

He held out his hand to her. She took it and stood up. He was right, her feet did feel as if they were in prison.

'I'll clear up here,' he said. 'You go and get ready. A taxi will be here when you come down.'

'This is mad.'

'Of course.'

'Grace may be angry.'

'You won't come to any harm with me. Why should Grace be angry?'

'Why indeed?'

Mimi climbed the stairs. At least, she thought, maybe I'll have a bit of fun.

On the landing a young man was standing, wrapped somewhat defensively in a large bath towel. He looked startled to see her. I must be getting used to manifestations, she thought, I'm not a bit alarmed.

She smiled at him.

'Ah . . . good morning,' he said. 'I'm . . . ah . . .' He gestured towards Polly's room.

'Are you also an angel?' Mimi asked him politely.

'Ah . . . no. I . . .'

'That's all right. I just wondered.'

She crossed the landing and went into her own room and closed the door.

Polly was asleep. She lay on her back, one arm slung above her head as if she were waving goodbye. Her mouth was slightly open.

'Polly.' Paul called her name softly. There was not even the flicker of an eyelid.

An angel. How about that?

He laughed.

He walked round the room for a few minutes wondering whether to go. Go now. Quietly dress and get out. Before she woke up. He could if he wanted be back in London in five hours' time; giving his agent a bell; making himself available.

I wouldn't want to do that to Polly, he thought.

Polly's ace.

He walked round the room trying to make up his mind.

On the dressing table was a picture in a silver frame.

He picked it up, the better to see the two people in it.

The father.

He knew the father; Polly lived in the basement of his house in Hampstead. The father smiled and was handsome. The father crushed your hand in his powerful grip. The father looked deep into your eyes, judging your suitability to touch his daughter. By and large, pretty hateful. A man who believed in the importance of knowing the right people. Paul doubted if he came into that category.

The mother.

Now, he had also met the mother, albeit in her dressing gown . . . and cross. Boy, had she seemed cross. Quite rightly so, if you thought about it.

In the picture, she stood beside the father, her face made up to the nines, every inch the star. She smiled, but there was a caution about her; between them there was light, not even the suspicion of their clothes touching. He wondered about the occasion of the picture. It had a formality about it that indicated some important moment in their lives, or the life of one of them anyway.

For some reason he touched the mother's face with a finger and quickly put the picture down.

I think I should go.

Why?

Polly's ace.

The sound of a car drew him to the window.

He had already heard Grace leaving earlier, in his half-sleep and wondered with a sudden anxiety if she was now coming back. He should have gone. After he had heard her car leave the driveway, he should have leapt out of the bed and gone.

A taxi drew up at the gate and sat there with the engine ticking. The old lady that he had met on the landing came out of the hall door and walked along the drive to the gate. She walked with great caution, leaning on a stick. She seemed to have pain in all her bones.

The taxi driver got out of the cab and opened the back door for her.

She smiled at him as she lowered herself into the seat, a smile of great sweetness.

Jesus God, he thought, what are these people?

I have to go.

The taxi moved off and he turned back into the room, his mind made up.

Polly's eyes were now open and she smiled at him too.

'Darling Paul,' she said.

That was that.

She held out her hand to him and he sat on the edge of the bed holding her warm fingers and wondering what to say.

'Who was the old lady who has just driven off in a taxi?'

For a moment she didn't say anything. She frowned slightly.

'Mother,' she said at last. 'Great. She must have changed her mind about letting us have the car. Good old mother.'

He shook his head.

'No. Your mother's not an old lady. This is an old lady. Very old. I met her on the landing when I was coming out of the bath.'

Polly sat up, alarmed.

'Mimi? Oh my God, it couldn't be Mimi.'

She pushed back the bed clothes and got out of the bed.

'It couldn't be Mimi.' She repeated the words as she pulled a dressing gown around her and rushed out of the room.

'Mimi,' she called on the landing.

He heard doors opening and shutting and then Polly's bare feet on the stairs.

'Mimi. Mimi, darling. Are you there? Mimi.'

Doors opened and the voice disappeared out into the back garden. No one answered.

Paul started to get dressed. It was better to be dressed rather than undressed if there was a crisis.

Polly came back into the room.

'I can't find her anywhere.'

'I told you,' said Paul. 'She drove away in a taxi.'

'Why didn't you tell me?'

'Be reasonable, Polly. I am telling you. There didn't seem to be any harm in this old lady walking down the path and getting into a taxi.'

'You should have stopped her.'

'Look, if you had said to me last night, by the way, if you see an old lady walking down the path and getting into a taxi, stop her, then maybe I'd have stopped her. Maybe not. Chill, Polly. She looked fine to me. Mind you . . .' He stopped.

'What?'

'Oh, nothing.' He didn't think this was the moment to mention angels.

'What will I do? Oh, don't stand there grinning, Paul, this could be serious. What will I do?'

151

'Well, I suppose there are three things you could choose from. Ring the police . . . a bit extreme. Ring your mother at the theatre. Probably also a bit extreme.'

Polly nodded vigorously.

'That I do not want to do,' she said.

'Nothing.'

'What do you mean, nothing?'

'Just that. Get dressed. Have breakfast. Get on with the day. My guess is that she will come back in the taxi and life will go on as normal. Maybe this is normal. You don't live here. Maybe she does this every Friday. The taxi driver was very nice to her.'

Polly considered this. Her face lost some of its anxiety.

'Mother has never mentioned . . .'

'The old lady just leads a secret life of her own. After all, why not?'

'She's a bit . . .'

'A bit what?'

'Well, you know. A bit potty and very shaky. We do have anxieties about her. Maybe, you know, the time has come for her to . . . You know, Daddy thinks she should go into a home. A really nice one . . . Mummy is hopeless when it comes to making decisions.' Her voice faltered away. 'It's difficult to know what to do. We want her to be safe.'

'She looked perfectly safe to me.'

Polly went over and looked out of the window, just in case she might see her grandmother walking slowly up the path.

'She probably hasn't got any money.'

'Don't worry. After all your mother leaves her here every day.'

'I think she just sits and watches television.'

He sighed. He couldn't go now. He couldn't just leave her in a bit of a state. Somehow he would have to work out how to get away before evening.

'What time does . . . ah . . . your mother get home?'

Polly shook her head.

'I haven't a clue. It all depends on her schedule. She did say she was very busy today. Probably about six thirty. She comes home always to cook Mimi her dinner. She's quite good like that. I do hope Mimi's not going to be troublesome. Not till after the first night anyway.'

'First night?'

'Yes. She's playing Gertrude at the Abbey. I think they open in about three weeks.'

She picked up her hairbrush from the dressing table and began to brush her curly highlighted hair.

His eyes were drawn to the photograph.

She saw him looking at it.

'Mum and Dad,' she said. 'I'm going to have a bath. Why don't you go down and make us some breakfast.'

'They look like they're at a party or something. A celebration.'

'It was, really. It was the fifth anniversary of their divorce and Daddy and Pauline's wedding day. He was an awful ass to invite her. She arrived looking like a bloody film star and did her luvvie bit all over the place. It was terribly embarrassing.

Pauline was offended, my father was angry and she had a whale of a time. All Daddy's old friends that she hadn't seen for years were crawling all over her. She can be quite hateful at times.'

'Gertrude,' said Paul.

'Yes. Oh God, how I wish I had a normal ordinary mother who stayed at home and loved a whole pack of children and Dad. Cherished Dad. He's got all that now, with Pauline and the kids, and I'm left on the outside. Sometimes I feel they just want me there because I can babysit for them, not because they . . .'

She stopped and threw the hairbrush onto the bed.

'Sorry.' She came over to him and put her arms around his neck.

'I am sorry. They just cut me in half from time to time and I really hate that. I want to be whole. I don't want to have to think about them. I hate having to dream about the perfect family.'

'There is no such thing.'

'I love you,' she whispered. 'We could perhaps be perfect.'

'Dear Polly.'

He pulled her to him and held her tight. Over her shoulder he caught the eyes of the mother and father in the photograph. He shut his eyes and kissed Polly.

This is the road down which I wish to travel, he told himself. This is perhaps my perfection. He licked salty tears off her cheeks. He felt whole.

'I love you too, dear Polly,' he whispered into her warm ear.

\* \* \*

The awning out over the street made her think of Paris, and then briefly of Benjamin.

She shook her head to dislodge the thoughts. She didn't want to think of Benjamin.

Because of the awning the restaurant was quite dark inside, but nicely cool.

She was quite tired now and her heart beat rather frantically against her ribs. She would be all right once she sat down.

He pulled out the chair for her and helped her into it. He took her stick and leaned it against the window by her side.

Outside, people chatted to each other and a little wind scurried from time to time around them, causing skirts to ripple and secrets to scatter among the tables.

In here they were safe.

He sat down across the table and smiled at her.

'You are tired. I'm sorry. I didn't realise just how hard it would be in this city to buy a decent pair of shoes.'

'Well, I'm over-excited rather more than tired. It's been such a long time since I've been into town. I feel a bit like a child. I'd be lost in a moment if you weren't with me.'

'The feet?'

She smiled and looked down at the taupe suede boots folded neatly just above the ankles.

'As you said they should be, just like gloves. My feet, I'm afraid, are old and rather useless . . . but I suppose they might as well be comfortable.'

He handed her a menu. She shook her head.

'No. You do it. I'm sure you'll choose a delicious meal.'

Benjamin had always chosen for her; that had of course been in earlier years when he had taken her out to restaurants, before he had withdrawn from that sort of life, to his garden and his whiskey bottles and his prayers.

Bonifacio was talking to the waitress.

Mimi calculated that he was over five hundred years old, not a touch of grey even in his hair. He must have left the world quite young, she thought.

She had been to Rome once . . . such a long time ago. Not all that long after the war really. Grace, she remembered, had taken her first steps while they had been away. She also remembered the slight pain of not having been there to see that miracle happening. A tattered-looking city it had been, full of tattered people; grey and tired she had found it. A sharp, cold wind had blown dust constantly in her eyes. They had had an audience with the Pope. The Holy Father as Benjamin had insisted on calling him.

That was when Benjamin had been locked into religion as he had later become locked into alcohol.

She couldn't remember which had been the more tiresome, Benjamin holy, or Benjamin pickled.

Benjamin had taken her to a shop near the Spanish Steps and bought her some rosary beads that looked as if they were made of coffee beans and silver and she had held them out for the Pope to bless. She had closed her eyes as he had approached their small group and held the beads out in her cupped hands. She remembered composing her face into what she had hoped was an attitude of beatific humility, as seen in medieval Italian paintings. She had hoped that he didn't have x-ray eyes.

She hadn't seen those rosary beads for years.

'Maybe I gave them away,' she said aloud.

'Where have you been?' Bonifacio put a small glass of white wine in front of her as he asked the question.

'It's so hard to get rid of the past. Thank you. It's like a web all round me. I keep trying to escape and I can't.'

She took a sip of the wine.

'I'd really like to be able to forget it all and just be aware of this glass of wine. You. The sun or the rain. If only everything I do didn't carry something else with it. I find that quite tiring. That makes my head as well as my body ache.'

Grey tears trembled in her eyes.

He leant across the table and touched her hand.

She felt the warm shock of his energy run through her.

'You know,' he said, 'it is quite possible that you forget everything. That there is nothing in your life but the moment you live. You could walk out of this restaurant and never remember that you have been in here. You can finish this meal and never remember that you have eaten it. You can go home and not remember the sounds and smells or the people. I can arrange that. If that is what you want.'

She looked at him thoughtfully and shook her head.

'Haven't I just spent two hundred and fifty pounds on this idiotic pair of boots? Where would be the point in my not getting the best value out of them possible? I want to see the look on Grace's face when I tell her how much they cost. I always want to have the possibility of buying another pair when these are worn out. I think I'd better stay the way I am.'

He smiled and lifted his glass towards her.

'Wonderful Mimi,' he said.

She gave him one of her most charming smiles.

The waitress arrived with plates of fish salad; curled prawns, rings of calamari, crabclaws, smoked salmon, clams in tiny shells like finger nails and dressing in a bowl.

'My dear Bonnyface,' was all that Mimi was able to say.

'*Buon appetito*,' he answered her.

In a bar not far away Gertrude was having a glass of wine and a sandwich with Polonius. They were old friends, old colleagues, you might say, together again in a play after many years. They talked *Hamlet*, they talked the director, they talked the bloodyness of the theatre, they talked how much they disliked big-headed young actors who thought they knew everything, they talked London, they laughed. Pals they had always been, and were pleased to be together again. Secure for the time being in all those things you need to be secure in and also in that familial friendship that happens when a play is being made.

'And the divine Mimi? Still motoring?' he asked.

Grace sighed.

'She's getting on, you know. I get quite scared sometimes leaving her on her own all day.'

'You make her sound like a dog, darling. Do you have to dash home and take her for walkies?'

'I suppose I should really. She's okay at the moment, but it's just a question of time. In the summer it's not too bad. She potters in the garden and I get home about six. Mrs O'Brien is there three days a week, so that's not too bad, but the rest of the time she's alone. Quite shaky. Isn't it awful? That prospect in front of us all. How will we manage when faced with helplessness?'

'I intend to have a succession of healthy, beautiful young men beating a path to my door. They will cater to my every wish. I advise you to start making your own plans. Never throw yourself on the mercy of your relations. They have none.'

She laughed.

'It's much easier for you lot to make plans like that. There's a kind of solidarity amongst gays that we seem to lack.'

'Don't believe it, darling. It's a myth we put out to stimulate the jealousy factor. We have to get our revenge where we can.'

'It is good to see you again. You must come out and have dinner and meet Mimi. Not tonight. I think I may have a Polly problem tonight.'

She told him about the arrival of Paul.

He laughed.

'Paul who?'

'Hemming . . . Hemmings — something like that.'

'Yes.' He thought for a moment. 'I've seen him in something at the Court . . . yes, some sort of ghastly modern-dress *Seagull*. He was good. About the only good thing in it. He played Constantin. Stressed out. I remember that. A whole lot of stress. I thought Polly preferred rich kids. Her sensible father's daughter. Mind you, that lad will probably be rich before too long. A bit of a dish.'

'I wasn't seeing straight. Come on. We'll be late. We're going to have to run.'

'At our age, darling, and arrive sweating and tousled? Never.'

She got up and walked lightly across the bar and out into the sunny street. He followed her. Outside he took her arm.

'Darling, you don't look a day over forty-seven. I thought I'd play Polonius young . . . ish, you know. After all, why should the old bugger be seventy-five? He's always played seventy-five. Doddery old bore. There are young bores too. We meet them all the time. You actually married one. What do you think? After all, he has those two sprightly children. I can't see him a day over fifty. Just think of all those youngish political schemers you see around. What about John Redwood, for instance? I'm sure he might sacrifice his daughter to keep in with the mighty ones. What do you think? Do you think I could play him à la Redwood?'

'I presume you've made your mind up already. I'll tell you something though . . . you're not to play him a day younger than me.'

'I promise.'

They did run then, skittering down Grafton Street, past the American tourists and the crowds of Spanish students and the beggars and the stalwart women carrying bags from Marks and Spencer.

That delicious smell lingered.

It was in the hall and the sitting-room and even remotely in the kitchen.

The house was clean and calm.

Grace poured herself a glass of wine and sat down in a chair by the sitting-room window.

A mellow wind rustled in the garden.

She wondered where everyone was, but didn't try to find out by calling. She wanted — just for a few moments — to relish solitude. Tomorrow she would let Polly have the car. Take that chap off into the Wicklow mountains, go to Brittas Bay. It was no longer possible to fuck in the sandhills. No solitude there. Not much joy in fucking in sandhills anyway. Serious discomfort, sand grinding and itching in secret places.

Elsinore.

She saw stone flagged floors and echoing halls; shadows in which spies could lurk. Always wind and outside drifting, shifting sea and sand, long acres of mournful sand. A very uncomfortable play. I think we should all be cold, always drawn towards heaped fires and safety from the wind.

Sand would be everywhere there too, drifting in the wind. Gritting into your eyes and teeth.

I'd better go and put the chicken in the oven. Fetch herbs from the garden, rosemary and fennel.

She laughed inside herself.

She had played Ophelia at the Oxford Playhouse, aeons ago, almost straight from school, wet behind the ears. That was when she had met John.

'*Nymph, in thy orisons, be all my sins remembered?*'

He had said that to her the first time they met.

Was it the first-night party?

Why had that impressed her?

She couldn't remember.

From this distance, and no longer wet behind the ears, it seemed a pretty tacky sort of thing to say.

He had been so handsome and so unactory.

She had presumed him, from that very first moment, to be without sin.

Not a very sensible presumption.

No, indeed.

It had been a terrible production.

She had been a terrible Ophelia.

Meeting John had made everything seem better though.

For a while.

For fifteen years, in fact.

Not too bad, under the circumstances.

It was a bit here, there and everywhere, she thought.

Mimi warned me.

Mim had always been a good warner.

Mother's role.

'Now I,' she said aloud, 'have never warned Polly about anything.'

She got up and went into the kitchen.

Perhaps that had been a dereliction of duty.

I used to so resent Mimi's warnings.

She flung open the door of the fridge and stared into it. Great bright red American fridge. You could live in it. She got pleasure every time she looked at it; bought after a six-month run in London and then New York of *Hedda Gabler*. Awful woman. Great fridge.

She took out the chicken and put it on the table and then the bowl of Polly's peperonata.

Salad, new potatoes, raspberries and crème fraîche.

She looked at the food spread in front of her.

Food always made her feel safe, made her want to sing.

She took out a plate with five skinned and sliced smoked eels.

Lemons.

Cheese.

Take the cheese out now or it will still be chilled at dinner-time.

I wonder will those lovers come home?

Bloody better.

Herbs.

Then I must call Mim. She must be sleeping. No sound of the telly.

She switched on the oven and opened the back door.

The evening sky came into the kitchen and everything became for a moment bright.

She stepped across the terrace and began to gather parsley, rosemary, thyme and mint.

One very bright star pierced the blue sky.

'Mimi.' She called up towards her mother's window, softly at first then once more, louder.

There was no reply and she went back into the kitchen.

She poured herself another glass of wine and began to assemble dinner.

Chop this and that.

Pound herbs into the butter.

She heard a bump and then a slight shuffling upstairs.

That was okay.

She was always relieved to find Mim alive each day when she arrived home.

The smell of herbs now battled with Father's Albertine.

She kicked off her shoes and began to massage the butter into the chicken.

I wonder why I thought of John?

Ophelia, I suppose.

Mim said it wouldn't last.

Unless . . .

Yes, Mim had said, unless. She had known what men expect. Not that John was remotely like Father.

Poor old Father.

At least he kept his problem to himself; well, the safety of the nest. He was a dignified drunk. He didn't drink for fun or blokeish reasons; he was never the life and soul of any party. He just drank. He remained upright, polite, buttoned into his tidy suit, until he fell down asleep and when he woke up, he put on his smart suit and started all over again.

Why?

Was that to do with expectations too?

Mim would never speak about it. She would answer no questions.

'He's gone. Leave him be,' was all she ever said.

Maybe she just didn't know either.

She wiped her greasy fingers on a cloth and then put the chicken into the oven.

She heard Mimi's cautious steps on the stairs.

'In the kitchen,' she called out. 'Come and have a glass of wine, darling.'

The old lady's stick tapped on the hall floor.

She was walking across the hall to the drawing room.

'Mimi.'

Tap, tap and a soft shuffle.

Grace picked up the bottle and a glass and went to look for her mother.

She was standing by the window looking out at the garden. The sea was still lit by the sun.

'He's gone,' said Mimi.

'Wine?'

Mimi nodded.

'I have been asleep. Wine at lunch always makes me sleep. Wine in the evening wakes me up. It's a funny thing that, isn't it?'

She turned away from the window.

'No point in expecting him to be out there now.' She spoke the words and put her hand out for the glass of wine.

'Thank you, my dear. I must say I am very well looked after.'

She sat down in her high-backed armchair, the one it was easy to get out of. She took a sip of wine. She crossed her ankles.

Grace glanced down at her mother's feet.

'Mimi . . .'

Mimi took another sip of wine. The hand that held the glass trembled slightly with expectation.

'Those are nice boots. I don't think I've ever seen . . .'

She moved towards Mimi as she spoke.

They were very nice boots.

'Where . . . ?'

'I can't remember the name of the shop. It was Italian. Anne Street or Duke Street. Flavio. Ruffio, something like that.'

'Mim . . .'

The hall door opened and Polly's voice called out, 'Yoo-hoo.'

'Florio,' said Mimi.

Polly came into the room, followed by Paul, who hovered by the door.

'Hello, Mum. Marvellous smell. Hi, Mimi. Glad you're back safely. God, I'm zonked.' She threw herself on a chair. 'We've done the whole bit. The Castle, St Patrick's, Davey Byrnes. Trinity College. The whole bloody tourist trail. My feet are dead.' She kicked off her shoes. 'By the way, this is officially Paul.'

She waved a hand in his direction.

'A drink is . . .'

Paul bowed in Mimi's direction.

'Yes, Florio,' said Mimi.

'I'm really glad to see you back, Mimi,' said Polly. 'I was really scared of having to tell Mum . . .'

'Red or white?' Grace asked Paul across Polly's head. 'Just a second, Polly. Let's all have a drink first, then there's something that needs to be cleared up.'

'White,' said Paul.

'We met on the landing. I remember that.' Mimi raised her glass towards him and gave him a big smile.

'I'll have white too,' said Polly.

Grace left the room and went into the kitchen.

As she passed Paul in the doorway he put out his hand as if to touch her and then quickly drew it back again.

Had they taken Mimi into town and then abandoned her? she wondered.

She took a bottle from the fridge and picked up two glasses.

I'll kill them if they did an irresponsible thing like that.

She marched back into the room.

'Cleared up,' said Grace.

She put the glasses on the table and took the cork from the bottle.

'I was just telling you, dear, when they arrived. I think I'll change to white if I may. Summer drink. Wouldn't you think?'

She smiled across Polly's head again to Paul.

'I had a wonderful day.'

'Polly . . .' Grace handed her daughter a glass.

'It had nothing to do with me. Don't glare at me like that. She went off in a taxi. Didn't she, Paul?'

Paul didn't say a word. He moved to the table and took the glass that was there, full almost to the brim.

'I am totally confused. Mimi, did you go into town on your own, in a taxi?'

Mimi nodded happily.

'Firenze. That was the name of the shop. I remember it now. I believe that's the Italian for Florence. That's where I bought the shoes. It is very difficult to buy a decent pair of shoes in Dublin. These shoes.'

They all looked at her shoes.

'Well, they're boots really. My feet feel quite at home in them. Now, young man, if you could give me some white wine . . .'

Paul looked towards Grace. She nodded and he picked up the bottle and went over to Mimi. She held her glass towards him and he poured some wine into it. There was already a few sips of red still in the glass and the white coloured faintly as he poured.

'Are you all playing a joke on me?' asked Grace.

'We saw her go down the path and get into a taxi. That's all I know. I wanted to ring you up, but Paul . . . well, Paul . . .'

'Mimi. How did you get a taxi?'

Mimi looked out of the window without speaking for a moment.

'Is there any reason why I shouldn't get a taxi?'

Nobody spoke.

'I needed to get a pair of shoes . . .'

'I could have brought you in tomorrow.'

'I don't like the shoes I get with you. You can probably come with me next time, now that I know where to look. Soft suede, hand stitched. Like you see in medieval Italian paintings. Isn't it surprising that they still make the same sort of shoes nowadays?'

There was a long silence.

'They're lovely shoes,' said Polly at last. 'They look like Gucci.'

'That's right,' said Mimi. 'Gucci is the name all right.'

'Yes,' said Paul. 'They're lovely. They're very stylish. Lovely colour. They look really comfortable.'

'Only the Italians know how to make shoes.' Mimi wiggled her feet up and down as she spoke. Then she looked up at Grace. 'Are you angry with me?'

Grace shook her head.

'I'm just a bit confused, that's all. If you'd told me . . .'

'I didn't need to tell you. I went into town and I came back. My shoes cost two hundred and fifty pounds – I presume you want to know that bit of information. At this moment I have no intention of doing it again, but you never can tell. Two hundred and fifty pounds.' She spoke the figure with a certain pride. 'I really enjoyed myself.'

Grace put her glass down on the table and went over to examine the shoes. She bent down and ran a finger from toe to ankle.

'They're lovely, darling. Health to wear them. I must visit Firenze myself one day.' She touched her mother's shoulder. 'I just worry about you from time to time.'

'No need any more.'

She turned towards Paul and held out her hand. '*Je m'appelle Mimi*,' she said, and they all laughed.


By the time they finished dinner Mimi was tired out and slowly climbed the stairs to her room.

The sky through the window was a mass of stars and a lop-sided moon hanging so close to the earth that Grace felt she would be able to touch it from the top of Killiney Hill.

'I'm going down to swim. The sea will be full of stars. I love it like that.'

'You're as mad as Mimi,' said Polly.

'I'll swim too,' said Paul.

Polly looked at him with astonishment. 'Holy God!'

'You can come if you like,' said Grace. 'But I must warn you, I'm going now. This minute. There should be no delay when you decide to do something like this. Otherwise the idea grows cold. Pleasure fades away. It becomes some sort of chore. I'll meet you at the car in three minutes. I will drive off if you are not there.'

She left the room and ran upstairs.

Polly looked at him.

'It'll be freezing.'

'I feel like being frozen. Where will I find a towel?'

'Hotpress. Up beside the bathroom.'

'Will you come too?'

'You must be joking. I'm going to watch telly.'

Luckily they met no other cars on the winding road down to the sea. Grace drove in the middle of the road, quite fast, as if she might at any moment have second thoughts. She didn't speak. He watched her face as they moved from the pools of street light into the dark bends and under the overhanging trees. He couldn't think of anything to say. Some moments her eyes glittered in the light, then they were dark again. She seemed to have forgotten that he was there.

She pulled the car in to the side of the road and got out and slammed the door. She had left the keys in the ignition. He didn't know whether to remind her or not. He closed his door and followed her down toward the long beach.

He almost had to run to keep up with her.

The sea was black with long rippling silver waves. A lighted train tacked along the rails at the back of the sand. He wondered if the passengers were looking down at them. Probably not, he thought. The sound of the train faded and only the sea was left sighing as the silver waves broke on the shore.

She just stripped off her jeans and sweatshirt. She was wearing a black bathing suit underneath. Without even a glance in his direction she ran towards the sea. Away along the beach he could see a man walking with a dog and the clustered lights of houses spreading back inland.

The sand was gritty under his feet as he stepped out of his shoes and socks. He dropped his clothes beside hers on the rocks and ran after her, regretting his foolishness. It was cold. The sand had a residual warmth, but there was a chilly little wind which made his flesh cringe.

She had been right; the sea was filled with stars.

He watched her as she swam out from the shore, each move of her arms made dazzling by phosphorescence.

He ran into the water and followed her.

Along the beach the dog barked and another train rocked along the track, this time heading out of town. He watched the lights disappearing down the coast.

She was coming back towards him. She was a good swimmer. As she reached him she turned over on her back and smiled.

'I'm sorry,' she said. 'I really am quite graceless from time to time.'

She lifted a hand from the water and poured a cascade of

stars over his head. '*Benedictus, qui venit in nomine Domini.*'

She turned over, displacing light, and swam back towards the shore.

His eyes stung.

*Benedictus.*

What did she mean by that?

Latin.

Church words.

Nothing probably.

Naturally nothing.

All the time people said words that meant nothing.

She just said those words because they sounded good.

*In nomine Domini.*

He rolled over and over with the waves to the sea's edge and then scrambled to his feet.

*Hey there, you with the stars in your eyes.*

He ran up the beach to where she stood fastening her trousers and then suddenly became aware of his nakedness. He snatched up his towel and pulled it round him.

'Do you do this a lot?' he asked her.

'What? Swim? Whenever I have the time. You can walk around like a zombie all day and then get into the sea and you feel alive again. It's a very simple and cheap form of therapy.'

'Why did you say that to me?'

'What?'

'Those Latin words.'

She shook her head and silver sparks flew from her wet hair.

'They were church words, weren't they?'

'Probably. That doesn't mean anything though. Sometimes words just come out of my mouth without my willing. I'm always afraid this might happen on stage. You know, something quite irrelevant. Imagine that! Imagine the dagger looks from whoever else was on the stage.' She threw back her head and laughed. 'I know very little Latin. I hated my Latin teacher.'

She bent down to put on her shoes, brushing the damp sand from one foot and then another with the fingers of her right hand.

'They were church words,' he repeated.

'I know less about the church. I quite like to live without a safety net. My father was a passionate church goer. He used to get up every morning, even in his last couple of years when he was . . . well, pretty . . . mouldy – hungover to be truthful, and plod off to church. He never went in the car. I think the walk was some awful penance. I don't know how he managed it sometimes. Batter, church, batter, church. That seemed to be his system.'

'Batter?'

She straightened up.

'Drink. It was himself he battered. Like a man in a locked room banging his body and his spirit against the wall.'

She picked up her togs from the rock and folded them into the towel.

'How did the wonderful Mimi deal with that?'

Grace smiled at him. There was a trace of her mother's warmth in the smile.

'She's something else, isn't she? I wasn't around much in the last few years of his life. Marriage, work, all that . . . and to be perfectly honest I couldn't bear to be in the same house with them. They were both so diminished by despair. I never knew what it was all about. I never asked her to this day. I don't suppose she'd tell me anyway.'

They began to walk up the path towards the car.

'She was too old by the time he died to return to some sort of cheerful equilibrium of living. She'd been out of it all for too long. Her friends had all moved in other directions. I think they found her need a bit unnerving. Now she's imprisoned by her own infirmity. I honestly don't think she has much more life in her.' She sighed. 'Perhaps I'm not as good as I ought to be. Perhaps . . .' She caught her foot on a rock and stumbled.

He put out a hand to steady her.

'Thank you.' She turned to smile at him and instead of letting her go he pulled her against him and began to kiss her.

Oh dear God, he thought, why am I doing this?

She pushed her way out of his arms and let him have it in the face with the palm of her right hand.

Then she began to run to the car.

'What the fuck do you think you're at?'

He stood there rubbing his cheek and wondering the same thing.

He watched as she opened the car door and then got in, slamming it.

She drove off, without apparently looking to left or right, leaving him standing there, with a wet towel in his hand not knowing how to get back to the house.

# Two Moons

✳ ✳ ✳

Grace drove the car through the gateway and then turned off the engine. She sat staring at the right hand that had hit him. The palm was still stinging. I expect, she thought, I hurt myself more than I hurt him.

Damn.

Little fucking bastard.

How dare he?

How

dare

he.

She was shaking.

Something was hammering in her head, trying to split open her skull. It was the twenty-seven fists of anger.

Chill Gertrude, she shouted inside her head to herself.

Then she laughed.

Was it my fault?

Did I misguidedly and unknowingly smile too warmly in his direction?

Naaah.

The guy's an asshole.

Polly always picks on assholes.

Not normally assholes who have designs on middle-aged ladies though.

The front door opened and Polly stood in the light.

Her shadow spilled out down the steps.

She peered towards the car.

Now what? thought Grace.

She got out of the car and shut the door. She stood, the keys in her hand, looking up towards Polly.

'Hi. I thought maybe you were drowned. Where's Paul?'

'He's walking.'

'He's what?' Polly came down the steps.

'He just said he wanted to walk. It's a lovely night. If I hadn't had the car . . .'

Polly snatched the keys from her.

'For God's sake, Mother, you're as bad as Mimi. He doesn't know the way.'

'He found his way yesterday from the airport.'

'Hopeless.'

Polly got into the car and started the engine. She wound down the window and stuck her head out.

'You haven't had a row with him or something?'

'Of course not, darling.'

'I do not understand why things always get so complicated when I come over here. In England . . .' she put the car into reverse and backed towards the gate '. . . everything is so simple. I like things to be simple.' She shouted the last six words and drove away. 'So I do.'

So do I.

Grace went up the steps and in the door. She closed it behind her and leaned against it, like, she thought, Joan Crawford, Bette Davis, Barbara Stanwyck; they had all leaned against doors from time to time. Perhaps even Gertrude had. Unlikely. A drink would be a good thing, but foolish. The least foolish thing she could do now was to go to bed. Read a thriller. When in doubt read a thriller. Even one you had read before.

Maybe, she thought as she went up the stairs, he just kissed me because he loves Polly so much.

I love Polly, so I must kiss her mother.

Hello, Polly's mother.

Perhaps I am out of things, old-fashioned. Maybe a kiss means nothing anymore. *A kiss is just a kiss* . . . Oh for God's sake, Grace!

*I know a hawk from a handsaw when the wind is in the east.*

It was a kiss.

If anyone else had kissed me like that I would have been flattered; well, almost anyone else. Even at my age you have to be a bit selective.

I wonder what he'll say to her.

Suddenly she started to giggle. She dashed across the landing and into her room. She closed the door quietly so as not to disturb Mimi.

Mimi woke up very stiff.

All that excitement . . . she thought . . . all that scurrying round, wine, taxis. My life hasn't been like that for . . . she pondered on that as she dressed slowly . . . was it ever carefree?

She shook her head in answer to her own question.

Not since Benjamin came into it.

I suppose, she thought, I could divide my life into Before Benjamin and After Benjamin.

BB I was definitely carefree and then he came along carrying care secretly with him. Carrying a burden that he refused to share with me.

She sighed and the sigh caught at the back of her throat and she began to cough. She sat down on her bed. Her whole body shook and for a while she felt quite feverish, then it passed and she sat there bewildered. I mustn't think about Benjamin. I must find my new boots and go downstairs and see what today will bring.

That's a good idea.

The boots were a comfort to her feet.

She opened her bedroom door. The smell of coffee drifted up the stairs. She was a tea-for-breakfast person, but the smell was very seductive.

There was no sound from any bedroom, no open door, so she presumed that Bonifacio was making some wonderful Italian breakfast.

She started on the slow descent.

He came out of the kitchen door and looked up at her.

'I smell coffee,' she said.

'It is good.' He held out his hand and helped her down the last two steps. 'You have slept well?'

She nodded.

'I'm stiff. I think I did too much yesterday.'

He settled her into a chair at the kitchen table, put a cushion behind her back and handed her a cup of coffee.

'It is my fault, Mimi. I take the blame. Today we will be quiet. We will sit in the garden and listen to each other and your bones will rest.'

She smiled at him.

'You do say such nice things.'

She decided she wouldn't tell him that she preferred tea to coffee at breakfast.

He put a plate of hot buttered toast down in front of her and then sat down.

'No one's up?'

He shook his head.

'Such a lovely day,' said Mimi. 'When I was young I would have been up and out in the sun. I think that is what I remember. Sometimes I'm not quite sure if I remember the truth or what I would have liked the truth to be. Is that odd?'

He shook his head.

'Not odd at all. There are lots of people who rewrite their past and, what's more, believe it themselves. Now that is odd.'

She took a bite of toast and butter trickled down her chin.

Soft footsteps shuffled in the room above them.

'Someone,' said Mimi.

She took another bite of toast.

'I will be in the garden when you feel like coming out there.'

'Don't go.'

'I must. Suppose one of them was able to see me. Where would we be then?'

She laughed.

'What fun it might be.'

'In the soup,' he said and vanished.

He was quite careless though, she thought, noticing that he had left his cup, half-filled with coffee, steaming on the table.

That friend of Polly's, lover, whatever he was, came barefoot and silent into the room.

She picked up the coffeepot and leaning over filled Bonifacio's mug to the brim.

'Have some coffee,' she ordered, 'and some toast. Sit down there and tell me what your name is. I connect you with Polly, am I not right?'

'Good morning.'

He walked past her and as he moved she smelled the smell of sleep and bedclothes and early morning from him.

The smell of sex, perhaps, but then she realised that she no longer remembered what that smell was like.

'Paul,' he said, picking up his coffee. 'God, this smells good. I smelt it all the way upstairs, creeping through the floorboards.'

'Italian,' she said with a little smile. 'Don't you just adore Italian coffee?'

She raised her voice as she spoke.

'You're an actor? Have I got that right? I think someone said you were an actor. I rather like actors. Mind you, I don't know very many of them, in spite of Grace. You do know that Grace also acts? She's rather good, I think. I won't go and see *Hamlet* though. I've always found it a rather boring play. Do have a piece of hot buttered toast, at least it *was* hot buttered toast.'

She glanced out of the window to see if Bonifacio was to be seen.

He took a piece of toast.

'Is no one else up?'

'It's Saturday.'

'Ah.'

'Why get up, if you don't have to? Do you think that Grace will mind if I don't go to see *Hamlet*?'

'I don't really know. You ought to ask her.'

'How about you? Would you mind if your mother didn't come to see you in *Hamlet*?'

He chewed for a moment.

'Yes, perhaps I would. Perhaps indeed I would be hurt by the fact of her disinterest. I wouldn't mind if she thought I was good or not. I think I would just feel lonely if she didn't come to see it. Families have obligations towards each other.'

'Are you going to marry Polly?'

To her intense surprise he blushed.

'I'm sorry. I shouldn't have asked you that. Old ladies can be so tiresome. We are impatient to know so many things and time is so short. Yes.' She poured herself another cup of coffee. 'I do have to say you're a cut above the others.'

There was a laugh from the doorway.

They hadn't heard Grace coming barefoot down the stairs and she stood now behind them in the doorway. She was dressed in jeans and a tee-shirt and her hair hung down around her shoulders.

'Darling Mim, you shouldn't say such things.' She walked across the room and kissed her mother. 'Polly would kill you, if she could hear you.' She took a cup from the dresser and poured herself some coffee. 'This smells great. Who made it?' Mimi spread her hands wide in a gesture that meant nothing.

Paul stared at the table.

'She's right, of course. You are a cut above the others. But we won't let it go beyond this table.'

He looked up at her. She stood with her back to the window and he couldn't see her face.

'You got safely home, I see. The silly boy decided he wanted to walk home from the beach last night, Mim. There was nothing I could do to dissuade him.' She took a sip of coffee. 'Polly was quite cross with me when I arrived home without him.'

'She was quite cross with me too. But that's all okay now. She thought that I must have been rude to you.'

'Yes,' said Grace.

'But, as I say, that's all right now. I have apologised to her.'

'And to me?'

Mimi looked from one to the other and then slowly got to her feet. 'You are talking riddles. I am going to sit in the garden. Riddles confuse my brain.'

She groped for her stick and headed for the door out into the garden. She wondered as she went what he felt he had to apologise for. She hoped it wasn't anything substantial.

Bonifacio was sitting at the bottom of the garden in the shade of a tall magnolia tree that had been planted by her father on the day she was born. He got up when he saw her come out of the house and came up the grass to meet her, taking her arm carefully when he reached her to help her down the steps.

'I can't apologise to you.'

He spoke the words after a long silence.

She bent her head towards her cup and inhaled the strong fumes of the coffee.

Outside in the bright sun, she saw Mimi walk carefully across the grass. She was nodding her head and smiling towards some invisible being.

Oh Mimi, she groaned inside herself, don't go loopy on me.

'Do you understand what I am saying?'

She was startled by his voice; she had for a moment forgotten the embarrassment of his presence.

'Sorry.' She turned towards him. 'I didn't hear what you said. I was . . .' She gestured towards the garden. 'Mimi.'

He wasn't listening.

'You see,' he said. 'I could do it again now. I thought last night it was some sort of madness that had come over me. Wine, the sea, the way you . . .' He shook his head. 'The way you smiled at me.'

'No. It was nothing to do with that.' Her voice was angry. 'You're not going to bloody blame me for your . . . your . . .' She couldn't think of the right word.

'Oh no. Nothing is further from my mind. I just can't apologise. You can only apologise for your unacceptable actions if you don't intend to repeat them.'

'Unacceptable action.' She nodded.

'Grace . . .'

'Don't let's make a big issue out of this. After all *a kiss is just a kiss . . . as time goes by.*'

He joined in singing the last few words and then they both looked at each other and laughed.

The telephone rang.

Grace put her cup of coffee on the table and went across the room and picked up the telephone. He watched every move she made. He watched the way her head dipped and how she rested her cheek against the fingers of her right hand as she spoke into the receiver.

'Hello.'

A male voice squawked.

'Darling. How lovely. Yes. No. No problem . . . I can't think of anything nicer.'

Paul got up from the table and went into the hall.

She heard him running up the stairs, across the landing and into Polly's bedroom.

'Dear Charlie, see you tonight then. About eight. Mim'll get very over-excited. It's an age since she's seen you.' She made kissing noises into the telephone and put it down.

She went over to the kitchen door and called down the garden to Mimi.

'That was Charlie Benson on the phone, Mim. Remember Charlie? He's coming to dinner tonight. He can't wait to see you.'

Mimi waved a hand in her direction to show that she had heard.

Food.

I must think food and then Gertrude.

I must not allow myself to be confused by the unacceptable behaviour of silly young men.

Or touched. Heavens no. I must not allow that.

Actors. Silly young actors.

I suppose one might as well say silly middle-aged actresses who smile at people.

May I never smile again?

Now that sounded a mite Shakespearean.

I'll do something with a chicken.

Lots of herbs and garlic and a chicken.

Thick rich creamy sauce . . . Charlie will like that . . . and rice.

'It's such a lovely day, I thought, Mum, if I can have the car, that we might go to Brittas Bay.'

She hadn't heard Polly come into the room.

'Not if you call me Mum.'

'Mothah. Will Mothah do?'

'It's preferable. Charlie Benson is coming to dinner. Will you be . . . ?'

'Great. How nice to see Charlie. It's been ages. Is he in the show?'

'Polonius.'

'An old friend of Mum's.' She spoke to Paul who was standing just behind her shoulder. 'Maybe you've come across him. Sweet old pouf.'

'Enough of that old stuff. He's the same age as I am. Especially if you're going to borrow my car.'

Paul muttered something that Grace could not hear.

Polly laughed happily.

'We're going now. Now. He's such a bully. He won't even let me have some breakfast.'

'Take a banana,' suggested Grace.

'I have the keys.' Polly jangled them as she ran across the hall after Paul. The hall door slammed behind them.

'*Stay not upon the order of your going, but go at once,*' muttered Grace to her cup of coffee, which was now cold. She emptied it into the sink, looked for a moment at Mimi laughing in the garden and decided to immerse herself in Gertrude.

'We used to go to the beach,' Mimi said. 'On days like this. When we were young. Well, perhaps I should say, younger. Yes. Younger. When Grace was a child. Why not escape? I used to say. Benjamin never came. He hated the beach. He hated taking off his shoes and socks. He hated sitting on the ground and eating sandy tomatoes. He loathed the sea. He never, never got pleasure from looking out of the windows of this house and seeing . . . all that.' She waved a hand towards the sea.

'I would love now to walk on a beach, in my bare feet. I wouldn't want to spoil my new shoes.'

A spasm of pain shot through her back.

She closed her eyes and in her lap her fingers groped at each other for comfort.

He took her right hand and held it gently, like a lover or a mother delivering comfort through stillness, and after a few moments the pain passed.

She opened her eyes and smiled at him.

'There is no answer to that,' was all she said.

'Like Benjamin,' he whispered, 'I have never been into the sea. Don't think the worse of me for that. It was never an occurrence that came my way.'

She smiled.

'You could try it here.'

He shuddered slightly.

'My body, dear Mimi, would disintegrate. Where I come from the sea is like polished metal when the sun shines and steam rises from the shallow pools left when the tide goes out. We never went near it. We were never allowed. We kept to the shade. My mother warned us always about the sea and the sea beasts and the little stinging flies in the marshes behind the sand dunes and the reptiles and the watching fish that caught you by the leg and carried you down into the water and fed on your flesh when you were dead.'

'My goodness,' said Mimi. 'Where on earth did you live? Here the sea, if treated with respect, is therapeutic and a great source of entertainment.'

'We didn't live close to the sea, so we only knew those frightening stories that people told us about it. My mother was a very nervous person. She wanted her children to live for ever. She believed the stories and we were warned and warned, and threatened and made to swear all sorts of outlandish oaths.' He laughed suddenly and squeezed her fingers tight. 'She was so funny really. We used to laugh at her. Don't go near the sea, she used to say whenever we went anywhere . . . like to visit my uncle in Arrezzo. Don't let the sea get you. Promise me that. She had never seen it. She didn't know where it lay. She only knew how dangerous it was. We lived, you see, right in the centre of Italy. She thought of the sea as some huge creeping animal. I laughed so hard when I first saw it, one of those days of hammer heat. It was too hot to laugh, but I couldn't help it. But I still have inside me the notion that maybe she was right.'

'Right in the centre of Italy.'

'Yes. A small town called Borgo Sansepolcro. Many miles from the sea. My father was a shoemaker. A master.'

'Ah,' said Mimi. 'I should have guessed.'

'I too. But I was never a master. I loved the feel of the soft skins. I loved the coloration of them.' He paused for a moment and wondered if he had used the right word. 'Yes. The different dyes. The fine colours. You know what I mean? They were never just brown or black. They were really joyful colours. You know the paintings of Piero della Francesca? His father also was a shoemaker. I was apprenticed to him for three years, to learn the secrets of the colouring. He too in his day was a master, that shoemaker. And his son, one of the great masters that boy became. I have no recollection that he ever painted the sea. Lake Trasimene perhaps, but not the sea. Perhaps his mother too had her fears.' He laughed. 'Sometimes in those pictures, maybe they wore shoes made by me. Maybe they did. Isn't that a good thought? I have perhaps that immortality.'

'Angels are immortal anyway.'

He shook his head.

'Not I. Oh, not I. I have suffered death.'

He took off his little hat and fanned at his face with it.

His eyes looked immortal, she thought.

How silly. How could they look immortal if he had suffered death? Maybe they just look aware.

Benjamin's eyes had been blue, a grey-blue as if washed by

tears. She had never understood why he had needed to cry so much. Not, mind you, that she had ever caught him at it; he wasn't one for crying in public.

'I suppose I'm not a real angel anyway.'

'A fake? A cheat? A pretender?'

He laughed.

'No, no, no. Nothing like that. It's all in order, you know. I was sent. I was summoned from the shadows and I will go back to the shadows. I just said I was an angel to put you at your ease.'

'Shadows?'

'Peace perhaps.'

'Is there such a thing?'

'That's all there is.'

She nodded.

'No God? No hierarchical system of angels and archangels, saints and sinners?'

'I have never come across it.'

She looked out to sea. The usual boat was heading for England. What seemed like a squadron of yachts skimmed across the bay, their white sails leaning landwards.

'Yet you say you were summoned . . .'

'Yes.'

'By whom?'

'By you.'

She considered this notion.

He carefully put his hat back on again and watched the yachts with interest. The three in the lead went about, displacing water and readjusting their sails.

'I heard this voice in the shadows . . . I didn't have to pay any attention . . .'

'I never called. I have never called for help. It's not part of my nature. Anyway, I don't need help. There have been other times when I could have done with it but now . . . It's a bit late really to be calling for help? Wouldn't you think?'

'What are they doing?'

She looked towards the boats. One after another, they swooped and then turned, pushing back the way they had come, fighting against a stiff little breeze.

'They always race on Saturdays. In the summer, that is. Do you mean to say that you are merely a figment of my imagination?'

'I never suggested any such thing. Some voice in you called and I came.'

'That I am potty?'

'Please?'

'Crazy. Mad. Unhinged in some way.'

'Do you not like me?'

'Yes, I do. I really do.'

He smiled at her.

His teeth could have been better, she thought.

He spread his hands in a generous gesture.

'Then, dear Signora Mimi, enjoy.'

She frowned for a moment.

'I suppose I should have asked you for some sort of proof . . . like a badge or something. We're always being told to ask people for their credentials . . .'

'I have no credentials. I have no badge. But I haven't shown myself to be some sort of a dangerous person. Have I?'

She shook her head.

'Good,' he said. 'That's all right then. We don't have to worry any more. We can enjoy our acquaintance with each other.'

'Yes, I suppose that is the right thing to do. I must say it's very nice to have someone to talk to. Grace is always so busy and most of my friends are . . . well, all of them are gone. You know what I mean?'

He nodded.

'Dead.'

They let the word lie between them for a moment.

'Dead, death, dying. No one uses those words nowadays, you know. I expect they were used more liberally when you were alive. Looking back at that time from here death seemed to be around every corner. At least that's what history tells us.'

He laughed.

'Nothing changes that much, Signora Mimi.'

'*This fell sergeant, death, is strict in his arrest.* Shakespeare said that,' she said quickly, in case he thought she'd made it up herself. 'I don't know what fell means, unless it is that he fells his victims. I must ask Grace . . . if I remember.'

She glanced up towards Grace's bedroom window. It was open and a pale curtain stirred slightly.

'I do admire Grace . . . really I do. She can conjure up such courage when it is needed. I was never able to do that. I have always been a fearful coward. I presume you were a courageous man.'

He shook his head.

'No. I never liked the notion of being hurt . . . or indeed even hurting someone else. I shied from all that element that seems to be in men. I joined no armies. I carried no weapons.' He laughed. 'I never even fought over a woman. All my friends did that from time to time. Part, you might say, of the ritual.'

'You made beautiful shoes for your ladies, instead.'

'How did you know?'

'Personally speaking, I'd have preferred a man who made beautiful shoes for me, rather than one who laid about him with a sword.'

'Your husband was a gentle man?'

She thought about Benjamin.

'Yes. I do have to say that. I don't think that to be violent in any way would ever have occurred to him. He was very hard on himself.'

'Hard?'

'He thought it was important to live within a certain set of rules; his God's rules, his society's rules. I think he believed in hell. Actually, looking back, I think he might well have been a little touched in the head. I've never thought of that before. Odd that he should be so much in my head at this time.'

She stopped.

Why should she speak to this stranger about Benjamin?

'It was like he carried some terrible burden around all the time. In the end he took to silence.'

Where was the harm in speaking out? No one could be harmed.

'He neither spoke, nor did he like being spoken to. Words seemed to hurt his head.'

'You must have found that difficult.' His voice was sympathetic.

'Let's talk about something else. You don't have to feel sorry for me. I have led quite a good life . . . I don't mean that I have been a particularly good person or anything like that. I mean that life has been very good to me. It's quite easy to be happy, you know, if you go with the flow.' She laughed. 'That's a new expression I heard recently on the TV. Go with the flow. I rather like that.'

They sat in silence for a while.

He watched the boats and the seagulls and the rippling sparkles on the surface of the sea and she looked inward into her life and wondered why she was telling him lies.

Above them, from her bedroom window, Grace looked down at her mother, apparently about to nod off into sleep, her head sinking lower and lower onto her chest. She thought of calling down to her and then thought better of it. She picked up her book and pen from the table and went down the stairs. She took Mimi's big straw hat from the hall press.

As she walked down the steps into the grass, she heard her mother's murmuring voice. 'Have you x-ray eyes? Can you see into my head?'

'I can see you getting sunstroke, if you sit there for long without your hat on,' she called out. 'You will boil your brains.' She waved the hat at her mother as she spoke.

Mimi looked slightly displeased.

'Thank you, dear. I was just about to ask him to get it for me. Or the umbrella. The umbrella might be better.'

Grace handed her the hat, which she clapped onto her head.

'I'll get the umbrella. I thought I might come and work here beside you, keep you company.'

'I don't think I need you to do that, dear. Just get me the umbrella. I am quite happy here, just talking things over.'

'What sort of things are you talking over?'

'Just this and that. Things that need seeing to. I have a lot of things in my head that need seeing to.'

'I'll get the umbrella.'

'And while you're in the house, there's a bottle of white wine in the fridge. Bring that out too, if you will, and two glasses. Thank you, dear.'

As Grace walked towards the house she heard her mother laugh.

'Might as well be hanged for a sheep as a lamb,' she heard her say to the thin air.

Everyone arrived at the same time: Mimi came slowly and majestically down the stairs in a lot of black and beads just as the doorbell rang and Grace's car turned in the gateway.

Grace suddenly felt harassed.

All steamed up from cooking, she thought to herself.

'I'll get the door, dear,' called her mother from the hall.

She had spent most of the afternoon sleeping off the effects of too much white wine drunk in the noonday sun.

She didn't seem any the worse for wear.

Grace wondered about the two glasses for a moment and then the noise in the hall chased all other thoughts from her mind.

Mimi, Charlie and a large bunch of flowers were tangled together in a huge embrace.

Polly and Paul were having trouble getting into the hall. Their faces were burnt by the sun and tiny particles of sand shone on the skin of their faces and arms, making them look as if they had been gently sprayed with golden paint.

Charlie held Mimi away from him at arm's length and looked her up and down.

'My darling,' he said. 'You divine ageless creature. How I've missed you.'

He bent and kissed her hand and then handed her the flowers.

'Greek. You look like a magnificent Greek goddess.'

Mimi tossed her head.

'Greek? Surely not Greek. What about Italian? I'd rather look Italian.'

She handed the flowers to Paul who had just stepped past Charlie into the hall.

'Put these in water, there's a dear. This is Polly's latest. Hello, Polly. You're all covered in sand.'

'Why don't you all come in to the sitting-room and stop clogging up the hall? Everyone can kiss everyone else in here.'

No one was listening to Grace except Paul. He was standing on the bottom steps of the stairs, just outside the laughter and the embracing and he was staring at her. He looked slightly absurd clutching the huge bunch of flowers in front of his body, his face speckled with glittering sand.

'Everyone can kiss everyone else?' He mouthed the question at her as she looked in his direction.

She gestured down the passage.

'In the kitchen you'll find . . .' She looked at the flowers, '. . . all that sort of thing.'

He stepped down from the stairs towards her.

'I'm very bad at finding things.'

Her instant reaction was to take a step backwards, away from what suddenly seemed to her to be some terrible danger. She hit the side of the door and stood there for a moment trying to calm her panic.

She took a deep breath and put her hand on Charlie's arm.

'You haven't said hello to me yet. Polly, you're spreading sand all over Charlie's clothes. Go and show Paul where the vases are and then both of you get tidy for dinner. Go, go, go.'

Charlie's arm was round her and he pulled her tight to him.

'*Calme toi, ma belle.*' He kissed her cheek. 'How beautiful you all look tonight. I feel privileged to be in such beautiful company. I didn't bring you flowers, my darling. I thought a couple of bottles of champagne would be more digestible. I suggest the young man, to whom I have not been introduced, might put them in the fridge.' He held a hand out towards Paul.

'Paul Hemmings,' said Paul, taking it.

'Paul,' said Polly and Grace simultaneously.

'Paul something or other,' said Mimi.

'I thought I recognised your face,' said Charlie, holding

Paul's hand. 'I saw your Constantin at the Court. Great performance.' He dropped Paul's hand. 'All things considered.'

He swept Grace and Mimi into the sitting-room, leaving
Polly, Paul, the flowers and the champagne in the hall.

As those evenings go it was a success; quite a lot of laughter,
quite a lot of theatrical jokes and gossip, the occasional prickly
silence which caused Charlie to glance quickly from face to
face. Damn him, thought Grace, the old assessor, seeking out
everybody's secrets, plaiting threads even we do not see together.
He flirted with Mimi, was avuncular with Polly and flattered
Paul.

Each one was delighted by his attentions.

Grace held her breath.

About eleven o'clock Mimi rose from her chair. She found
it hard to straighten her back and as she walked across the room,
she looked tired and very frail.

'I must go to bed. It has been so good to see you again . . .'
She paused for a moment and a shadow crossed her face as she
groped for his name. 'Forgive me. I never thought I would come
to this, searching for the names of old friends. Charles.' She
spoke the word with triumph.

He got up and took her hand.

'Mimi, my dear Greek goddess, I would forgive you
anything. We haven't seen enough of each other over the years.
I hope to rectify this. I will make sure that Grace invites me
regularly over the next few weeks.' He bent and kissed her hand.
'Perhaps you might even be persuaded to come out and dine
with me one evening. I would enjoy that so much.'

She smiled at him.

'What fun that would be. I might have to bring Bonnyface. I think you might like him.'

She left the room.

Paul got up and followed her into the hall.

'You look tired.'

She looked up at him.

'Yes.'

'Can I help you up the stairs?' He smiled slightly. 'I could carry you.'

'I think I can make the stairs tonight, young man.' She grasped the knob at the bottom of the banisters. 'Look to Polly,' she said and started her climb.

He stood for a moment watching her before he went back into the sitting-room. He crossed the room without speaking and sat down beside Polly. The window behind them was open and soft night sounds came with the gentle breeze into the room. Across the room in the semi darkness of the shaded lamps Grace and Charlie leaned towards each other, hands touching, their voices low and intimate. His eyes filled with stinging tears. This is so bloody unfair, an almost childlike voice in his head spoke, I have become the victim of a terrible joker. Grace put out a hand and stroked Charlie's face and they both laughed. Paul closed his eyes. Polly took his hand and rubbed the back of his fingers with her thumb.

'Darling,' she whispered. 'That was kind. That was good.'

He looked at her, puzzled. Her thumb still had particles of sand on it and they grated into his skin.

'What?'

'Mimi. It was good of you to follow her like that. Grace just takes her for granted. I think she thinks that Mim is indestructible, so she ignores her a bit.'

'She's a great old girl. I just thought she looked worn out all of a sudden.'

'Who do you think Bonnyface is?'

She held his hand up to her warm face and rubbed it against her cheek. Last week he would have found it a charming gesture.

'I once had an imaginary friend called Fred.' he said. 'He came everywhere with me. I had to have a plate for him at the table when I ate.' He laughed. 'I remember my mother saying, "One for you and one for Fred," as she put food onto our plates. But, of course, the food she put on his plate was imaginary too. "Look," she'd say, "Fred's plate is empty. He's eaten all his tea. Fred is a good boy."'

'What happened to Fred?'

'He got run over by an 88 bus.'

'How horrid? Why?'

'I couldn't think of any other way to get rid of him, so when I was walking down the Holland Park Avenue one day, I caught him unawares and pushed him under a bus.'

'You murdered him?'

'I suppose so. It was quite quick. He didn't feel a thing.'

'What did your mother say?'

'She never knew. I didn't tell her.' He thought about his mother for a moment. 'She might have been cross. I don't really know. I must have been about eight. He was getting to be a bother.'

She kissed his fingers.

'I didn't realise you were such a ruthless person.'

He pulled his hand away from hers.

'Yes, Polly. I'm afraid I am. Quite ruthless. Come on.' He stood up. 'Let's go to bed. All that sea and sun and gambolling in the dunes has worn me out.'

She laughed happily and stood up.

'Yes. I'm worn out too, but happy. I'm terribly happy.' She took his hand again and squeezed it. 'Thank you.'

'How wonderful you both look standing there together in the damned moonlight,' commented Charlie in his best Noël Coward voice.

Polly ran over and threw her arms around him.

'It is lovely to see you, Charlie. Give me a ring when you come back to London and let's meet.'

'You've better things to do than waste your time on old men, my dear. But maybe I will, and bore you with too much gossip.' He waved a hand at Paul. '*There's metal more attractive.*'

'Good old Shakespeare. Night, Mum. Great evening. Great, great day.'

The young people left the room hand in hand.

'Brandy?' Grace asked Charlie.

'Why not?'

She got up and went to the cupboard to get the bottle and glasses.

'Is Polly thinking of marrying that young man?'

She poured quite a large amount of brandy into the two glasses and then walked back across the room and handed him his. She sat down beside him again.

'I don't know.'

'I do hope not.'

They sat in silence for a long time, sipping at the brandy.

'She's not cut out to be an actor's wife. That's not a criticism of her, darling. She's great, a lovely young woman, but she's been living in that house in Hampstead too long to be able to fit into the real world. A good solid banker, that's what she needs, or, perhaps a barrister. Someone solid, safe, like Daddy.'

Grace sighed.

There were two moons again out beyond the window. She tried to concentrate on that fact. She thought of Li Po who died drunk trying to embrace the wrong moon. My sweet embraceable moon, she sang in her head. Charlie was talking but she didn't want to hear what he was saying. He took her glass from her hand and put it down on the table.

'You're not listening to me.'

She shook her head.

'Why not?'

'I'm tired, Charlie. I think we should ring for a taxi for you.'

She got up and walked over to the window. The moon in the sky hung over Bray Head, like a lantern, the moon in the sea seemed to breathe, a living face just below the surface.

'What is going on?'

'Nothing is going on, Charlie.'

'My dear girl, I have been around too long not to know when things are going on.'

He heaved himself up from the sofa and came over to her. He put his arm around her shoulder.

'What a moon.'

'Two moons,' she said.

'He never took his eyes off you all evening. He could hardly speak . . . and your sweet Polly noticed nothing, only her own happiness. Oh God, I'm so glad I'm not young any more. I have left behind all that capacity for terrible happiness and terrible pain. Swings and roundabouts, my darling. I sometimes regret the happiness, but not all that often any more.'

'You sound more and more like Polonius.'

'What did you do to him?'

'Nothing.'

She turned and pressed her face into his chest.

'Nothing. I promise you that. I gave out to him the night he arrived. I have hardly spoken to him since. Hardly. For God's sake, Charlie, he's only been here for two days. He's . . . he's . . . What should I do?'

'Send them both packing.'

'Yes. That's what I should have done, at once.'

'What do you mean, at once?'

'The other night on the beach. He . . .'

She said something into his chest that he couldn't hear. He bent towards her and took her chin in his hand, turning her face up towards his.

'What?'

'He kissed me on the beach. I . . . ah . . . gave him a wallop across the face and then left him to walk home. I should have sent him packing then, but I didn't know what to say to Polly and I thought . . . well, it was just cheekiness of some sort.'

'Ooo la la.'

He let go of her and went back to his brandy.

'You don't . . . ?'

'No. No, of course not. No.'

She turned once more towards the window. 'I just want them both out of here. Everything will be all right when they've gone back to London. I just don't know how to get rid of them without having a huge row with Polly.'

He gulped down the last of his drink.

'I'll deal with it, darling, in the morning. In the morning. Now, give me a bed for the night, there's a dear, and another drop of that divine brandy and I will deal with it all, in all sobriety, in the morning. Trust me.'

She began to laugh.

'I never trust anyone who says, trust me.'

'Well, you're going to have to this time, aren't you?'

He yawned.

'I do love a bit of a problem. See, I am in my Polonius mode, but I won't hide behind the arras. I doubt if you have an arras anyway. No one has such wall hangings anymore. I will so look forward to breakfasting with Mimi. By the way, who is Bonnyface? It seems to me that this house is coming down with a thousand secrets.'

'Mim is becoming a bit unreliable. I'm not sure what to do.

She went off into town on her own yesterday and bought a pair of boots. They cost two hundred and fifty quid.'

He laughed.

'Good old Mim. That's the sort of thing I like to hear.'

She shook her head.

'Don't joke, darling. Perhaps the beginning of a slippery slope . . .'

'Perhaps on the other hand she just wanted a pair of boots. She got home safely.'

'Exhausted.'

'So?'

She didn't reply.

He took her hand.

'Let her be. Let her be happy. Let her be a little crazy, because that's the way she likes to be. Let her . . .'

'I want her to be safe.'

'If that's all you want for her, then lock her up. That's simple. I mean somewhere nice, of course. There are lots of nice places for old ladies who have a few bob, whose families want them to be safe.'

'Oh shut up,' she said, crossly. 'I haven't the slightest intention of putting Mimi in a home.'

'There's no need to be pompous or holier than anyone else about it. We've all done it, darling. I've done it. I felt rotten, but I did it. I put my old mum in a home. A great place, just outside London. Full of ancient actors and people in the business. She adored it. I felt guilty as hell.'

He drank down the last of his brandy.

'I'd probably have murdered her, darling, if I'd had her to live with me and that wouldn't have been very nice for any of us. Apart from anything else, she couldn't tolerate my sexual habits.' He rolled his eyes. 'She said that to me once, years ago. "I do have to say, Charles, that your father and I deplore your, *harrumph*, sexual habits." They always called me Charles.'

Grace laughed.

'To give Mimi her due . . .'

'One of the reasons I love your mother passionately is that she is so totally unlike my mother. You can count yourself lucky.'

'Why on earth did you put her into a home full of old actors?'

'For purely selfish reasons. It made visiting days quite tolerable for me. I always met someone I knew, or who I'd worked with. We could have a bit of a giggle. We must go to bed, my darling, otherwise, I'll drink more brandy and then I'll feel like hell in the morning and I won't be able to cope with your admirer.'

Mimi dreamed of Benjamin.

I have too much drink taken, she thought to herself as she half-woke and then was pulled unwillingly back down into sleep again.

He was kneeling on the floor by the window, his hands uplifted in prayer, his face silver in the light of an enormous moon. The moon in fact filled the whole window and she wondered as she looked at him what grief was in his head. That was the whole of her dream. No one stirred. He was trapped in silver. And in her dream she had to stare, she was not allowed to close her eyes, she was not allowed to wake. She was not allowed to call out to him. Was he talking to God or the moon, or merely to himself?

Was he drunk or sober?

In the last ten years of his life it had been hard to tell.

He now turned his head slowly and stared across the room at her, and as he moved his hands fell one by one to the ground and his body began to disintegrate in front of her, till all that was left were his eyes, two grey stones, and then they too were gone and she found herself awake staring at the window with a pain in her left arm and that frightened her even more than the dream had done. She lay quite still and slowly the pain receded.

I do not want to die with that vision in front of my eyes.

She forced a little laugh into the silence of the room.

'You can't frighten me like that. I refuse . . .' She stopped. She realised that her voice was coming out loud and strong. She didn't want to bring any of the others in on her.

No.

She rearranged her pillows and switched on the light. The moonlight departed; the room became friendly once more.

I wonder why I have to think about him now?

In the last few days he has entered my mind far, far more often than he has done in ten years. I do not want him in my mind. There are moments like this when I think it would be quite useful to believe in God. You could lean your troubled head against his bosom . . . that's what they are always exhorting you to do. *Come unto to me all ye who labour and are heavy laden and I will give you rest.* Something like that. I remember church so well, all those churches that he dragged me through, here, there and everywhere. Dark churches, light churches, high, squat, ornate and plain, Roman, Anglican, Lutheran, no matter. He would kneel and pray and I would sit beside him with my hands clasped in my lap and look at the architecture, the frescoes, the wood carvings, the tall coloured windows. He always wanted me to pray too. I could have pretended, but it seemed a pointless thing to do. I always used to hope that my lack of obedience didn't make him in any way feel diminished in the eyes of his God.

Her eyes drooped.

She could feel her lashes brush the top of her cheek bones and she gave a contented smile; her lashes, thick and black, had always been a cause of pleasure to her. She had looked closely at those false lashes that some women stuck on their faces and she had been happy that she hadn't had to put herself to such discomfort.

Even now
here in
bed almost . . .
almost drifting into sleep,
she could feel the pleasure of
her brushing lashes.
Yes.
Thick and black.
Yes.
Thick and . . .

✳ ✳ ✳

Bells begin to ring early on Sunday mornings.

Forget sleeping late, they say.

They clang and clatter.

There is very little dignity left in the chattering of the bells. Only cathedrals now or very wealthy parish churches have bell ringers; most bells these days have an electronic peal, a bar or two of some well known sacred hymn perhaps, or a falling peal, or there is the lone bell, come, come, come, it calls impatiently, the rope pulled by some sexton or other, his head throbbing perhaps after the excesses of Saturday night.

Grace was awakened by the clanging from the local church, halfway up the hill behind her house.

> *Hamlet, thou hast thy father much offended.*
> *Mother, you have my father much offended.*

*Come, come,* in time with the bells, *you answer with an idle tongue.*

*Go, go . . .*

She opened her eyes. The wind blew at the curtain.

*. . . You question with a wicked tongue.*

How superior, she thought with a giggle, to wake up quoting Shakespeare.

She stretched her arms and legs. The joints cracked and crackled in an alarming way and she thought, as she did quite frequently these days, of old age waiting for her. There's not much that happens after Gertrude and Arkadina. Mother Courage perhaps, then downhill all the way. The nurse in Romeo and Juliet, various aunts and ancient queens, and that thought reminded her of Charlie and she wondered if he had done as he had promised. She wondered what time it was. That bell could mean eight, nine, ten, eleven. Oh God, it couldn't possibly be eleven. Could it?

The bell stopped its clanging.

She pushed the bedclothes down and lay naked on the bed and let the wind that rippled the curtain touch her also.

I have never had a lover with fingers like the wind, she thought.

How remiss of me.

The door opened. Polly put her head round and then came into the room, closing the door behind her.

She looked at her mother without speaking. Her eyes moved from her mother's feet up along her body to her face. There she caught Grace's eye.

'Well?' said Grace.

'What are you doing?'

'I'm just lying here, as you can see, thinking about parts for ageing actresses. I have known those who have gone for Juliet at the age of fifty, but I don't think that's my scene. Bernarda Alba . . . now there's one I hadn't thought of. Grace DuBois . . . the list gets longer. Maybe there's life after Gertrude.'

'There's a draught,' said Polly. 'You'll catch a chill.'

'Rubbish. A little touch of the wind never did anyone any harm. What time is it? Is everyone up? How about Charlie? If he's going to invade my room too, I'll pull up the bedclothes.'

'Charlie?'

'He spent the night.'

Damn, she thought, the bugger's still asleep. I should have known better than to trust him an inch.

'An inch.' For some daft reason she spoke the words aloud.

'What?'

'Nothing.'

Polly looked exasperated.

'Honestly, Mum, it's like a mad house here. You're nearly as bad as Mimi.'

'I'm preoccupied.'

'I've noticed.'

'I'd like a cup of coffee. Who made that lovely coffee yesterday morning? That's what I'd like. Any possibility?'

Polly shrugged.

'I've no idea who made it. Must have been Mimi.'

Grace laughed at the thought.

'No hope of coffee then?'

'We're going.'

Wow.

Inside Grace's head the word exploded.

'Going?'

She sat up and looked at her daughter.

'Yeah. Paul only told me half an hour ago. He's got an interview first thing tomorrow morning.'

There is a God!

'Oh darling, what a shame. I'll drive you to the airport. What time's your flight? What time is it now anyway?'

She thought of swinging her legs over the side of the bed and standing up, but the thought of her daughter's critical eye on her body stopped her.

'Ten.'

Charlie asshole, Charlie nincompoop. Everything is going to be . . .

'We thought we'd go out as soon as possible and get whatever we can in way of a flight.'

. . . All right.

Oh boy.

*Stay not upon the order of your going but . . .*

'He wants me to go back with him. He wants me to be there. So . . .'

. . . *go at once.*

'. . . Yes. Thank you. It would be kind of you to . . .'

Grace gestured somewhat wildly with her arms and Polly retreated towards the door.

'. . . drive us.'

'I'll just have a quick bath. You . . . someone . . . make some coffee and then we'll be off.'

Polly opened the door.

'You can't wait to get rid of us?'

'Heavens no. It's been lovely . . . lovely . . . Great he's got an interview. It's just when something's been decided . . . Oh my dear, it is such a shame you can't stay longer.'

The door clicked shut.

She was talking to an empty room.

\* \* \*

'We'll bring Mimi. Do you want to come to the airport, darling? Just for the ride?'

They were drinking indifferent coffee in the kitchen.

Charlie was hiding behind the *Observer*.

Mimi shook her head.

'I think not,' she said.

'Why not? You usually like a little drive.'

'I think not this time. Thank you all the same. I will sit in the garden. I will indulge myself in conversation.'

Everyone looked at her, even Charlie.

There was a long silence.

Charlie folded the paper neatly and then stood up.

'Well then, if Mimi isn't going with you, you can drop me at the Shelbourne. Unless . . .' He turned and bowed towards Mimi. 'You wish to indulge yourself in conversation with me. If so, I am yours to command.'

'Certainly not,' said Mimi. 'Now, if you'll excuse me. I must go. It's late already.' As she pushed herself up from her chair she smiled at Polly. 'Goodbye, my dear. Have a good flight. Give my regards to your dear father.' She held out a hand to Paul. 'I don't know what all this rush is about. No one tells me the whys and wherefores of things. I hope we meet again. Before too long. My time is probably quite short now, you know.'

'Such nonsense you talk, Mimi,' said Charlie. 'You'll outlive us all.'

She blew him a kiss.

'Don't be such a smartass.'

Charlie hooted with laughter.

'Mim,' said Grace severely. 'You mustn't say things like that.'

'You do.'

Everyone applauded.

Paul got up and opened the garden door for her. He touched her arm as she walked past him.

'It has been really nice meeting you.'

'You'll be back.' She stared him in the eyes. 'Oh yes, you'll be back all right. I can tell. I hope you'll be in time.'

She moved off, very slowly, down the steps and across the grass. The two chairs were where they had been left the afternoon before, slightly in the shade of the magnolia tree.

Charlie walked over to where Grace stood by the window. He put an arm round her shoulder and they both stood looking out at Mimi as she walked across the grass.

'Doesn't she look wonderful? She's all dollied up,' said Charlie. 'She looks like she's expecting someone.'

Grace nodded.

Charlie pulled her close against him and whispered in her ear. 'Darling, am I a broken reed?'

'Yes,' she said. 'And a smartass to boot. Mimi was right.'

'Are you two fighting?' Polly came over and joined them at the window.

'Certainly not.'

'Yes.'

They both spoke at once and then laughed.

Polly linked her arm through Grace's.

'I was just getting used to you all again. It's a shame we have to go.'

Charlie turned his head slightly and looked at Paul.

'Come and join us. Much as I love all the women in the house I long for the touch of male flesh. Come and press against me. Save me. Help me keep my sense of proportion.'

Paul scowled at him and remained by the door.

Mimi settled herself down in her chair and then turned and waved towards the house, acknowledging most graciously their interest in her.

'It's time to go.'

Grace disentangled herself from Charlie and Polly. 'If you really want a lift, Charlie, you have exactly five minutes to get yourself into the car.'

'We're going to get married, Mum. That's why he has to go back to this interview. He's got to stop being picky about work now, don't you, darling?'

Polly turned round and smiled at Paul who had been sitting silently in the back of the car.

After they had dropped Charlie at the Shelbourne Hotel, Polly had got out of the back of the car and had come to sit with her mother in the front.

At the moment when Polly said those words Grace had been negotiating the turn into Dorset Street and she had said nothing. She avoided a bus and a man on a motor bike neatly. Then she looked in the mirror. Paul's face was white.

'Polly . . .' He spoke the word and then stopped.

'I'm sorry, darling.' Polly leaned over the seat and stroked his arm.

Grace concentrated on driving.

'We had decided to tell Dad first. All that sort of formal nonsense that he likes so much. But I couldn't bear the thought of telling you over the telephone. I am sorry, Paul. I should have given you some sort of signal that I was about to be unreliable again.' She laughed happily.

Grace cleared her throat.

'Isn't this all a bit sudden? I mean . . . I'm thrilled. But have you pondered long enough? Marriage is . . .' She drew over to the kerb and stopped. 'I only want you to be happy.'

'I am happy. I really am.'

'Yes? Well that's wonderful. I'm delighted.'

She was getting *nul points* for this she realised. She leaned forward and kissed her daughter on the cheek.

'I do hope you'll be very happy, my darling.'

She turned to Paul.

'I'm delighted,' she repeated. 'I hope you'll be very happy.'

'Thank you,' he whispered.

'I hope you'll make Polly happy.'

She hadn't intended to sound threatening but she suddenly became alarmed that perhaps she had. 'I . . .'

'Of course he will, silly Mum. Just because you couldn't hack marriage, doesn't mean . . .'

'Your father will be delighted.'

As she spoke she put the car into gear and shot out into the traffic again. All she wanted to do now was to get rid of them as fast as she possibly could.

Talk about a scumbag! She accelerated and scooted around

a bus about to move off from a stop.

Talk about a scumbag.

Her hands on the steering wheel were trembling.

'Hey, Mum, mind out. We want to live till the wedding!'

She slowed down.

'I bet you wouldn't pass a driving test in England.'

'Well, luckily I haven't the slightest intention of taking one.'

She smiled and smiled.

She drove with more care.

In the mirror his eyes were staring at her.

She put up her hand and adjusted the mirror slightly so that she couldn't see them.

'So. Tell me your plans. I presume you're not thinking of rushing off to the nearest Register Office. Your father wouldn't like that at all. He likes a wedding to be a wedding.'

'I suppose it depends a bit on Paul's work, but we thought late autumn. *Hamlet* will be over then, won't it? End of October probably. We don't have to look for anywhere to live. Paul's flat has heaps of room for both of us.'

'October.'

'We'll have to see what Dad says. I suppose Mim will want to come?'

'Wild horses wouldn't keep her away. She'll love a wedding and she'll be thrilled to see your father. She's always loved him.'

'We'll have to have it in London, of course.'

'Of course.'

'Pauline's an amazing organiser. Anyway, Dad will want that. That won't bother you, will it?'

'No. Why should I? I can just enjoy myself.'

'And of course, all our pals are there. It would be hideously expensive to expect them all to come over here.'

'I don't mind, Polly. Really I don't. You don't have to go on . . . Mimi and I will enjoy a jaunt to London. I don't think she's been over there since . . .'

The traffic lights were changing in front of her. She put her foot on the accelerator and shot over the crossroads.

'. . . Benjamin.'

'I'll tell you one thing, we won't let you drive the wedding car.'

'I've never had an accident yet. Not a scrape, not a dent. Nearly thirty years of driving.'

She raised her voice as she spoke the last words.

'Thirty years.'

Just in case.

Polly laughed and thumped her on the shoulder.

'Poor old Mum.'

'I don't have a problem.'

Like hell I don't. We all have a problem here.

She drove the rest of the way in silence.

She drew up behind a taxi at the departure doorway and turned to Polly.

'Darling, I do hope that you'll be terribly, terribly happy.' She put her arms round her and hugged her.

Paul was taking their cases out of the boot.

'It just came as a bit of a surprise. That's why I was a bit . . . well, astonished. Mim will be thrilled and I'm sure Daddy will too. Keep in touch about all your plans . . . please.'

'Of course I will. Take care. Sorry we couldn't stay longer.'

Polly jumped out of the car and picked up her case. Paul leant in through the door. He took her hand for a moment and then dropped it.

'Good-bye. Thanks for everything.' And suddenly they were both gone. On the seat beside her hand lay a gold pen. She frowned. She picked it up and looked at it. In fine letters running down one side of it were the words . . . *for darling Paul from Mummy and Daddy* . . . and underneath the date 5th March 1988. It was warm in her fingers. She wondered what to do and decided to wait for a few minutes, and see what happened.

I could post it.

No.

He will come almost at once. If he doesn't then I will post it. She tapped the pen against the steering wheel. I will tell him just what I think of him. Rotten little . . . I will count to ten and then I will go.

One, two . . .

He pulled open the door and was in the car beside her.

'I didn't know what to do.' He took the pen gently from her and held her hand in his. 'I don't know what to do. I am so sorry. My darling Grace.' He held her hand against his cheek. His cheek was hot and almost feverish. 'Please don't despise me. I have no time. Polly's in the queue for tickets. I just ran. Don't hate me, Grace. I simply can't work out what is going

on. I . . .' He put a hand over his face and she thought he was
going to cry.

She touched his shoulder and then very tentatively the side
of his jaw with a finger.

'It'll be all right,' she said. 'When you get back over there,
everything will be all right.'

'How can it be?'

'Go now.'

He nodded.

He took her hand and kissed it; her fingers and her wrist
and then the palm.

'I love you.'

'Go.'

'Grace.'

'Please, go.'

'Do you understand . . . ?'

'No. Get out of this car, you little jerk, and go and sort out
your head.' She pulled her hand away from him. 'Sort out your
life and Polly's. Think about what you're doing to Polly. God,
you are a scumbag.'

He got out of the car and stood looking down at her.

'Yes,' he said. 'I think I must be.'

He put the pen into his pocket and turned and went back in
through the door again.

Her heart was hammering with such anger that she had to
sit quite still for a few minutes until it began to beat normally
once more, then without looking in her mirror she drove away
from the kerb, narrowly missing a Mercedes Benz.

\* \* \*

'I think of Benjamin a lot these days. I wonder why. For years I haven't given him a thought and now, suddenly, here he comes, back into my life again.'

Bonifacio lay on the grass out in the full sunlight. He had taken off his shirt and exposed a mat of curling hair on his chest. He had also thrown his little round hat on the grass and she was amused to see a circular patch of baldness that had been well covered before. Balanced on his chest he held a half-empty glass of red wine. Full bodied, fruity, Italian . . . a bit like himself, she thought. His black eyes stared right up towards the sun, something that she had been told always was not just hard on the eyes, but positively dangerous. She remembered having tried it once or twice and her head had become invaded each time by a brightness that was so intense that she thought her brains might burst.

She took a sip from her glass. This was really very pleasant, almost sybaritic, sitting in the garden like this and sipping wine.

This could be a comfortable way to die, she thought. Found dead beside an empty bottle of full bodied, fruity, Italian wine. Why is it . . . she became irritated for a moment with herself . . . I can never concentrate on the important matters?

'Have you an explanation?' she asked him.

He turned his head towards her and smiled.

'Of course.'

'Well?' She waited for him to speak.

'It was he who called me.'

'Who? Benjamin?' She laughed. 'I don't believe this.'

'I think you should.'

'I don't think that Benjamin, for all his religiosity, would have believed in apparitions.'

He looked upset.

'Is that what you think about me? My dear signora!'

He sat up and leaned towards her. He tapped her knee with a finger.

'I am not an apparition.'

'He always mocked the moving statue, the bleeding hands, the tears of blood. In fact such manifestations made him quite angry.'

'I am not an apparition.'

She nodded.

'You say he called you.'

He took a gulp from his glass and lay back once more on the grass. 'On mature reflection, yes. I think that's who it must have been. If not you. It must have been Benjamin.'

'You really ought to get your story straight. You seem to be a bit muddled about the whole thing. It doesn't exactly inspire confidence.'

'One voice sounds much like another.'

'What rubbish.'

He closed his eyes.

A wasp buzzed dangerously around the rim of her glass. She put out a hand and waved it away.

'I don't mean to be rude, but on the face of it, my voice and his voice would have little in common. I am, after all a . . .' She waved her hand in the air, '. . . and he was, well you know, a man.'

'A voice in the shadows is a voice. It fills your head. It has no gender, no tone, no pitch. When it stops it leaves an echo as if your mind was a deep valley, full of reverberating sound.' He opened his eyes suddenly and looked up at her. 'I did ask. I did say why. And the echo died away. That was all that happened. I could be forgiven for thinking it was you. I should be forgiven for my confusion.'

The wasp came back, daring to dip inside her glass. She flicked the outside angrily with her finger and the wasp fell into the wine.

'Damn.' She picked up the glass and threw the wine, wasp and all onto the grass. 'I hate wasppsss. It's all right. I have always been filled with confusion myself. It is not a condition that I can carp about. Get up, Bonnyface. Put your hat on, or the top of your head will get sunburned and you will suffer, and please pour me another glass of wine. What is it called? It is very delicious.'

He got up and put his hat on, well trained by his mother no doubt to obey the commands of old ladies.

'Vino Nobile di Montepulciano.'

She repeated the words. 'CI as in cheese, church, cheetah, I presume?'

He laughed.

'I suppose I don't have enough time left to learn Italian?'

He didn't reply.

'I take a long time to learn things. As you get older the mind seems to work in fits and starts . . . not that I've ever been intellectually gifted. No.' She shook her head and smiled to herself. 'I never minded that when I was young and sprightly, but now perhaps it would be a help.'

'What sort of help?'

'I might have the company of the scholars and thinkers. That might keep loneliness at bay.'

'It might not.'

'Perhaps he thought I might need company. It would be nice to think he had such a caring notion in his head. It was quite hard, you know, to understand what he had in his head. He protected himself very well. I was less lonely after he died than I was when he was alive. Were you married?'

'Yes.'

She thought for a moment.

'Were you happily married?'

He didn't answer.

'I don't mean to pry. Some marriages are happy. I would like to think that yours had been. You seem to be a nice man.' She laughed a little. 'Or angel. Or apparition. Or even figment of my imagination.'

'I had a good wife.'

'Is that all you're going to say?'

'I was perhaps not a very good husband. So it is maybe that I was happy and she was not. I never gave it much thought. She was a good wife, except for one thing. She had no children. I would like to have had a son. Every man wants a son. Every man needs to know that he will be immortal. For that you need a son.'

'Or daughter,' she suggested.

He shook his head.

'No. A daughter will produce someone else's immortality. Certainly, I would have loved a daughter, but she would have gone. Daughters always go. She would have belonged to someone else. She would have had his sons. They would have been no part in my life.'

'What a peculiar way of thinking.'

'It is just the way I am.'

They both sat and sipped their wine in silence for a few minutes.

'What was her name?'

'Maria Rosa Franceschi. She was a distant relative of that great man, Piero. She was sometimes his model. In our small town we were all related to each other. By degrees, you know. So in some of his paintings you can see her face.' He gestured with his hands. 'You see, she has her own immortality. Women always win in the end. I was not unkind to her.'

'I'm sure you weren't.'

'I just liked other women and . . .'

'And?'

'So. That was the way we lived. I made for her the most beautiful shoes. Not for the others. She had always the most beautiful shoes in Borgo Sansepolcro.'

'That must have been a great comfort to her.'

'You are cross with me?'

'No. Why should I be?'

'Sometimes people get angry when you tell them things like that.'

She put her hand on his.

'I like you.'

'Thank you.'

'If I may ask, what age were you when you . . . ah . . . you know?'

'Died?'

She nodded.

'I was not old. I was as I am now. Forty-two and three months.'

'Oh dear, how sad.'

'I had a fever for six days and then . . .' He snapped his finger and thumb together.

'It was a summer with many mosquitoes. A plague you might call it of mosquitoes. Many people died. I died before my father did. An extraordinary happening, except in times of war. They carried a disease, the mosquitoes, and many people died. It was quite normal for those days.'

'And your wife?'

'She minded me well. She put cold cloths on my head and tried to wave air through the room when I couldn't breathe.'

He stood up and whirled his arms windmill fashion, displacing the warm air. He looked absurd as she must have done.

'That is how I remember her, standing there in our room trying to make the air move. Such wasted effort.'

'I wouldn't say that.'

'I died.'

'Forty-two years and three months.'

'That's right.'

'Perhaps you were lucky. This isn't much fun you know, hanging around waiting to be felled by the sergeant. Filled with silly anxieties about falling in the bathroom or setting the house on fire. People always seem to think that old people will set the house on fire. It seems to me a bit absurd. Of course, I am a bit absurd now. I see that in their faces. People like Polly, I see it in her face. I'd rather not, I do have to say. When I was young, the world was full of terribly handsome old men. I used to flirt with them. There are no handsome old men now. What has happened to them, I wonder?' She laughed. 'They were probably only fifty. It's such a shame that handsomeness, beauty, leeches away with age. I was stopping being beautiful just when I had the freedom to enjoy it. "How lovely your mother must have been when she was young," I hear people say to Grace, as if I wasn't there listening. Good Lord, how I hate my invisibility.'

'I think you are beautiful.'

He took his hat off with a flourish and knelt at her feet.

'I don't think you are invisible.'

He took her hand in his and kissed it.

'You are over four hundred years old.' As she spoke she leant forwards and ran a finger round his tonsure. 'And invisible to everyone except me, so we're in the same boat, really. Get up, get up. Thirty years ago, I would love to have had you at my feet. Now it is a delightful joke.'

He stood up, continuing to hold her hand. The warmth spread up through her arm and relieved the pain, and then round her shoulders and down the other arm.

I recommend angels for the relief of pain, she said to herself in a TV advertising voice.

She gave his hand a little squeeze and then removed hers.

'I think maybe we've had a little too much to drink. We'll go in and get some coffee.'

She pushed herself up from her chair with her painfree arms and they began to walk slowly across the grass.

'In case I gave you the wrong impression,' she said, 'I was never unfaithful to my husband. That seemed important at the time. Now, I feel, it was probably foolishness.'

As they came to the bottom of the steps, he held out his hand to her.

'No, thank you. Today, I can manage quite well.'


I am making a fool of myself.

Over-reacting.

Overacting.

A short sharp laugh at this moment.

That's what it is: I am seeing myself in some tear-jerking role. Am I Meryl Streep or Bette Davis? God, that shows my age anyway . . . *Darling, we have the stars* . . . et cetera, et cetera.

This will be a joke.

Yes.

When?

Fool!

Such stupid questions you ask yourself.

Tomorrow.

Next week.

In three months? A year?

When I am Mimi's age and the grandmother to his children we will be able to say, remember those idiotic few days in Dublin.

And we will laugh.

A very private laugh.

Oh boy, yes, a private laugh; this would be one joke that Polly would not forgive me.

She's forgiven me a lot.

Not my driving.

Another little laugh here.

I must not grow to enjoy this role. I must not make my complacent little jokes. I must confidently eschew this role. It is not my scene.

I never wanted to play Natalya Petrovna in *A Month in the Country*. Passion can be so ruthless. Ingrid Bergman was such a star in the part. Wrong though.

I'm getting better.

How long ago was that anyway? Early seventies? Late sixties? I think Polly was a tiny baby. What was I doing? Yes. Yes. Bianca in *The Shrew* at Stratford. The baby and I spent the season there. John had hated that. 'And who will look after me?' he had said. Quite reasonably, I suppose. I didn't think it was reasonable then. I seem to remember I used a lot of four letter words. He always hated that. He never came to terms with the fact that the Irish swear in all circumstances. It is part of the pattern of our language.

It was then I saw Bergman. Everyone in the theatre was in

love with her, so I suppose it didn't matter whether she was right or wrong for the part.

It will be all right.

It will be.

She laughed aloud in the car outside her house in Killiney.

It will be.

She picked her bag up from the seat beside her and got out of the car. She shut the door and locked it.

I must recognise that I have for a few moments been in great danger of making an eejit of myself. A total fucking eejit.

Gertrude, come between me and all harm.

She walked towards the house.

I must take the shears to Albertine, she thought.

A good normal thought.

She opened the hall door and went into the hall.

The wonderful smell of roses pervaded the house.

The sun shone in broad bands through the open doors of the sitting-room and the kitchen beyond. Dust particles drifted in the brilliant light.

'Yoo-hoo,' she called. There was no reply.

She slung her bag over the newel post at the bottom of the stairs and went into the kitchen.

In her big chair by the window, in full dancing sunshine, Mimi sat, her head slumped forward towards her chest, her hands folded politely in her lap.

'Jesus!'

Grace walked slowly across the room.

My heart's having a bad time today. Just calm down, heart.

Here we have one old lady asleep in her chair. No need, heart, for panic. No need at all.

She bent down and put her hand on Mimi's shoulder gently.

'Mother.' She surprised herself by her use of the word.

A thin trail of saliva between the left-hand corner of Mimi's mouth and her chin glittered in the sun, looking as if it had been laid there by some marauding snail.

'Mimi.'

There was a little snort and Mimi opened her eyes. She looked for a surprised moment at Grace and then smiled.

'Sloshed,' she said and closed her eyes again.

'Oh, Mimi.'

Grace staggered to a chair and sat down and burst into tears.

After a moment she began to laugh.

'Oh God, Mim, I thought you were dead.'

'Well, I'm not.' Eyes still shut as she spoke.

'You gave me such a dreadful fright. I don't know when I've ever had such a fright. When I saw you . . .'

'I'm not dead. I'm sloshed. It's rather nice.'

'How . . .?' She looked around the room and saw the glasses, the empty bottle, the coffee cups. 'Who . . . ?'

'Vino Nobile de Montepulciano,' said Mimi happily. 'Perhaps half a bottle in the sun is too much for an old lady. I shall sleep a little more, my dear.'

Grace picked up the bottle and looked at her mother.

'A whole bottle, in the sun.'

Mimi smiled in her sleep.

There was, however, coffee left in the coffee-pot. Good coffee, not yet cold.

What goes on in this kitchen when I'm out? wondered Grace.

Who does she invite in?

Tramps?

Neighbours?

The milk man?

She got a cup and poured herself some warmish coffee.

Whoever it was could make coffee, that was for sure.

As she stood sipping at it she looked across the room at her mother. She just had the air of an old lady asleep.

I want her to be safe.

She sighed. Bloody Charlie was right; that wasn't enough.

I want Polly to be safe too.

Hateful word, safe.

But then Polly's safety is her own business, whereas Mimi . . . ?

Whereas Mimi?

I want to play Arkadina at the National . . . if it comes my way. I want to play Medea, I want to play Clytemnestra. I want to immerse myself before it is too late and work and work, because that is when I'm not just another butterfly. That is when I almost believe I understand something about being alive. I live through other people's words and ideas.

Sod it.

Can't even write my own dialogue!

She took her cup over to the sink and turned on the tap, then gathered the cups and glasses and began to wash them.

Down the garden the two chairs were in intimate proximity under the magnolia tree and she began to wonder again about Mimi's visitor.

'I feel better now. Quite recovered. Pretty sprightly, in fact. I'm sorry Charlie has gone. He makes me laugh.'

Grace turned round and looked at her mother. She was wiping at the corner of her mouth with a tissue.

'I dribbled,' she said. 'How disgusting.'

'Polly and Paul are going to be married.'

Mimi scrunched the tissue up and put it in her pocket.

'I don't expect so,' she said. 'I can't see that happening.'

'Polly told me in the car. In the autumn. In London.'

'Can you?'

'Can I what?'

'See it happening.'

'I . . .'

'You should never have married John.'

'That's true.'

'I told you that at the time. He was nice, I liked him . . .'

'You said all that.'

'But he was wrong. This chap, this whatever his name is, he's nice too, but he's wrong. I can tell. Polly's really quite like John. Anyway, you don't have to get married these days. Did you tell her that?'

'I think they know that.'

'They could shack up.'

Grace laughed.

'I do love you, Mim,' she said.

'Thank you. So you should. If this is going to happen I'll have to spend a lot of time in town. I'll have to buy a hat, and another pair of shoes, gloves . . . a whole outfit. I would like to be well turned out.'

'When we know a bit more about it, I will bring you in one day.'

'No, thank you dear. I will be able to manage without you. Do you think that Giorgio Armani makes suitable clothes for old ladies?'

'Mimi!'

'I like Italian clothes. I will take advice from Bonnyface. I think I'll go up to my room now and have a little rest. Stretch out. I find being upright makes me so tired.' She got up slowly from her chair.

'Who is Bonnyface?'

'My friend. You don't have to worry, Grace dear. He is quite an appropriate companion for me.'

'Who is he, Mimi? You keep dropping his name into conversations. Where does he come from?'

'I don't really want to talk about him. I don't want you looking askance at me. He is my angel. Don't say a word. I see by the look on your face that you were going to say something silly. Don't bother. I can handle this. You must let me do that. Guardian angel. There are such things you know. He is someone to whom I can talk. You should be pleased. His presence should relieve you of a lot of bother.'

She moved on slowly across the room in silence. At the door she turned towards Grace and smiled.

'No need, my dear, to look so upset. I am temporarily quite happy. Yes. That is correct. Quite, quite happy.'

She left the room and closed the door.

*Grace,*

*I can't attach an adjective to your name, because if I write the ones that fill my head you would be angry with me. Maybe, even now, you will throw this letter away unread. Please don't do that. I am masochist enough to want to imagine you reading my inadequate words.*

*I don't know how this has happened: I am neither a fool nor a teenager, expecting to be struck by eternal love, as if by a bolt of lightning, so when it happened I was, and still am, totally incapable of dealing with such a situation.*

*I was sure I was in love with Polly; delightfully in love with her, enough in love to consider spending our future together, having children, and all that sort of thing. Of course I have had affairs, but lightweight and unthreatening. Folly is different . . . or rather that was what I felt until . . . I don't have to say any more. Maybe it was the shadow of you in her that made me think I loved her.*

*The present situation is untenable; it was the result of total panic on my part and is unforgivable, except that I hope in the fullness of time you will forgive me, even if Polly never does. Untenable is not the word that I really mean. I mean, unbearable.*

*I think of you all the time. I pray, because I am an old-fashioned person at heart, and I believe that there is a God, and I believe in the power of prayer, that God will erase the images of you from my mind and my heart. I pray that He will remove the sound of your voice from my ears. I pray that He will remove the terrible agony of sexual desire. And when I have prayed, I do have to say, I pray again that He will pay no attention to my prayers.*

    *I know it is too much to expect that you will ever think of me with anything other than contempt . . . It was right, if somewhat unromantic of you, to call me a scumbag. I have not behaved very well. I have no excuses. I love you, Grace. Keep reading. I, the scumbag, love you, want you, need you to comfort me. I feel like a branch that has been broken in a storm and hangs by a thread from the tree. I had no notion of such storms until last week.*
*Please, Grace, do not hate me.*

It was unsigned.

*Dear Paul,*
    *I don't think of you with contempt.*
    *Anger and alarm for what you are doing to Polly.*
    *I loathe treachery, conniving and lies.*
    *Please don't write to me again.*
    *Please don't attempt to see me again.*
    *Please, please, don't tell Polly about all this. I love her and need her in my life. She will recover from this nonsense and so will you.*
*Please leave me alone.*

It was also unsigned.
    And unsent.
    Grace went even to the lengths of putting a stamp on the envelope. She walked to the letter box on the corner of the road

and at the last moment she put the letter back into her bag. Each time, for several days, that she opened her bag, to root for money, find her lipstick, blow her nose, write a note or a date in her diary, the letter caught her eye. She began to feel the weight of it pulling her down as she walked with her bag slung over her shoulder. After about a week she went down one night to the beach to swim. The moon was now a sliver and the sea was black and full of stars. She took the letter and tore it into tiny pieces and spread them as she swam among the cold needle points of light.

She didn't feel any better.

For the next few days a sharp wind blew from the east, from England, or from the Russian Steppes as Benjamin used to tell her. She had never quite believed him.

It was unseasonal. The sun still shone in the bright, clear sky, but the wind curled around the garden and made it uncomfortable for Mimi to sit outside. Instead she sat in the bay of the sitting-room and watched the dancing leaves on the magnolia tree; she listened to the rustling of Albertine against the glass; she thought from time to time about Benjamin.

She sighed and looked at Bonifacio who was sitting opposite her in the bay, his legs stretched out before him. The picture of content, she thought.

'I have never liked waiting,' she said to him. 'Never. It is impossible to settle to anything when you are waiting. Grace used to drive me wild. She was never punctual. Benjamin was always early, on the other hand. That used to annoy people too.'

'What would you be doing now, my dear lady, if you weren't waiting? How would you be filling your days?'

She shook her head.

'I don't know. I had lots of things to do when I was younger. I can't remember any longer what they were. They were certainly of very little importance. I led a pleasurable life, you know.'

She sighed again.

'Well, let's say that I had little cause for complaint.'

She was tempted to sigh yet again, but thought the better of it. Self-pity was something she had very little time for.

'You want me to talk about Benjamin, don't you?'

'Perhaps. I think we should go for a walk. Up to that hill, behind the house. It would be good for you.'

'I couldn't manage that. My legs won't carry me so far these days. Not even on the flat.'

'If you take my arm you will be all right.'

He stood up and held out a hand towards her. For a moment she hesitated.

'Trust me,' he said.

She put her old gnarled hand in his and again she felt his warmth surging through her, and the pain became lost in the warmth. She stood up. She threw her head back and laughed like a young girl.

'Why didn't you come earlier, Bonnyface?'

'There was no need.'

'I would have enjoyed your company.'

'Thank you. I think though when you were younger, you had many friends, many companions.'

They were walking, almost striding, Mimi felt, on the grass below the obelisk; around and below them was the circle of sea and the hills. The wind folded and unfolded the shining surface of the sea and tugged at her hair. Her hand lay light in the crook of his elbow. Some children kicked a football away to the left and she could hear their shouts being blown towards her. She considered their situation with a certain astonishment and then decided that to enjoy what she had at that moment was the most important thing that she could do.

She patted his arm with her hand.

'How clever you are,' she said.

He laughed. 'I like being able to perform such tricks. A bit of harmless fun. I'm afraid I can't stop the wind blowing though. I do hope you're not cold.'

'I am filled with angelic warmth.'

They walked in silence for a moment or two and then she spoke.

'About Benjamin.'

'Yes.' His voice was very gentle.

'He was quite a wretched man . . . I mean when I say that, that he was filled with wretchedness. I saw that from the moment that I met him. It was like some awful challenge. I felt I, I alone in all the world, could make him happy. Such vanity. How do you cope with such vanity?'

He shook his head.

'So when nothing worked . . . you know when I discovered after a time, that nothing was working, I thought it was my fault. Blame, blame, blame. I heaped blame on myself. He became locked in some terrible contemplation of God and then he began to drink. For years we never spoke. We went to all those places together . . . you know those places that cultured people need to go to, Paris, Rome, Bayreuth . . . He loved opera . . . Milan . . . loved opera. He couldn't even talk to me about that. I could always feel him beside me disappearing into the music. He cried when Maria Callas died. The only time I ever saw him cry. Though I know he used to cry at night. Maybe it was just the drink running out of him, but I could hear the sounds of weeping if I passed his bedroom door at night. I never knew what to do. So, like all sensible people, I did nothing.'

She stopped. She stood for a few minutes or perhaps even half an hour and she looked into the past. She felt cold suddenly; the wind had become cold. She couldn't remember where she was for a moment. The past or the present. She felt that if she moved her head quickly Benjamin would be there beside her. She felt he might hold his hand out towards her and that she wouldn't be able to take it. She needed to go home.

Bonifacio spoke.

'I think, signora, that you should go home.'

She nodded.

'Yes.'

He held out his hand and she took it.

The lights in the house were on. The evening sun shone through the leaves of the chestnut tree by the gate, splattering the path with light. She walked slowly towards the hall door. She stumbled on the first step and saved herself from falling by catching the railing.

The door opened and Grace came out.

'Mimi! Where in the name of God have you been?'

She took her mother's arm and almost hauled her up the steps and into the hall.

Mimi's legs were trembling and she sat down on the chair by the door.

'I've been going crazy. Do you know what time it is? I was just about to ring the police. Mimi. Where have you been?'

Mimi shook her head. She waved her hand at Grace to try and stop the indistinguishable words.

'Please . . .' she managed to say at last, 'I'm all right. Here I am. Stop carrying on.'

'It's six o'clock. I drove round and round looking for you. I went into the Byrnes. They said they hadn't seen you since lunchtime . . .'

'Let's go into the sitting-room. Let's have a little drink. I just took the notion to go for a walk. What's so bad about that?'

Grace helped her up and they went into the sitting-room. The windows were closed against the wind and the roses tapped against the glass. Mimi sat on the sofa and Grace took two glasses and a bottle of wine from the cupboard. Her hands were shaking.

'Mimi, I don't know where the hell you've been, but you've frightened the life out of me. I searched the house. I yelled your name. I thought I was going to find you . . .' She took a deep breath and poured the wine.

'I'm all right. I'm here.'

Grace handed her a glass.

'Yes. But where were you?'

'I went for a walk on Killiney Hill.'

'Don't be silly.'

'I'm not being silly. I tell you that's where I was. I didn't notice the time pass. I'm sorry.'

'Mim, you can hardly walk to the bottom of the garden. How could you possibly get to Killiney Hill?'

'Bonnyface . . .'

'Truth, Mim.'

'That is the truth. I went with him. He took my hand. That was where he wanted to go. He suggested it. I thought to begin with it was a foolish notion, but it wasn't. I'm sorry I gave you a fright.'

They stared at each other in silence.

Grace sat down and put her hands up in front of her face.

'Are you crying?' asked Mimi, concerned.

Grace shook her head.

'Thinking.'

Mimi watched her think. After a while Grace took her hands from her face.

'You know, I think I must tell Dr Browne about this.'

'Why?'

'I think he ought to know.'

'It's none of his business.'

'Of course it's his business. You disappear off for hours. You talk about this . . . this . . .'

'Bonnyface. Of course dear, he's not really Bonnyface, that's just my little joke. Bonifacio. That is his real name.'

'You frighten me to death . . .'

'It seems to me you need to talk to Dr Browne about your fear. I don't need the doctor. I am quite well, thank you. I hate going to doctors. They have no longer anything they can offer me. I'm a trifle tired perhaps. I think I will go up and have a quick nap.'

She looked at her daughter thoughtfully.

'I'm sorry dear, if you have been upset. I know this is a stressful time for you. Rehearsals get so tense about the third week, don't they? Next time we decide to go off on a little adventure, I'll leave you a note. I promise. That way you won't have to worry about me. Give me a hand up, dear.'

'Mimi . . .'

'Hand up, dear. I cannot get up without your hand. I would like to stretch out on my bed. There are things I have to think about.'

Grace took her mother's arm and pulled. With pain, the old woman stood up.

'Thank you. I can manage quite well now on my own . . .' She set off slowly across the room, leaning on her stick. 'You know, when Bonnyface is with me, I feel no pain. Isn't that strange? I find it strange. You look quite peaky. You should have an early night. It's odd, when you look peaky, you have a look of your father that I have never noticed before. Something to do with your cheekbones.'

She stood at the bottom of the stairs gathering her strength to start the climb.

'I don't think I ever told you, your father cried when he heard that Maria Callas was dead. Did I ever tell you that?'

'No.'

'It was the only time I ever saw him cry. You don't expect men to cry. Did John ever cry?'

'Mimi . . .'

'I asked you a question.' Mimi's voice was sharp.

Grace shook her head. 'No.'

'I often thought that he wouldn't have cried like that if I had died.'

'What rubbish . . .'

'He was, of course, drunk when he heard the news. Tears come easily when . . .'

'Mimi. I hate this sort of talk.'

'Yes.'

She hauled herself up the first step.

'He didn't like me very much, you know.'

'He loved you.'

Step two.

Will I make it to the top? she wondered.

'You don't know. You went away. Perhaps I should have gone away also.'

Step three, four.

'That, I think is what he really wanted me to do.'

Five.

'But he never had the courage to say so.'

Six, seven eight. A little run.

'Go and learn your lines.'

'I know my lines.'

'Just go then. I prefer to finish this climb without you there.'

* * *

Grace went into the sitting-room and poured herself another glass of wine.

She listened to Mimi's faltering footsteps in the room above.

She wondered whether to ring Dr Browne.

She decided against it.

Not just yet. She's all right now. Here.

Will she be all right tomorrow?

How the hell do I know?

I know my lines. My moves. I know the rhythm of the play. I know the feel of Gertrude's body.

I know what Dr Browne will say.

I know everyone's lines except my own. Grace's lines escape me.

*Hamlet, thou hast thy father much offended.*

He will say the thing he has hinted at for so long now. He will be sensible. He will be rational.

*Mother, you have my father much offended.*

Perhaps she's right, perhaps I am the one that should be treated by Dr Browne.

He will just laugh at me in his usual reassuring, charming way. The way in which he treats ladies of a certain age; the way in which he treats actresses, and other women who wish to push out the frontiers of their lives.

Smile.

I know Gertrude's smile. I know it's changing pain as the play goes on.

She will be all right tomorrow.

Paul.

What a strange word to come into my head.

*Come, come, you answer with an idle tongue.*

I should have sent that letter. That would have been that. It was unequivocal.

I will write another. This time I will post it and then I will never call the word Paul into my mind again.

That made her feel better.

It made her move into the kitchen and start chopping vegetables for a good nourishing soup.


The telephone rang. It clanged its way into Grace's ear less charmingly than the Sunday morning bells.

It clanged into her undreaming sleep.

Someone's dead, she thought, sitting up abruptly, unsticking her eyes.

This was the way she had received the news of her father's death; the urgent ringing and then Mimi's composed voice. Then she had been in London, Hampstead to be exact, and the birds in the garden had been sleepily waking, as they were now. The moon was vanishing into the pale sky and she could see the sun's rays pushing their way up beyond the rim of the sea.

'Hello?'

Her voice was anxious, fractious too, and full of the thickness of sleep.

There was a long silence.

That probably meant, she thought as she waited, that no one was dead.

'Hello?'

'I have been waiting for your letter.'

She was right, no one was dead.

She toyed with the notion of putting down the receiver, but she wanted to hear the sound of his voice again.

'What letter?'

'The letter you haven't written me.'

'Do you know what the time is?'

'No. I can't sleep. Do you know why I can't sleep?'

'I'd rather not know.'

'It's such a bloody waste of time. I don't dream of you. I dream of nothing. I prefer to lie awake and think about you. All I do the whole night through is think of you.' He crooned the words into her ear.

She laughed, in spite of herself.

'You'll never make it in musicals.'

'You never can tell. Think of Rexie.'

'I eat my words.'

'Do you realise you haven't hung up on me?'

'Yes.'

'Why not?'

She didn't answer.

'Well, thank you anyway.'

'How's Polly?'

'Ouch.'

'I'm going to . . .'

'Her father's a pompous bastard.'

'I could have told you that for nothing.'

'How did you ever get yourself mixed up with a turd like that?'

'Ever heard about love?'

'I don't believe it.'

'He's very handsome, very sexy . . .'

'Very pompous . . . Very rich.'

'Did I once call you a scumbag? Goodbye.'

'Don't go, for just a moment. I want to ask you something. One moment. Please. Are you still there?'

'Yes. But you'd better make it snappy.'

'Had things been different . . .'

'Things aren't different.'

'. . . is there any possibility that you . . .'

'No.'

'. . . might have liked me? Thought of me as a friend?'

'I don't see why not.'

He laughed suddenly. She couldn't think why. She felt he had pulled a fast one on her.

'I don't know you.'

'I love you. Go and swim. Dear, lovely Grace. It would make me happy to think of you swimming.'

He put down the receiver.

She sat in bed holding the telephone and the sound of his voice hummed in her ear.

'What a good idea.'

She put the telephone down and got out of bed as if she had

thought enthusiastically of the idea herself.

She found her togs and wrapped herself in her towelling dressing gown and went out onto the landing.

Mimi was standing by her bedroom door.

'I heard the telephone.'

'Yes.'

'Is there a problem?'

'No. Go back to bed, Mim. I'm going for a swim. I'll get breakfast when I get back.'

'It's only five thirty.'

'Yep. Nice time for a swim. Just me and the birds.'

She started down the stairs.

'Grace.'

'Yes.'

'Who was it?'

'Paul.'

'Paul? Oh yes, Paul. Are you sure there's no problem?'

'No problem. He just wanted a chat. Go back to bed.'

'I'll never sleep now. I'm sorry about yesterday.'

'That's okay. Just don't frighten me like that again.'

Just oyster catchers and gulls.

The wind had died and the sea barely moved. Only the oyster catchers moved like dancers at the sea's edge; they were unperturbed by Grace's arrival. Several gulls stood on the rocks, their eyes malevolent and others floated on the surface of the sea. They too, remained quite indifferent to her. In fact she felt they were unaware of her presence.

She swam straight out to sea; something she had always been told not to do.

'Parallel to the shore,' her father had always warned her. 'Never out to sea. Only maniacs swim straight out to sea.'

He would scrunch backwards and forwards along the beach waiting for her to come out of the water and then without a word, he would turn away from her and walk home, not waiting for her to dry herself, or even slip on her shoes.

She had hated his presence there on the beach, like a prison warder, inhibiting in some way her freedom.

'I'll never drown,' she had said to him one day, a squally day with little waves snagging on the stony shore. He had said nothing, just caught his muffler and tucked it more firmly into the collar of his coat.

'And what could you do anyway, if I did start to drown or get swept away round Bray Head? What on earth could you do?' He had indicated with his hand that she should go about her business of swimming and when she had come out ten minutes later, squeezing the water from her hair, she had seen his grey figure climbing the steps towards the road.

Now she swam strongly out towards the sun, watched by unfriendly seagulls and ignored by the oyster catchers.

When she came out the rock on which she had put her clothes was shining pink and the bird on top looked like a marble carving, every feather delineated in the strong light from the low sun, the eyes like shining stones. She looked down at her body and she too was pink and glistening with salty drops. She wished that Paul was there with her and then squashed the thought, blotting and rubbing at herself with her towel.

'*All I do the whole day through is dream of you.*' She danced a few tentative steps on the sand.

'Da dee da dee dadada.'

The seagull looked at her with contempt and flew away.

'Eat your heart out, Debbie Reynolds,' she said and went home to cook breakfast.

'God, you're so lucky that you die early in the play. I really hate that pile up in the last ten minutes. Crash, crash, gurgle, all the major players are dead. *Let four captains bear Hamlet, like a soldier to the stage,* all the rest of us scattered on the floor, martial music, curtain, thunderous applause.'

'We hope.'

'We certainly do.'

'Ever seen the Reduced Shakespeare Company?'

She nodded.

'Now that's the way to do it.'

'They could do all of Chekhov in fifteen minutes. *The Three Seagulls in Vanya's Orchard.*'

'Are you all right?'

They were sitting upstairs in Bewleys at a table that was just too small, looking down on the mêlée of Grafton Street. Everyone down there looked so young, she thought, and so unburdened. Three young musicians were playing Bach just down the street and a small group of people had gathered around them to listen.

Charlie tapped her hand with a finger. She smiled across the table at him.

'Oh yes, thank you, Charlie. I'm fine. I think we have a play. Bits and bobs to be . . .'

'You know what I mean.'

She stared at him not speaking.

'Grace.'

'Mim wandered again. Not into town this time, but the other day I came back and she wasn't there. Oh God, Charlie, I thought she was dead. I expected to find her body each time I opened a door. Then just as I was about to ring the police, in she comes as cool as a cucumber. I could have killed her.'

'Where had she been?'

'She mumbled on about Killiney Hill and this *doppelgänger* or whatever you'd call it of hers. Mind you, she's been angelic since. Full of remorse and charm.'

'That's Mim.'

'I haven't time for this now. That sounds terrible. I simply cannot cope at this moment. Once the show is on . . . then . . . then . . .'

'Then?'

'I'll have time . . .'

Her voice trailed away.

Outside in the street the Bach came to an end and there was a scattering of clapping.

'I feel both inept and guilty. I've never really confronted the problem. Just gone my own sweet way and thought, one day, one day I'll get stuck in to dealing with Mim's life. Now my inertia or carelessness has caught up with me. Everything seems so easy when everything's going right.'

For a moment his face splintered in front of her, the cups and plates on the table might be about to disintegrate. She closed her eyes for a moment and when she opened them again the equilibrium of Bewleys, of Charlie across the table from her, had been re-established. She picked up a paper napkin from the table and blew her nose.

'Sorry,' she said.

He nodded.

He leant forward towards her.

> *'My liege and madam, to expostulate*
> *What majesty should be, what duty is,*
> *Why day is day, night night and time is time,*
> *Were nothing but to waste night, day and time.*
> *Therefore, since brevity is the soul of wit*
> *And tediousness the limbs and outward flourishes,*
> *I will be brief . . .'*
> *'More matter with less art.'*

Two women at the next table had stopped talking to each other and were staring at them.

'Fuck duty,' said Grace.

The two women re-started their conversation.

'You don't really mean that, do you?'

Grace shook her head.

'I want to work. I really do. You've no idea, being a man, how grim the prospect is of . . .'

'Old age is not sexist, my pet. It comes to us all.'

'Women get forgotten quicker than men. Your self-esteem leeches away, when managements aren't battering at your door.'

'My dear girl . . .'

She grinned at him.

'Girl?'

'In a manner of speaking.'

She took a lump of sugar and put it in her mouth.

Scrunch.

'I want to work. We have to soldier on, Mimi and I, but I want to work.'

Scrunch.

'Very bad for your teeth, darling.'

'As if I didn't know.'

Scrunch.

Her hand hovered over the bowl and he slapped her fingers. The two ladies at the next table were watching openly.

'Anyway, that's not what I was asking about. It's the other.'

He leant towards her. 'What about the other?'

She sighed and then put out her hand and touched his face.

'There is no other.'


'Bonnyface.'

'Signora?'

'Is being dead more satisfactory than being alive?'

They were walking gently along the beach.

She held his arm for support: it wouldn't do to slip on the stones and have to be carried home by strangers. Besides, as usual, it was only when she was held by him that she was pain-free. I could stride out, she thought, holding his arm like this, in my fine suede boots, but better be safe than sorry.

The susurration of the sea was like music whispering in her ear, the music, she thought, of all those seductions she had never known.

He laughed, a little nervously, she thought.

'I found being alive very satisfactory.'

'That's no answer to my question.'

He said nothing.

She pulled at his sleeve impatiently.

'You forget that I died young. My life was active, perhaps you might have thought it uncomfortable, a bit vicious at times, but on the whole I found it satisfactory. I was never a contemplative person. I had very few aspirations, signora. In those days we knew where we stood. Perhaps if I had had the eyes of Piero the painter, I might have been less satisfied.'

'You're not going to answer my question, are you?'

He shook his head.

'How tiresome of you.'

'I do not have the right.'

They walked in silence for a few minutes.

'I'm really thinking of Benjamin, more than myself. I do hope that he found some sort of peace. He believed in heaven and hell, you know. Punishment, all that sort of thing. I used to pull his leg about it . . . early days . . .' She sighed. 'Yes, in the early days I used to pull his leg about a lot of things. Maybe I wasn't very kind. It is quite difficult, don't you think, when you are young, to be very sensitive to the pain of others?'

He didn't reply. He wasn't in a very chatty mood, she thought. She smiled at him and gave his arm another little tweak.

'Are you getting fed up?'

'Fed up?' He looked puzzled.

'Bored with being here. Wanting to move on. There's not a lot happening. I mean . . .'

'No. No, signora, I am very pleased to be here with you. Bored. Not bored. You are a very easy person to watch over.'

'I wish you could communicate that to Grace. I think she finds me a heavy burden. I think we should go back home now. Just in case she comes home early. I don't want to upset her again. There is just one favour I'd like to ask.'

'What's that?'

'I don't want Grace to be worried or upset in any way before the first night. Do you know what I mean?'

'First night? What is that?'

'The play opening. We must keep things calm for her until the play opens.'

She looked at him anxiously.

'After the first night actors become reasonably normal people again. They can think again about the real world. Until the next time. We must go home now. I can't have her upset.'

He held out his hand.

There should be sparks, she thought as she took it, stars between his hand and mine, neat zigzags of lightning to show that something untoward is happening. There was nothing, not even an exhilarating passage of air. She only closed her eyes.

She opened them as she heard Grace's key in the door, Grace's voice yoo-hooing in the hall, the door's slam. She heard all these sounds at once as she dragged her eyes open and felt once more the nag of pain.

'Yes,' she called rather breathlessly. 'I am here.' She was reassembling herself as she spoke.

She was sitting in her place by the window, her hands clutching at the arms of the chair, her face flushed, her hair, she could feel, tangled by the wind.

'I am here,' she repeated, as Grace came into the room. 'Yes. Hello.'

'Hello, darling.'

'Everything go all right?'

'Oh, I dunno. I dunno. I can't see the wood for the trees at the moment. I have to have a glass of wine. How about you? It will be all right on the night.'

She opened the press and repeated the words very slowly, each word floating on its own in the still air of the room.

'It will be all right on the night.'

'It always is.'

Grace laughed and poured wine.

'Not true, Mim, as you well know. Think of all those ghastly, terrifying failures.'

She picked up the two glasses and walked over to her mother. She handed her a glass.

'Are you okay, darling? You look a little flushed.'

'I think I must have been asleep.'

Grace sat down and stretched her legs out in front of her.

'This won't be a ghastly failure.' She took a gulp of wine. 'Just one of those, "why?" productions. Why did they bother? Why do *Hamlet* without a prince? Why now? Why waste all that money on astonishing costumes? Ha! I know the answer to *that* question anyway. To seduce people into thinking that what you see is what you get. Well, I suppose, why *not*? If you can get away with it.'

She yawned and then smiled at her mother.

'Maybe it's not that bad. Maybe I'm just suffering from exhaustion, nerves, confusion and hunger. I'm going to whizz up and have a bath and then I'll take us both out to eat. I haven't the energy to cook.' She yawned again. 'Okay?'

Mimi didn't answer. She had just noticed that the floor by her feet was sprinkled with a dusting of fine sand and pebbles.

'Mim?'

'Gently.'

'What does that mean?'

'Gently out. Yes. Go dear, and now go and bath. Or bathe. Perhaps you might bathe. Swim.'

'I swam this morning. Do you feel up to going out?'

'Gently out. I feel up to that. Yes. I have been asleep all afternoon. All. I never moved. Go dear, and have your bath. I will . . .' She picked up her glass from the table and looked at it. '. . . Pebble.'

Grace looked at her for a moment and then got up.

'Oh my God,' she said and left the room.

* * *

It was all right.

They went gently and ate and talked with amiable disengagement about topics that at that moment interested neither of them. *Hamlet*, weddings, death and the other anxieties were left to one side.

They went home and went to bed at nine thirty.

There was no longer either sand or pebbles on the floor.


Three mornings passed before she was again woken by the phone. Sharp disappointment had grated at her mind until each day the density of work had taken over all her thoughts.

'*Readiness is all*,' Charlie had muttered to her the evening before as she was dashing from the theatre.

She had scowled at him.

'Even our infant prodigy is beginning to take on the look of a pear about to drop off the tree.'

'Piss off, Charlie.'

There had been a scattering of rain in the night and even before the ringing had woken her she had been able to smell the grass refreshed, and the leaves and Albertine in the dying moments of her dreams.

She was filled with comfortable happiness as she turned over and reached out for the telephone.

'Yes.'

It was Polly.

'Mum.'

She sat up, punching her pillows into shape behind her.
'Darling.'

'I'm sorry to ring you so early, but I knew you'd be going out and . . .'

'Darling.'

An explosion of tears.

'Darling. What is the matter? What has happened? Are you ill?'

Unintelligible words.

'Darling Polly, stop that sniffing. I can't hear a word you're saying. What is the matter?'

The crying stopped.

'Paul.' She just said the one word. It hovered on the wires like a tightrope walker, somewhere between London and Dublin.

'What about Paul?'

'He's broken off our engagement. He said last night. Oh Mum, he doesn't want to marry me.'

The crying started again.

Oh God!

A beat, two, three, filled with tears.

'Ehm, darling, you had a row. Everyone has rows.'

'No, no, no. We had no row. He just took me out to dinner and then . . .'

'I'm sure he didn't mean it. He just has something on his mind. Work. It's a . . .' She groped desperately for the right words and came up with the wrong ones, '. . . a little hiccup.'

'No. Take me seriously, Mum. It's over. That's what he said, quite, quite calmly. It is over. He . . . he said he was sorry but it was over. OVER. Got it? Mum?'

'I've got it.'

There was a long silence.

Grace stared out of the window at the rosy sky.

'He was quite polite. It was not a row. After all, Mum, what could I say?'

Grace didn't answer.

'But why? I asked him that.'

'What did he say?'

'He just shook his head. He just repeated, like I said, it's over. That was all. It was not my fault. He said that too. Not your fault, Polly, please believe that. He kissed my hand and left the restaurant. I haven't slept a wink all night, Mum. What will I do?'

'Nothing. Have a bath, put some slap on your face, go to work and pretend that nothing's happened. After a while you'll mend. Everybody mends.'

'I expected more from you than that.'

'Darling, what more can I give? If you were here I would hug you to death. All I could say, though, would be the same words. I'm sorry. You'll mend. It may take an age, but . . .'

'Could you speak to him?'

'What?'

'Could you speak to him . . . please, Mum? He liked you. He told me how much . . . he might tell you things he won't tell me and I could put things straight. Please, Mum.'

'No, I'm afraid I couldn't do that.'

'Why not?'

'For various reasons that you know quite well. I have no

intention of interfering in your personal life. And there's *Hamlet*. For heaven's sake, Polly, we start previewing the day after tomorrow.'

The tears began again.

'Polly . . .'

'It's all right. That's the way it has always been, isn't it? No room for me. Plays, bloody plays. Polly can wait until the play is over. Not now, darling, I'm going to be late for my rehearsal. Come back later, darling, I'm learning my lines. Go away, darling. Interviews, darling, first nights, darling, dress rehearsal, darling . . .'

'You're being . . .'

'Most unfair. Of course, of course. Don't be unfair to Mummy, she starts previewing in two days.'

'Well, thanks for all that.'

'Yes.'

'Perhaps you'll feel a bit better with that off your chest.'

'Oh, my God.'

Polly slammed down the receiver.

Grace got out of bed and moved over to the window. Her legs were trembling. Every part of her was trembling. She leaned on the window-sill. The moon was a pale disc in the pink sky.

She tried some deep breathing, unsuccessfully.

The man in the moon smiled at her.

'Sod off,' she said.

The telephone rang again. She ran to it, filled with tenderness and forgiveness.

'Hello, darling.'

'Grace?'

It was Paul.

'Sod off,' she yelled and put down the receiver.

'These mornings I keep hearing the telephone.'

Grace didn't reply. She was running over in her mind the things she needed to bring with her: script, Nurofen, change of shoes, Kleenex, Rescue Remedy, two Cox's Orange Pippins, ciggies, just in case of some dramatic crisis, *Irish Times*, Nurofen . . . said that . . .

'Grace.'

'Yes. Oh yes, darling. Sorry. Mind elsewhere. I may be late. Mrs O'B will be here from eleven until about seven. She'll get you your supper and then go. Will you be all right?'

She picked up her bag and slung it onto her shoulder.

'You look exhausted.'

'Thanks.'

'Someone keeps ringing up in the middle of the night.'

'Darling, it wasn't the middle of the night. It was five o'clock.'

'Same thing. I never get back to sleep again after.'

'It was Polly.'

'How strange. Is she all right?'

'She's not getting married after all.'

'I didn't see that lasting. I suppose she's very upset.'

'Yes.'

'Poor Polly. I could have told her.'

'Lucky you didn't. Do you want a ticket for the first night?'

'What is it?'

Grace sighed.

'*Hamlet*,' she said.

'I've seen *Hamlet* sixteen times.'

'Is that a yes or a no?'

'Probably not. I'll discuss it with Bonnyface. He might like to see it. He's lived through all that sort of thing, you know.'

Grace sighed again.

'Well, let me know, when you make up your mind.'

'Someone else rang as well.'

'Wrong number.'

Grace bent and kissed her mother and then left the house.

Liar, thought Mimi, as she watched her go.

Something's up. Not just first nights and all that.

Benjamin came in the door and walked towards her.

'No,' she said. She closed her eyes and then opened them again. He stood about three feet away from her, staring past her out of the window.

'Albertine's done well,' he said.

'Benjamin . . .'

'Could do with pruning. I see that you and Grace have let the garden go to rack and ruin.'

'You might at least say, Good morning Mimi, how are you?'

'I can see how you are. Not very well. Not long for this life, I would say.'

'You haven't changed much.'

'I certainly am identifiably myself.'

'Where is Bonnyface? I hope you haven't chased him. I like him.'

'Bonnyface? Oh, you mean that Italian fellow. More your type than mine. I think he's in the kitchen making coffee. Anything to drink around here?'

'No.' With great difficulty she struggled to her feet.

'No, Benjamin. Absolutely no. I will not have that starting all over again.'

'What?'

'Drink, drink, drink.'

'If you don't want me to have a drink, I won't have a drink. I never knew what else to do when I was with you. Drink was my one protection.'

She looked at him, aghast.

'There you go again, blaming me for everything.'

'I told you I hadn't changed.'

'I don't know how they put up with you.'

'There is no one. You know that. You always told me that.'

'You never believed me.'

'I couldn't. I had to believe in repentance and forgiveness.'

'You never asked me to forgive you.'

'I thought God was more important. I thought that one day I would be embraced by his divine love. The sinner would become undefiled.'

She put out a hand and touched his shoulder. She recognised at that moment his neat grey suit that in the last couple of years of his life he had always worn to church. She felt flattered that he had put it on for her. He flinched at her touch and she remembered that too. She removed her hand.

'You were never a sinner. You just despised yourself for what you were and you hated me for what I was not.'

'A simplistic view, if I may say so.'

'You may. I would like you to go away and not be bothering me. I have enjoyed the last few weeks. I would like to continue to do so. I'd rather you stayed in outer darkness and I don't want Grace upset. She has a first night. Just in case you were thinking of manifesting yourself to her.'

'No. That hadn't entered my head.'

She moved towards the kitchen door.

'I am very tired these days. I sleep a lot. I need to be treated with benignity. Bonnyface suits me fine. I am glad that he has come into my life. I really don't need you, Benjamin.'

He laughed. 'Do you remember the first time we met?'

'Yes. Nine Arts' Ball. 1932.'

'I sat and watched you dance with every other man in the party and I thought, I will be safe in her hands.'

'I loved dancing. I miss that. I have missed it forever. You never took me dancing.'

'No. I was afraid.'

She looked at him in silence for a moment.

'Afraid of what?'

He walked over to the window and looked out down the sloping lawn towards the magnolia tree. She thought that maybe he was going to disappear without answering her. That would be like him all right. Her life with him had been filled with unanswered questions.

'I could have taught you to dance,' she said, to break the silence.

'I was afraid you might find someone more suitable than I. That you might go. Leave me to my demons.' He gave a short bitter laugh and turned to look at her. 'Both real and imaginary.'

His body was cracking up; through his neat grey suit she could now see the window frame, the curtains moving slightly as a breeze stirred through the room. She heard the hall door open and close and she saw his hands rising up and disintegrating in front of her eyes. She thought she might fall heavily onto the floor and break something in the falling and she grasped at the tabletop to steady herself.

Mrs O'Brien popped her head around the door.

'There you are, m'dear. I'll be witcha in a second. I have to run to the toilet. I thought I'd never make it up the road.'

Slowly Mimi made her way back to her chair and slowly sat down among the soft cushions that comforted her back and shoulders. Her eyes drooped, she thought only for a moment, but when she opened them Mrs O'Brien was standing in front of her with a cup of coffee steaming in her hand.

'Didja have a bad night?'

'Well . . .'

'I see you were making coffee. You should have left that to me.'

She put the cup on the table close to Mimi's hand.

'No point in overdoing things and me here to give a hand. It's that nice strong stuff. I could smell it the minute I opened the door. I prefer that to th'instant, but you couldn't get Joe to let it past his lips. Wouldja eat a biscuit?'

Mimi shook her head.

'Sure? Chocky? There's a whole tin of them Belgian ones on the table. She knows I have a sweet tooth. You could save me from temptation by having a few yourself.'

'No thanks, Mrs O'Brien. I think I'll just drink my coffee and have a little sleep.'

'That's a good girl. She's left a list for me on the table so I'll take a run down to the shops before I take my shoes off and you can have a little snooze before I do the hoovering. I thought I'd give the bathrooms a good scour out today and wash some blankets while the sun is still shining. I can hang them in the garden and let them have a good blow. I'll just take a sup of that coffee and get on with my schedule. You give me a shout if there's anything you need.'

She bustled back into the kitchen.

Mimi lifted up her cup carefully. A toast. Thank you, Bonnyface.

I long for normality.

I would like a life where there are no surprises.

Boring; I might almost like a boring life.

She turned the key in the door and went into the house.

The hall light was on and upstairs the lighted landing waited for her. A lamp glowed dimly in the sitting-room.

Everything in fact was as it should be, normal, no surprises. On the table a tray was set with a plate of sandwiches, some fruit and a thermos of coffee.

God bless Mrs O'B.

There was a note propped against the thermos flask.

> *She went to bed at 6. She is tired out these days. I took her*
> *some supper on a tray. There's no denying it, she likes her food. A*
> *gentlyman rang for you. He didn't leave his name. He says he will*
> *ring again. He sounded English is all I can say.*
> *Yours truly Mrs J O'Brien.*

Grace laughed.

Mrs O'Brien's notes always made her laugh.

She poured herself some coffee and then took a huge bite of a chicken sandwich.

It had been a day filled with intolerable pauses. She had smoked fifteen cigarettes, each one more unpleasant than the last, each one more necessary than the last.

Never again.

I will never walk into that trap again. Never have that first one again.

She paced around the room, chewing, too tired to even sit down or perch on the arm of a chair. Her legs insisted on her moving, round and round.

All her life she had lived in this house, except during her brief excursion into marriage. All her life it had been here waiting for her to put her key in the door and turn.

It had been so easy after Benjamin's death to slip back in again; smell the same old smells, eat off the same plates, touch the same furniture and watch from the windows the same old moons. Two old moons, waxing and waning, regular as clockwork.

We only wane, she thought as she paused by the window.

She began to laugh. She had to put the cup down on the table so as not to spill the coffee.

'We only wane,' she said in her best movie star voice. Bette Davis?

No. That wouldn't do.

'We only wane.' Katherine Hepburn? That's better. I am at last beginning to relax.

The telephone rang.

She picked up the receiver and put it on the table. She crossed the room and switched off the lamp. She poured herself some more coffee and took a couple of sandwiches in her hand. She left the room. She could hear his diminishing voice, 'Grace. Grace. Grace.'

She closed the door and went up the stairs.

She could hear his voice in her head.

'Grace. Grace. Grace.'


'Grace.'

At the sound of her mother's voice she sat up in bed and unstuck her eyes.

It was more than broad daylight.

'Coming,' she shouted.

She looked at the clock by her bed.

Shit. Quarter to eleven.

Oh my God.

It's okay. Calm yourself.

No rehearsal.

Preview.

'Coming,' she called again and pulled on her dressing gown.

Mimi was standing at the bottom of the stairs.

'I didn't know what to do. It got later and later and then I took my courage in my hands.'

'You're a star.'

Grace kissed her mother lightly on the top of her head as she went past.

'I might have slept all day. Have you had breakfast? I think I'd like the works. Then I'll go down and swim it off.'

She went into the kitchen, followed by her mother.

'Someone,' said Mimi, 'left the telephone receiver off the hook. I heard this awful howling noise when I opened the door this morning. I ...'

Grace was filling the kettle and swinging her head from side to side to loosen up the neck muscles.

'It must have been me. I was really knocked out when I got home. I just thought I didn't need the phone ringing in the morning. Polly ... someone ringing. I wanted to sleep forever. So I ... you know.' She switched on the kettle. 'It was a dreadful dress. Everything that could go wrong went wrong. We never got a really good run at it. Lights ho ... no lights. The ghost which is all done by electronics went berserk and Hamlet fell into the grave and nearly killed Ophelia. All's going well, Madame la Marquise.'

Mimi laughed.

'As you all say nowadays, so what's new?'

'Bacon, eggs, sausages, tomatoes, fried bread. What do you say? A killer meal. But who cares? Sit down, darling, before you fall down.'

'I'm all right. I will lay the table. I feel sprightly today. Well, not exactly sprightly, but clearer in my head than I have done for some time.'

Slowly she began to move around the room, collecting cups and plates, knives, forks, all the accoutrements of meal times and laying them on the table.

'I would like to talk to you about your father.'

Grace pulled the frying pan off its hook and slammed it onto the stove. She didn't say anything. She got the butter from the fridge and picked up a knife.

'May as well be hanged for a sheep as a lamb,' she said and cut a lump of it into the pan.

'He was here yesterday.'

'Mimi . . .'

Luckily the phone rang.

Grace pushed the pan off the heat and picked up the receiver. She held it tight against her ear so that the sound might not creep out into the room.

'I am cooking breakfast, I don't want to speak to anyone,' she said.

A laugh beat into her ear.

'I'll get a cab at once.' It was Charlie. 'I feel just like a good big breakfast. Don't start without me.'

She put the receiver down and turned to Mimi.

'Another place. Charlie's on his way.'

She went back to the pan.

'Darling . . . after the first night. There's a lot of stuff has to be cleared up, after the first night. Problems to be addressed.'

'I just wanted to have a conversation with you about your father.'

'Yes. I just don't want to have it today, or tomorrow or the next day. After that I will be at your disposal.'

'Your problem has always been that you put your work first.'

'Yes. It's a decision that I had to make a long time ago. It's never been a problem to me. It's just the way I am. I have to keep that clear space for work. My work.'

Mimi dropped a cup. It bounced on the tiles and then broke up and settled like a fallen flower. Mimi stood quite still and looked down at the debris.

'I'm sorry. I . . . Sometimes my hands don't work. I . . .'

'It's all right, Mim. Don't worry. I'll clear it up.'

Mimi stared at her reprehensible hand with anger.

'I hate this,' she said.

'It's all right, Mim. What's a cup, for God's sake?'

She opened a cupboard and took out a dustpan and brush.

'I hate not being in control of my own hands.'

She shook her hands angrily in front of her face.

Grace wasn't watching her, she was bent over sweeping the china petals into the dustpan.

'Just sit down, Mimi. Don't get all upset.'

'How can I not be upset? Benjamin was here yesterday. I think it must have been yesterday. I hated that too. I was saved by Mrs O'Brien. I do not like being left alone. I do not like being at the mercy of people like Benjamin.'

Grace stood up. Her head was a little dizzy from the stooping. She brushed the broken china into the dustbin.

'Benjamin is dead.'

'I never said he wasn't dead. I just said he was here. I know he's dead. I sat beside him and watched him die. You weren't here.'

Grace took her mother's arm gently and brought her to a chair. She realised suddenly how thin the old lady had become: her arm seemed all trembling bone.

'Sit, darling. Let me tuck these cushions round you. There. This is all my fault. I should have woken up in time to get you your breakfast. I'm sorry.'

'I'd like a glass of wine. If you look around you might find some Vino Nobile di Montepulciano.'

'After breakfast, perhaps. I really don't think you should be drinking wine before breakfast. Charlie will be here soon. That will cheer you up.'

Mimi slumped down into the chair.

Grace went back to the frying pan.

After a few minutes silence Mimi began to sing.

'Come into the garden, Maud,
The black bat night has flown.
Come into the garden, Maud.

*I'm here at the gate alone.*
*I'm here at the gate alone.'*

Grace scooped fat over the frying eggs.

'We had lamps when I was a child. You know, polished brass lamps and cut glass ones. Heavy cut glass, the light made rainbows on them. My papa used to take one of those lamps out into the garden and sing that and Mama would run out in her long dress and stand beside him looking up into his face, all lit by the lamplight. Well, maybe he didn't do it all that often, but he did it once. I remember that as if it was yesterday. Do you have such happy memories of your father and mother?'

Grace scooped the eggs and bacon onto a dish and opened the oven door.

'I'm sure I would if I thought about it.'

'No. I don't think so.'

The doorbell rang.

*'And the woodbine spices are wafted abroad,*
*And the musk of the rose is blown.'*

Charlie stood on the doorstep a full blown rose in his hand.

Grace recognised it at once. It came from the tall bush by the gate.

*'You come most carefully upon your hour.'*

'I love to come into a singing house. I haven't heard *Maud* for years. Since I was a child. Bravo, Mimi.'

He walked down the hall and into the kitchen.

'*There has fallen a splendid tear from the passion flower by the gate.*'

He joined in.

'*She is coming, my dove, my dear;*
*She is coming my life, my fate:*

'Darling Mimi, I am transported. How wonderful you are. Let me give you this token of my admiration.'

He handed her the rose. She laughed and tucked it behind her ear.

'What a delightful old cod you are.'

He looked offended.

'Old?'

'Oldish, if you prefer.'

He shook his head.

'It doesn't appeal to me either. Just think, Grace, I came all this way in a taxi to be reminded, as I walk in the door, of my own disintegration. Let's have breakfast.' He sat down beside Mimi and looked expectant.

'You arrived just in time. I was getting at her.' Mimi spoke the words happily.

Grace clattered plates and dishes onto the table. They were all enfolded in the glorious smells of a fried breakfast.

'How very disagreeable of you,' said Charlie. 'Oh God, darling, think of all that cholesterol. We may not make the first night. Have you an understudy waiting in the wings . . . an *All About Eve* person, waiting to pounce? I don't. But I think

Rosencrantz may have been learning my lines. I saw him giving me a sinister look the other day.'

'Or *gentle Guildenstern?*'

'Definitely Rosencrantz . . . He's the small dark one, isn't he? I don't accept cups of instant coffee from him.'

Grace laughed.

'See, Mim, how paranoid we're getting? It's the play. Suspicion, corruption, murder, all at large among the cast. Fried bread, Charlie?'

'Yes please. May as well be hanged for a sheep as a lamb. Are you coming to the first night, Mimi?'

Mimi shook her head. 'If Polly was coming over I would go with her. She could put me in a taxi if I wanted to leave at half-time, and I probably would. *Hamlet's* fearfully long. She's not engaged any longer, you know.'

'Who?'

'Polly. I don't really understand why they get engaged these days. They're all sleeping with each other anyway.'

Charlie was staring at Grace.

'True?'

'Of course it's true,' said Mimi. 'I wouldn't have said it otherwise. I told Grace it wouldn't work out. Didn't I, Grace? Nice young man. Wrong girl. That's what I said, wasn't it, Grace? Not that I could say that I know him well, or anything like that. But, I have an instinct for these things. I know.'

Grace wondered if Mimi had already been at the Vino Nobile di Montepulciano. I must have a little look around her bedroom, she thought. Maybe this is the answer to her odd behaviour. Mrs

O'B would have told me, unless of course she had some notion in her head about protecting us all from ourselves.

Charlie and Mimi were laughing, their heads leaning close together. Charlie's lips shone with butter.

What was so funny? she wondered. What have I missed?

Do they notice that I'm not with them? Probably not.

'Isn't it silly,' Grace said. 'We eat and sleep and go to work and then eat and sleep and it goes on and on and then we die.'

They both stopped laughing and looked at her.

'What would you suggest we do instead?' asked Charlie.

He popped half a sausage into his mouth and chewed while waiting for her to answer.

'I suppose people who have really exciting jobs are the lucky ones. Otherwise I can't see much point in the whole carry on. Can you?'

'Well, there's sex, darling. That's not bad. Food, drink. A few of life's cheerier ephemera. Take heart. Only forty-eight hours to blast off.'

'She's rather oofy today,' said Mimi.

'What the hell's oofy?'

'See what I mean. Crotchety, if you prefer.' Mimi turned to Charlie and spread her hands wide, in a gesture she thought she must have learnt from Bonifacio.

The telephone rang.

Grace jumped to her feet.

'I'll . . .' She swept a plate with toast and marmalade onto the floor. 'Shit. I'll . . .' She looked round as if to find the nearest telephone and then, ignoring it, she ran from the room, closing the door behind her.

'Grace.' He didn't wait for her to speak. 'Don't put the phone down. I won't say anything untoward. I just want to know if you're all right. I want to know how the play is going. I want to know if you've spoken to Polly. I want . . . I want . . . oh bloody hell, Grace, I want you so much. I can hear the gentle susurration of your breath.' He laughed. 'How about that? Lovertalk. Oh, beautiful Grace, I want to engage, so much, in lovetalk with you.'

'I am really angry with you.' Her voice was a whisper. She could feel the silence in the kitchen as Charlie and Mimi tried to hear what she was saying.

'Yes. You must be angry. I understand. But you would be far more angry if I hadn't done this. Polly will recover. Give her six months. Less . . .'

'We can't talk about this now.'

'People there? Ears? Of course, what an ass I am. We'll talk about everything when I see you.'

'You won't be seeing me. You may not, you *must* not come over here. Do you understand me, P—?' She stopped, afraid to speak his name aloud.

'No.'

'I insist.'

'There is no insisting. Abyssinia.'

He hung up.

'This is all totally absurd.'

She walked across the room and looked out into the garden.

She pushed open the glass doors and stepped out onto the verandah.

I am too old for this sort of nonsense.

Angrily she snapped a dead rose from its stem and threw it down onto the wooden step.

I do not want this sickness visited upon me. She took a deep breath of the sunny salty air.

'It will all pass. It is absurd. It is not a sickness, merely an absurdity. Polly will never know. No one will ever know and one day it will . . .'

'Mimi wants to know if you are talking to this person of hers called Bonnyface.'

Charlie was standing behind her, one hand on her shoulder.

'Just to myself.' She laughed suddenly. 'I just felt like a little conversation with myself.'

'May one enquire . . .?'

'No. Absolutely not.'

She gave him a pat on the arm.

'Why don't we go for a drive? Take Mim into the country-side. The Sally Gap or perhaps the waterfall at Powerscourt. It's an age since I've been there. What do you think? Let's go and find out where she'd like to go.'

She pushed past him into the house.

'Only if you'll let me drive,' he called after her.


Mimi sang all the way.

'*Birds in the high hall garden* . . .'

Just audible. Toning in with the sound of the engine, the

ticking of the wheels. The sound would have inhibited conversation, if anyone had wanted to talk.

They drove through the Glen of the Downs and then forked left for Delgany. There were touches of yellow in the chestnut trees.

'Mim, it's so lugubrious,' said Grace at one moment.

'I like it. I haven't thought of it for years. *Maud has a garden of roses and lilies fair . . .'*

Grace glanced sideways at Charlie, who gave her a little wink.

On the edge of Greystones he turned in through a gateway and stopped the car.

He turned to Mimi who seemed quite oblivious to the fact that the car had stopped.

*'A voice by the cedar tree . . .'*

'I am going to walk for a few minutes on the beach, before we go home. Will you come, Mimi? We will take great care of you.'

Mimi opened her eyes. 'I think not. Where are we?'

'Greystones,' said Grace. 'The south beach.'

'I am comfortable where I am, thank you. I will remain here.'

Grace and Charlie got out and walked under the railway arch onto the long bleak beach. Everywhere children ran, dug, cried, laughed, hopped and scattered the grey edge of the sea with colour; somewhat disconsolate mothers sat on tartan rugs surrounded by wet and sandy clothes and perhaps dreamed of Barbados, Lanzarote or merely Grafton Street.

Charlie tucked his arm through Grace's and they walked down to the edge of the sea.

Two children were building a castle, while a third fruitlessly and enthusiastically filled the moat with water from a bucket.

'I'm sorry,' he said to her, squeezing her arm against his side.

She shook her head.

Out on the horizon a boat trailed smoke.

'Is he becoming a pest?'

She didn't answer. She picked up a stone and threw it into the sea, narrowly missing a man in a black bathing cap.

'It's not that,' she said at last. 'I am beginning to need to hear the sound of his voice.'

Gulls bobbed like wavelets, close in to the shore, hoping to scavenge from picnickers.

Why did I say a stupid thing like that? It is not in my nature to blurt.

'Don't tell anyone, Charlie. You can be such a gossip. Please don't make a fool of me. There's Polly to think of. There's . . . there's . . .'

She didn't look towards him as she spoke. She wondered why the man was wearing a bathing cap. Ear problems? Vanity? Perhaps he wore a wig?

'I am offended.'

'Why, darling?' She leant towards him and kissed his cheek. 'Don't be silly. We all know each other's little weaknesses. You are a news gatherer and disseminator *par excellence*. Just a bit of discretion is all I'm asking. Because of Polly.'

He took her arm and they turned and walked back up the beach towards the archway.

'If you want my advice, which you probably don't, have a bit of fun, darling. Let your hair down for once. After all, it's not every day that one is hotly pursued by a handsome young thing. I should be so lucky. Any time a dish like that gives me the eye, he turns out to be terminally stupid. Just a pretty face. That's okay for one-night stands, but beyond that it's a bit tedious. Maybe I'm getting old. As they all say now, chill out. Don't take things so seriously. Fling, darling.'

The swimmer with the bathing cap panted past them, a small towel draped around his shoulders. He was wearing a pair of black plimsolls which squelched as he ran. He still had the black cap on his head. He ran under the railway arch, leaving a trail of drops on the sand.

'But on the other hand,' Charlie continued, 'if you really want rid of the little beast, I can arrange for him to be offered a year's contract in Sydney; I'm thinking of going out there myself for a while. I rather fancy lounging on Bondi Beach watching those gorgeous surfers.'

Grace laughed.

'I thought the Aussies were seriously homophobic.'

'Don't you believe it, darling. Nothing could be further from the truth. Mimi seems to be waving at us.'

Across the car park they saw Mimi flapping her hands at them, nodding her head up and down. As they got closer to the car she began to mouth words at them.

'Home.'

Charlie opened the door and got into the car.

'I really hate this place. This horrible grey stones place.'

Grace got into the back and put a hand on her mother's shoulder.

'I really hate it. A grey stones car park. And you left me sitting there.'

'Mim, we asked you . . .'

'I can't walk on all that sand. I remember that place, all grey stones and sand. We used to come here when Grace was a child.'

'I am Grace.'

Charlie backed the car carefully out of its space and drove onto the road.

'Home?'

'I never liked it. Benjamin liked it. I used to say, I don't want to go to that grey stones place, but he wouldn't heed me. So exposed to the east wind. He used to go to the golf club and would leave us here on the beach. Grace and I. Exposed to that awful east wind. And here you go and do the same thing. Did you go to the golf club?'

'No, of course we didn't. We were only gone about five minutes.'

'How was I to know? I was waiting for him to come back all the time and I didn't know what I would say to him. I told him to go away the other day.'

She clasped and unclasped her hands on her knee as she talked. Her fingers were like twigs, dry brittle twigs, in danger, Grace thought, of snapping at any moment.

'We're all here now, Mim. We're going home. Everything's all right.'

'And not come back. I said that to him.' She thought for a

moment. 'I think I said that to him. I meant to say that to him, but then I always meant to say things to him and I never did.'

They drove in silence through the wide main street of the little town.

Good, ordinary women in cardigans were doing their shopping. They were pushing prams and had dogs on leads. The station, the fish shop, the grocer, the butcher, a chemist and, after a while, among its trees, the Protestant church.

Then she spoke again.

'I should have stayed at home. I am afraid now away from home that something may happen.'

'Nothing will happen. We're all here together.'

'People go away.'

Her hands fell, still, down into her lap.

Grace spoke too brightly. 'Did you know that Greystones once had more Protestants than Catholics living here? Sixty per cent. Something like that. Did you know that?'

Charlie started to laugh.

'How hateful you Irish are. Always on about the same old thing.'

'What are you talking about?'

'Just a joke, Mim. I thought it was time for a joke. A little local-colour joke.'

'I said, people go away. That wasn't a joke. Die, for instance.'

'*To sleep, perchance to dream.*' Charlie took his hands off the steering wheel and sawed the air.

'Benjamin never wanted Grace to go on the stage. Sometimes I remember everything. It's as if a bright spotlight lit my whole past. I can see every detail. She went away then. Just like I said . . . went away. She never really came back.'

'I am here, Mim.'

Charlie turned slightly towards her and frowned. Grace sat back into her seat and closed her eyes. Too many things were fighting in her head. Grace, you have your father much offended. Spinning colours, red and gold and stars and two moons, waxing and waning to the sound of her mother's voice. Grace, you have your . . . In the full moon the shadow of Paul's face and then the waves splitting and wrinkling that image and white, gold and green birds swooping into the sea, pecking with ferocity at the remnants of his silver flesh. Grace . . .

'Grace.'

She opened her eyes, startled by Charlie's voice.

She looked around. They were nearly home, running now along the new road from Shankill to Ballybrack. Five, six minutes more, then she would gather her wits together and then, as Mimi would say, she would be going away again.

'I'm sorry. I fell asleep.' She shivered slightly, nothing to do with cold, but with recollection of her dream. 'Did I miss anything?'

'He was speaking Shakespeare to me,' said Mimi. 'It was lovely. *The wind sits in the shoulder of your sail, and you are stayed for. Hamlet* . . . but of course you know that. How foolish you must think me. He spoke it so well.'

Charlie acknowledged the compliment with a little bow in her direction.

Neat low walls, neat gardens, neat houses all the same; the

road swooped down and then up a little, no trees, just neatness.

'A bit like England,' commented Charlie.

'It used to be fields,' said Mimi. 'Cows, trees and some high grey walls that you couldn't see over. I remember that. Cow parsley in the summer. A bit like the country really. Do you remember that, Grace?'

Grace didn't reply.

Mimi waited a moment or two.

'Grace doesn't ever remember anything. She expunges all memories from her mind. Life is easier like that. Remembering things isn't always fun, you know. I don't have the energy to do much else these days.'

'I remember my lines,' said Grace, again too brightly.

'*I am slain.*' Charlie screamed the words in agony.

> '*O me, what hast thou done?*'
> '*Nay, I know not. Is it the king?*'
> '*Oh, what a rash and bloody deed is this?*'

'Very good, dears. Thank you. I didn't like Laurence Olivier in that film. A bit old, I thought. Heavy. He was a bit heavy. I liked him better in *Gone With The Wind.*'

Charlie laughed. 'Memory letting you down there, darling.'

Mimi thought for a moment.

'Clark Gable.'

They turned in the gate.

Mrs O'Brien was standing on the doorstep polishing the brass knocker with a big yellow cloth.

'What,' asked Mimi, 'is she doing here?'

'She's come to get your supper.'

'Why, may I ask?'

'Because, darling, I have a preview. I have to fly away now . . . and Charlie. We'll have to scuttle you into the house and go. We have a word call at five thirty.'

'Scuttle,' said Mimi with disgust. 'I can get my own supper. You can put everything on the table and all I have to do is eat it.'

'No.' Grace got out of the car. She walked towards Mrs O'Brien who put the duster in the pocket of her overall and wiped her fingers on her skirt.

'I thought as you weren't here I might as well get stuck in. I cleared the mess you left after your meal. I didn't think you'd want to come back to that. What time will her nibs want to eat? I like to have a little sit down and watch *Neighbours*. The kettle's on, do yez want a cup of tea? I had one and I got here, I can make more in a flash.'

Grace passed her and went into the hall.

'I hope she won't be difficult.' She almost whispered the words. 'She's a bit cranky today.'

'Upset tummy, perhaps?'

'Well . . .'

'As you get older the tummy gets more and more unreliable. I had a terrible time with my old mam. Mind you, she was ninety when she went. I suppose you can't . . .'

'I just think she's tired.'

'Ah, the pet . . .'

Mimi and Charlie came slowly in through the door.

'Are you tired?'

'No.'

'Would you like if I tucked you into bed and brought you up a little something on a tray?' Mrs O'Brien turned and smiled at Grace and Charlie. 'God, there's days I'd give a fortune for someone to say that to me.' She laughed, showing white slabs of teeth that shone with scrubbing.

She must be the cleanest woman in the world, thought Grace; Brilloed all over first thing every morning, disinfected, polished, scoured inside and out. Only failing, she thought, that weakness for chocolate biscuits.

Mimi had turned into a charming child.

'Mimi would like tea in bed.'

'Right you be, Missis Pet. Up we go then. Take my arm. We'll have you all tucked in and comfy before you can say Jack Robinson, whoever he is when he's at home.'

'She is going away again.'

'Goodnight, Mimi. I won't be late,' Grace called from the doorway.

'Sometimes I think she will never come back.'

'Never mind. Can't we manage without her very well? Upsadaisy. I'll bring you up a nice cup of tea and then after *Neighbours* is over we'll have a little chat about your supper.'

Charlie took Grace's arm and they left the house.

After her cup of tea, Mimi fell asleep.

She was wakened by pain. It pounded the length of her

spine and up into the base of her skull.

She wondered whether it was night or day.

She wondered where she was, but gradually the familiar feel of her sheets, the composed and friendly smell of her pillows told her that she was in her own bed. Carefully she opened her eyes; the sky was still blue, but the sun had moved behind the hill. Benjamin's Albertine was still stirring outside the window that faced the garden.

It had always been her room. It was from this window that she had watched her father sing to her mother in the garden below, lit by a cut-glass lamp and the moon. She had missed its intimacy when she had moved into the big bedroom across the landing that she had shared for years with Benjamin.

Until I could no longer bear it, she thought, no longer bear to lie beside the restless, angry man in mother's four-poster bed. One morning she had gathered all her clothes, her bits and pieces and moved them across the landing to what she always considered to be her own room. They had never discussed the move. It was as if they had never shared a room at all.

She had thought after Benjamin's death that perhaps she might lock the room up, like a room in a fairy story, and leave it just as it had been on the day of his death, a macabre memorial to her husband. But common sense had prevailed and she had sold the bed and called in the painters. Even after the smell of paint had evaporated and after the room had become quite, quite new she had been assaulted, each time she had opened the door, by the stale smell of whiskey and black depression. Fancy, all fancy, she thought. But the notion had always persisted in her head.

Fancy.

It was a spare room now.

The room where Polly and her whatsisname . . .

Polly.

More like I was than her mother.

Oh, God!

Bonnyface and I must try and have another little run into town. How I enjoyed that little spree. I enjoy spending. That seems pretty silly at this stage of my life. I would love to spend for a whole day and then come back and lay out everything that I had bought in this room, cover the chairs and tables with extravagances. Open boxes and bags and scatter the room with their contents. Then I could lie in bed and admire the colours, the textures, the way the light from the windows picked out a shade here, a shade there. I would murmur to myself, 'All my lovely things. All my lovely things. All my . . .'

Polly was never like Grace. She will settle down. I think that is what is in her mind, settlement. She is a sort of dreamless young woman. Intelligent, charming, all the things she ought to be. She is lucky really to have the sort of father who will always protect her from the vagaries of Grace.

Dreams only lead to trouble.

Dreams . . . her mind faltered off into sleep again.

When she next woke the pain had eased and Bonifacio was sitting in a chair by the bed watching her. From the room below she could hear the murmur of the television, the laughter, the little pattering of applause.

She smiled at him.

'I'm glad you came back. I thought he might have chased you away. I thought I might never see you again.'

'I wouldn't go like that, signora Mimi. Abandon. I wouldn't abandon. I was close by, you know. I was making coffee, to surprise you, and then he came, so I waited and then *she* came. That woman. So.' He spread his hands wide and rolled his eyes.

She laughed.

'Help me to sit up. I feel so silly lying here as if . . . as if I were a baby or something.'

He leant over her and eased her up, re-arranging the pillows behind her.

She felt well, almost young again, ready for living a long life as he moved his hands, tucking, pulling, smoothing, bending down towards her, his breath now on this side of her face, now on the other.

'I would like another little excursion into town. If it could be managed.'

'I think anything can be managed.' He stepped back from the bed and smiled at her. In one hand, however that had happened, was a bottle of Vino Nobile and in the other which he stretched out towards her, an empty glass.

'A little wine? Better than all the pills in the world to bring comfort.'

'Yes, please.'

He poured the wine and handed her the glass, a heavy crystal goblet. She and Benjamin had bought two of them in Venice. She hadn't seen them for years.

'I thought they were broken,' she said. 'I think I remember Grace dropping them on the kitchen floor. A long time ago. I think . . .' She frowned with the concentration of thinking. 'Yes. I do remember. We swept up all the pieces and threw them away, but he discovered them and blamed me. He always liked to do that. Why did you do it? He always liked to say that to me. Anyway, here they are again . . .' Bonifacio also had one in his hand. 'Resurrected.'

He filled his glass and put the bottle down. He held his glass up.

'Resurrection!'

She shook her head.

'I won't drink to that.'

'What then?'

'I don't know. I know very little, Bonnyface. I seem to have spent my life learning very little. People aren't like that any more. They seem to want to discover things all the time. I was never intrepid. You know when Grace scooted off all those years ago to become an actress, I honestly thought she was mad. Why is she doing this? I thought. Why is she creating problems where there are none? Why doesn't she sit tight and let life happen to her and probably enjoy it? Of course, I understand now, but I didn't then.'

'See! You have learnt something.'

She smiled a little sourly and took a drink.

'It doesn't make for happiness, you know.'

'What?'

'Being intrepid. Grace isn't happy. I was happy once. I remember that so well. When I was first married to Benjamin, I didn't think life could be better . . .'

'Memory plays funny tricks.'

'I was happy.'

She stared at him over her glass, tempting him to contradict her.

He shook his head.

'I was happy.' She screamed the words at him.

He got up and moved slowly towards the window.

He seemed to be fading into the evening sky. The room was almost dark now.

'You don't remember.'

His voice was almost a whisper.

For a moment she thought it was Benjamin again, standing there, a shadow by the window.

With all the energy she could summon she hurled her glass across the room. As the door opened she heard it breaking, disintegrating on the floor.

'All in the dark?'

Mrs O'Brien switched on the light and the room became calm once more and empty.

'I heard you call out. Did you have a little dream? I thought maybe you'd taken a turn and fallen out of the bed.'

She coaxed Mimi with her hands back down into the pillows again.

'My mother fell out of the bed once and broke her hip. It nearly finished her off. Hospitalised she was for near on three months. That was before they took to throwing people out the minute they come out of the anaesthetic. That's what they do now. Believe it or not. Two days in and home you go. Heartless, people have got these days. That's what I say to Mr O'B. Heartless. There you are. Comfy? I'll run down and mash the spuds. There's a nice little bit of fish for your tea. Would you like a little tincture of wine with it? She said you could have that if you wanted it. Where's the harm? I said to her. There's no harm at all in moderation. I say that to Mr O'B from time to time. "What's moderation when it's at home." That's all he says. God love him. Are you all right now? Don't go nodding off again and have more bad dreams.'

She smiled down at Mimi.

Mimi thought the best thing she could do was smile back. What a waste of a bottle of Vino Nobile, she thought as she smiled. Maybe I'm going mad. There's a thought.

'Please leave the door open,' she said.

Mrs O'Brien nodded.

'No problem.'

She sailed towards the door, creaking and rustling.

'I'll be right witcha.'

She left the room and Mimi listened to her creaking and rustling down the stairs.

'I don't mean to upset you,' she whispered to the empty room. 'I didn't want you to run away.' There was no reply. 'After all, you silly sausage, you are here to mind me. You told me that yourself.' More silence.

Below Mrs O'Brien turned some knob or other and music flared for a moment and then died to a soft murmur.

'Silly sausage,' Mimi giggled.

What a silly childish thing to say!

I don't like being alone any more. I am afraid. That seems to be the bottom line.

I am afraid.

I am afraid to die alone.

I sat through those hours with Benjamin. I didn't dare to get up and call someone, or go to the loo even. I was afraid I might miss that snapping of the thread.

Perhaps he hated me being there. I never considered his point of view. Perhaps there was someone else he would rather have passed his last moments with. I never considered that either.

Grace was otherwise occupied.

Grace was always . . .

Ah no. Unfair thoughts.

What did I expect from her?

A whole load of grandchildren perhaps? I could have doted on them. All my unused love could have been expended on them . . . Polly used to bite her nails. I used to reprimand her for that. 'They're my nails to do what I like with', she said to me once. I couldn't argue with that. I could never argue with Polly. God love her. I hope she's not crying her eyes out at this moment in time; her heart broken by that feckless actor.

Whatsisname?

She stared at the window for a while thinking nothing.

She could smell the sea. Sometimes you could do that; the breath of salt faintly on the air. It usually meant the weather was going to change.

Bonnyface was right.

I shouldn't have shouted at him. I want him to come back. I will apologise. I will say . . . what will I say?

I knew almost at once that he didn't love me. Even in those days when I was young and knew so little, I knew that.

I could have made so many other men love me, but that was not in my nature.

He wanted to bind me to him and then not love me. It was like a prison. Nowadays people talk about such things; there are counsellors, head shrinkers, therapy sessions, drugs, pills, potions. Get it off your chest, examine it, debate, talk, listen, talk, listen, and finally understand. I simply cannot understand. Maybe if I had believed in God I might have been able to understand something.

It's a bit late to be thinking that now.

He did. It didn't help him.

Did nothing for him at all. In fact it only seemed to make him more and more and more unhappy. Eternal penance. Praying and drinking. And then carried off in the end, unshriven. Is that the right word?

I suppose that was my fault. I should have summoned a priest at some stage. I just couldn't bring myself to do that. Was that evil? I must ask Bonnyface. I must say I never felt guilty. Even now I don't feel guilty, merely curious about my own motives. Was I getting my own back by withholding the possibility of eternal life from him? I do hope that I am not so cruel.

I could do with that glass of wine.

I hope Mrs O'B won't be too long.

Perhaps I should get up and go downstairs. I have been disgruntled all day but that's no good reason to lounge in bed. It would be so easy to stay here, never get up again, dwindle daily among the bedclothes.

Mrs O'Brien however was on the stairs, singing and laaing to herself as she mounted, holding the tray carefully out in front of her.

'*It's someday I'll go back again* laaalaaa *to watch the sun go down of* laalway *bay*. Laa.'

She swept into the room and put the tray on the end of the bed and then settled and ordered Mimi into a comfortable position for eating.

'Missis Pet,' she said, punching at the pillows. 'Never get downhearted. That's what I always say. Where's the point? Mr O'Brien suffers from a bit of the old depression. Just from time to time. Down in the dumps he gets. Sits around the place with a long face on him. There's nothing I can do or say will rouse him up or put a bit of energy into him. I used to think it was the drink, but no, the doctor says it's the depression. Don't we all get depressed at times, I said to him. We can't just sit around like that and moan. Wouldn't the world come to an end if some of us didn't get up each morning and get on with life. God! When I think about it, there's times I could have set fire to myself. But I didn't, did I? I'm here, amn't I? Tell you what I do. I pop into the chapel and light a candle in front of the sweet Mother of God and tell her all about it. Just whisper you know, not loud so the whole world would know my business. She always looks so gracious. I always get the feeling that she understands. Of course youse wouldn't do a thing like that. The couple of Protestant churches that I've been in are cold old places, aren't they? Not like ours. I like the statues we have. Blessed people and saints. I like to feel them all around me. There we are. Nice little bit of fish that. I dipped it in flour and pepper and salt and gave it a quick fry. I have a bit below for myself. I've even poured myself a drop of wine. Why not?'

'Why not?' said Mimi, reaching out for her glass.

'I'll leave you in peace to eat it all up. Fuel. You know a good meal is fuel. We need that to keep going. I'll pop down and tuck into mine before it gets cold. Give me a little shout if there's anything you need.'

'We need to keep going,' repeated Mimi.

Mrs O'Brien gave a little shout of laughter and her teeth clattered.

In fact for a moment Mimi thought they were about to fall out.

'That's the ticket, Missis Pet. I'll leave the door open . . . then you . . .'

'Close it over, please,' said Mimi. 'Draughts.'

She spread the napkin over her chest and picked up her knife and fork.

Mrs O'Brien pulled the door to behind her.

'You can come out now, wherever you are.'

'What's that?' Mrs O'Brien shouted from the landing.

'Nothing, just a little ahnh ahnh anhn. Cough. Clearing of the tubes. Angh anghg. Thank you all the same.'

There was a little laugh from the window.

She looked across the room. He was standing between her bed and the window. Just the outline of a man. Bonnyface. She hoped it was Bonnyface and not the other. It had to be Bonnyface. The other would not have laughed like that. He had found little in his life to laugh at and Mimi presumed that he would find equally little in death. She watched the light fading; she watched the shadow become corporeal.

Bonnyface still held the glass in his hand.

'What a lady,' he said. 'She might be like my mother. I like to think that.' He walked towards her as he spoke. He waved the glass in his hand; the wine twirled up inside and then twirled down again as his hand moved. 'I like to think that there are still women in the world like my mother.' He laughed, throwing back his head with joy. 'My mother too, would have said that. There are times when I could set fire to myself. You are never thinking things like that.'

Mimi shook her head.

The fish was tasty. Mrs O'Brien was definitely handy with the frying pan.

He sat down on the end of the bed. She felt no weight, no shifting of the springs.

Mimi took a gulp of her wine.

'All right,' she said. 'So I wasn't happy. I pretended here, I pretended there. What was wrong with that? Why do you want such nonsense out in the open?'

'It's good housekeeping.'

She looked at him and laughed and then finished the wine in her glass.

'More,' she said like a child.

He bent down and took the bottle of Vino Nobile from the floor by the bed. He reached over and filled her glass almost to the brim.

'Aaah,' she said with pleasure as she watched the wine splash into the glass. 'I was never a good housekeeper, even at the best of times.'

He nodded and held his glass up towards her.

'Cheese,' he said.

'Cheers,' she corrected him.

'Cheers. Three cheers.'

They drank.

'Well?' The word came out of her mouth like a small explosion. She took the corner of the napkin and wiped her mouth. 'I want to know why you have upset me by exposing me to that man. That dead man. I have not felt right in the head since he appeared. I thought you were what you said you were . . . an angel . . . a guardian. Now you seem to have some connection to him. I find that quite disagreeable. I do have to say that.'

The wine was oiling her vocal chords. She felt the syllables slipping from the darkness of her throat and through her mouth with a speed and ease that was not normal for her. She held the napkin to the side of her face as if she might have to catch an overflow of words that might spill out across her chin and down her neck.

'I have to say that. I do not like being upset. I have never liked being upset. If you have come here to upset me then I would like you to go away. I would rather be by myself. Alone. I would rather be alone. Yes. Alone. Even, even, even . . .'

She stopped and stared at him. She wasn't quite sure any longer which of them it was.

'Even,' she whispered and put the glass down on the tray.

There was a long silence; a drift of music from the TV downstairs; someone a few gardens away calling to a child for bedtime.

The man, whoever he was, got up from the bed and lifted the tray from her knees and carried it across the room to the table.

'Even what?'

'Every bit of furniture in this room belonged to my mother and father.' She thought for a moment. 'Not this bed. No. I bought this bed for myself about twelve years ago. Some demon of extravagance took hold of me.' She giggled. 'Long before you came into my life. I've always had a weakness for spending money.' She looked past him, out of the window. She wondered to herself what she was talking about, and then remembered.

'Even . . . She'll eventually put me in a home, you know. That's just common sense really. She will have to do that. I can see the necessity for that.'

There was a roar of laughter from the TV and then applause.

'Well, what I was really trying to say was that I'd rather suffer that solitude, that indignity than have you and that dreadful man upsetting me.' She reached out and touched his hand.

'It's not you, Bonnyface. I love you. You make me feel good, but I think that maybe you're in cahoots with him. You'd better give me another glass of wine. Maybe my wine-drinking days are numbered.'

'I have never heard of cahoots,' he said as he got up to fetch her glass from the tray.

'Plotters. Are you a plotter, Bonifacio? Were you a plotter in your youth? Does it come naturally to you? Thanks.'

She took the glass from his hand. His fingers lingered on hers, spreading that warmth into her bones that she had come to expect from contact with him.

'Don't bother to answer that,' she said, before he had time to open his mouth.

'I am all betrayers.' He spoke the words in such a matter of fact way that she thought she hadn't heard him correctly.

'What an odd thing to say. I don't quite grasp what it means. Can you explain? How can you be all betrayers? That's such a silly thing to say.' Her voice was angry. 'You're not supposed to be upsetting me. I am all betrayers, indeed. If you had an air you could sing that.'

She took a gulp of wine and closed her eyes.

There was total silence.

A laugh came bubbling up from her gut and an air.

*Voi ché sapete.*

Good old Mozart, never lets you down.

'I am all betrayers, all betrayayayers.'

She slitted her eyes and peeped towards him through her lashes. He sat there, weightless, looking at his hands, a slight smile on his face.

'You know,' he said, after she had stopped singing. 'I

probably would have loved you. I loved my wife, but I would have betrayed you, as I betrayed her. I would have enjoyed that. I enjoyed the deceptions, the lies, subterfuges, whatever you like to call them. I got so much pleasure from the energetic betrayal of my wife.'

'And she . . . ?'

He shrugged. He raised his hands and held them out towards her. 'I think she was not happy.'

'I presume she was faithful to you.'

'I would have killed her if she had not been.'

Mimi sighed.

'I didn't mind about her happiness until that last moment as I watched her trying to move the air in the room with her hands and then I thought, how sad, just for pleasure, to have caused her such pain. A passing thought. It was too late for more than that.'

'I think I will never understand men. I was brought up to believe that to make a man happy, to keep him by your side in utter content, you only had to manifest your love for him in the most comfortable and charming ways possible.' She sighed again. 'Maybe I wasn't listening correctly. Maybe I misinterpreted my own parents' marriage.' Again she had that little flash of her father singing in the garden and then thought with irritation that she should have in her mind somewhere more than one memory of her mother and father. 'They seemed to have a perfect relationship. I think perhaps that I was too self absorbed to understand anything about them. I wanted so much to live happily ever after.'

Bonifacio reached out for the bottle and poured them each another glass of wine.

'I never asked for more than that,' she said.

They sipped their wine in silence.

'He didn't seem to want anything I had to offer. Anything.' She gave a little giggle. 'Anything, you know what I mean?'

He nodded.

The room was almost dark by now.

The moon was becoming visible, still coloured though with evening warmth.

'Hold my hand,' she commanded. 'I have no pain when you hold my hand.'

He put his hand on hers. She gave a little laugh.

'Maybe we could have had a little romp. I think I would have liked that. I always wanted to do that, but never had the courage. He knew. He knew that I eyed men with that in mind and though he didn't want me himself he wouldn't have countenanced that. Like you. He wouldn't have killed me, but perhaps he might have killed himself. That is comfortable, your hand on mine. How wonderful at this stage in my life to feel love for an angel. I think I may go asleep now. I am tired today.'

A little comforting laugh. He stroked her fingers. His face glimmered, pale as Benjamin's had been, deep furrows from forehead to chin; little fires sparked in his eyes. The glass toppled in her hand and she felt the softness of the wine flowing across her wrist, staining the sheet. Staining her nightdress and staining the sheet, she thought as she drifted into sleep. What will they say about this?

Blackness. No moon edging in, lighting corners with its cold beam. I have never liked the moon all that much. Never could sleep with the moon on my face. Never could face the cold moon. Never really found it romantic. Never could. Never . . .

Grace closed the door softly behind her and kicked off her shoes. Her feet seemed to grow several sizes larger with relief. They spread comfortably on the cool floor. She dumped her bag on the end of the stairs and went into the kitchen to get herself a glass of wine from the fridge. As she walked across the kitchen, Mrs O'Brien's note in the middle of the kitchen table caught her eye. Large blue letters straggled on the white paper; her best paper, she noted, taken from her desk drawer; headed, thick, expensive paper for writing letters to posh managements: the RSC, the National, producers, directors and theatrical knights and dames. One of her minor follies. I am someone, she sometimes thought, when she took a piece of that paper from the drawer. Only sometimes, of course; the rest of the time she laughed internally at her folly. Anyway, Mrs O'Brien was no one to be swayed by such foolishness. A piece of paper was a piece of paper to her. Grace picked it up and walked with it in her hand to the fridge. She opened the door and took out a bottle of white wine. Perhaps, she thought, bottle in one hand, letter in the other, a cup of tea might be more sense.

Oh, fuck sense. She took a glass from the cupboard and sat down at the table. She poured a glass of wine and put the letter carefully down in front of her, for some reason squaring the edge up with the edge of the table.

She took a drink and let the cool wine refresh for a moment or two the inside of her mouth, stale with cigarette smoke and too many words.

*Dear Mrs Grace, as per usual I took her up her supper on a tray. She ate the lot, a nice bit of fried fish like you said. I left her to her own devices, the poor woman was worn out by all that walking or whatever you did during the day. When I went up to get her tray and tuck her up for the night, taking you at your word that I could go at half ten she had poured wine all over herself, sheets and blanket included and was asleep or passed out, I wouldn't know which. I don't know where she got the wine I gave her the one glass of white on her tray as per you said I should. I didn't want to wake her so I have not changed her bedding. She looked quite happy I just slipped out and left her in peace. I hope I did the right thing. She had a little smile on her face and wasn't snoring or anything like that. There was a bottle by the side of the bed and I put it in the bin I'll see you tomorrow all things being equal.*
*Yours sincerely Mrs J O'Brien.*

Whatever that means. All things being equal. Most of the time things are pretty bloody unequal.

She went over and looked into the bin. Plonked down into the plastic bin liner was a bottle. She stuck her finger in the top of it and pulled it out.

Vino Nobile di Montepulciano.

She dropped it back in again and slammed the door of the bin cupboard.

'I feel a bit inadequate,' she said aloud.

She looked at her glass of wine on the table and decided she didn't need it. She picked it up and poured it down the sink and then went around the kitchen turning off the lights.

This has all got to be sorted out.

Moonlight shone on shining taps and glass doors.

All, she thought, it all has to be sorted out. After the first night, she thought, all things being equal.

As she passed Mimi's door on the way up to her room, she paused for a moment. She heard no sound, no cause for alarm, unless silence was one. Quietly she turned the handle and opened the door a crack; she heard the gentle rise and fall of breath.

'Sweet dreams,' she whispered. Gently she closed the door and went on upstairs.

The telephone began to ring as she approached her room. She turned and went into the bathroom. She turned on the taps, she flushed the loo, then brushed her teeth and washed her hands and face; by the time she had finished all that the ringing had stopped and then she went to bed.

Again and again she couldn't sleep.

She would get to the edge and then voices tumbling in her head called her back again to wakefulness. Mimi, Polly. *Confess yourself to heaven; repent what's past; avoid what is to come.* Paul. And for some inexplicable reason the sound of her father's laughter punctuating the words in her head. He had so seldom laughed. Way back when she had been a child maybe . . . yes, yes, for sure, not exactly light-heartedly, more a sober laugh. There, the sound passed for a moment by her ear, then words, more words. *Be thou assured, if words be made of breath, and breath of life, I have no life to breathe what thou hast said to me.* And Paul. Mrs O'Brien is sitting at the table scratching away on the wood with a bright blue pen. That must mean that I am asleep. Mimi is asleep. Polly is asleep and Paul is singing, *all I do the whole day through is dream of . . . The Queen carouses to thy fortune, Hamlet.*

She got up at about six thirty, feeling like death warmed up, and put on her bathing togs and, over them, her dressing gown. Barefoot, she ran down the stairs and out of the door.

She knew, she had been told so many times, that it was dangerous to drive in her bare feet, but what the hell.

The air was cool and the sun was just beginning to rise, casting long shadows on the silent roads that curled down towards the sea. She drove in the middle of the road, frisking the tail of the car round the corners like a racing driver. 'Stirling Moss,' she sang aloud. 'I'm the tops. Jacques Villeneuve. I'm the tops. Mike Hawthorn. I'm the tops. Rudolf Caracciola.' She couldn't think at that moment of the names of any more racing drivers. She narrowly missed a milkman in an electric van as she swung into the car park above the beach.

The tide was out and the sand was cold and gritty. The usual early morning birds, oyster catchers she thought they were, pecked delicately for worms at the sea's edge. An early train moved towards the city and out on the horizon, silhouetted against the golden sun, the usual boat was heading for England. Everything was as it ought to be; the same as yesterday and the day before. She glanced back towards the beach before throwing herself forward into the water and saw a man, like her father, walking along on the dry sand, his hands behind his back, his shoulders slightly hunched. She swam parallel to the shore, as she knew she should. Maybe he was one of Mimi's hallucinations, maybe an innocent beachwalker. She wondered idly about hallucinations, ghosts, figments, Hamlet's father, *I am thy father's spirit, doomed for a certain term to walk the night* . . . et cetera, et cetera. I don't believe in spirits, phantasms.

The man on the beach had disappeared when she turned back. She swam to the shore and ran to where her dressing gown lay and crossed the tracks of his human feet, size eleven trainers, going down the beach towards Bray and coming back again. Palpable footmarks. In about half an hour the water would cover them. Size eleven trainers . . . phhht!

She drove home with sobriety. The milkman was halfway up the hill as she went past. He waved at her. She raised a finger from the steering wheel in acknowledgment.

Mimi was on the telephone in the kitchen when Grace arrived. Her nightdress was stained with what looked like blood, but then Grace remembered the Vino Nobile.

'It's Polly.'

Mimi held the telephone at arm's length towards Grace. 'She didn't wake me up. I was all ready down here, about to make myself a cup of tea. You woke me up, leaving the house at that unearthly hour. I heard you.'

Grace took the phone from her.

'Darling. Hello. Are you all right?'

'You slammed the door,' said Mimi.

There was silence at the other end of the line.

'Polly? Are you there?'

'Of course she's there,' said Mimi.

'Yes.' Polly's voice was very low. 'Where on earth were you? I rang at this hour because I thought I'd be sure to get you. I rang last night and no one answered.'

Grace felt instantly guilty.

'I was afraid that something might have happened.'

'No. Nothing. Preview last night. This morning I was swimming. Are you all right? I have been worrying about you.'

'If you really want to know I feel bloody awful. I can't get my head together at all. I can't remember when your first night is. I just wanted . . .'

'Tomorrow.'

'Well . . . to wish you luck. We were going to come . . . he and I . . .'

'Darling . . .'

'Surprise you . . . He booked the tickets and . . .'

'Don't upset yourself. It's so nice of you to ring. I really appreciate that.'

'He . . .'

'Yes?'

'. . . had booked the . . .'

'Yes. You said.'

There was a long pause.

'I keep crying.'

At this moment, Mimi, who had been fumbling in the

fridge, dropped a jug of milk on the floor. The jug broke most gracefully in four pieces and a few slivers, and the milk began to spread across the tiles.

'Mimi . . .'

'I'm so sorry . . .'

'Mum . . .'

'. . . my dear. My hands . . .'

'Hang on a second, Polly.'

'. . . don't work very well these days.'

'Mum . . .'

'Mimi, sit down. I'll deal with it in . . .'

'Mum . . .'

'Yes, darling. In a minute. Mim, sit down.'

'I'll . . .'

She looked like some heroine of Grand Opera, standing there, Grace thought, hair uncombed and bloodstained gown, her fairly useless hand raised slightly in the air.

'Mum . . .'

'Sit down, darling Mim, please do sit down. Sorry, Polly. I'm with you now. What were you saying?'

'Nothing.'

'I'm sorry, darling. Mimi dropped the milk jug. Nothing serious. A little minor drama.'

She smiled across the room at Mimi.

'Drama, drama, drama. So what's new? I'm talking to you about something serious. My life. Your daughter's life, and Mimi drops the milk jug. So what's more important to you, your daughter's life or a bloody milk jug?'

Wham.

Grace looked at the dead receiver in her hand. It is much more fun, she thought, to slam a door than a telephone receiver. She hung up and looked at Mimi.

'She's upset,' she said.

Mimi nodded. 'It's that man. Whatsisname. The man she shouldn't have got engaged to.'

'I've never been much help,' said Grace.

She got a floor cloth out from under the sink and a bucket and a plastic bag to put the broken china in. 'Out of the sea and into a milk jug.' She got down on her knees and began to clean up the mess. 'Why don't you go up and get dressed? You look as if you'd been stabbed.'

Mimi patted at the stain.

'I really don't remember . . . I was talking one moment and then . . .'

'Talking?'

Mimi moved slowly towards the door. 'You never believe me when I tell you, so I won't say a word. I will keep my lip buttoned.'

'Suit yourself,' said Grace, squeezing milk into the bucket.

'We all do that really, don't we?'

Grace caught a little sliver of china on the end of a finger and a bubble of blood appeared. It didn't look at all like wine.

'Bugger,' she said. 'What a way to start a day.'

In the end of all the day wasn't bad.

Grace cut the grass, pushing the lawn mower, tick tack

across the lawn and back again, the lines quite straight; Father might have approved.

She clamped Hamlet firmly into the front of her mind and thought only in little word bursts of the play.

Mimi sat under the magnolia tree, sometimes with her eyes closed, sometimes with them open but not seeing the garden around her. There were no manifestations, no unsober moments, no scowls, no ugly silences.

At about five thirty they ate scrambled eggs and bacon at the kitchen table.

'I wonder a lot about Gertrude,' said Grace to her mother.

'Gertrude? Oh yes, Gertrude. Sorry, dear I keep forgetting these days. All sorts of important things. Gertrude. What about Gertrude?'

'It's the half-good and half-bad thing I can't quite get a hold of. Did she connive at her husband's death? She was obviously having an *affaire* with Claudius, but how much did she know? Is she a murderess?'

'Do you have to know?'

'I should by now and I don't. We open tomorrow night, Mim, and I still haven't got the heart of the play. I'm all right but I am performing. I'm glossing over the heart of the person.'

'No one will know.'

'I will.'

'Does that matter? Aren't you just being a little . . .' She waved her fork in the air, unable to find the right word.

Grace waited to see what the word was going to be, but only silence hung between them.

313

'It's my truth and her truth,' Grace said eventually. 'If I can't get those two knitted together, then I'm a failure. I'm just someone doing what they're told to do.'

'Do you think Shakespeare knew?'

Grace laughed.

'*Ay, there's the rub.*'

She noticed for the first time how the fingers of Mimi's left hand seemed almost welded together. The hand lay on the table as if it was too heavy for her mother to pick up, made of lead, no longer flesh and bone.

'Sex,' said Mimi.

I wonder if she's had a little stroke? Maybe something like that is at the root of all this. The day after tomorrow . . .

'Sex,' repeated Mimi. 'Something you don't know very much about.'

'Come off it, Mim . . .'

'You married John because you thought he would keep you safe.'

Grace looked cross. Mimi leaned across the table and tapped her hand.

'Well? Didn't you?'

'I was in love with him.'

'Rubbish. You needed him at that moment in time. I always rather liked John. I probably liked him more than you did. You certainly weren't crazy wild about him.'

'Oh, Mim, for heaven's sake. Sensible people don't go crazy wild.'

'Yes, they do. That's Gertrude's problem. She's crazy wild

314

for Claudius. Not just in love and a bit confused . . . she's really . . . well, besotted. To the point of not seeing him clearly. I've seen the play umpteen times. I know I'm right. She can only see her own obsession. Until . . .' She sighed, a long deep sigh. 'Until.' She smiled one of her most charming smiles at Grace. 'It's amazing how tangled up we get with our children.'

She looked up quickly towards the window as if she had seen something there. Her face for a moment became quite without colour, as a cloud moved across the sun. Her head drooped and her voice was so low that Grace had to strain her ears to hear it.

'If it hadn't been for you I might have run away from all that hatred.'

'Mim, what was that? I didn't hear.'

'It was a foolishness, my dear. Just a foolishness.'

'What hatred? That was what you said, wasn't it? No one has ever hated you.'

'I perceived hatred. That's all. I'm tired. I get so tired and so confused these days. Go to work, my dear. Mrs O'B will be here soon. She will keep me safe.'

'Mim.' Grace got up from the table, making a list in her head as she spoke of all the things she needed to bring with her. Here we go again, Nurofen, Kleenex, toothbrush, Ballygowan fizzy water. That reminded her. 'There's to be no drinking bottles of wine and all that nonsense tonight. Just be as good as an angel. Please.'

'An angel.' Mimi laughed. 'There are bad angels as well as good ones, remember that.'

Grace kissed the top of her mother's head. There was a slight smell of mustiness from her thick hair.

'Just try and be a good one.'

Mrs O'Brien and her chatty tongue had gone, leaving the kitchen shining and Mimi sitting in the drawing-room by the window, a warm puff of a shawl tucked round her shoulders, a book that she wasn't going to read on the table by her side. She had refused to go to bed; refused with charm and a degree of firmness that had surprised Mrs O'Brien.

'I am not in the least tired,' she had said. 'I prefer to stay down here for a while. I will read my book. I may watch the television. I may just sit and think. I have a lot of things to think about. If I go to bed, I will merely fall asleep. That is not what I want at all.'

She gave a clear smile, a young beauty's truthful and illuminating smile, and Mrs O'Brien gave in.

'Suit yourself, Missis Pet. If that's the way you feel, I'm not going to have a row with you about it.'

After she had gone; after she had clicked the door shut and given it a little push just to make sure that the lock had clicked home; after she had clicked herself in her new high-heeled slingbacks down the path to the gate and then headed off up the road to the pub in the village at the top of the hill, where she planned to have a couple of quick gins before going home to either ignore or pacify the fellow and to bury away, at the bottom of a drawer where he couldn't find them, the crackling new notes that she was now receiving every day from Grace;

after all that, Mimi smiled again as Bonifacio strolled through the door.

'What have you been doing all day?'

She held her good hand out towards him. He bent and kissed it and she felt, as she had hoped, the surge of energy run through her body.

'Waiting for this moment, dear signora.'

'I made a mess of things yesterday, didn't I? Spilt wine all over the bed. Ridiculous thing to do. Were you there when I did that? Do I have you to blame?'

He laughed.

'No one was to blame. You just fell asleep.'

'I wasn't happy yesterday. I've got used, over the last few weeks, to feeling quite happy. Who are you?'

'Can I get you something? Coffee? Wine?'

She shook her head.

With great care she raised her left hand slowly, supporting its weight with her right hand.

'I can't use this hand any longer. That's a sign, you know. I have been waiting for such signs. I know that very soon Grace will call in the doctor and a whole programme of terrible things will happen. Hospital, tests, drugs, probes, nurses, whispering. All that sort of carry-on is guaranteed to frighten an old woman like me out of her wits. What use will you be to me then, you so-called angel? Answer me that.'

He shook his head.

He took her left hand between his two hands and held it.

She felt nothing, no warm flooding through her blood, no

tingling, not even the comfort of flesh on warm flesh.

'You disappoint me.'

'Why?'

'I thought maybe that you might have performed that small miracle.'

'I did warn you. Inconspicuous miracles are all I'm good for. I can't bring the dead back to life, or make the blind see.'

'No one can.'

He didn't say anything.

'Can they?'

He shook his head.

'I don't know.'

'In other words, you're a cod.'

He looked startled.

'I don't know what that is, a cod?'

'A fraud.'

'I'm just like you said, a messenger.'

'Well, I think it's time you delivered your message.'

She held up her good hand, like a policeman on point duty might have done.

'Just a minute before you say anything, if it's to do with . . . you know . . . death. Please remember what I said about the first night. Is that too much to ask?'

He let go of her hand and stood up.

'I could take you to the first night. That is the sort of magic I can do. Would you like that?'

She shook her head.

'Oh, God, no. I'm too old to see that play again. I'd like to go to the pictures though? How about that? We'd have to circumvent Mrs O'B though. I don't know how we'd manage that. Do you like the pictures?'

He spread his hands wide and smiled at her.

'I have never been.'

She banged her good hand on the table.

'Great. We'll do that. Tomorrow. You must work a miracle. We'll have supper out and go to the Forum in Glasthule. There's a film there Mrs O'Brien tells me would shock me. I can't remember what it's called, but I'd quite like to be shocked. Now, you must tell me your message. You can't get out of it that easily.'

He turned his head away and looked out of the window, or rather, it seemed to Mimi, he looked at the reflection of himself in the dark glass.

'Where is Benjamin?' She was watching his face in the window as she spoke.

He looked momentarily startled. 'Benjamin?'

'Yes. I know he's lurking somewhere, waiting to upset me. He was always trying to upset me.' She laughed briefly. 'He succeeded very well. I didn't demand anything from him. My expectations, like most of the women of my generation, were negligible; a family, a reasonable life, safety, with luck, for ever. In return we ran good homes, were loyal wives, loving mothers, smiled at the right people; we saw our men right. It sounds pretty despicable now, but then it was the natural scheme of things. Most of the time it worked all right. I thought he loved me. I thought that we would live happily ever after. I was wrong.'

319

She put her hand over her face so that he wouldn't see the tears that flooded from her eyes. He moved over to her and put his arm around her thin shoulders, she leaned her head against his chest and they sat in silence for a long time.

'How I hate people who moan,' she said at last.

He pulled her hand away from in front of her face and opening it out, pressed it against his face, absorbing her tears into his skin. He held her tight and she felt young again and as if the world was full of possibilities.

'He gave me one child as if it was a duty and then left me to all intents and purposes. He became obsessed with religion, with rules, with outward appearances. We had to appear perfect. I think he gave up loving me in case some of my imperfections would wipe off on him. Do you think that might be right?'

He kissed the palm of her hand and then touched her face. 'I don't think that could have been right.'

He ran a finger across her forehead, he smoothed her hair; age and time for a few moments meant nothing, her brittleness became subsumed into his warmth. Just her one hand remained cold, foreign, almost like a warning. How silly I was, she thought, not to go down this road before it became too late.

She pushed herself out of his embrace and settled herself more comfortably in her chair.

'We could have run away together, you and I,' she said. 'All those years ago. Where would we have run to, I wonder?'

He shook his head.

'I know nowhere. I never even went to Rome. I always wanted to travel to Rome and set up there in my trade, make beautiful shoes for all those rich people, and soft leather gloves and velvet purses for the ladies, glittering with jewels. No more did I get to Florence. Just imagine what it would have been like to have made just one pair of riding boots for Lorenzo di Medici.'

They both started to laugh, amused and also a bit embarrassed by such a flight of fancy.

'I think you'd better tell me whatever it is,' she said gently. 'Cough it up. Get it off your chest. Then we can be friends. I do have to say that I have really enjoyed the last couple of weeks. Thank you.'

'So have I.' He looked at her thoughtfully for a moment. 'Yes,' he said at last. 'You're right, it is Benjamin. I told you that day in the garden. I told you that I heard his voice calling me. Now, I assure you, my dear lady.' He leant forward and took her hand once more. 'I assure you that I have no idea why he called to me. I merely obeyed the impulse of his voice.'

'So I have to wait until it suits him to tell me what all this is about.'

'I'm afraid so. Yes.'

The telephone rang. They both jumped as its strident tone hit the silence of the room. Mimi got up slowly and crossed the room. She picked up the receiver.

'I hate people who ring late at night or early in the morning,' she said across the room to Bonifacio. 'I'm always afraid they're going to say something I don't want to hear. Hello?'

There was only silence, the silence of someone holding their breath, the silence of expectancy.

'Hello. Hello,' she said, encouragingly.

There was a breath of a sigh and then a click as whoever it was at the far end put down the receiver. Mimi hung up.

'You know,' she said to Bonifacio, 'I think Grace has a lover. Not of course that it's any of my business.'

She looked past him at the window, at the reflection in it of the old woman and the angel, lit warmly by low lamps, and someone else, standing slightly behind her and to the left between her and the door. A shadow almost. She wondered was it possible to see the reflection of a shadow. I suppose, she thought, that with ghosts, spirits, angels and that sort of thing, anything was possible; no rules applied.

'I see you there lurking, at the corner of my eye, so I do. Are you waiting your turn to speak, or merely snooping? Huh?' Anger made her voice shrill for a moment. 'Why can't you rest peacefully in your grave like most people do? Maybe I should have had you cremated, but we weren't allowed that right in this country then. Anyway it probably wouldn't have pleased you. I did try very hard to please you. First of all because I loved you and then later because it seemed the proper thing to do.'

She turned back towards Bonifacio.

'I don't want to talk to him now. The daytime is best. Now, I feel tired and in a fearful muddle. I think I need my head clear to cope with him. To understand him. Are you listening, Benjamin? Are you getting my message?'

Suddenly the room was empty; the window only reflected one old lady, stooped, one hand hanging quite helplessly by her side.

There was the sound of the key turning in the front door.

'Damn,' muttered Mimi.

The door opened and Grace came in to the house. She dropped things on the hall floor, a bag, a coat, several books, a pair of shoes, a sponge bag, the *Irish Times*; they all spewed across the floor.

'All the lights in the house are on,' she called as she stepped through her own debris. 'Why? Is there some sort of a crisis?' She came round the corner into the sitting room. 'Mim! What on earth are you doing up? It's almost twelve. Are you all right?'

'I am all right.'

'You ought to be in bed. Why did Mrs O'B not tuck you up before she left?'

'I didn't want to be tucked up, thank you. How was . . .' she thought for a moment, and frowned slightly, '. . . the show? The . . . *Hamlet*?'

'Pretty bloody awful. I really hate previews. Neither one thing nor the other shows. That's what they seem to be. Dodgy. Come on, darling, it's time for bed. Let me give you a hand.' She put an arm around her mother's shoulder and began to draw her towards the stairs. Mimi moved with her, uncomplaining, thankful in fact for the support of her daughter's arm. They moved slowly and silently up the stairs. At the top Mimi moved away from Grace's protection.

My mother looks so small, thought Grace. How is it that I have kept my eyes shut for so long? Small, frail, a bit crazy. She is under my protection now. I am becoming the mother, she the child.

'It'll be all right, Mim. We'll both be all right.' She wondered if they were the right words to say.

Mimi turned and shuffled towards her bedroom door.

'Yes. Once I hear what your damn fool father has to say, I'll be all right sure enough.' She stopped and looked back at Grace. 'After all I have only one way to go.' She pointed into the darkness of her bedroom. 'By the way, someone telephoned.'

She laughed a little inside herself at the look of alarm on Grace's face.

'Who . . . ?'

'The same one. The one that rings in the middle of the night. Not a word was spoken, but I knew.'

She went in to her room and closed the door.

'It was probably a wrong number.' Grace said the words loud and clear and went back downstairs to turn off the lights.

Carefully Mimi got out of her clothes, unbuttoned, unwrapped, unfastened; she bent and stretched, folded her sleeve slowly down over her useless arm, wondering as she did so if she should take the rings from her wedding finger; thought, not really, where was the point?

She washed her face and teeth and put cream on her face. That was perhaps a little absurd, she thought, as she felt the scented cream sink down through her pale skin. I like that feeling; it is, though, an optimistic gesture. At last she switched off the light and lay her head back amongst the pillows. Moonlight, cold and clearly, lay in a stripe across her bed, the rest of the room was dark. Her hands lying outside the bedclothes were silver, each gnarl and wrinkle carved with skill. As her eyes began to close she felt someone gently take her right hand and hold it, her fingers intertwined, in his. There was nothing left for her to do but sleep.

Rain came the next day; scudding up the coast driven by a sharp south-easterly wind. The landscape became shadowy green and turbulent as the wind stretched the branches, and bent the tall palm trees in the normally sheltered gardens on the hillside above the sea. The sea and clouds reflected each other; there seemed to be no horizon, just the grey swelling of cloud and water, merging together.

Grace was awakened by the rattling of rain on her window. The sun had been with them for so long that it took her several moments to recognise the sound. The curtains were flapping into the room and raindrops were splattering the floor. She got out of bed and closed the window.

No swimming. Bad start to day.

She leaned her head against the window-pane and stared down through the bursting rain into the garden. Albertine looked as if she might be blown off the wall. Must get up a ladder sometime and . . . and what? Hammer nails into the wall? Tie twigs with bits of green string?

Father would have known. He wouldn't just have known, he'd have done it. He'd have been up there on his ladder, snip, snip, snipping, his face unsmiling. His sense of order had never been dented, even at the worst of times.

She wondered about him. Is he here in this house, upsetting

Mimi? What bloody awful headaches he must have carried in his head as well as his anger, his piety, his black silence. All the things he didn't allow himself to think about.

Ay, there's the bloody rub.

Quickly she thought of Charlie, breakfasting in bed, alone, she presumed, in the Shelbourne Hotel; reading the *Irish Times*, the theatre reviews in the quality English papers, telephoning his friends, networking, setting up his future life in Australia ... heck! For a moment the sliding drops formed a likeness on the glass, the glimmer of Paul's eyes as he stared at her through the window of the car. Heck!

I am going potty, like Mim.

Why do things explode?

Why can't we just lead quiet lives and get on with our jobs? Get on with living and dying?

I am not going potty. I am suffering from pre-first-night stress. I am not thinking at all about that blasted boy. And anyway why has he not rung me up to wish me luck? I want him to do that. Just to show there's no hard feelings. I don't want there to be hard feelings. I want us both to ... Oh fuck! She laughed aloud. Yes, unfortunately ... all things being equal ... I want him to ring me up, nothing to do with good wishes, nothing to do with hard feelings, I want to hear the sound of the little bastard's voice.

She remembered a prayer suddenly that had been part of her childhood learning ... *Oh God, unto whom all hearts be open, all desires known and from whom no secrets are hid.* That was how it had started. I do not want to be burdened as my father was burdened, by a secret that I cannot face. If You exist, and Mimi would deny Your existence most vehemently, scrub my heart and soul and body clean of this insidious longing. I'm not like him. I don't want this to be happening to me. I want rid of all thoughts, pure or impure of that . . . Paul.

She waited for a few minutes, her mind a blank, just the sound of the rain in her ears and the impatient tapping of Albertine on the window. God did not speak, nor did the telephone ring. Exasperated with herself, she put on her dressing gown and went to get the breakfast.

She didn't get dressed until it was time to go to the theatre. Where was the point?

No reason to put a nose outside the door on a day like this.

Mimi sat in front of the television set, sometimes alert, sometimes nodding into a half-sleep from which she would awake with a little start.

Grace went about her household chores in her bare feet; beds, clean the bath, wash up the breakfast things, make coffee, read the paper, muttering in her head as she moved around the house, Gertrude from her first words . . . *Good Hamlet, cast thy nighted colour off, and let thine eye* . . . to the last, *Oh my dear Hamlet . . . oh my dear Hamlet* . . . stare into fridge, more coffee, try to read a book, cook lunch and prepare supper for Mrs O'B and Mimi, answer the occasional questions thrown to her by Mimi, answer the telephone, her heart thudding with fear each time she ran to answer it.

Polly.

'Mum.'

'Darling.'

'Sorry about yesterday. I'm just in a bit of a state. Good luck. Oh golly, I wish I was there with you. Are you okay? Are you, Mum?'

'I'm fine, darling. Thanks for ringing.'

'Dad wants a word.'

'Grace?'

'Hello, John.'

'Good luck. Break a leg and all that.'

'Thanks.'

'We'll all come over and see it. Poor Poll's in a bit of a state at the moment. Bloody actors. Ha ha. No offence meant.'

'Oh, John . . .'

'I know how you're feeling old thing, all tensed up. I remember. I'll not drone on. We'll be over though when things settle down. Look forward to that. Kiss, kiss.'

'Thank you.'

'Love to Mimi.'

'I'll tell her.'

'John sends his love,' she said to Mimi.

'I always liked John. Polly's very like her father.'

'Am I very like my father?'

Mimi looked at her.

'Why do you ask?'

'Just natural curiosity. I don't really remember him very well.'

'You look quite like him. Same nose. Same colouring. He was a good-looking man.'

She returned her concentration to the television.

'I was thinking more about personality, character.'

'This man is teaching me how to stuff red peppers. It's very interesting.'

Charlie.

'Morning, my darling, or is it afternoon? I am spending the day in bed.'

'Hello, Charlie.'

'Why get up, I said to myself, on a day like this?'

'Why indeed?'

'Are you all right?'

'I'm fine.'

'Mimi behaving?'

'We're all fine.'

'You're a star.'

'So are you.'

'Just checking. See you this evening. Love you, doll.'

'Go back to sleep.'

'Charlie,' said Mimi. 'Did he ask after me?'

'Yes.'

'Pity he's queer.'

'I don't think it bothers him.'

'He'd have been a nice man for you.'

Agent from London.

'Gracie?'

'Henry. Hate being called Gracie. Please don't call me Gracie just before a first night.'

'Sor-ee. Just ringing to wish you all the best. We sent you a collective message to the theatre, but just in case it doesn't arrive, good luck, good luck.'

'Thank you, collectively. I hope it arrives. I do like lots of messages to stick around my dressing room. I feel as if it's Christmas and everyone loves me.'

'Talking of which, Arkadina is coming up roses. It's a big yes, yes. We'll get down to brass tacks after tomorrow, but this is just to make you feel good. I'll be over at the weekend to see the show, we'll talk about it then. So smile, Gracie. I mean Grace.'

Silence.

'You don't say anything.'

'I've lost my voice. Are you pulling my leg?'

'Why would I do a thing like that? I'll see you on Saturday. Lunch in the Shelbourne at one. Collective love, darling. Bye.'

'And who was that?'

'Henry.'

'Henry?'

'Agent Henry. Just wishing me luck.'

She went across the room and kissed her mother.

'I do wish you felt up to coming.'

'Fiddledy dee.'

'I really mean it.'

'I have other plans.'

Grace looked alarmed.

'Mim . . .'

'Nothing for you to worry about.'

'Mim, I don't want you to go upsetting Mrs O'B. We really need her, you know. If we didn't have her around, we might have to think about tiresome alternatives. You know what Doctor . . .'

'Run along and have your bath. I'm not going to upset any-one. I promise you. I might go to the pictures. There's something at the Forum that Mrs O'Brien recommends. We might go to that. I haven't made my mind up yet. Things are a bit tense around here, Mrs O'Brien says it would take me out of myself.'

Grace stood silent and confounded, staring at her mother.

'You must admit,' said Mimi.

'Admit what?'

'Tense. I am not a fool. I am not losing my mind. Nothing like that. I just want to have a bit of fun. Before . . .' She stopped. She stared defiantly at Grace. Then, after a long silence she repeated the word. 'Before.'

Grace cleared her throat.

'Yes, well . . .' She paused for a moment. 'Look here, Mim, I have to go and have my bath, I know I have been pre-occupied. I know . . . well, we'll get everything sorted out tomorrow or the next day. We'll talk about . . . well . . . we'll talk about everything then, but I do have to ask you not to do anything silly tonight. I don't think I could cope with that worry on my mind. We'll go to the pictures if you really want to tomorrow afternoon, or . . . we'll ask Charlie to come. We'll have lunch out and then . . .' She pulled herself together and looked her mother in the eye. 'Promise me, Mim, that you won't go out tonight. Promise me that you'll stay here with Mrs O'B. Please. Otherwise . . .' She couldn't think otherwise what. 'Please.'

Mimi sighed.

'Very well dear, if you insist. It will mean though that I have to have a conversation with your father that I feel a bit ambivalent about. You know, I need to know and I don't need to know. I do not like being bullied, my dear, but as it's your first night . . .'

'Oh God, I'm sure I've forgotten my lines.'

'Don't be silly, dear,' said Mimi.

'I don't think you handled that very well.'

It was several hours later and Mimi had just finished her grilled lamb chops and mashed potatoes, with a small plate of lemon meringue pie to follow. Her coffee was on the table by her hand and Mrs O'B was watching *Brookside* in the kitchen.

The curtain would just have gone up, thought Mimi, Grace would be on stage by now, transformed, and soon the first night would be over.

Bonifacio walked from the darkness of the hall across the room to where she was sitting. He stood looking down at her, then he took off his hat and laid it beside him on the table and smoothed at his dark shining hair with a hand.

'I don't think you handled that very well.' He smiled at her. 'I was rather looking forward to going to the cinema. I was looking to performing my little miracle. I get a great sense of well-being from performing little miracles.'

'You heard?'

'I hear most things.'

'Yes, I knew the moment after I'd said that, that I'd been rather foolish, burnt my boats, so to speak. I'm sorry.'

'Never mind.'

He had a bag slung over his shoulder, which he put now on the table beside his hat.

'You didn't promise not to have a drop of wine.'

'I did not, but what about . . . ?' She nodded her head towards the kitchen.

'There will be no problem. As long as you don't spill it all over the place again.'

She laughed.

He went over to the cupboard where the drinks were kept and took out two glasses and the corkscrew.

'That's *Brookside* over.' Mrs O'Brien put her head around the door. 'There's not much to it. Not near as good as *EastEnders*. *EastEnders* is more like real people and that. Are you all right there? More coffee?'

'No, thanks. I'm all right.'

Bonifacio stood quite still with the glasses and the corkscrew in his hand and a little smile on his face.

'I'm just going to pop up and give her room a good do. Shift the bed. That bed hasn't been shifted for ages. Hang up her clothes, she's a terror for leaving things lying. Unless you want the company? We could play a little game of cards if you liked?'

'Ah . . . no, thanks, Mrs O'Brien. I'm quite happy. I have a lot to think about.'

'That's all right then. You know where I am if you need me. Then before I go we'll have you tucked up in bed. Snug as a bug in a rug.'

She disappeared and Mimi could hear her bumping the terrible Hoover up the stairs.

Bonifacio put the glasses on the table and unwrapped the wine.

'How clever you are,' said Mimi.

Carefully he pulled the cork from the bottle and filled the two glasses. He handed one glass to Mimi.

She held it up to the light. 'It's like a glass full of jewels. Look at that. I feel drunk just looking at it.'

He clinked his glass against hers.

She raised the glass to her lips and took the merest sip and then put the glass down on the table.

'You know,' she said, 'things are going to change round here. After tomorrow. Do sit down, Bonnyface, you're making me nervous standing there. Sit here, close to me so that I can touch you if I want to. I have been through all this before, so many times.'

He pulled up a chair and sat so close that their knees were touching.

'She falls so eagerly into the rhythm of working; those voyages she makes. I don't mean physical voyages, though she makes them too, I mean each part she plays. Do you understand me? The whole pattern of her life exists in that world.'

She took another little sip of her wine, dipping her head forward to the glass as a bird might do. Her left hand lay dead in her lap. 'I watched her move away out of my world, with sadness, I do have to say, as I had no one then who might love me as I wished to be loved. I don't mean when she moved away from Ireland, but when I realised that neither Polly, nor I nor any man could ever mean as much to her as her work. That strange ephemeral work she does.'

She thought for a moment or two.

'After tonight she will coast along for a while, she will become for a while a normal person. She will worry about me and Polly; try to organise our lives so that we can all be content with each other and then, one day the hunger will start again and, she won't forget us, she never does that, but she will belong somewhere else.'

She became silent. Upstairs the Hoover hummed and Mrs O'Brien's footsteps were heavy.

'Old ladies like me can go on for years and years, you know. My left arm doesn't work any longer. You know that, don't you? That must mean something. God knows what will go next. There's not much point in worrying. I've had such fun over the last few weeks. Look at my lovely boots.'

She stuck her feet out towards the light.

'I've only taken them off to go to bed since the day I bought them. We could do lots more things like that? But we can't really, can we? Even now, she thinks odd things are happening in my head.'

She gave a little splutter of laughter.

'I suppose they are. But no more odd than Gertrude and all those other people she has floating inside her. Are you listening? Or have I sent you asleep with my wanderings?'

She looked outward from her thoughts and saw Benjamin

there, sitting knee to knee with her, a glass of Vino Nobile in his hand.

He put the glass down and leaning forward he took her hand between his two. She felt nothing.

'You can't work miracles,' she said.

He shook his head.

'I used to pray that I would be able to.'

'You weren't very nice the last time you manifested yourself. If you're going to be like that again, I'd rather you went away.'

He pressed her hand. His fingers were restless. She felt nothing, just saw his fingers moving on her flesh, his fingers encircling her wrist, touching her fingers, smoothing the pale dry skin.

'That was a speech you made.'

'So?'

He looked puzzled.

'What does so mean?'

'It's what they all say now. So? It's taken the place of strings of words. It needs a question mark after it. I think I meant, why are you questioning my right to make a speech?'

He put his glass down and clapped his hands.

'*Bravo*, Mimi.'

'Are you Benjamin or Bonnyface?'

He spread his hands wide, the gesture used by Bonifacio.

'At this moment I am Benjamin. That is all you need to know.'

'That's what you always thought. She doesn't need to know. What she doesn't know won't hurt her. Now you're playing more games with me. I do wish you wouldn't.'

She heard the slight sound of grievance coming into her voice and she stopped talking. She folded her lips neatly together and looked more closely at him. He was wearing that same suit, the grey flannel one that he had been wearing the last time he had appeared. She wondered what she had done with that suit all those years ago. St Vincent de Paul probably. She nodded to herself, yes, that was it. There had been so much stuff that they had come and collected it from her, hangers full of suits, and cardboard boxes of shirts and woollies. She had thrown away the intimate stuff and the things that smelt incurably of drink. Now he looked tired, pale, with deep circles under his eyes. She felt a little lurch of love in her heart, but she kept her lips folded.

They sat for a long time staring at each other, and the bumps and clatters of normal domesticity continued over their heads.

He spoke at last.

'I thought he would be more acceptable to you. I thought he was the sort of man that you would like; warm to. I thought . . .'

He cleared his throat and sat in silence again.

'I need you to help me. I need . . .'

'You look tired,' she said.

He nodded.

'Tired. Yes.'

'How can you be tired if you have been enjoying eternal rest?'

He didn't answer.

'I'm sorry,' she said. 'I know that frivolity always upset you. I will try to . . .'

'It's all right.'

'Bonifacio,' she said. 'You were telling me . . .'

'Yes. I just remembered the sort of men you used to like.'

'I used to like you,' she said softly.

'I thought that if I came. If I . . . You might not . . . You might have closed your eyes and ears to me. I thought that.'

He thought he had explained something to her.

'You never used to let me ask questions,' she said. 'You would brusquely wave me away when I did. Not now, you used to say, and I knew there was no point in asking when. What did I do to make you despise me? I'm asking that question now and I'd like an answer. Now. Not later.'

His eyes were a washed-out blue. She had remembered them as being brighter, snapping with anger, unwelcoming eyes.

'I never despised you. Not for one single second.'

'You could have fooled me,' she muttered under her breath.

'I'm going to make my speech now. It's the only way I can do this, Mimi; take a run at it, like a horse in a race, no matter if you win or lose, you have to get to the finish.'

She gave him a quick little smile, before folding her lips tight again.

'You said in your speech that no one loved you as you wished to be loved. That, I suppose was true enough, but I loved you. I really would like you to believe that. And I watched myself make you so unhappy. I couldn't bear that, but there wasn't anything I could do about that. That's what I thought. Now I see things very differently. I suppose there's no harm in telling you now the way I was, but I couldn't have done it then.'

He looked at her and said again, 'I need your help.'

'How can I help you, if I don't know what you're trying to tell me?'

But she put out her good hand and touched his face gently. 'Tell me,' she said. 'We no longer have anything to lose.'

'Once upon a time. Mimi, will I start by saying that? The good old formula.'

She nodded. 'I suppose it's as good a way as any.'

He closed his eyes and began almost to chant.

'Once upon a time there was this person ... man. I must say man. A man. He was a man and I was a man. We were no longer boys who didn't know what from what. We discovered that we loved each other.'

He paused and opened his eyes and looked at her.

She nodded again.

'It was the most hateful and the most wonderful thing that I had ever known. We tried not to meet, but we found that was impossible. We used to meet in all sorts of secret places. Sometimes horrible places. I remember so well the terrible fear of being discovered, the terrible humiliation of how we were compelled to behave. After love, I used to curse him. Stand in the middle of the floor and curse him, to his face. Blame him for the way I was and the way he was and swear that I would never see him again. Then, maybe a week or ten days would pass and we would find ourselves in the same room, we'd meet in the street maybe, or perhaps with friends. There were times, indeed, when I would try and engineer a meeting, without letting on to myself that that was what I was doing and we would start all over again. I used to pray that I would die. But when I was with him . . . you know what I mean . . . I wanted to live forever.'

He stopped and gave her a wry smile.

'That's the substance of it.'

She didn't say anything.

'Are you so shocked?'

I suppose I am, she said inside her head. Shocked that now, at this tailend moment of my life he could tell me this story, when he might have told me when we were young and had energy and might have cried together, or laughed at the foolishness of the world and love. I could have lived with that. I think. Once I had got used to the idea. That might have taken a long time, but I think I could have got used to it. We would have had a secret, he and I, instead of which, we had nothing.

He was waving a white handkerchief in front of her.

'Here,' he said. 'You're crying.'

She took it from him and wiped her eyes.

'I'm sorry,' she said. 'I'm very sorry.' She looked at the handkerchief: in one corner was the letter B, ornately curlicued and surrounded by a garland of flowers. She remembered stitching it for him, during her pregnancy, thinking as she worked on it, how it was too feminine a piece of decoration and that he wouldn't be able to use it in the office. 'You'd better tell me the rest of the story. Did this go on after . . . after we . . . ?'

'No, no. Of course it didn't go on. Nothing like that, ever. I promise you that. He went away. He gave me absolutely no warning. I suppose that was the right thing to do. But I didn't think so at the time. We drove out to the Pine Forest. It was a Sunday evening, I remember. He called for me at Mother's. He had this little Morris car. A funny little car with a leather roof and we puttered up there. Not many people went there in those days. We climbed up, sliding ... do you remember how you used to slide on all those needles, feet deep, centuries deep, almost to the top and we lay in a hollow under the trees. It was quite warm and the needles were dry and comfortable.' He gave a little laugh. 'Until you took your clothes off and then they stuck into you like little splinters. We lay there for a long time, and it got dark and he took my face between his two hands and he said, "Tomorrow, I'm going to England. Don't say a word," he said, "until I'm finished. I've got a job in the legal department of the British army and they're sending me out to Sicily to work in the military commission there. When the war is over I'm going to stay over there. I'm not coming back. I'm going to find myself a nice girl and get married and live a ... normal life. That's what I have to do. And you should do it too." He was crying as he spoke. We lay there until it was quite quite late, just holding each other and then we went home and I never saw him again.'

'Never?' A whisper from her.

'I heard of him from time to time. That was all. He did what he said he was going to do. Whether he was happy or not, I have no idea. No idea at all.'

'I can't think of anything to say. Why did you pick on me?'

'I was so lonely, so very unhappy, and burdened by all that façade of normality that I had to keep up. One part of me shouted that he was right, to be normal, to be like everyone else, that was where happiness had to lie. The other part just longed for him, to even be able to speak about him. Then, at that dance I saw you. You were so charming, Mimi, and so warm, I thought that I would be safe with you, just like I said.'

'It never occurred to you that maybe I might be better off with someone else. Someone . . .'

'No. My own safety was all I was thinking about. I . . . Well, we were happy for a while, weren't we?'

'Maybe you were, but I always had this feeling that something was wrong. If only you could have told me.'

'If I had you might have left me.'

'I might. I don't know. I didn't know too much about such things in those days.' She sighed. 'I don't really know much more now. But I do know that people have more open minds. I just would like to have known that you didn't hate me for some reason that I couldn't fathom; that you weren't running away from me. I wanted you to love Grace too.'

'My dear Mimi, I did. You were both my precious objects and I couldn't bear the thought that you might look on me with disgust.'

There was a rumbling and a slight crash from upstairs.

'What's that?'

Mimi began to laugh.

'It's Mrs O'Brien moving Grace's bed. She doesn't have much finesse. A bit Wagnerian.'

How daft that she should have said that. She remembered how much he had loved Wagner; the visits to Bayreuth; Benjamin enraptured by the music, his face losing its anger as he sat in the vast auditorium. But, now, to her surprise he laughed too.

'Thunderingly Valkyrian, really, I'd say. Not exactly the background music I would have asked for.'

The moment of laughter eased them both.

'I was so disgusted with myself,' he said. 'Neither prayers nor drink saved me from that disgust. And I saw what I was doing to you, how I was destroying your life and I thought, well, hell, why not? I am suffering so why shouldn't she? Why should anyone near me be happy?'

He looked anxiously at her.

'I have worn you out. Perhaps again I have misjudged things.'

'I'd love a cup of coffee. You were never able to turn your hand to such things. I presume . . .'

'I'm sorry. Have a drink instead.'

She shook her head.

'No. I'd rather not. You've given me rather a lot to think about. I must say you've lifted some burdens from my back, but maybe you've handed me other ones. I don't know yet. My head is aching.'

She put out her good hand and touched his face, unlike Bonifacio, his skin was cold. He put his cold fingers on hers and pressed them against his cheek.

'Mimi . . .'

Above them a door slammed and Mrs O'Brien's feet marched towards the stairs.

'Benjamin.'

He was no longer there. Her hand felt the cold imprint of his fingers. His handkerchief lay on her lap, and on the table lay Bonifacio's cap.

'That's a good job of work done.' Mrs O'Brien put her head round the door. 'The room is as good as new and I did her bathroom too. Are you all right, missis? I'll just wash my hands and then I'll make a cup of tea. Would you eat a samwidge? I'm going to have a samwidge. About this time of the evening I like something with a cup of tea. Carries you through the night.'

'Just a cup of tea would be lovely, thank you. I'll come to the kitchen and have it there with you.'

'Suit yourself. It'll be ready in two shakes of a lamb's tail.'

The head disappeared. Mimi folded the handkerchief carefully and put it in her pocket, then she got slowly up from her chair.

'Bonifacio,' she called softly. 'You've left your hat behind.' She wondered whether to put it away in a drawer, so that no one would see it and wonder about it, but then thought that the best thing to do was leave it where it was. She wanted to go to bed and when she reached the hall she started on that journey, up the stairs.

'Mrs O'Brien,' she called out as she put her foot on the bottom step. 'Mrs O'Brien.'

'What's that?'

'I think I'll go on up to bed. I'm really . . .'

Mrs O'Brien appeared at the kitchen door.

'. . . very tired.'

Mrs O'Brien bustled to her side and slipped an arm around her waist.

'I shoulda seen. You're grey with it. Just grey. I told her the other day I thought your colour was very bad. My old mother went like that. I knew when I seen her colour go the way it did that she wasn't long for this world. God rest her. I'll see you to your room so, and bring you up a nice cup to the bed. Then a good night's sleep and you'll be right as rain in the morning. There's nothing like a good sleep to get you back on form again.'

Up and up they went.

'I'll leave a note for her telling her that you're all safely tucked up. She likes the little notes I leave. She said that to me . . . oopsy daisy, up we go.'

It was over.

The dead had raised themselves up again and taken their curtain calls. They had bowed to the audience and to each other. They had held hands and bowed and bowed again. They had smiled and smiled and had finally left the stage.

Grace rubbed at her face with a bundle of tissues, up to where her hair was held back by a wide band and down around her neck. She always felt like a ghost after she had taken off her make-up, her face like some pale, wan thing in the mirror, no vitality, no character left.

Cards, flowers, telegrams were scattered round the room, giving me a headache, she grumbled to herself, throwing the tissues into the wastepaper basket and pulling some more out of the box. From everyone in the world, she thought, wishes, loving messages, kind words, remembrances; but nothing from that bastard, not a word, not a rose. Bastard. She took a deep breath and muttered in her head; asshole, dick head, mother fucker. That one stopped her short and she looked at herself in the glass.

'Well, he didn't fuck this mother,' she said aloud and then smiled rather dismally at herself.

There was a knock at the door.

'Who is it?' she called. She hated people coming to her dressing room after a show, preferring to meet friends in the bar when she had time to become herself once more. She gave a final rub to her face.

There was no reply.

She pulled the band off her head and began to brush her hair, counting to herself as she bent forward and brushed with long strokes.

One, two. I will then go home. Go to bed. Six, seven, eight. Put all these flowers in water, the house will be like a bloody undertaker's parlour. Fifteen. Why am I such a cranky bitch? Twenty. Maybe if the rain has stopped I might have a swim. That thought pleased her. Twenty-four, twenty-five. She sat upright and shook her hair which stood out round her head, stiff with static electricity. There was a slight sound behind her. She turned, instinctively putting up a hand to try and control her hair. He was standing by the door.

'Oh . . . oh . . . I . . .'

She got unsteadily to her feet.

'I thought . . .'

He moved slowly towards her.

'You know,' he said in a conversational way. 'You're just as beautiful as I remembered.'

He stood in front of her quite close, not touching.

'What on earth are you doing here?'

'First night. Remember? I came to see you.' He laughed uneasily. 'I had tickets for Polly and me and then . . . well, I came on my own. I had that accusatory empty seat beside me all through the show. Are you pleased to see me? Perhaps I shouldn't ask.'

'Yes.'

He put a hand out to touch her and then froze, hand midair.

'Will you hit me?' he asked anxiously.

She shook her head. 'Probably not.'

He took her hand in his and gently kissed her knuckle bones.

'I wish you hadn't come,' she lied.

'You're trembling.'

'I'm tired. I'm rotten tired, Paul. I . . .' She pulled herself together and snatched her hand away from him. 'Let's get out of here. We've got to talk. You gather all the flowers up, would you? I have to bring them home for Mim to see.' She slipped her feet into her shoes. 'And the cards. Bring the cards too. Now where the hell's my mac? Well get out as fast as we can.'

The door opened and Charlie put his head into the room.

'I know you hate people in your dressing room, darling, but I heard voices and . . . well, well! Look who's here.'

'Good evening, Charlie,' said Paul. 'Great performance.'

'That's more than he's said to me,' said Grace. She stood somewhat aggressively with her coat on and her bag over her shoulder, waiting for him to go away.

'Thank you, dear boy,' said Charlie. 'What did you think of our hero?'

'Not now, Charlie. We're going. I promised . . .'

'I thought we might have crossed the road and had a sordid drink in the Tide, but . . .'

'I promised Mimi that I'd . . .'

'. . . you seem to be otherwise . . .'

'. . . Mim, that I'd go straight home. So . . .'

'. . . occupied.'

'. . . another night, Charlie. Another night.' She moved towards him, her eyes staring straight into his. 'Charlie.'

'I'm going. You leave me no alternative. I'll have to go and mingle.'

'Charlie.'

He smiled at her and nodded. He made a movement with his hand as if he were cutting his throat and then left the room without another word.

'Can you manage all those? My car's in the lane. We'll go out the stage door and avoid the crowd in the bar. Come on.'

It had stopped raining and the air was mild and still.

They packed the flowers into the back of the car without speaking and without speaking she manoeuvred the car out of the lane and over Matt Talbot bridge and left down along the quay.

'Did you promise Mimi that you'd go straight home?' he asked at last.

'No.'

'Will I talk about the play or about us?'

'There is no us, Paul. There will be no us.'

She turned right, narrowly missing a lorry that was parked without lights beside the old gas-yard wall.

'Would you let me drive?'

'I have never had an accident. I've told you before. I don't know why everyone goes on at me about my driving. I have driven for nearly thirty years. My licence is uncontaminated. My no claims bonus is intact.'

'There's a first time for everything.'

'I have driven in France, Italy,' she veered over onto the right-hand side of the road, 'America . . . all over the place. I have survived.'

'Grace . . .'

And then veered back again.

'Where are we going?'

She nodded towards the hills ahead of them, not too far away.

'Somewhere we won't be interrupted by Charlie or Mimi or any of Mimi's ghosts. Not far. Don't worry. You will survive also.'

'We.'

She shook her head and then smiled towards him. He closed his eyes as if he couldn't bear to feel the smile slicing through his eyes and down into his heart.

'We can't just do this in silence,' she said after a while. 'Rush like this through the streets of Dublin, not speaking. What can we speak about that doesn't really matter? I don't know anything about you, inconsequential or otherwise . . . except . . .'

She put her foot on the accelerator and they rushed across a crossroads as the lights were changing.

'Except Polly,' he said.

'I don't really know all that much about Polly either. I do

have to say I was pretty inattentive when she was growing up. Does she like Ella Fitzgerald, for instance?'

He laughed. 'Is that important?'

'I think it's quite important to know such things about your children. Their terms of reference. There have to be little islands on which you can stand together. Do you have parents?'

'Yes.'

'Brothers? Sisters?'

'What is this?'

'An interrogation.'

'I love you.'

'Does she like Judy Garland? Do your brothers and sisters, if they exist, like Judy Garland?'

'I do.'

'Well, that's something anyway.'

'I mean I do love you.'

'*Somewhere over the rainbow,*' she began to sing.

The houses were thinning out now; they were quite high above the city and looking back Paul could see the carpet of lights stretching down to the blackness of the sea. Trees leaned over old stone walls and then more rows of small houses sloped down the hill to the right. The street lights had ended and the road became narrower and steeper.

'*Somewhere over the rainbow . . .*'

'Are we nearly there?' he asked like a small child. 'I want . . . to be there, wherever that is going to be.'

'A few minutes. The Pine Forest. Just around a few more corners. My very first boyfriend, when I was still at school, had a motor bike and we used to come out here sometimes on Sunday afternoons and sit under a tree and talk about how we were going to change the world. We never got up to any devilment, only really innocent kisses. The place was filled with young couples just like us. Whispering voices. The whole forest was filled with whispering voices. A kiss or two was very exciting then, you know.'

They turned a corner and the darkness of the wood rose up on each side of them.

'I am jealous,' he said.

She pulled the car in to the side of the road and then leaned forward and kissed him on the mouth.

He pulled her against him, but she struggled away and got out of the car. The air was fresh and smelt of pine sap and needles and there was a great silence all around them. She turned away from the car and walked into the darkness of the wood. She went upwards through the trees across the slithery needles. After a moment or two there was no light at all and he had to follow the sound of her steps and the panting of her breath as she scrambled over some rocky outcrop.

'Are you still there?' she whispered over her shoulder to him.

'Yes. Forever,' he whispered back.

Before they reached the top she stopped. There was enough light now to see; it was as if they were in a huge cave with the great branches of the pine trees spreading out over them and the white light of the moon casting long black shadows on the floor of the forest.

She sat down with her back to a tree and held out her hands

towards him. The ground was soft and dry and scented. He took her hands and knelt down beside her.

'You are all silver.'

He turned her hand over and kissed the palm. She could feel his face was wet with tears.

'Grace, oh my dearest Grace. I have been so lonely. I never thought I could ever be so lonely.'

She rubbed at his cheek with a thumb.

'Don't cry. Please.'

'I have to. I didn't know what you'd do when I went into your room. Throw me out? Swear at me?'

'What a monster you must think I am.'

'So I have to cry. Here we are together. I have thought of this moment, dreamed of this moment and I have to make a fool of myself by crying.'

She put her arms around him and pulled him close to her.

'There,' she murmured into his ear as if he were a child. 'There, there. If I weren't given to swearing and hitting, I would be crying too.'

'Do you love me?'

Slowly, arms tight around each other, they toppled down onto the bed of needles, which perniciously began to work their way into their hair and skin and through their clothes, into pockets, seams, creases. They were invaded by an army of pine needles.

'Yes.'

'Yes.' He stretched his head back and gave a huge cry of joy.

A bird, startled from its sleep, flew out from the tree above them into the moonlight.

'See what you've done.' She pulled him down against her once more. 'You're upsetting the locals.'

The moon seemed very close to Mimi's window. Like a searchlight, prying, she felt, into her head. She didn't like that. Was it night still, or had they passed into morning? She hadn't heard Grace come in so maybe it was still night. Or maybe Grace was cavorting, releasing the tensions of the last few weeks.

Her head throbbed. Too many thoughts struggled in there. If only that stupid man had told me all that . . . then . . . when? Way back one night as they were holding hands under a benign moon. How would I have felt?

Did we ever hold hands under a benign moon? She couldn't remember. They had never gone out to the Pine Forest and lain together under the trees, she at least remembered that. Their courtship had been quite politely conducted in the drawing-rooms and restaurants of Dublin, and under well groomed trees in gardens and parks.

He was probably right. I would have laughed in his face and gone looking for my future in safer hands. Or slapped him. Perhaps I might have done that.

Would I have been shocked? Angry? Filled with sorrow for him? How can I tell looking back from here? I was a different person then. It was another country in which we lived.

Now I am too tired to know how to feel. I have no energy

left for anger and barely enough for forgiveness. Just enough though. Just enough.

She beat with her good hand on the bed.

Just enough.

His cold fingers caught at her hand and held it imprisoned on the blankets. His face hovered like the moon before her eyes.

'If only you had trusted me,' she said. 'We could have managed.'

'Yes. I see that now. We probably might have managed. I couldn't believe that then, though.'

He leaned his head on her imprisoned hand. She pulled herself free of his fingers and laid her hand gently on his hair.

'I forgive you,' she said. 'For not trusting me. All the rest is nonsense. Absolute nonsense.'

A cloud covered the moon, the room became dark and she fell asleep.

The geography lesson was over and at last they lay still. The moon shone on the hills, chasms, lakes and boglands of their bodies and a dog fox walked softly past unnoticed by them, intent on his own business, his paws scattering pine needles as he moved. She sat up and began to grope around for her clothes.

'Don't move.' He put a hand on her arm.

'We have to go. I should have been home hours ago.'

'I could lie here forever.'

'Noodle.'

'Do you love me?'

'What do you think? Yes, of course I love you. Come on, we

have to go.' She leaned down and took his hand. 'Get up.'

She pulled and unwillingly, he scrambled to his feet.

'These bloody little needles. They're everywhere.' He brushed ineffectually at himself.

'Don't worry. They'll wash off in the sea. And in months to come you will find some stuck in your pockets. They'll remind you of me. Such foolish things.'

'The sea,' he yelled. 'I'm not going near the sea.'

'Of course you are. The great end to the mating ritual. A lep in the sea.'

She was away, down into the darkness, and he was after her, hopping and hobbling, happy as he had ever been in his life. Once they were in the car and turned safely pointing down towards the city, he asked, 'What will we do?'

'Do?'

'Yes, Grace. Do about us?'

'I told you there is no us.' She turned towards him. 'No us. You must see that. There can't be.'

'Watch the road. You mean . . .'

'I mean just what I say. Oh God, Paul, I've thought about this so much. I love you. Don't think anything else. I've not been able to get you out of my mind for weeks. If there had been no Polly, perhaps then we could have embarked on some mad sort of adventure. Extreme happiness or extreme misery, who knows? But there is Polly. I love Polly. I couldn't do that to Polly. I couldn't build that wall between us. What we've done tonight is bad enough, but only you and I will ever know about that. Our great and wonderful secret.'

'I thought when you said you loved me that you meant it.'

'I did. I do. You must believe that.'

'Then . . . this is absurd. How can I believe it, when with such . . . ease you just throw me away. Like a used up piece of Kleenex or something.'

'Ease!'

'It seems like ease to me. It seems like you're playing a game with me. A bloody awful game that only you can win. You've made up the rules.'

He sat in his seat staring out of the window and seeing nothing, and she flicked around corners, sliding down, through the streets of sleeping houses towards the sea and Mimi and work and Polly.

After a long time he said, 'I'm sorry. I didn't mean all that. I'm sure there's some way we can arrange things. Some way we can meet . . . just from time to time, if that's the way you wish it. I can't . . .'

'There is no way, dear, dear Paul. There are some secrets that are too debilitating to carry around all your life with you. My back is not strong enough to carry that one.'

'I can't live without you.'

'Of course you can and I can live without you. We can both work. We have friends. You will have lovers, a wife, children. Maybe I will have lovers. And we'll both have a wonderful but not too burdensome secret that we can pull out and look at when things get low. You thought I was going to throw you out when you came to the theatre. I didn't. Let's be thankful for small mercies.' She swung across the road and switched off the engine. 'Come on. Let's enjoy the last fifteen minutes that we will ever have together.'

They walked hand in hand down onto the beach.

Little crisp waves wrinkled across the face of the moon in the sea.

'Two moons,' she said. 'I always love that.'

She took her clothes off and threw them onto the rock and turned and held out a hand to him. He nodded and stripped quickly and they ran together into the sea and out towards the moon that lay folding and unfolding on the surface of the sea.

'Beat you to it.' He plunged and began to swim out to sea.

'No,' she called. 'Don't be silly.'

Back on the shore a man, hands clasped behind his back, walked slowly towards Bray.

'Paul.' Her voice echoed like some lonely seabird; the walking man lifted his head, a cloud edged its way across the moon and the sea became dark. She could see the flash of Paul's arms and the little ripple caused by their movement. Slowly he turned and began to swim back towards her.

'*Somewhere over the rainbow . . .*'

She began to dance in the water, to keep herself warm.

'*If birds fly over the rainbow . . .*'

He was close to her now.

'Do you know, I honestly thought I would swim on and on until I died.'

She stopped dancing.

'But then I got too cold.'

He started to laugh.

'I got too fucking cold to kill myself.'

He grabbed hold of her.

'Come on. You owe it to me to warm me up. *'We're off to see the wizard!'*

They capered and leapt and fell into the water and rose again and swirled the sea around them like a glittering cape. They waltzed and polkaed and jived.

They whirled onto the sand and stood, arms wrapped around each other, their hearts thundering and dancing.

'You meant what you said?' he asked.

She nodded.

'We are absurd,' he whispered.

'Yes.'

They kissed and their mouths and their teeth and tongues tasted of salt.

The walker passed them, unnoticed, as the fox had done, his hands still clasped behind his back, his head poking slightly forward. He went up the slope towards the road.

She dried herself briefly with her blouse and then handed it to him.

'We can ring for a taxi from the house,' she said.

He shook his head.

'No. I'll wait at the station for the first train. I'd prefer to do that. There has to be a first train.'

'But . . .'

'No buts . . . Just stand there and count to a hundred and I'll be gone. Remember those games? Hide but no seek. Remember how you used to gabble those numbers. Start gabbling now.

I will probably love you forever and I will always believe that we might have made it work. We might have been the happiest people in the world.'

He put his hand for a moment on her shoulder and she began to count, staring out at the two moons.

'Twofoursixeighttentwelve,' she shouted out aloud, cheating, as she had always done.

But even then she knew that he was gone into the darkness.

She picked up her raincoat and threw it round her shoulders and still counting, she went towards the car.

'Twenty thirty forty fifty.'

It was raining the next day, but the house was radiant with flowers.

'It's like a bloody florist,' said Grace as she brought the last vase into the sitting-room. 'Have you examined all those cards?'

'So many people wish you well. That must make you feel wonderful.'

Grace laughed.

'I expect some of them could do me a serious damage, but they send me flowers instead.'

'This one,' Mimi held up a card, 'says, Looking forward to working with you in London and the Big Apple.'

'That's a bit premature, Mim. I've been offered the possibility of . . . well, of Arkadina. I haven't made my mind up yet. I don't think I'll take it though.'

'Why not? You've always wanted to play that tiresome woman . . . I can't imagine why.'

Grace picked up Bonifacio's hat from the table and examined it. 'Who owns this?'

'It's mine. Just put it back where you found it.'

Mimi's voice was sharp.

'Yours?'

'Mine. Answer my question, if you please.'

Grace whirled the hat round on a finger. She frowned. 'I thought perhaps I'd take a few months off or so. A year perhaps.'

'Your father says you should do something about the garden.'

'Who?'

'He's really a bit displeased about the state of it. He put in so much time, you know.'

'My father's dead.'

'I think you should tidy up his garden.'

'I don't give a fart about his garden. It's just somewhere to sit on sunny days.'

'Sometimes you can be so crude.'

'Yes. I quite enjoy it. Sorry.'

She put the hat back down on the table.

'We'll go to the doctor tomorrow.'

'I don't want to go to the doctor. I know what he'll say and do. He'll probably kill me with all his treatment. That's what doctors do; they kill you with treatment.'

'Look, Mim, I want to stay here with you. In this house. We'll tell him that. I won't let him do anything you don't want. Mrs O'Brien and I will kill you with our treatment instead.'

Mimi laughed.

'Arkadina . . . ?'

'Arkadina can wait. And I'm not so old that I can't wait also. Who owns the hat?'

'Bonifacio. He left it there last night. I expect he'll come back for it. He doesn't seem to have a change of clothes. You know you hate not working. You're never at your best when you're not working. Down the years I have been aware of that.'

'You'll just have to put up with me, so you will. We have a call for notes at twelve. I must fly. I shouldn't be too long. I've left you some cold ham and salad on the kitchen table. I'm pretty certain I'll be back by about two. Maybe Charlie might come back with me and we can all have tea together.' She crossed the room and kissed her mother lightly on the cheek. 'Take care. You and Bonifacio and whatever other people gallivant around this house when I'm not here. Take bloody care.'

The pain woke Mimi from the comfortable snooze into which she had fallen after Grace had gone.

It was like a huge hand squeezing her heart, wringing, mangling all life out of it. She sat quite still for a few moments, not even daring to open her eyes in the hope that it would go away. The arm that she had thought was already dead throbbed and burned from elbow to shoulder.

'Take bloody care,' was what Grace had said. How can I take bloody care, when I can't even open my eyes? That's what I'd like to know. That is the question.

She heard a sound, a footstep, a breath close by. Carefully she opened her eyes. Bonifacio was standing in front of her.

'Have you come for your hat?' she whispered. 'It's on the table.'

He didn't speak. He stretched his hand out and touched her arm and then her head and she felt laughter bubbling up inside her.

'We never got to the pictures. Wasn't that a shame? We should have made a more strenuous effort. Will we go now?'

He didn't answer.

He took both her hands in his and drew her to her feet.

'Let's go now. Not to the pictures. Go. Go away,' she said. 'I can walk anywhere in my lovely boots; up mountains, on beaches, through the city, even on the moon I'm sure I can walk. I can run. I can dance. I know I can dance. I used to be a wonderful dancer. I was as light as a feather. I used to fly in the arms of my partners. I can do all those things again. I can show you how well I dance. Let's go now, Bonifacio. Let's go to Rome and Venice and Borgo Sansepolcro and dance in the streets. I can do it. I know that I can do it. I know.'

In the following essay, Dr Adrienne Leavy discusses the work of Jennifer Johnston, examining the themes explored in her oeuvre. It was first published in *Reading Ireland: The Little Magazine* and later published in the *Irish Times*.

Adrienne Leavy is originally from Dundalk, in County Louth, Ireland. She studied law at Trinity College Dublin, and the Honourable Society of Kings Inns. After being called to the Irish Bar she immigrated to the United States where she practiced law in Phoenix, Arizona, before returning to University to study literature. Adrienne is the publisher and editor of the on-line literary magazine, *Reading Ireland: The Little Magazine*, and the founder of www.readingireland.net, a website devoted to promoting Irish literature and contemporary Irish writing.

# In Praise of Jennifer Johnston

Widely regarded as one of Ireland's foremost contemporary novelists, Jennifer Johnston occupies a curious place in Irish literature. Although her talent is widely recognised, and she has won many awards, her works have so far rarely appeared in critical studies of contemporary Irish literature.

Born in Dublin in 1930 to the playwright Denis Johnston and the actor and producer Shelah Richards, Johnston was educated at Trinity College Dublin, and lived for many years in Co Derry before returning to Dublin, where she now lives. Her first novel was published in 1972 when she was 42, and since then she has published 18 novels, including *Naming the Stars*.

Her awards include *The Evening Standard* Best First Novel Award for *The Captain and the Kings* (1972), The Whitbread Prize for *The Old Jest* (1979), and her fourth novel *Shadows on our Skin* (1977), was shortlisted for the Booker prize. In 2012 she was awarded a Lifetime Achievement Award from the Irish Book Awards and she was one of the writers nominated in 2014 for the position of first Irish Laureate for Fiction.

For the many fans of her work, Johnston's skillfully constructed novels, with their elegant economic realism and tight storylines, constitute a distinctive and sophisticated voice in Irish literature. Writing about the impact that Johnston's debut novel *The Captain and the Kings,* had on him, Dermot Bolger recently described how he loved the book for 'its sparse intensity and intimacy and how the simplicity of the writing belied the complexity of her characters'.

The qualities that were evident to Bolger in Johnston's first novel have manifested themselves to equal effect in each of her subsequent novels. Broadly speaking, Johnston's work deals with family sins and human frailty within the context of the turbulent history of 20th-century Ireland. The scope of her novels includes examinations of gender, class, religion and politics. Her stories involve characters on both ends of the aging spectrum, from youth and adolescence to old age and inevitable decline. They are Protestant and Catholic, male and female, urban and rural.

As one critic has noted, her novels 'record with great care the ways in which individuals recoil from, or attempt to meet, the political, economic and cultural exigencies that impinge so crucially, and so damagingly, on their lives'.

## Big House

One of the narratives of Irish history that Johnston frequently draws upon is the literature of the Irish 'Big House'. Fictional representations of the social and cultural organisation of the Anglo-Irish or Protestant Ascendancy class dates back to Maria Edgeworth's Castle Rackrent, published in 1800, with perhaps the most well known exponent of the genre being Elizabeth Bowen.

Contemporary novelists such as William Trevor and John Banville have also used the motif of the Big House in their work; however, Johnston's imaginative incorporation of this theme is far more extensive. Her Big House novels highlight the destructive effects of the religious, economic and class divisions on those who inhabit and also those who surround the Big House. In these stories, her characters appear to be prisoners of both personal and political history, trapped by family expectations and pre-ordained societal expectations. Often, these novels revolve around a female character struggling to establish a voice in post independent Ireland, with an elderly patriarch in the background, irreparably damaged by the events of war.

Irish independence dovetailed with the collapse of the social organisation of Anglo-Irish life, and by 1922 the events of the previous decade had rendered the Ascendancy class 'nervously defeatist and impotent'. Terence Brown sums up the new political reality thus: 'The establishment of the Irish Free State found Protestant Ireland in the 26 counties ideologically, politically, and emotionally unprepared for the uncharted waters of the new separatist seas, where they comprised what was seen by many of their nationalist fellow citizens as an ethnic minority.'

## Wartime Ireland

Two novels in particular, *The Old Jest* (1979) and *Fool's Sanctuary* (1987), exemplify Johnston's treatment of wartime Ireland and its aftermath. Set in 1920, *The Old Jest* centres on Nancy Gulliver, a young Protestant girl who unwittingly becomes ensnared in the conflict between nationalists and the English army during the Anglo-Irish war. Nancy longs to grow up, and her sheltered life is dramatically shattered when she befriends a mysterious stranger hiding in a deserted beach house near her grandfather's home.

The man is Major Barry, an IRA commander on the run, and Nancy's innocent attempt to escape her insular world results in tragedy when she agrees to convey a message from Barry to one of his contacts in Dublin. As a result of his instructions, 12 soldiers are shot in Dublin. In one of his few lucid moments, Nancy's ailing grandfather, who spends his days mourning the death of his son on the battlefield of Ypres during the First World War, tells the authorities that he had seen his granddaughter talking with the fugitive.

The novel closes with Nancy witnessing the execution of Barry when he is discovered on the beach, and it is unclear to what extent if any this experience will galvanize her into political action.

*Fool's Sanctuary*, which is also set during the War of Independence, is narrated in the form of a flashback by Miranda, a young Protestant woman who lives on a large estate with her parents. Her father Termon realises how unjust his position of privilege is and tries to compensate by devoting his life to preserving and improving the land for ultimate redistribution to the new Irish nation. Both he and Miranda are sympathetic to the republican cause, but they are not in favour of violence.

As a young woman from the Ascendancy class, Miranda

feels excluded from the political events taking place around her: 'I felt briefly at one time a longing to fight for freedom, but I merely cried for freedom; an inadequate contribution to the struggles of a nation.' Miranda is in love with Cathal, a Catholic tenant whom her father is subsidising through college. Tragedy ensues when Miranda's brother, Andrew, and his fellow British army officer Harry, return to Ireland and to the estate for a visit.

Cathal, a republican sympathiser, is also a childhood friend of Andrew's, so when the local IRA men plan to kill the two British soldiers, Cathal comes to warn them and is himself killed for being an informer. This eruption of violence, which robbed Miranda of her chance for love, stunts her development and she remains alone on the estate for the rest of her life, trapped in a hyphenated identity, belonging to neither side of the class or political divide.

In her essay 'Jennifer Johnston's Irish troubles', Christine St Peter's reading of this novel underscores the impossibility of resolving the ideological contradictions and class barriers which the doomed lovers face: 'Cathal is obliterated by an act of noble self-sacrifice that perpetuates class privilege, and by a narrative necessity that demands punishment for two violent acts: belonging to the republican cause during the civil war and daring to love a woman from the landed class.'

The theme of problematic and dangerous interactions between the Anglo-Irish and the native Irish is also evident in Johnston's early work. In *The Gates* (1973), Minnie McMahon, a young woman on the verge of womanhood, returns to Ireland to the care of her elderly uncle, 'The Major', after completing her education in England. Free from the domineering clutches of her English aunt who has ambitions to make a socially acceptable marriage for her, Minnie develops an attraction for Kevin, the son of one of the tenants on her uncle's estate.

Between them, they hatch a plan to steal and sell the ornate gates that adorn the entry way to the estate. Minnie's intention is to invest the money in the estate's farming potential, whereas Kevin seeks only to escape from the grinding poverty of his family. The gates symbolise this Ascendency family's slide into genteel poverty, as they are the only remaining item of value on the estate.

The position of the Anglo-Irish in the new Independent Ireland is deftly conveyed with poetic symbolism: 'Just off the road leading to the Major's house, the Protestant church crouched like a little old lady, embarrassed at being found some place she had no right to be, behind a row of yew trees. The other end of the village, on a slight eminence, a semi-cathedral, topped by an orange gold cross, preened itself triumphantly.'

When the young couple succeeds in their plan and Kevin drives away to deliver the gates to their potential buyer, the reader guesses before Minnie does that only heartache and betrayal will be her recompense.

## In the trenches

In one of her early stories, *How Many Miles to Babylon* (1974), Johnston moves the setting of the novel from the initial background of a rural estate, to the battlefields of Flanders during the First World War. The possibility of communication across class or religious divisions is usually explored in Johnston's novels through two lonely individuals, and in this instance the protagonists are both male.

Alexander Moore, the only child of parents in a loveless marriage, grows up lonely and friendless on his family's estate in Co Wicklow. When he befriends Jerry Crowe, a stable hand who works on the estate, his mother forbids all interaction with Jerry because he is socially inferior. When Jerry enlists in the British Army because his family needs the money, Alec impulsively enlists too.

Alec's action is prompted by his mother's revelation that his father is someone other than her husband. In the trenches the two friends are separated again by class and now also by rank. They are commanded by Major Glendinning, a ruthless officer who shares Alec's mother's belief in the class system. When Jerry is tried and convicted as a deserter after leaving his unit to search for his father, Glendinning orders Alec to command the firing squad. In an act of mercy, Alec privately kills his friend and he in turn is arrested and condemned to die.

The flare up of sectarian violence in Northern Ireland in the 1960s, which continued for several decades, prompted a number of interventions by a diverse range of writers, artists and intellectuals from both sides of the border. Johnston turned her attention to contemporary Northern Ireland, specifically the violence in Derry in the early 1970s and the machinations of the IRA in the early 1980s, with two novels, *Shadows on our Skin*

(1977), which was shortlisted for the Booker prize, and *The Railway Station Man* (1984).

In *Shadows on our Skin*, Johnston explores the relationship between a young working class Catholic boy in Derry, Joe Logan, and Kathleen Doherty, the teacher who befriends him. Joe lives with his beleaguered mother and an ailing embittered father who is living in the past with a heroic fantasy he has constructed to maintain his self-esteem. Mrs Logan, who has been hardened by poverty and a loveless marriage, is fiercely protective of Joe, and tries to shield him from the conflict that destroyed her husband and threatens to engulf her older son Brendan.

Her character is in many ways reminiscent of the inner city mother figure featured in Paula Meehan's poem, 'The Pattern', who also sublimates her frustrated energies into constant cleaning and scrubbing. When Brendan returns from England he encroaches on his younger brother's relationship with Kathleen, and eventually confides in Joe that he dreams of a future life with her. In a jealous rage Joe tells Brendan something about Kathleen that only he knows: she is dating a British soldier. Unbeknownst to Joe, Brendan is involved with the IRA and having confided in Kathleen, he panics when he finds out about her boyfriend and disappears. Joe's revelation results in a devastating punishment for Kathleen, similar to that described by Seamus Heaney in his poem 'Punishment'.

*The Railway Station Man* begins in Derry with the news that Helen Cuffe's husband has been accidentally killed by a terrorist when visiting a pupil whose father was in the RUC. Helen leaves Derry for the quiet coastal village of Knappogue in Donegal, a move calculated to insulate her from the violence she suffered in Derry. Helen retreats from the world through her painting, and avoids all efforts by her son to jolt her into political awareness.

In this isolated area she meets an Englishman, Roger Hawthorne, who is devoting himself to reconstructing a disused railway station. Roger, who was pressurised into fighting in the Second World War by his imperialist family, is both physically and psychologically damaged as a result. A tentative friendship grows into a more serious bond, and for a brief moment it appears that these two characters will be able to find peace and exorcise their ghosts.

Like the character of Mrs Logan in *Shadows on our Skin*, Helen wishes to avoid any interaction with the politics of Northern Ireland, but when her son and lover are accidentally killed in an IRA explosion, she is forced to confront the political realities of the world around her.

Writing about *Shadows on our Skin* and *The Railway Station Man*, Neil Corcoran points out Johnston insists on drawing attention to 'the complications and confusions of motivation, desire, and involvement which should corrupt any stereotyped conception of "terrorism"'. In Corcoran's view, 'these novels draw their strength from Johnston's long engagement with transgression, rapprochement, and catastrophe in Irish history'.

Politics and personal life also intersect in a more modern context in *The Invisible Worm* (1991). In this novel, which is another story about arrested female development, Johnston explores the intersection of various conflicting ideologies: Catholicism, nationalism, Protestantism and unionism. Like the character of Miranda in *Fool's Sanctuary*, the female protagonist of this novel lives in a fog of reminiscence because of a past trauma. Laura Quinlan has become emotionally crippled by her father's sexual abuse. Johnston places Laura's rape within a specific political context as her father is a former IRA man turned Senator, and Ireland is presented as run by men like him. As Heather Ingman points out, 'Laura comes to symbolise all the abused children, battered women, and incest survivors whose stories bear witness to the underside of Irish nationalism, stories that men like her father wish to suppress because they do not fit into the image of a glorious new nation.' And in fact, Quinlan warns her not to tell anyone about the rape, stating: 'we have to keep our suffering to ourselves'.

## Ageing

A recurrent preoccupation for Johnston is the subject of ageing. For the many elderly characters that populate her novels old age is not a dignified state; they have trouble moving, sitting, sleeping, eating, and remembering to stay focused on the present instead of the past. The limitations of old age are elaborated on in typical Johnston style, with great economy of language and a refusal to either sentimentalise or patronise.

An example of what it's like to live in an ageing body appears in *Two Moons* (1998). This story, which involves three generations of women, two of whom live together, continues

Johnston's interest in female relationships in multi-generational Protestant families. Mimi, the elderly grandmother, is typical of Johnston's heroines in that she is quirky, outspoken, fragile and brave. She lives with her daughter Grace, a stage actress, who is preparing for an upcoming role in *Hamlet*.

Mimi spends her days drinking too much and communicating with an angel she names Bonifacio, whom only she can see. This fairy-tale conceit does not detract from the rich portrait Johnston draws of an ageing character confronting the pain of her past and the inevitability of her future demise.

## Family secrets

Recent work deals with families struggling with secrets in contemporary Ireland. In *Grace and Truth* (2005), Johnston writes about incest, a subject rarely broached in Irish literature. Her skill as a master storyteller prevents the drama that unfolds from descending into lurid sensationalism. One of Johnston's strengths as a novelist is that she always makes her characters matter, no matter how reprehensible their behaviour, and the subtle cameo portraits one finds in this novel are drawn with great skill and control. Her characters are psychologically convincing, even when engaged in self-deception.

The uneasy accommodation that Protestant families have had to make in Catholic Ireland is subtly conveyed in *Shadowstory* (2012), in which the typically benign grandfather of the central character Polly, rails against the possibility of his son marrying a Catholic woman. What concerns the old man is the thought that future generations of his family would be brought up Catholic because of the Vatican's Ne Temere decree, which demanded that children of mixed marriages be raised in 'the one true faith'.

In his mind, the minority thus becomes further marginalised through forced indoctrination into the Catholic Church. Although set during the Second World War, the impact of the Ne Temere decree was felt for many generations in Ireland, and remained a source of resentment for the Protestant community.

## Conclusion

Johnston is a chronicler of Irish families, and her imaginative preoccupation with family dynamics and relationships has resulted in a body of work that ranges across a century of Irish history. Individual life is often emblematic of national struggles, ranging from the Irish volunteers who fought alongside the British in the battlefields of the First World War, to the recent 'Troubles' in Northern Ireland. Very often in her work the past reshapes the present, and family secrets are shown to be just as damaging as a corrosive political legacy. Johnston's fiction reminds us of the indeterminacy of the past, and the dangers of idealising any one version of Ireland's recent history, or our own family history.